Dear Linda,

GIRL
ANONYMOUS

So many thanks!

CHRISTINA
DODD

Chris Dodd

CANARY STREET PRESS

CANARY
STREET
PRESS™

ISBN-13: 978-1-335-46352-4

Girl Anonymous

Canary Street Press
22 Adelaide St. West, 41st Floor
Toronto, Ontario M5H 4E3, Canada
CanaryStPress.com

Printed in U.S.A.

To Scott, love always.

And yes, he always does help me with my research.

CHAPTER 1

SAN FRANCISCO, CALIFORNIA
THIS MORNING

In the fourth-floor library of the Arundel mansion

"Interesting piece, isn't it?"

Maarja Daire of Saint Rees Fine Arts Movers didn't start at the sound of the man's voice. When handling a painting by one of the Three Kingdom masters, or an antique statue raised from the depths of the Aegean Sea, or *this* miniature pitcher of fragile red glass, one did not physically startle.

Yet she realized how deeply she'd fallen into her vision of the past, for how else had this man managed to position himself close enough behind her without her hearing his approach? *This* man, of all people?

She swiveled to face him. "You are...?" She did know who he was: scarred, unsmiling, pulling darkness around him like the black Armani jacket he wore with his blue jeans and worn white running shoes.

"I'm Dante Arundel. We spoke on the phone."

"Yes." His voice was distinctive: slightly accented, deep, and so soft she should have had to strain to hear him, yet so resonant she heard every word inside her head, as if a specter of the past communicated through a bond so ancient she had thought—hoped—it was broken. "You're Mrs. Arundel's son?"

"I am. Pronounce your first name for me."

She blinked at him, drawing on her acting skills to subdue the primal chill that warned of imminent danger. "I introduced myself on the phone."

"I like to be sure."

Strangers frequently asked how to pronounce her name. But he hadn't asked, he had demanded. Based on nothing more than that, she diagnosed him as an obnoxious bastard, intent on throwing her off-balance. Ridiculous on her part, but when a woman worked in this field, obnoxious bastards proliferated like the weeds in her garden.

The question was, why did he want her off-balance? Was he like this with every woman he encountered?

Or did he recognize her? "My name is *Mar-ja*."

"It's Estonian for Mary."

"Yes." She smiled again, pleasantly, and thought, *If you know that, you could have found the pronunciation online.*

He smiled, too, the sharp, toothy smile of a circling shark. "Is your family Estonian?"

"My mother liked the name." Not an answer, but a mind-your-own-business nudge.

She didn't think he'd take the hint, but he followed with, "I appreciate the care you use to move my mother's possessions."

She gazed down at the tiny pitcher she cradled in one palm. "That's my job."

"You've worked for her before."

Annoying man; he knew very well she had. "Saint Rees Fine Arts Movers are the best fine arts movers in Northern California, and your mother demands the best for her possessions."

"You're the best at Saint Rees Fine Arts Movers?"

"Yes." The job had landed in her lap in the summer after her high school junior year, and Saint Rees had quickly recognized her spookily accurate talent for antiquities.

"You're not modest," Dante said.

"I know my worth." She'd had to pass inspection with Mrs. Rees, the power behind the throne, and a deal was struck. She'd worked for Saint Rees Fine Arts Movers in the summers while attending college, and they contributed financing toward her studies. After five years, she still had her instinctive perceptions about authenticity, a new art degree that gave her cred with the clients, and she loved her wildly lucrative job so much she'd brought her foster sister Alex onto the team.

"You're in charge?" Dante was like a dog gnawing a bone.

"Yes." She was done with his unwarranted interrogation. "And yes, this is an interesting piece. One of the earliest works from the Italian island of Murano, stopper missing, assumed broken, its contents sealed with wax."

"That's a lot to know by casual observation."

"I don't observe casually." She observed with her vision, of course, but also through the past that whispered as it sank into her skin and shrieked in her nightmares. He didn't observe casually, either, for his knowing gaze flicked between her face and the pitcher cupped in her hand. "In my family, there's some discussion about whether or not *la Bouteille de Flamme* is genuine."

She nestled it into the tissue paper, then surrounded it with enough bubble wrap to fill the box. "It's genuine."

"You know this because…?"

She taped the box closed and her fingers lingered as she placed it in her staging area. "When one often handles antiquities, one develops a sense about them."

"Does one?"

"Yes. One does." She grinned at him and thought, *I'm still skinny, but I'm way taller and twenty-three years ago for Christmas I got my two front teeth…recognize me now?*

He didn't say anything. Or rather—he didn't admit anything.

Good. Mrs. Arundel didn't say anything. She didn't admit anything. Maybe, hopefully, neither one of them *knew* anything. Maarja had put great effort into being nondescript. She liked to think she'd succeeded, and if she hadn't quite…she could distract Dante. "Almost everything in this library is genuine." At his quick critical glance around, she realized probably she shouldn't have said it quite like that.

"What's not genuine?" He shot words at her like bullets.

Nope, definitely shouldn't have said that. She gazed around the airy, gracious, classically decorated library with its first editions sheltered in locked glass cases, its artfully lit old master paintings, BCE vase fragments and statues. "The Chinese scroll."

"Damn it," he said without heat. His face had not so much been formed; instead his sharp cheekbones and thin nose looked as if they'd been carved from some cruel and ancient stone. The artist that carved that crook in his nose and the long scar that slashed his forehead and cheek had been intent on warning all who viewed him that he was a survivor, a man to be feared.

"You acquired it?"

"I bought it," he corrected. "From a highly respected auction house."

"Mistakes are made."

"Not when you sell to me." Behind his brown eyes, so dark they were almost black, she caught glimpses of gold, as if molten lava emotions moved beneath his surface. It would be nice to think so; that would make him almost human.

Perhaps better to backpedal. "I might be wrong."

"Are you?"

"No." Surely he wasn't the type to kill the messenger.

"I'll have it reappraised. At the same time, I'll have my appraisers reappraised."

Her gaze dropped to his hands. Broad-palmed, long-fingered, big-boned. They could form a fist that would take a man down with a single punch. More than that, he sported the ridged calluses of a dedicated self-defense practitioner. The only thing that kept a person working at the sport was a respect for its real-life potential. She knew; she had a few calluses herself.

Dante looked toward the door and called, "Nate."

The biggest man she'd ever seen stepped into the room. In his dark suit, white shirt, and nondescript tie, he looked like one of the Aryan villains in an old Bond movie, exaggerated in his bulk, his height, his stolid lack of expression. She would bet he had calluses all over his body.

"Did you hear what Maarja said?" Dante asked.

Nate nodded, a stiff movement that barely stirred his muscled neck.

"Check on it, will you?"

Nate put his hand to his earpiece and stepped back into the elevator foyer. She heard a low rumble that might have been an approaching earthquake but was probably his voice.

She hoped Dante Arundel's appraisers survived; cheating him, or even not giving his purchases the care he required, would be a risky business, as she was sure they knew.

She moved farther into the room, into the corner where five large paintings and three eighteen-inch-tall statues waited to be boxed. She ran the tape measure on them; the dimensions matched up with those Dante Arundel had sent. She checked them again, because one didn't make mistakes when handling priceless art, and sent Alex a text instructing her on the sizes of the packaging for the larger pieces. She got a thumbs-up text and 5 minutes.

Arms folded, Dante watched as she started the process over again with a Shakespeare Second Folio and a framed Picasso sketch.

She wondered if he intended to shake her composure with his silence and his judgmental gaze, and she wanted to tell him to knock it off. She'd had far more imposing scrutiny from far more imposing watch groups.

She didn't say a word. It was his stuff, or rather his mother's, and if he wanted to observe, he could. Probably he hadn't identified her; in her loose white coveralls with her name stitched on, her white running shoes, and her short dark red hair covered in a blue bandanna, she was a far cry from the little girl wearing her Sunday dress and jumping over the black tiles onto the white tiles, using the parquet floor as if it were a giant hopscotch.

She pushed her glasses down her nose to read the tape measure and jot them down, and when she was done, again checked them against the measurements Dante Arundel had sent.

He unfolded his arms and plucked her glasses off her nose, a presumptuous move that left her startled and blinking. He held them up to the window and squinted through them. "Why do you wear these? There's no correction."

"Blue-light protection."

He glanced at her tape measure and her pen and paper. "From what? You're low-tech."

"Blue light on my phone. My tablet." She nodded at her devices. "I'm back and forth all day. It's easier to wear them than to not have them when I need them."

"The glass is so lightly tinted, I can hardly see it."

"My eye doctor prescribed them. One assumes he knows what he's doing." A lie; she'd bought them online, but she itched to slam Dante Arundel down.

"Hm." He placed the black frames on the side table and viewed her face as if he were appraising a piece of art, with sharp interest but no emotion. "Your eyes are an unusual color. Violet?"

"Just blue." She heard the elevator door ding and hoped to hell it was Alex.

It was. Alex walked through the library door pushing the luggage cart piled with the boxes, paper, and bubble wrap. She kept glancing behind with an alert, wary expression; none of the company's movers related well to burly men in dark suits who loitered in foyers, but Alex more than most.

She saw Dante, appraised him in a single glance, and said, "Ah."

He stepped forward. "I'm Dante Arundel."

Alex shook hands with him. "A pleasure." Obviously, it was not.

Together she and Maarja began the arduous process of packing the larger paintings and highly breakable pieces of art.

"The truck is in the drive? Unguarded?" Dante let it be known he was critical.

Alex's gaze sliced toward Maarja. She seldom spoke to the clients; tact was a skill she'd not chosen to learn, and the extremely wealthy expected to be treated with the delicacy of their art objects.

However, few of their wealthy clients irritated and presumed quite like Dante, and Maarja had to consciously regulate her tone to answer him. "A van. We have a van. Serene is with it. She'll be fussing with the contents, making herself appear busy to any eyes that might be observing, but in fact she's our lookout and security."

"She's armed?" Dante asked.

"We're all armed, but while we're in a safe environment— your estate—Alex and I concentrate on packing and transporting to the truck, so while we're aware of our surroundings, we're focused on the objects."

"Three women think they can safeguard treasures worth millions?"

He really needed to watch his attitude.

Not that he would. He was one of *those* guys, but Maarja wavered between wanting to punch him right between the eyes or ask him, *Do you know who I am?*

CHAPTER 2

The last impulse alone told Maarja clearly that she needed to finish the job and get out the door. "After a couple of attempted robberies, I convinced Saint Rees that armed male guards make people pay attention. Women are perceived as harmless, so a woman puttering around a large white van marked *Junk* means the contents aren't valuable and not worth bothering."

"Anyone who thinks you're harmless is a fool." Dante chuckled, a deep warm trickle of mirth at odds with the ruthless persona he presented.

The comment and the amusement made her pause, look at him, acknowledge that she might have misread him. In her business and with her past, she'd learned that such a misreading could put her at a disadvantage. She kept her tone pleasantly neutral as she said, "I know how to protect the objects I'm sent to guard."

He kept his gaze on her face, observing her as he dug beneath her skin. "And how to protect yourself."

He struck emotional gold, for she snapped, "What do you mean by that?"

"I mean you have the look of someone who puts a lot of time and effort into self-defense."

Since Maarja put a lot of time and effort into disappearing into the woodwork, she didn't appreciate *that* comment.

Alex interrupted, "Do I look as if I put a lot of time and effort into self-defense, too?" She posed, hand on her hip, and smiled invitingly at Dante.

A behavior so at odds with Alex's usual quiet professionalism and hands-off attitude, Maarja had to look twice to realize Alex was running interference.

Dante accepted the invitation and ran his gaze up and down her; her curvaceous body could not be disguised by the loose white coveralls. "You don't, but I wouldn't dare jump you in a dark alley."

Alex winked. "Best to wait on an invitation, and never in an alley."

"That's my rule." Down the hall, the elevator dinged. He glanced out the door and faced back to Maarja, and he was not amused. "That's Serene, I assume?"

Maarja gave in to her knee-jerk reaction. "No, she would never—"

Serene strolled into the library.

Serene always lived up to her name. Deep insights, lots of meditation, never surprised, never the best fighter, but always fighting to win. Tall, willowy, blonde, older than Maarja but not as experienced as a mover. She looked around the library in calm interest like a tourist on a house tour. She nodded as if the place was exactly as she expected, and to the speechless Maarja, she said, "Saint Rees sent a male guard. Were you expecting him?"

"No! Who?" Maarja shot a horrified glance at Dante.

He observed the play between the women without expression, and yet at the same time he exuded displeasure. Neat trick. Scary aura.

"That guy Morrison. Scrawny, fast with his hands, thinks he's handsome." Serene's low placid voice contrasted with her scathing appraisal.

"I know him." Maarja took a breath and tried not to shout. "You shouldn't have left him alone with the van. What are you doing up here?"

"I was interested in this house. It's on the National Treasury, you know."

"I do know, but we don't have rights to tour a client's home without invitation, *and* we don't leave a man alone with the van. You know the message that sends."

Dante crossed his arms over his chest and silently critiqued Maarja's in-charge position.

"A lot of security out there. A lot of security in here." Serene jerked her head toward the door where Nate's shadow lurked. In her own relaxed and soothing way, Serene was undermining any confidence Dante Arundel might have had in Maarja and in Saint Rees Fine Arts Movers. "I sense this operation is blessed."

"Serene, this is Mr. Arundel."

Serene started forward, hand outstretched.

Maarja stepped between them. "I sense *he* is displeased. Return to the van. Do the job for which you were hired."

Serene pulled up short. She smiled pleasantly. "Of course, Maarja, but sometimes it's best to put your trust in the universe. I certainly have. *Namaste.*" She put her palms together and bowed, and strolled out as gracefully as she had strolled in.

Alex followed her, and from the elevator lobby Maarja heard her giving Serene hell. The bell dinged, the doors closed, and the women's voices were abruptly cut off.

Maarja turned to Dante. "I do apologize. In the past, Serene has been completely reliable, but she marches to a different drummer and unfortunately the beat unexpectedly caught up with her. I'll speak to her, as will Saint Rees."

"Make sure you do."

The elevator bell dinged again.

Maarja heard the sound of Mrs. Raine Arundel's mechanical wheelchair.

Dante smiled, and that smile transformed his face from Sir Grumpy Black Armani Jacket to Mr. Loving and Living in Old Running Shoes.

Points to him. He adored his mother.

Mrs. Arundel paused and greeted Nate.

Nate rumbled back a few words in a polite tone.

Mrs. Arundel rolled in, followed by her long-time assistant, Béatrice, a wispy woman with a face as expressionless as Nate's. In her case, Maarja suspected an addictive use of Botox and a vacuous mind.

Maarja had met Béatrice during prior moves. Her thin blond hair draped around her long pale face making it look longer. She wore a pale pink lipstick and a bright pink blush, her eyelids drooped like a basset hound's, and she always sniffed so much Maarja wanted to snap at her to blow her nose. But that was all external; Maarja didn't like her because of her morose air; with her, she carried her own personal gray sky, and Maarja was convinced Béatrice remained employed based on Mrs. Arundel's soft heart.

Dante beamed as he leaned over and kissed his mother's cheeks. "Mère, did you come to say goodbye to your cherished library?"

She cupped his face in both her bony sun-marked hands and patted his cheeks. "I'll miss San Francisco and my lovely townhouse, but I know you'll recreate the library in my new home in Montana."

"Every bookshelf," he promised. "Every cove molding. Every hideous leering cherub on the ceiling."

Maarja hid a grin. Good to know she wasn't the only one who thought the naked cherubs on pink clouds were a little over the top...as it were.

"They're not leering." For such a small woman, Mrs. Arundel had a full-throated voice. "Those are the satyrs."

"Those, too." He straightened up and flicked the button on her wheelchair, putting it into manual.

Before he could move her, Béatrice said, "Mrs. Arundel, do you mind if I go back down to the office? Standing hurts my back."

"Of course, dear. Go on." Mrs. Arundel gestured her out.

"I'll catch up with you there. Remember to sort the mail while you wait for me."

"Yes. The mail…" Béatrice used a die-away tone as if sorting would ruin her manicure, which was beautifully done with a light pink gloss, and drifted from the room.

"She's having a bad day," Mrs. Arundel confided to no one in particular.

"Does she ever have a good day?" Dante asked irritably.

"She couldn't sit down in here?" Maarja must have thought it a little too loud.

Or Dante had his own psychic moments, for he replied, "Exactly, Maarja. Mère, we pay Béatrice to be your companion and assistant, not to watch videos on her phone."

"You know the result of her injuries, poor thing." Mrs. Arundel really sounded compassionate.

Dante did not. "Yes. Her lover left her after the explosion. Which proves he was the shallow bastard Father told her he was. Maybe she should have listened to her younger and smarter cousin." He maneuvered Mrs. Arundel close enough to watch the packing. "You know Maarja?"

"I love Maarja. She's moved things for me before."

Maarja came to kiss Mrs. Arundel's smooth cheek and face the same scrutiny she'd given her son. "Young lady, you're more beautiful each time I see you."

"I was thinking the same thing about you." Maarja judged Mrs. Arundel to be about sixty, thin and groomed, her skin glowing with her inner spirit and perhaps an advanced skin-smoothing laser treatment. Her stylish green T-shirt dress was ruched to emphasize her well-toned figure, and around her shoulder she draped a black throw that weighed heavily on her shoulders and down her back.

The elevator dinged again, and Alex strode in. She nodded decisively to Maarja and moved into position beside her.

"Mrs. Arundel, this is Alex. We've worked closely together

many times, and you can be assured we hold your belongings as dearly as our own."

"Alex—" Mrs. Arundel extended her hand "—it's wonderful to meet you." She smiled again, a mother's tender version of the smile that transformed Dante's face into something vaguely acceptable.

Alex lightly embraced Mrs. Arundel.

Which showed the happy power Mrs. Arundel exuded, for Maarja had known Alex since their teens, and Alex was chary with her hugs.

Mrs. Arundel utilized her wheelchair to allow her guests a sense of height, to put them at ease, to encourage them to speak tenderly, and to undermine any anxiety about dealing with a woman who'd suffered a broken spine and lost the ability to walk. "Alex, you don't look like Maarja, but you share the same gestures and expressions. Are you sisters?"

The other thing about Mrs. Arundel: she observed what most people never did.

Alex glanced at Maarja. "We are sisters of the heart. We were raised in the same foster home."

Mrs. Arundel leaned her head back on her headrest. "For you both to be such lovely young ladies, your foster mother must have been an amazing woman."

"She was," Maarja said. "She is. She—" *Wait.* How had Mrs. Arundel known a *woman* had given them their foster home?

Dante's phone squawked like a chicken laying an egg. He scowled and looked at the screen. "Mère, did you change my ringtones again?"

Mrs. Arundel laughed with delight. "You're too serious, always busy, you never make cheer. You need a little levity in your life."

"Chickens are not levity. They're food and feathers."

Maarja did not grin at his irritation, but it was a near thing.

"I need to make a call." He kissed his mother. "Are you going to be all right by yourself?"

"Of course, dear. The girls will be here with me, and after that, I want a moment alone to say goodbye to my beloved book nest." She patted his cheek. "Take that unfriendly behemoth with you."

"Nate isn't supposed to be anyone's friend. He's my bodyguard." Dante placed his hands on the arms of her chair and looked into her eyes. "I should insist on getting a bodyguard for you, too."

"Once I'm in Montana, there'll be no need. I'll miss the city, though…" Mrs. Arundel sighed.

Maarja exchanged glances with Alex. Yes, she knew the Arundels were scary people, but who would threaten a sweetheart like Mrs. Arundel? She gave Dante the side-eye.

What had he done to cause trouble?

"Movers, are you almost done?" he asked.

Movers. How charming. He'd already forgotten their names. "Yes, sir," Maarja said. Two could play that game. "This is the last piece."

"Another ten minutes at most?" He wasn't estimating. He was demanding.

Maarja looked at Alex, who was even now carefully placing Mrs. Arundel's bubble-wrapped and boxed treasures onto the luggage cart.

Tight-lipped, Alex nodded. She was done talking to him.

"That's right, sir," Maarja said. "Ten minutes."

"Make sure you pack everything." He picked up the small box with the tiny Murano glass pitcher and handed it to Maarja. "Especially this. *La Bouteille de Flamme* has special meaning to our family."

CHAPTER 3

Maarja accepted it. "Yes, sir. I know."

Dante shot her one of those dark glances that slashed at her presumption, or maybe warned her of the danger she courted with her admission of knowledge.

Alex interceded again. "Everything will be safe in our keeping."

He nodded, but he didn't take his menacing gaze from Maarja.

She smiled brightly. "Measuring me for a coffin?"

Alex moaned softly.

He answered without an ounce of humor. "That's the undertaker's job. I'm involved with the other end of the death business."

"Dear boy!" Mrs. Arundel rubbed her fingers on her temple as if he gave her a headache.

Dante inclined his head to Maarja, walked through the elevator foyer, yanked open the stairway door, and descended the steps.

When the door slammed behind him, Mrs. Arundel said brightly, "Do hurry, young ladies. I do love this room and while my darling Dante will make everything the same in my new home, I'm feeling sad and, of course, I don't want him to know."

"I'll do it for *you*," Alex mumbled.

Mrs. Arundel watched as they got the luggage cart packed, and Maarja carefully placed the package containing the small pitcher in another larger padded box at the top.

The library shelves were still full of books, a few lesser paintings still hung on the walls, but regular cross-country movers were scheduled to handle all that.

Mrs. Arundel kissed Maarja and Alex before they left her sitting with her back to the windows, looking wistfully around.

As they moved the cartload into the foyer and toward the elevator, Alex said, "What a sleazeball that man is."

Maarja didn't have to ask what man. She knew. His personality left an imprint as clearly as the glass pitcher or the Picasso or any of the other genuine works she'd so carefully packed. "Yes." She pushed the down button. "Good-looking men often are."

"You thought he was good-looking? The body, sure, but the face? Talk about a sneering satyr! His mother's a buttercup, though." Alex pushed the lit button several times, as if that would hurry the elevator along. "What happened to her? What's with the wheelchair? Was she in an accident?"

"Years ago. There was a bomb. It exploded. She was too close."

"A bomb." Alex meditated on that while they waited for the aging elevator to make its majestic ascent. "Because the Arundels are the sort of shady people who get bombed a lot?"

Maarja glanced around for cameras; although she didn't see them, she knew they were here, and microphones, too. She lowered her voice. "They were. For years. Noble French immigrants who made their fortune with some disreputable dealing. It was my understanding they've gone legitimate. But don't quote me on any of that."

"Because of the bomb they've gone legitimate?" When it came to this stuff, Alex was a good guesser.

"Brat Benoit Arundel was old country, a golden bully."

"A godfather?"

Together they'd seen the movie enough times to appreciate its wisdoms. "Collector, scavenger, profiteer, criminal. Yes, a godfather. But he didn't claw his way to the top. He was privileged right from the get-go. The explosion that killed my mother killed him." Maarja could see Alex wanting to ask questions, but Maarja shook her head. She'd said more than she'd ever said, and probably unwisely. "Dante was about nine at the time."

"You know a lot."

"Front-row seat." Now Maarja punched the elevator call button as if that would make it arrive in a hurry.

"Oh." Alex contemplated Maarja as if that explained a lot. "Is that why you flinch at loud sounds?"

"Could be." The door opened and the women maneuvered the luggage rack inside.

Alex pushed the starred button. "He's in charge now?"

"Looks like it. I don't know the details. First I was with my aunt, then..." Maarja shrugged.

Alex shrugged back. She comprehended in a way most people could not.

"Eventually I ended up with Octavia. Best thing that happened to me." The doors began to slowly close, and Maarja reached up to adjust her glasses. She touched her bare temple. "Damn it. He took my glasses and put them on the table."

"He? Dante Arundel took your glasses? Off your face? Really, a flaming pustule of a sleazeball. Go get them back!"

"You can handle this?" She indicated the luggage cart.

"Even the Arundel family package full of special meaning." Alex managed sarcasm well. "I'll wait for you on the ground floor by the elevators. We'll go out to the van together."

Maarja caught the door before it slid closed. She touched her hand to her chest over her heart, and pressed it to Alex's outstretched palm. They nodded at each other, sisters of experience if not blood, and Maarja ran toward the library.

She caught Mrs. Arundel in her wheelchair in the middle of

the room, looking sorrowfully about her. In a concerned voice, she asked, "Young lady, what are you doing back?"

"My glasses." Maarja picked them up, stuck them in her pocket with her carpenter's pencil...and lingered. "Are you sad at leaving your home?"

"It's become necessary." Mrs. Arundel smiled bravely, but glanced around again, avoiding Maarja's gaze. "Don't they need you downstairs to help load the van?"

"Only an emergency would make them leave without me." Maarja took Mrs. Arundel's frail crumpled hand. "Is there anything I can do for you?"

"No, dear, really. A few moments alone is all I need."

Mrs. Arundel looked so anxious, almost on the verge of tears, that Maarja took pity on her. "Of course. I understand. I'll see you on the other end, in Montana." She walked out the door and down the corridor to the elevator. She pushed the button and waited, and as she did, she heard a muffled crash behind her.

Had Mrs. Arundel somehow fallen?

She turned in time to see a blinding flash of light, hear the roar of an explosion.

CHAPTER 4

The floor rippled beneath Maarja's feet.

She shouted, fell. As heat rolled over the top of her, she covered her head with her arms. In her head, she heard her mother's voice.

Run, Mary. Run and never look back.

She had to run!

Maarja half rose and turned toward the elevator.

Another explosion shook the floor. She fell hard, flat on her face, knocking the air out of her lungs. Angry red stars swarmed her vision.

She lost consciousness, but in that loss she heard her own five-year-old self screaming, *Mama! Mama! Mama!*

And—

My fault. Mama, I'm sorry. My fault!

Maarja regained consciousness, and the panic remained, but had been transformed by memory into determination.

Dear God. Flames would engulf that faded kind woman in the wheelchair. Someone had to save her.

Maarja had to save her.

Maarja crawled toward the library, ears ringing, blinking to clear her vision. "Mrs. Arundel," she shouted. "Mrs. Arundel, I'm coming!"

Sooty smoke rolled out of the library, blackening the ceiling. Scarlet flames roared, reaching high out the broad doorway, blistering the pale cream paint until it turned a gruesome brown and peeled off.

Fear writhed in Maarja's gut. She had trained in every aspect of security. She knew what to do to rescue endangered art. When she thought about it—and she did—she had expected her childhood experience to armor her against the shock and horror. She hadn't foreseen she'd hear her mother's voice in her head, commanding her to run, or that her childhood obedience would be replaced by the terror of knowledge.

She'd been here before.

Not here, not in this place, but staring into the flames, into the madness of shattered glass, shards of furniture, and broken bodies.

Desperately Mary wanted to go to her mother's rescue. In despair, she realized what Mama had done, and why she had drilled those words into her little girl's head.

Run, Mary. Run and never look back.

Maarja wanted to run, to obey her mother's never-forgotten directive, but Mrs. Arundel was somewhere in that library. All Maarja's old guilt strengthened her resolve. Mrs. Arundel could not be left to burn.

In the library, flames scraped the ceiling, blackening the toes of the artfully painted cherubs, and Mrs. Arundel's wheelchair stood empty. For one cowardly moment, Maarja thought, *She's gone. I don't have to—*

She caught sight of the woman sprawled on the carpet face down, her black shawl covering her face and back, the hem of her green dress charred and smoking.

Gone? Of course she wasn't gone. Maarja mocked herself with scathing intolerance. What was Mrs. Arundel going to do, get up and run?

The force of the blast looked as if it had come from the

outer wall of the library, probably a projectile incendiary blasted through the window. Mrs. Arundel had been knocked out of her wheelchair, was probably now unconscious. Fire consumed books and shelves, advancing across the hardwood floor toward Mrs. Arundel's prone body.

Maarja glanced around the elevator foyer, grabbed a quilted blanket used for moving, and used it to cover her head and her face. She took a long deep breath of oxygen, then kept low as she ran into the library and dropped to her knees beside Mrs. Arundel's still figure.

She pushed the heavy wrap off her face—and jumped when Mrs. Arundel opened her eyes and snapped, "Maarja! What are you doing back here?"

"Rescuing you." Now that she'd plunged into the inferno, now that she'd replaced the old terror with this moment, Maarja could place her anxiety on ice.

"No!" Mrs. Arundel took a hard breath, coughed, and dropped her forehead onto the carved rug and mumbled...something that sounded like the F-bomb.

She'd probably suffered a blow to the head. That compounded by oxygen deprivation would explain her odd behavior.

Maarja looked around for the wheelchair. It was close at hand, overturned when Mrs. Arundel had been hurled out. Smoke rose from the leather seat, but otherwise it was intact. Thank God. Unthinking, Maarja reached for the metal frame.

Mrs. Arundel snapped again, "Don't touch! You'll burn your fingers."

"Right." That was so right. Maarja realized that here and now, the wheelchair would serve as a roasting pan.

Mrs. Arundel painfully lifted herself onto her elbows. "Maarja, I beg you, save yourself!"

Steadily, Maarja replied, "And *you*. I will save *you*."

Mrs. Arundel stared at her in frustration, then gave a little laugh. "*Of course* you have to save me." Tears sprang to her eyes, and she wiped at them. "That's fate, is it not?"

Maarja's hopes for anonymity were dashed. Mrs. Arundel did know, and Maarja felt sick. "I guess it is." An admission the flames would consume if Maarja failed Mrs. Arundel now.

"Can you drag me out of here?" Mrs. Arundel asked.

"Yes." In the short run, that made more sense than the wheelchair. Yet Mrs. Arundel and Maarja were about the same height and weight. No way Maarja could perform a fireman's lift. How would Maarja get her any farther? Into the elevator? Or, if the elevator had been sabotaged—for this bombing was a malevolent act—down the stairs?

One problem at a time, Maarja. "I'll use your throw to pull you."

"Good idea!" Mrs. Arundel pushed herself over onto her back. "I trust you. Move briskly, young lady!"

Maarja removed the moving blanket from her own head, felt such heat from the fire she knew her eyebrows had singed. She covered Mrs. Arundel to protect her from the flames. Grabbing the throw in her hands, she braced her feet and yanked.

Mrs. Arundel moved about twelve inches.

The flames leaped twenty-four inches.

Incentive.

Moving in jerks, walking backward, one pull at a time, she hauled Mrs. Arundel across the rug. Mrs. Arundel's dark scarred, emaciated legs dragged limply behind them. When they reached the hardwood floor, Mrs. Arundel's body slid more easily, they moved more quickly, out of the library and into the elevator foyer.

The air was better here.

Mrs. Arundel pushed the blanket off her face. "There. I'm safe! Now you run!"

Maarja did. She ran to the elevator and pushed the button.

It didn't light up. Of course not. The system had shut down. Maarja reported, "Elevator's unavailable. We'll take the stairs."

"I can't take the stairs! I can't walk. You saved me." Mrs. Arundel made a shooing gesture. "Go get help!"

Inside the library, the flames crackled with joy as they consumed the books, shelves, paint and furnishings. With every passing second, the heat and smoke grew exponentially, greedily sucking up the oxygen.

Oh, God. Dear God. Let me do this!

"You are not safe, and I'm not leaving you!" Maarja leaned down, grabbed the throw, and once more started the process of walking backward, yanking Mrs. Arundel toward the stairs. She had no idea how she was going to get the fragile lady down three flights to the ground floor. She wondered if, hoped that, Alex would run up the stairs, open the door, and arrive to help Maarja carry Mrs. Arundel down.

She wouldn't; they'd trained for such a situation and Alex would perform her duty. Right now, Alex and Serene were thrusting the fine art into the van, locking everything and racing away, down the road to some random destination. There they'd be joined by other Saint Rees Fine Arts Movers guards and everything would be taken to a safe, hidden place and stored until this crisis, whatever it was, was over.

Maarja would somehow make this work…because she had to.

The stairway door slammed open, slapping the wall, barely missing Maarja's butt.

Dante Arundel stood framed, shoulders hunched, flexing his fists. "You! The stupidest damned—" He glared at Maarja as if she'd somehow been responsible for the crisis.

"Dear boy, she wouldn't leave."

Maarja waited tensely for Mrs. Arundel to explain why.

Right now, he didn't care. Reaching down, he lifted his mother, placed her over his shoulder, and commanded Maarja, "Follow!"

As if she was so witless she'd stay on this floor if he didn't tell her to escape.

He also said, "Shut the door behind you!" and "Don't collapse now, I can't carry you both."

As if she would leave the door open to allow the fire to use the stairwell as a chimney. As if she was weak enough to—

She staggered, grabbed the handrail, and stopped to regain her balance.

All right. She might be suffering from delayed shock. But she wouldn't collapse! As if she'd allow Dante Arundel the satisfaction.

Dante took the corner for the next flight of stairs, and below, she could hear his deep voice murmur to his mother and Mrs. Arundel's lighter tones murmur back.

They sounded so normal.

Later, Maarja told herself how normal they sounded.

Maarja started down again. She might not have eyebrows, but by God she'd saved Mrs. Arundel's life today!

Anyway, who needed eyebrows? Or eyelashes? Or—she shook her head and watched as singed bits of hair floated past—bangs?

Just like before.

She staggered again, her knees buckling. She gripped the handrail tighter, and paused to let the wave of grief and horror pass. It had been so long she thought she'd forgotten. She told herself she'd forgotten, because why dwell on it? When would something like an explosion reoccur in her life?

Never. Never. She put her hand to her aching heart. *She should have told Saint Rees he had to replace her on any job concerning the Arundels. But who could have imagined this?*

She continued down and around the corner, then down and around the corner, then down and around the corner—all those landings, and she never caught a glimpse of Dante and Mrs. Arundel. Her isolation began to feel like a haunting. Had she died up there in the flames?

She got to the ground floor, slammed through the door into

the foyer, saw smoke billowing down the curved staircase, heard a series of explosions above.

The front door stood open.

Thank God. Dante and Mrs. Arundel had left the building.

Maarja spent one second with her hand on the stitch in her side.

One second too long. Another explosion rocked the old and revered mansion.

She ran onto the raised porch.

Behind the ornate iron fence that encircled the property, people milled in the street, gawking and exclaiming. Everywhere she saw phones raised to film the event, as if this tragedy was nothing more than a drama for their entertainment.

Two people in particular, a man and a woman, stood at different angles and filmed, their eyes narrowed and their expressions intent. Whenever someone got in their way, they moved enough to produce an uninterrupted eyewitness account.

Reporters, she thought in dismay. *How did they get here so soon?*

Police shouted, moving them back behind a line. Sirens shrieked as fire engines worked their way through San Francisco's ever-congested traffic.

A woman screamed. Stopped and screamed again.

Maarja looked for the source.

There she was, Béatrice, close to the ambulance parked on the lawn. Sitting on her knees, placing an oxygen mask on her face, taking it off and giving a shriek, putting it back on again.

Drama queen. This wasn't about her. It was about—

Maarja's gaze shifted to the crowd of EMTs leaning and kneeling and speaking in concentrated tones…around a woman's sprawled body.

Gaze fixed, she clutched the banister in both hands and moved down the stairs. A woman's body in a green T-shirt dress. *Mrs. Arundel's unmoving body.* Her legs were akimbo, her limp arms had been pulled away from her chest. They were giving her oxygen, using a defibrillator.

Maarja didn't understand. "What's…happening?"

Nate stood, arms crossed over his massive chest, observing. In that ponderous voice, he said, "They're working on her. They might bring her back."

"Bring her back? From…?" *From death?* "What? No!"

He scrutinized her as if surprised by her outburst. "Mrs. Arundel was a fragile woman. Surely you observed that."

"She felt strong when I dragged her. She—" Maarja sprang forward, ready to aid the medical team. Distantly, she knew she wasn't qualified, but—

Someone grabbed her from the side, stopping her headlong rush.

A man. A man held her.

She punched him in the ribs, twisted in his grasp.

With her skills, she should be free. She wasn't. She looked up, saw the dark wavy hair, the scarred face. Dante. It was Dante.

He held Maarja with both arms wrapped tightly around her. He dragged her away from the house, toward the fence. "Maarja. Maarja. It's all right. You did the best you could. It's all right. You tried, but she was too fragile."

Maarja strained against him, struggled to go to Mrs. Arundel. "What do you mean? Your mother? She's not…"

"She's dead."

Maarja froze. "She…is…not! She's not. I saw her. I heard her. She was fine. You carried her. I heard you two talking."

In the background, she heard Béatrice shriek in between breaths. Glass broke as explosions rocked the house. People shouted in the streets as more and more police were needed to control the crowd, as more and more fire personnel in turnout suits streamed through the now open gate dragging hoses and equipment. One of the reporters used the confusion to slide into the compound and, still filming, focus on the EMTs around Mrs. Arundel. *The bastard.*

And Béatrice's periodic shrieks, slamming like bullets shot from the world's most irritating rifle.

Dante looked into Maarja's eyes, sympathy in his gaze. "She knew she was dying. She knew you saved her from the flames, and she thanked you."

"I don't want thanks." Maarja lunged toward the EMTs as they placed Mrs. Arundel on a stretcher and covered her face with a sheet. "I want her to be alive!"

He gripped her, turned her head, pressed her face against his chest. "She died in my arms."

"No. No, she didn't." Maarja still fought in disbelief. "You're lying!"

"Maarja, it was her heart."

"No, she didn't die. No, she didn't. She can't die." Maarja began to collapse, every hope broken, every grief reinforced. "She can't die. She can't." Tears smashed through the suspicion and heartbreak, and she sobbed out loud. "I tried so hard…"

CHAPTER 5

Of course, it didn't matter how hard Maarja had tried. What mattered was...what was.

Mrs. Arundel was dead.

After the ambulance had left with her body, Dante called the EMTs over to check Maarja. She found herself flat on her back receiving oxygen, having someone peer into her eyes and listen to her heart. She was diagnosed with shock, hooked into an IV, and given a drug to calm her.

"Who do you want me to call?" Dante asked as they placed her on the stretcher.

Maarja tried to think. She lifted her hand to rub her face and Dante caught it. "Don't. You're burned."

"Um. Call my mom. Octavia Maldovitch. Make sure she knows I'm going to be okay. I don't want her to try to get to the hospital. She's better staying close to home."

"Do you know her number?"

"It's on my phone. Autodial." She fumbled in her coveralls, trying to find it in her hip pocket.

The EMT handed a phone to Dante, who made a funny face.

"Also call Saint Rees. Leave a message. With the emergency van takeoff, he'll be concentrated on that. You know his number. Leave a message, tell him to send someone to take me home when I get out of the hospital."

"Right." Dante stepped back.

"Wait!" She took a quivering breath. "Ask if my crew is safe. Ask if Alex…is safe."

"Of course," Dante said.

As the EMTs transported her toward a second ambulance, she caught glimpses of a scowling Béatrice, still clutching her oxygen mask, of an impassive Nate, arms crossed over his chest. Someone held a phone high above everyone's shoulders filming *her* now as if she were a high-strung actress dealing with a contretemps on the set.

In the emergency room, she was immediately and thoroughly checked out, given pills for stress and to sleep, ointments for her burns, and more fluids. The doctor told her to go to her own doctor in the morning, and she was released. When she asked about billing, she was assured the matter had been handled. Which meant Saint Rees's well-thought-out insurance policy had kicked in. Julie, the young nursing assistant, told her she had a driver waiting, put her into a wheelchair and pushed her out the doors.

It was night, Maarja realized. Hours had passed since the explosion.

Grief had not passed. Drugs could only do so much. Time and again, she smashed into the unacceptable fact; she had failed to rescue Mrs. Arundel… *More blood on my hands. Always blood and heartache and the slow erosion of self caused by loneliness.*

There on the hospital's brightly lit sidewalk, she expected to see Saint Rees or one of the people from his firm.

Instead Dante Arundel leaned against a black sedan. He scrutinized her and frowned. "You look like you walked through hell."

She bit her lip and blinked away tears. "I'm fine."

Julie frowned as sternly as he ever did. "Shock is a terrible thing, Mr. Arundel, and that attitude won't help her."

"I'm fine," Maarja said again.

"Sure you are. So am I. We're both fine." She remembered how firmly he'd held her when she fought him, how he'd demanded she get medical help, be transported to the hospital, not rail at the villains who'd taken his mother's life. How did a man who had lost his mother today manage to infuse the situation with such biting sarcasm?

As Julie set the wheelchair's brake, he reached down to wrap his arm around Maarja's back and help her out.

She flinched.

He halted. "Are you bruised? Bones broken I don't know about?"

"No. No. I don't like…" She knew better than to give too much information. "Thank you for your assistance, but I can stand on my own."

"Mr. Arundel, you get in the driver's seat. I'll put her in the car." Julie replaced his arm with her own.

Dante nodded curtly, opened the passenger door, and went around.

In a low voice, Julie said, "You don't have to go with him if you're afraid."

"He wants to talk to me about what happened." As Maarja spoke, she realized that must be the case. "The explosion. What I heard and saw."

"You should be talking to the cops, not him."

"Sooner or later I'm sure I will, but right now—he's one of those men who gets his way. Surely you see that."

"I don't have to like him for it. Don't put up with any shit from him."

"I won't. I'm tougher than I currently seem." As Julie tucked her into the passenger seat, Maarja said, "Thank you. For everything."

"Hmph." Julie shut the door, whipped the wheelchair around and headed back inside.

Dante put his arm across the back of the seat and scowled at Maarja. "You don't need to act like I've got cooties. I'm not going to hurt you. I'm not going to assault you."

All right, fine. He was going to make a thing about her flinching at his touch, and surprisingly, having Julie instruct her to *not put up with any shit* made Maarja feel stronger. "It's not you. I don't like to be touched."

"At all?"

"When I was eleven, there was a...bad moment."

It took him a minute to realize she was done talking. Any conclusions he would draw would be right enough. "Good to know. I'll be more careful in the future."

"Thank you." She watched as he put the car in gear and drove onto the street. He took a route she didn't know, and she asked the question she should have asked first. "Are you taking me home?"

"You're in no shape to be alone."

"Someone will come from the firm."

"We're going to my condo in the city."

"What? No! I don't want—"

His hand slashed the air between them. "You put your life at risk to save my mother. I owe you everything. I owe you protection. I owe you my life, and I will sacrifice for you."

"No. You owe me nothing! I did it because she—" Maarja's voice stumbled. "Because she was a kind and lovely lady who—"

"It doesn't work that way. You know that." His low tone grew harsh. "You and I, we live in a world of revenge and reparation."

"What do you mean?" She spoke quickly, leaning away from his possible implication. "I don't live in that world."

"Look at politics. Look at the news. Look at the school shootings and the mass shootings in public places. You have no choice.

You were born to this world, and if you try to ignore it, you could be dead in truth."

She could slash her hand as well as he could. "I take care of myself."

"When you're recovered, you can take care of yourself." He glanced at her as the streetlights blew past, light angles changing, creating an eerie movie-like set. "Whether or not you want me to feel a debt, I do."

"I didn't do it for you."

"I know. Believe me, I know. Now close your eyes. You look like hell."

By the time they pulled into an underground garage and stopped, she'd fallen asleep half a dozen times, and when he helped her out she didn't have the oomph to argue. He didn't mock her, she could say that for him, but got her up the elevator forty stories, into his condo, tossed back the sheets on a bed, and left her to toe off her shoes and collapse. Which she did. She slept four hours before her bladder demanded she rise and empty it.

Damned intravenous fluids.

Dante had left the light on in the bathroom, and she stumbled in, locked the door behind her, used the toilet, and stepped to the sink to wash her hands—and gasped in dismay.

Her reflection in the mirror was nothing short of a horror show. Gripping the edge of the cool marble counter, she leaned in.

The staff at the hospital had wiped her face and hands, and anywhere they hadn't wiped was covered in black sooty streaks. She'd known the ends of her bangs had singed, and her eyebrows and lashes, but she hadn't realized her skin looked as if she'd stayed in the sun too long. No wonder Dante said she looked like hell.

She wanted to go back to sleep, but she couldn't. Knowing she was so covered with greasy smoke…she had to wash.

The bathroom was decorated in soothing shades of peach

with blue accents and European styling. The glass shower occupied one corner, the big bathtub occupied the wall under the
window, a bidet sat beside the toilet, and the whole place was so
luxurious she muttered about a fur-lined pee-pot, then decided
she'd grown sour and envious in her old age.

She took a few minutes to figure out the shower—it vaguely
resembled an airplane control pit—and started the water. She
stripped off, dropped her formerly white coveralls in a corner—
they were black and singed, too, and not worth saving—threw
her panties, bra, and socks on top, and stepped into the spray.
The spray that came from all directions. It rained on her from
above, from the wall in front, and one handheld sprayed at her
chest. On the wall to the side, another pulsed at her butt. She
used a washcloth to work the citrus-and-lavender soap into a
lather, and discovered it cut the sooty grease as if it had been
created for that—and the scent relaxed her with every breath.

Dante could have his fur-lined pee-pot with her blessing as
long as she could shower herself clean in here every day.

God. She spit on her palms and rubbed them together. An
old superstition, probably one she had wrong, but she needed to
cleanse the unruly wish away. She did *not* want to use Dante's
shower every day. She wanted nothing else to do with Dante
and his mother, which worked because his mother—

Grief and regret caught her, shattered her into tiny pieces.
Mrs. Arundel was dead. Killed by the blast, killed when her
heart stopped. Remembering how alert Mrs. Arundel had been
in that blast furnace of a library, how her eyes sparkled and her
voice snapped...Maarja couldn't believe it.

Dead. Mrs. Arundel was dead.

Sinking down on her knees, she sobbed. She clutched her
hair and beat her fists on her thighs.

It wasn't fair. Not to Mrs. Arundel, who sparkled with her
enjoyment of life, and not to Maarja, to have so many memories resurrected. To have the chance to change the outcome, to

think she had and then have her shining hope slammed down and broken.

The bits of the past always, always felt like broken glass in her mind, and now more sharp splinters tore at her composure, her peace, and she was disconsolate. She pulled her legs up, wrapped her arms around them, put her head down, and rocked and sobbed.

The click of the shower door made her look up in shock.

Dante Arundel stepped in.

CHAPTER 6

Dante wore a white short-sleeved T-shirt and gray sweatpants, and shut the door behind him. He knelt before her, not touching, and his dark eyes showed compassion and concern. "Please stop. You'll make yourself sick."

"I c...can't. You must see... I can't." She put her head back on her knees. All the old guilt rising and compounding the new grief... To cry in front of him lashed at her pride—yet the emotion could not be contained.

He gave a sigh, stood, picked her up, and sat on the shower bench with her on his lap. He rocked her. Which, for a guy who said he'd be more careful of touching her in the future, was wrong. On the other hand, there was not a hint of the sexual in his behavior. He offered pure comfort and really, what guy desired a woman who wept until her eyes were almost swollen shut and snot ran?

Yet the embrace was nice—and *nice* was not a word she'd ever thought to apply to Dante Arundel. His sweatpants provided a cushion against her bare parts. He kept his arms wrapped around her, pushed her head onto his shoulder, rocked her, and made low comforting sounds that came through as rumbling beneath her ear. The warm water cascaded over them, the steam on the glass enclosed them, and the first wave of her grief began to pass.

When her crying slowed, he held her until she lifted her head and sniffed, loudly, and wiped the back of her hand across her nose. Body fluids were so inconvenient and embarrassing.

He groped around and handed her the washcloth. "Blow."

She looked at it and looked at him.

"I've heard a crying woman blow her nose before. It doesn't matter. Other than being naked, you're hardly trying to seduce me."

"Being naked is how I take my showers." Snipping at him made her feel better, so she honked her nose and threw the washcloth into the corner. Leaning her head back against the wall, she looked at him beneath swollen eyelids. "Unlike you."

Everything he wore was soaked. "I took off my shoes and socks."

"How did you get in the bathroom?"

"I own this condo. I have the keys. I heard you crying and I couldn't stand it. Did you finish washing?"

"Everything but my hair."

He stood and deposited her on the bench, squirted shampoo into his palms, and massaged it into her scalp. Once again, the scents of citrus and lavender surrounded her. She closed her eyes against the bubbles and felt more acutely the way he dug his thumbs into the tense muscles at the back of her head.

As she relaxed, she burst out, "She...your mother... Who would do this to her? She was kind and smart, and already so helpless."

"My mother was *not* helpless. She was...amazing. Brilliant. Inventive. Up for any challenge. Tilt your head back." He pushed any unruly soap off her face and used the handheld to rinse her hair. "I am sorry about your hair. I'll have a stylist come tomorrow morning and cut it into some semblance of a style."

"My hair doesn't matter, or it wouldn't if I'd managed to save—" Her voice shook.

He took over the conversation before she could crumble again.

"Physically, sure, but Mère was smart and in her own way, ruthless. When my father…died…she decided to remake our organization, and she did."

She wiped her eyes and opened them, looked up at him. "From a wheelchair?"

"From her hospital bed. Then from her wheelchair."

"A woman of strong will." Maarja's opinion of Mrs. Arundel shimmered and shifted.

"A woman who engenders loyalty…and a woman who doesn't hesitate to enforce her decisions."

Code for *Do what I say or I'll kill you.* "Really? Mrs. Arundel? Really?"

"Really. She had enemies."

Maarja had never seen that in her, but—yes. As his father's heir apparent, Dante had been too young to take over the organization, but not too young to die, and Mrs. Arundel had been physically helpless. Someone had had to move swiftly to ensure their survival, and that somebody had to be Mrs. Arundel. "Is that why they wanted to eliminate her?"

"Yes."

The next logical question—"Who are *they*?"

"I intend to find out." Grim tone. "Some seek their own power. Some prefer the old ways. Some think anarchy will open up a brand-new world, so they'll bring it all down and start anew, and damned to who gets hurt." He finished rinsing her hair and returned the handheld to the hook. "If you can feel better about today's events, please know my mother is better off out of it."

Indignation made her want to slap him. "That's bullshit and you know it."

"It holds its own truth."

For the first time since he'd stepped into the shower, she looked at him, really looked at him. The man who had been everything that was kind and caring to her had been hiding his true emotions, for he strained like a black wolf, captured and at the end of his fetter. The muscles in his shoulders, arms, and chest flexed against the soaking white cotton, she could clearly see his dark hard nipples and... Her gaze dropped. She hadn't meant to notice, but his heavy wet sweatpants sagged low on his hips and only one thing was keeping them up.

Okay. He hadn't been aroused when she was a sobbing wreck—she knew because she'd been sitting on his lap—but she'd relaxed from her tight curl of misery, the snot had ceased running, and, oh, gee, as he said, she was naked.

She glanced up and discovered his lids half shuttered his eyes, allowing only a polished obsidian gleam to escape—and that gleam focused on her.

She was naked, he had noticed—well, sure, he'd been standing over top of her washing her hair—and to contain the sudden surge of her breath, she slowly reached up and touched her breastbone over her heart.

Her fingers caressing her own skin held a fascination for him, and he couldn't seem to look away.

This was it, then. The moment she'd feared and put off. But this time, the right circumstances: a cocoon of steamy safety, a past that unwillingly united them, and a dangerous man with a tender touch.

Abruptly, like a demon fleeing a burst of light, he turned and lunged for the door.

"Wait!" She grabbed for him, caught the sweatpants. The elastic released and left him standing in a pool of French terry. He wore soaked white boxers that molded his erection. "Dante, would you...?"

"No!" He stomped his feet to free himself from the heavy wet material.

She reached for him. "I want!"

"No. You don't like to be touched and I'm going to respect

that." The door latch clicked. The door opened. "As soon as I get out of here!"

"Dante!"

He froze. Every muscle in his shoulders, back, and neck flexed and strained.

She whispered, "Don't leave me alone now."

Still he stood, brittle with tension.

How to explain what she knew? "Dante, it's been a horrible day for you, too. You need me."

With a sigh, he turned and picked her up by the shoulders. "Yes. I do." He sounded almost…resigned.

He kissed her: lips formed to hers, tongue curious, gentle, alien to her. Breath that was not hers. Flames that kindled between them. A tangle of thorns. A thicket of passion. Emotions she had never comprehended, ever, in her whole life.

Before she could decide, he pulled back and stared at her, his dark eyes now wide, urgent, primitive. "Second thoughts. For me. For you."

"Not me." Why did he say that? Could he taste her uncertainty?

"You've had a terrible day. One shock after another. Grief and heartache. I shouldn't—"

"You've had the same day."

"I didn't face that explosion." With tender fingers, he traced the curve of her face. "Swollen," he said. "Like you were slapped. Why didn't you run?"

"I couldn't. I had to—"

"Save my mother." He stroked her face, yet although he watched her as if she were a mythical creature, a unicorn or a phoenix, he made no move to kiss her again. He kept a space between them, touching her only with his fingertips.

Yet that space hummed with vitality, need, an awakening that made her forget the past and find what she needed here and now. She caught his wrist and gripped it with all her strength. "I'd like you to kiss me again."

"You didn't like it."

"I...did." She winced. It sounded like a question.

"You stopped me. Did you mean to?"

"I didn't stop you. I let you kiss me."

"Fuck that. If you want me, kiss me. Open your mouth. Kiss me." He bent her over his arm and...oh, my. He was the kidnapping pirate, the ruthless magician, the prince who would turn the tide.

She yielded, opened her mouth to him, let him cup her breast.

Okay, there was no *letting*. He was doing what he wished with her body. She wasn't complaining or fighting. Of all the shocks of the day, this was the best. Or the worst. Or...the one that swamped all the other emotions.

Eventually he stopped kissing and whispered against her lips, "What do you want?"

This pirate, this prince, wanted her to make a decision. He waited on her decision.

Mostly.

Because while he asked, he lowered her onto the seat and spread her legs, and dipped his mouth and tasted her. The shock sent her reeling back against the wall, arms braced, slammed by sensation. She looked down at him; his eyes were blissfully shut, his lips moved and sucked and his tongue thrust into her...

She slammed back against the wall again.

What man did this? Pleasured a woman as if nothing else mattered? As if she tasted like ambrosia on his tongue?

According to her friends, between a man and woman, passion slowly built...if the woman was lucky.

Not here, not now. Passion *was*. She came hard and fast, clamping her thighs around his head and holding him in place while warm rain splattered, cool tile cradled her, and his finger—no, two fingers—pushed inside her as if he wanted to extend her pleasure. She whimpered and writhed.

He wrapped his arm around her waist, arched her spine, and pulled her forward to the edge of the bench. Taking her breast in his mouth, he sucked her nipple while stroking his fingers inside her and using his thumb to stroke her clit.

Too much. She couldn't keep track. He confused her senses. She knew only one thing: it hurt to want this much. "Please. Soon. Now." She groped her way down from his shoulders, slid her hand under the waistband of his shorts to his dick, touched it, held it.

He froze, waiting, watching her from those too-observant eyes.

She stroked lightly, enjoying the ridges, the silky smooth skin, the mushroom-shaped cap. "It's—"

"The biggest you've ever seen?" His tone held a cynical edge.

"Not at all." Did he think she was raised in a convent? "Have you ever *looked* online?"

He laughed, a brief explosion of amusement, and his shoulders relaxed infinitesimally. "Then what?"

"I'd like... Do you think we could... I'd like one moment in this day to be memorable not in a horrible way."

He got a funny look on his face, like he didn't know whether to guffaw or wince. After a moment's struggle, he said gravely, "Thank you for setting such a low bar."

CHAPTER 7

Maarja hated that this powerful, muscular man possessed a self-deprecating sense of humor. She wanted to *use* him, not *laugh* with him. If they went down that road, toward communication and mutual appreciation…that compounded the passion and made it…more.

She didn't know what exactly; she hadn't the experience to define it. But she knew it was…*more*.

He took his hands away and pulled off his T-shirt. "I promise to make it more than one moment, and yes, memorable in a way that will drive every other thought from your head."

Because she was a practical woman, she gave the sensible response. "I'm not expecting miracles! But—"

"Shhh." He put his finger over her lips. "Let me manage this. You just…relax. Crisscross your legs."

He'd already buried his face there, which made it a little late for caution. But what she'd learned in her youth couldn't be so easily dismissed, and she hesitated.

He tsked, took her ankles and crossed them under her, and turned her to face the wall.

Maybe she'd misunderstood the basics of human mating rituals, but this was weird.

His hands lightly stroked her shoulders.

She jumped.

He shushed her again, and nudged his fingers into the muscles and tendons of her neck. "Let me help you relax. I don't suppose you've ever had a massage?"

She shook her head.

"It seems like the antithesis of something someone who doesn't like to be touched would do. Lean forward." He urged her to put her head against the wall and stroked her spine. His hands slid smoothly along her skin; the scent of citrus and lavender grew stronger as the oil warmed under his palms. His thumbs moved more and more deeply along her vertebrae, down all the way to the crack of her ass, then up to her shoulder blades. There he dug under the bones and into the muscles, making small coaxing noises as if she were a new pet being lured to allow his touch.

It worked. She hovered on that plane between pain and relaxation. Every time he moved to a new position, her shoulders, neck, ribs, waist, he eased more tension away. "Breathe," he whispered. "Breathe slowly. Deeply. Do you meditate?"

She nodded.

"I knew you would. You do what's good for you, don't you?"

She nodded again.

"Let's allow those beta brain waves to take over now." He removed one hand, brought it back, and knelt behind her. Another wave of scent rose from her skin; his fingers glided around under her armpits. "Breathe." His voice crooned in her ear. "Breathe..."

Her chest rose, her breasts reached his cupped hands, and as she exhaled, he followed, his palms massaging, his rough-edged fingers stroking in circles that closed on her nipples until she wanted to scream at him to hurry. When he finally brushed the tips, she shivered convulsively.

"That's so good, isn't it?" His lips touched her at the base of her jaw. "Lean back, let me support you." He didn't wait for her to decide, but eased her back onto his chest.

He could see her now, his hands on her breasts and her legs spread. She felt his breath hitch and she whispered, "Breathe..."

He chuckled deeply and kissed her ear, then with his hand on her jaw, he tilted her head back. "Close your eyes," he whispered, and kissed her. She opened her lips for him and he used his tongue to tease her, and when she answered him, he hummed his approval. Breaking off, he said, "Look at you. Leaning against me, kissing me back, letting me pet your breasts..." His hand appeared with a bottle and he squirted the golden oil on her chest. "That rolls down, tracking toward your cunt which pouts with my neglect and begs for my attention."

She felt as if she should make a response. "Earth's gravity," she told him.

Briefly his chest shook.

He was laughing at her, but she didn't have time to tense before his palms had chased the droplets across her chest, breasts, belly, and stroked them across her clit. She watched his darkly tanned hands touch her in her palest, pinkest place—she refused to call it *that*—and rub and enter her again.

"Does it feel different when your legs are crossed wide than when they were close together?"

"Yes."

"How different?"

She swallowed. "I feel more exposed."

"More helpless? As if you couldn't shut me out?"

She grew tense, and she nodded.

He slid her around to face him. His grave expression frightened her; was he going to say it was too late? He shut her legs and pressed her knees together. "Say *no* whenever you wish. I'll stop. I'll understand."

She glanced down at him. Did he not really care if they—

"I'm as hard as I've ever been in my life. I want to lick you, suck you, take you in every way possible a man can take a woman. Then I want you to do the same for me." How did he know what she was thinking? The skin over his cheekbones had flushed a dark red, and so had his lips. His eyes observed her the way a predator observed its prey, and if anything, the sight of her body made his fingers twitch and reach. "I have committed my sins, Maarja, but I won't take you, no matter how much I want you. Do you understand?"

She nodded.

He sat back on his heels, so his head was below hers. "A man who can't control his urges isn't worth your spit."

She nodded.

"You have to tell me what you want to do. You can refuse me."

"I'm not refusing."

"You have to give me vocal permission."

She looked around the shower. "Are you *filming* this?"

He tossed back his head and roared with laughter. "No. I can see why you'd think so, but no. Nevertheless, I want the words. Refuse or, if you want to proceed, I want a spoken understanding."

"When I look at you, whether I like it or not, all I can think is...*I want to fuck him.*" She had to swallow before she could continue. "I don't know why. Why you?"

"I have some ideas," he said.

"I want to get on top of you, feel what you're like inside of me, ride you until we both collapse and the world vanishes."

"One moment in this day that's memorable not in a horrible way." He echoed her earlier words.

"Yes." She parted her legs and leaned forward. "I may have been misinformed, but as I understand it, your shorts have got to go."

He shed them in record time. He used the oil again, rubbing her until she was so aroused she was almost in pain, then coating himself. He knelt exactly in front of her and pulled her on top of him.

It was so simple. His erection unerringly found her and in slow, smooth small movements began the journey in. Her weight—and the aforementioned earth's gravity—pushed her onto him and the oil eased the way.

Her discomfort grew. She clenched and gave a weak struggle.

His fingers tightened on her butt cheeks. He stopped, glared, and clipped off one single word. "Virgin."

She stared back at him.

He waited.

She admitted the truth with one jerky nod.

"The Fates laugh." He tucked one arm under her bottom and wrapped the other around her waist, pulled her to his chest, and eased back so once again he sat on his heels. As he did, her feet slipped on the tile, she descended and...he was inside. *All* the way inside.

The shower rained down on their heads, a peaceful sound so the opposite of the harsh breathing from them both, and they stared at each other, her in shock, him in... She couldn't begin to decipher what he thought. Not what she'd expected. Not any rush of pleasure, certainly not ecstasy. Fury or grim determination. Or murderous intention.

What did that mean? Was he angry at her? Was he feeling trapped? Did men routinely look like sex turned them into maniacs? How would she know? And...it was a little late to wonder. She was here, now. Should she escape?

Tentatively she slipped her hands off his chest.

Stupid. Did she think she could leave and he wouldn't notice?

"All right?" He caught her hands and brought them up onto his shoulders. "Still hurts?"

She lifted her chin. "It's everything the first time is reputed to be, and that last was like ripping off the bandage."

In another lightning transformation, his expression changed from livid to amused. "Let's start at the beginning. Did you like the kissing?"

"It's interesting."

"You're going to turn my head."

She found her head in the crook of his elbow, his lips on her lips, his breath in her mouth, his tongue… This was no preliminary to sex. This was full-on mouth fucking: the thrusts, the sucking, the way he ran his fingers through her hair and wandered off to kiss her ear, then returned to her mouth as if he couldn't get enough of the sweet taste of her.

He moved inside her, too. Not thrusts. He was as far inside her as he could get. But as their bodies moved, angles changed, her discomfort eased, and she found herself shifting her legs as if she needed to reposition herself.

When she was panting and clutching, he eased away from her mouth, took her hands and kissed her palms, stroked up her arms to her breasts. "Small," he whispered. "Perfect. Responsive." She arched as he rubbed her nipples, over and around, then lifted her enough to lick and suck.

She thought his dick would leave her, but his hips followed enough to stay inside. He began a gentle rocking and she didn't like that, until he lightly bit her nipple and she surged up in surprise and then down on him.

He smiled. "I don't even have to ask if you enjoyed my mouth on your clit. You responded so quickly I never doubted you'd had experience. I'm an idiot. No experience, but you're sensitive, hmm?" He rose onto his knees, pushed her and placed her with her palms holding her upright, then spread her legs wide. "I can pull out and lick you now, or you can spread your legs wide and let me… Wider… There. Look. Look where we're joined."

Verbal record, now a visual record.

His excitement began to crackle in his voice. "Watch as I stroke your clit and you—please, yes. You move."

She had to. She had to move, to lift herself with her arms, lower herself onto his dick, wince and lift again. Varied signals bombarded her; the wild itch of passion, the need to move, to find completion, the pain of penetration, the citrus lavender scent of the oil, his fingers gripping her butt and moving her on him, the sight of his penis sliding in and out, his face, dark and intent, twisted as if he felt her pain. She could hear moans: his, hers, and her thighs ached with effort. Control had crept beyond them and in some lucid corner of her mind, she realized the previous hour could be measured in minutes.

This…this fucking must be measured as a 10.0 body-quake, the largest on record.

Adrenaline and desire had kept her moving; that vanished at the wrong moment and she lost her strength, collapsed into his arms. "I can't…do…anymore."

In a move of magnificent brute force and awkward gracelessness, he toppled backward, holding her firmly in place. "Ride!"

Tears welled. "I'm so close. Please. You do it!"

He rolled her underneath him and suddenly, no space existed between them. His weight held her in place, he held her knees bent over his elbows, his hips plunged in a rhythm whose music only they could hear, he watched her face as if nothing else mattered but the feelings they shared now, and now, and now. And—

She paused, hovering on the verge.

He released her hips. His guttural voice came from deep in his chest. "Fuck me *now*!"

On his command, passion shattered her, releasing a cataclysm that shattered the shell she'd built. She wrapped her legs around his hips and lifted herself, and gloried in his thrusts… and for the first time in her life, she lost herself to the moment and to the man.

CHAPTER 8

When Dante lifted Maarja to her feet, he leaned her against the shower wall and reached out to turn off the water…and she slid down to the floor. She giggled. "Sorry. I'm so sorry. I'm tired and so… Do I sound drunk?"

"Yes, but that's not the issue. You were hurt and grieved. You were in the hospital and they gave you drugs." He sank down beside her and peered into her eyes. "I should never have come on to you."

She was pretty sure he was checking her pupils, not flirting. "I fucked you. Remember? You told me to and I did." All in all, she was feeling quite pleased with herself.

"A virgin. A damned virgin! Broke every rule—" He looked down at his dick as if he blamed it. "How dare a twenty-seven-year-old woman who lives in twenty-first century America become a virgin?"

"I didn't become one. I never stopped being one. That not-touching thing." Her voice wavered a little.

"Right. When you said something happened when you were eleven, I thought—"

He had thought she'd been raped. She'd always been glad that she hadn't, but what had happened was bad enough to leave scars, some literal, some mental, some emotional. "I was at the bus station waiting for Aunt Yesenia to find me, as she promised, and a bunch of guys started to, um…"

"Touch you."

She nodded, feeling ill at the memory. "Mr. Caruthers stopped them."

Dante eased himself down beside her. "Who is Mr. Caruthers?"

"This old guy, a person of color. He'd been in the military and he was on the streets because he never quite left it behind. He saw things."

"Hallucinations?"

"More like the future. Anyway, he told the guys to go away, he focused on each one and told their fortunes, and they scattered. He scared them. He sat with me until the morning, then he took me to Octavia and told her she'd avoided her destiny long enough. When he left, I cried, and he said he'd let me know when Aunt Yesenia came into town. Mr. Caruthers didn't come back for two years, and then it was to bring Alex."

"Your aunt vanished."

"Abandoned me. I wasn't hers, I mean obviously, and whenever she drank, she said she wanted something more than dragging me around being scared all the time, that sooner or later you'd find us and—" Maarja snapped her mouth shut. The meds and the sex must have removed all good sense if she was going to admit *that* to Dante Arundel.

He nodded as if she'd shared what her aunt had said. She supposed he might have a fair supposition based on what he knew and how much, and she was half-inclined to ask him straight out…but what if he *hadn't* recognized her? *Didn't* remember that time before? He was, after all, scarred from the experience. Or from some experience. In his family's business, who knew?

She must have stared at him long enough and acutely enough that he felt he had to speak. "About the sex. I know at first it was uncomfortable—"

She snorted. "Uncomfortable? That's a euphemism."

"But you never seemed afraid or panicked. Did we manage to—?"

"It was memorable not in a horrible way." She rubbed his arm and smiled at him. "Thank you."

He picked up her hand and kissed it. "Generally, after sex a couple freshens up and in this case, there was blood because, you know—virgin."

She touched herself and stared at her red-tipped fingers. "How traditional."

For a long moment, he didn't move.

Sensing tension, she looked up. He had that look again: eyes at half-mast, color on his cheeks and lips, and—she dropped her gaze—his penis had grown in length and girth. "Oh."

"Don't be afraid. I'm not going to...allow you to fuck me again. You're too new and need to heal before we..."

"Do it again?"

"That's up to you, but I'm not a one-night stand kind of guy. Next time you'll be well, and I'll prepare like a normal guy instead of a horny thoughtless beast—" He stopped almost midword and developed this appalled glower that foretold disaster for someone.

"What's wrong?" she asked.

He stood up so fast his foot slipped on the massage oil and he slammed his hand flat on the wall, catching himself. He stared out the glass door toward the bathroom counter, then at his hand, then at his dick. He looked around as if he was looking for something and not finding it.

"What's wrong?" she repeated, more urgently.

He adjusted the water temperature on the handheld, unhooked it, and knelt beside her. As if he hadn't just experienced a twitch and bristle moment, he said, "As I was saying, generally after sex the couple freshens up so if you trust me to help you... Cool water should help with the irritation." He sprayed his own dick until it shrank to almost post-coitus size. "For me, cold would be better, but cool is good for you. After that we can get you into bed and you can sleep after your harrowing day."

She gripped his wrist firmly and shook it. *"What is wrong?"*

In a voice like doom, he said, "In a move of unforgivable carelessness, I didn't wear a condom."

She stared at him.

"I apologize. I swear I've never forgotten in my life. The stupidity—"

"I didn't think about it, either!"

"You're inexperienced, hurt, fatigued, grieved—you have every excuse."

"I'm not looking for an excuse. I may be inexperienced, but I know better." She took the handheld and sprayed her lady bits. She could call them that because, damn it, she wasn't a guy. "You must know I'm not diseased."

"Nor am I. I haven't been with a woman in two years. Two long hectic years." Grimly he paused as if he needed to count and confirm. "That's not my primary concern. If you're not on birth control for some reason, like to control your periods—" He waited hopefully.

She shook her head.

"Then—when was the last day of your last period?"

"It's not that easy. The bleeding kind of trails off, you know." His teeth clinked together in irritation.

"Um, a week ago?" she ventured.

"Five days? Eight days?"

"I don't pay attention. It's an annoyance."

"Don't you keep track on your app?"

"I've never had a reason to care! I'm pretty regular. When I go work out and I beat the stuffing out of the punch bag, I figure I should start carrying tampons. *Okay?*" She got progressively louder as she hefted herself to her feet. "Now that we've got that out of the way, I'm going to take my freshened up *honey house* and go to bed, and if I'm pregnant I will let you know when I damned well feel like it."

Although he hovered at her elbow, making sure not to touch her yet staying close enough to catch her if she collapsed, she climbed into bed (someone had changed the sheets when they heard the shower running). She tucked herself in and went right to sleep.

He dimmed the lights, pulled on a T-shirt and boxers, sat down on the chair beside the bed, watched her sleeping face, and remembered...

CHAPTER 9

Twenty-four years ago...

Nine-year-old Dante Arundel stood in his father's "office," actually
the expansive foyer of their San Francisco Pacific Heights mansion, and
watched Benoit Arundel deal with the business of the day. His father
was an important person, a feared man. Women called him handsome,
and Dante supposed that was true. Wavy blond hair swept his shoulders, shiny with the care his valet took of it.

Dante was the heir apparent, the legitimate son, so it behooved him
to pay attention to his father's mood, and to pay attention to events, for
at any moment Benoit could snap out a question and expect Dante to
figure out the answer.

Dante had seen men die for inattention.

Benoit's imposing velvet-cushioned antique chair—his favorite, and
worn around the edges—rested on an elevated platform. Dante's mother,
Raine Arundel, sat on Benoit's right, but down a step. She was also
an important person, although a woman. She was Benoit's advisor, the
person who decided who would be received and who would be rejected.
It behooved her to present the right people, the ones who brought gifts
and groveled with proper gratitude. Occasionally she got it wrong, but
not often. Benoit's reprimands were swift and painful.

Dante consulted his schedule as a thin worn woman, Pola Daire, arrived through the front door with her pretty, four-year-old daughter, Mary. He glanced at his mother.

She made the almost invisible gesture that told him not to worry.

But she was worried. He could see a tightness around her mouth.

No wonder. Romani. Benoit called them vermin, a scourge on the earth. He carried in him generations of old-world prejudice and, although Dante didn't know why, a particular loathing for the Daire family. Benoit wanted to eradicate them. He intended to eradicate them. Dante watched as the guards put the woman and the child through the metal detector, then wanded them, then ran their purses and shoes through an X-ray.

So Benoit feared them. As he should. Weeks earlier, Denny Daire had been slaughtered in his suburban Napa home while his wife and child were out running errands. Pola and Mary had disappeared; Dante had presumed his father's men had caught up with and eliminated them, too. Yet here they were, walking in as if they'd lost all good sense. As if Pola had lost all good sense.

At a nod from Benoit, Axel did a body search on the woman. The man was a brute, he enjoyed her humiliation too much, and when he removed a small wrapped box from her purse and started to untie the bow, she spoke in a low threatening tone that made Axel glance at Benoit, put the box through the X-ray again, and hand it back to her.

He leaned over the child. Mary was wide-eyed and skittish; she'd been taught not to let strangers touch her. Pola had to kneel beside Mary and speak quiet encouragement, and the look Raine gave the guard made him go over the child quickly and unobtrusively. He did examine Mary's necklace and ask her about it, and at her mother's urging, she spoke of it in a voice that tripped and stammered.

Axel laughed at her, imitated her stutter.

Mary hung her head.

Raine snapped her fingers, and Axel stopped laughing. Yet he still grinned as he dug through the capacious pockets on Mary's white ruffled apron and brought forth three small toys, meant to keep the child busy: a doll, a punch-button puppet, and a video game.

With a shrug at Benoit, he let them go, and Mary eagerly collected her toys and looked wide-eyed around the room.

Benoit leaned over and spoke a question to Raine, and she passed him the tablet with the application that had won Pola her chance to attempt to pass through hell. Benoit ran his eyes over the form. Dante knew the moment he read the information that had won her entrance; Benoit's eyes narrowed, he looked at Raine, who inclined her head, and he handed her back the tablet. He gestured Pola toward him.

She took a moment to speak to Mary, admonishing her to do as she'd been instructed. Mary looked concerned and confused, then she nodded, yet her lip trembled. Andere, their oh-so-dignified and formal butler, moved toward her in that unobtrusive walk of his. He moved quickly, but without drawing attention to himself. His full head of dark wavy hair was trimmed and subdued by his barber. He was tall, wore his suit well, never presumed, observed every situation, and responded accordingly.

Dante could not imagine him dressed in anything but black-and-white.

Andere knelt and spoke in a gentle voice, and offered Mary a handful of the lemon candies he always carried in his pockets. She looked up at Dante as if needing reassurance about taking candy from a stranger.

He nodded and smiled, giving her permission. He was well-acquainted with the restorative power of those French candies. Many a time after his father punished him, the sweet-tart taste of lemon had helped him regain the composure Benoit demanded of his heir. He hoped they gave the little girl pleasure now, in these decisive moments she couldn't possibly understand.

Pola walked toward Benoit with her shoulders back and her chin up. Benoit preferred to see applicants cower, but in the end, defiance or entreaty would make no difference. He would do what he would do. Probably she knew that, or possibly she didn't know how to grovel.

Pola stopped the prescribed distance away and offered the wrapped box.

Drawn by the sense that this moment had consequences he couldn't comprehend, Dante drew close enough to hear Pola speak.

Her voice was low, husky, vibrant. "Master, I brought a gift."

A bribe.

"It is the tribute you demanded of my husband."

"You are wise." Benoit accepted the box and flicked the bow open.

Dante exchanged glances with the bodyguard Benoit insisted Dante keep with him at all times. Nate was ten years old, tall and broad, stoic and taciturn. His last name was Arundel, so he was a relative of some kind, and he and Dante communicated without words. They both understood the significance of this moment.

"This small red glass bottle, the Bottiglia di Fiamma—"

Bottle of Flame, Dante translated from Italian.

"La Bouteille de Flamme," Benoit said assertively.

Of course. Pola gave it the Italian name, for it had been created in the fumes and furnaces of the island of Murano. Benoit was French and a bully; he had no respect for the origins and artistry.

Pola ignored Benoit's interruption. "The bottle, stoppered with wax—"

Benoit clamped his fingers over her skinny wrist. "Say it."

She stood straight and tall, unyielding, until Benoit began to grind and twist her bones, then she repeated, "La Bouteille de Flamme, stoppered in wax, gives honor to the blood of Jånos, the revered founder of my husband's tribe, a martyr who fought evil and won."

Benoit tossed her wrist aside. Lifting the bottle, he stared at the contents. "You exaggerate. All Jånos did was die." He showed it to the room. It was, indeed, a small red bottle, perhaps the size of little Mary's hand; it gleamed not like glass, but like polished rubies.

The sycophants in the foyer, and there were always sycophants present, applauded gingerly—vigorous applause might attract Benoit's attention, and that could be as painful as being ignored—and murmured their admiration and praise. Even Dante thought it beautiful and knew why Benoit had done so much to acquire it; it beckoned like a seductive woman.

Pola continued, "I bring dishonor to myself and my people by giving this into your possession, into the hands of a hated Arundel, worthy descendent of Èrthu the Pale, the legendary exterminator who raped and murdered, and skewered Rom babies on his lance."

Dante didn't know whether the woman praised Benoit and his ancestor, or spat on him. Nor could he tell if Benoit enjoyed her calm-voiced tribute, or would take a terrible revenge. Both, probably.

Definitely.

Benoit summoned Andere, who left Mary and in his unhurried pace came to Benoit's side. Benoit handed the box to him and spoke a single word.

Of course. Benoit trusted Andere as he trusted his wife. Andere had been a retainer to the family as long as Dante could remember, and moreover, he came from a family who had faithfully served the Arundels for generations. No one loved Benoit, but he commanded loyalty as easily as he demanded obedience.

Andere bowed to the man he served as master, and to Raine, the master's wife, and carried the box away to be put in the safe.

"Since the day Èrthu laid eyes on the vasi sanguigni—*"*

Blood vessel, Dante translated again.

"—so precious to my people, all the lords of Arundel have sought it, not for its holiness nor for its honor, but to own as a thing, a possession, a vanity. Now you have it, and tonight you may hold it and gloat, and in return, I seek a boon."

Tension coated Dante's tongue with the copper taste of blood, yet little Mary seemed unaware. She played hopscotch on the parquet floor. She turned her polished stone necklace to catch the light.

"In return for this tribute, I want you to guarantee my daughter's safety." Pola indicated Mary, who stood in the floor-to-ceiling mirror and admired her flowered dress and embroidered apron, her black patent leather shoes and white socks, the long blue ribbon threaded through the waves of her dark red hair. "Look at her. She's a child. When she was a toddler, she climbed on the back of the toilet tank."

"The toilet tank?" Benoit laughed.

"She fell. She hit her head. Since then, she hasn't been right."

Mary got the push-button puppet out of her pocket and made it dance in the mirror.

"You see her. She's not smart. She didn't speak until she was three,

and she stutters. Your man—" Pola indicated Axel "—laughed at her. She can't hurt you, Master. I beg you—"

Dante had seen this kind of desperation before; he held out no hope for the woman or the child.

Benoit interrupted Pola's plea. "Where's the stopper?" He leaned forward, watching her.

"I don't know."

"You bring me only half of what I desire. I want the stopper for the bottle. You know I must have it, for without that the bottle is worthless."

"Then return the bottle."

They engaged in a staring match, and to Dante's surprise, Benoit looked away first.

Dante realized this woman must have no real hope, or she wouldn't have come here, and most certainly she wouldn't have engaged Benoit in a war she refused to lose.

Andere returned and in his capacity as butler, he assessed the situation and moved to take Pola away.

Before he could reach for her, Pola said, "Benoit, my grandmother told me the stopper broke many years ago. That's why la Bouteille de Flamme is sealed with wax. Master—"

"I don't believe you." Benoit spoke each word clearly, a double death sentence. "No matter whether your daughter is defective. She's one of the Romani, the seed of the lice who crawl the earth, and as such, the sooner she dies, the happier I'll be. The safer my son will be."

"No." Pola sank to her knees. "No!" She crawled until she was beside him, lifted her hands in supplication.

Andere hurried forward.

The guards lunged toward them.

With a gesture, Benoit stopped them all. Pulling his big pistol from the holster at his chest, he pointed it at the middle of Pola's forehead.

Dante turned away; his father would say he was weak, for he couldn't stand to see the woman and child killed.

Pola screamed, "Mary! Now! Run!"

The little girl snapped out of her preoccupation with the puppet in the mirror. She dropped it, stared at her mother.

Benoit's pistol changed direction, pointed at Mary.

Of course. Benoit preferred to enjoy the greatest amount of suffering out of his executions, and having the mother witness her child's death would accentuate the sweetness of the bloodshed.

"Your son will pay for your sins!" Pola screamed, and slammed herself into Benoit's chest.

Mary put her hand in her pocket, pulled out her video game, fumbled with it, then turned and ran.

At that moment, Dante knew.

He sprang forward...as the explosion rocked the room.

CHAPTER 10

One angry early morning thought woke Maarja and brought her from a prone to sitting position. "You treacherous bastard!"

Beside her in the bed, Dante sat up. "What is it?" He spoke in a low voice, he held a pistol, and he held it pointed toward the door.

Where had he got the gun? Did he sleep with it?

She glared at him. "You keep massage oil in your shower!"

The pistol drooped in his grip. "Yeah?" As if he couldn't not, he glanced at her boobs, and his gaze lingered.

Even more offended, she pulled the sheet up, tucked it under her armpits. "How many women are you screwing in there?"

His jaw dropped. He rumbled like a volcano getting ready to erupt. "That's it? That's why we're awake at—" he checked the clock "—5:14 a.m.?" He slid the pistol into a pocket hidden in the headboard.

He'd climbed in bed with her while she slept. Fine. He wore a T-shirt and boxers. Fine. It was his bed, and a point might be made that she needed care. But this! Massage oil in the shower! "How many women…?"

His hand hovered over her bare shoulder. "You are the only woman I've made love to in my shower. Just you."

How likely was that? "Pull the other one."

"Look. I told you." He flung himself back on the pillows. "It's been two damned long difficult years of celibacy. I've been busy. Stuff has been happening. Business. Family. You can believe me or not. I'm a serial monogamist. Two years! I keep the massage oil in the shower to jack off. With the oil, it's easier. Glad you wandered in there to discover the conditions of my pitiful love life."

He was so indignant she had to give up her own indignation and grin. "I've heard if a man goes six months without, he's a virgin again."

"Who told you that?"

"My sisters and I were drinking with my mother—"

He rose from the bed, fetched one of his button-up shirts, held it so she could slip her arms in, helped her fasten it.

It was almost funny how careful he was not to touch her skin. It was not at all funny how much she wanted him to.

"Your mother?" he asked.

"My foster mother. Octavia. According to her own description, she's quite a broad."

"What do you say?"

"She is definitely quite a broad." She relaxed back on her pillow. "A woman of strength and determination who's not afraid of doing the right thing."

"She taught you a lot about doing the right thing."

"I've had many good examples in my life." *Pola, my birth mother.* "Even some men."

"Mr. Caruthers."

She inclined her head.

"I've got a few morals, myself." He sat up, rested his forearm on his crooked knee. "For instance, nothing could have convinced me to touch you if I'd known you were a virgin."

Irritation began to scratch at her mind. "But it would have been okay if I hadn't been?"

"Yes!"

"Because virgins are more valued?"

"Do you want the politically correct answer or the one that for me is the truth?"

Call her a pessimist, but this was not starting out well. "Give me the truth. I can take it."

He looked into her face. "You know who I am."

Slowly she sat up. He wasn't asking whether she knew his name. He was asking if she knew who he *was*. "I do." Should she panic?

"You know who my father was. You know who my family is. You know the war that lies in the long years of history between my family and yours."

That settled any question that lingered in her mind. He knew she was the child who...escaped. He knew what they shared; in the same instant, in a forceful explosion, their lives had broken in half.

How long had he known? Had he recognized her yesterday? Or had Mrs. Arundel known and told him?

So many questions, all of them horrible and terrible, all of them leading to pain and death...for her. She met Dante's gaze because she had seen her mother grovel, and what good had that done? If she had to die, she'd do it with her chin high. "I do know."

"You remember the explosion. That's clear."

"I don't remember my father at all, and I remember my mother only in flashes, but the explosion—yes, I remember that, all too often, in my nightmares."

"Our two families have driven each other almost to extinction. Ruthless killings, biblical in scope. An eye for an eye, a tooth for a tooth."

Bitterly she said, "And the whole world is blind and toothless."

"According to my father—he told this to me many times—the only way this can end is with one family victorious."

"The Arundels victorious." It wasn't a guess.

"Of course. That means that every person in your family is dead, slaughtered on the altar of a blood vendetta begun so long ago no one remembers the origins."

He was wrong. She knew. "This is quite a roundabout way of explaining why you would have kept it in your pants if you'd known I was a virgin."

He held up his hand, demanding her patience. "You have to know there's another way to finish this vendetta."

"I'm all for it, since from my point of view, I'm the one who's likely to end up dead."

He turned his head and looked at her, his eyes dark and inscrutable. "An unbreakable union between the two families."

"A contract between us promising we won't whack each other anymore? Like that's going to—"

He smiled a smile that mocked her foolishness.

She caught on. *Marriage.* He was talking about *marriage.* That kind of union. She hung on the realization as if it were a noose around her neck. "No, no. Don't be silly. That would be… medieval."

"Medieval as in how long this vendetta has been going on? Medieval as the traditional medieval way to end a feud?"

He leaned in close, close enough to make her feel threatened, and she was pretty sure that was what he wanted.

He asked, "Why should I even care whether we have a peace? You're the only remaining member of your family. If I kill you, the vendetta is over. The Arundels have won. That's one issue settled." He leaned back. "But I'm not my father. I'm not a vengeful bastard who justifies intercourse with the enemy before I snuff them out. Before I snuff *you* out. I actually have real human emotions, like compassion, which as far as I can tell, my father never did. No. I'll end the feud without more violence, and the only bloodshed is your blood in my shower."

Way to spell it out. He hadn't learned the lessons his father taught. Maybe he'd escaped soon enough. Maybe he hadn't inherited those character traits. Maybe his mother had instilled morals in him. Whatever it was, he wouldn't kill her...but he would marry her.

Medieval? Yes! This guy was medieval all the way. Firmly she said, "I'm not deliberately flinging myself on pointed bamboo stakes to heal the breach."

He lifted the covers and looked. "Did you hear that?" he said conversationally. "You've been compared to a pointed bamboo stake."

Cute. He was talking to his cock. She was *not* amused. "I'm not going to...to produce a child so we can declare that a ridiculous hostility is all better now. My God, would you want to spend the rest of your life with me?" Before he could answer, she answered for him. "No, you would not! We barely know each other."

"I know you deliberately faced the fire and explosion to save my mother."

"I didn't succeed!" Tears sprang to her eyes.

He took a breath, looked away, struggled with emotion she could comprehend only too well. "My mother died despite your efforts, not because of them."

"Yay me for not being murderous." She used the sheet to wipe her damp cheeks. "That doesn't bring her back to life."

"But a life may have already begun that will bring peace between the families—and you're the one carrying it."

"Unlikely." She waved an airy hand.

Yet he was starting to get to her.

"To return to the question about your virginity—you'll admit I had no reason to suspect you might be a virgin."

"I cannot believe I'm the only woman who made it to twenty-seven without—" she waved a hand "—sex."

"Nuns? Vestal virgins? Who? Who do you know—?"

"No one. All right? No one. I'm the only one." She crossed her arms over her chest. She wished he'd stop harping on it. Her sisters knew. Octavia knew. Other than that, she kept it pretty quiet because the one time she'd told a friend, the reaction had been incredulous. And loud. In a public place, and was one of the most humiliating moments of her life. She'd only been twenty-three, then. She could only imagine what it would be like now. She brightened. "On the other hand…it's now a moot point."

"And we're right back to medieval times."

"No blood on the sheets," she said in a deliberately over-cheerful tone. "No proof for the skeptics!"

"No skeptic would dare disparage my word."

No. She supposed not. She pulled the sheets up to her chin. Not when he wore the cold expression that clearly said he wouldn't hesitate to kill.

"Based on what you said, I believed that at eleven you had been—"

"Hurt. I was bruised and intimidated and fingered. I was mocked for my helplessness. That incident put the fear of men in me, the trauma lingered, and I never met anyone who I cared to put to the test." *Until you.* The unspoken words lingered in the air.

Some emotion brushed him, gratification, maybe, or confidence, or conceit. Of course, he pushed that aside and went right back to his line of reasoning. "Add in what your foster mother said, that after six months a man is a virgin again—"

"She was joking!"

"—we have a double-ancient-enemy-virgin-banging-without-protection. Which to me sounds like something out of a prophecy. Death or life, Maarja. That's what this has come down to."

"Superstition! This is not fate, it's nothing but superstition!" He opened his mouth again and she charged on. "Okay. Okay." She held up her hands in a stop gesture. Would he just *stop*? "Even if the gods are laughing, I do have one other suggestion, a possibility you haven't mentioned. Considered."

"Yes?"

"I'm a fine art mover. You're some kind of billionaire invested in…some vague thing that isn't illegal."

"And isn't immoral."

She hesitated. That sounded less like *We could do this thing to stop the nonsense* and more like *I'm trying to impress you with how appropriate I am as a husband.* She didn't know if that was better, or more alarming, and in the middle of this conversation, she didn't have time to decide. "I'm glad to hear that." Neutral enough. "We could just leave each other alone. Never see each other, pretend we don't know each other, go our separate ways…"

"We could. Unless there's—"

"A child. Yes, yes, I know. But if that's not happening—" *really, it was really unlikely, really* "—and we'll know soon enough, why should we give in to superstition? Why would we ever see each other again?"

"Because for the last two years, someone has been trying to kill my mother."

CHAPTER 11

Heartbeat.

Heartbeat.

Heartbeat.

Shocked deep breath.

"Two years? Two years someone has been trying to—" Words failed Maarja.

Dante nodded. "A runaway vehicle. A random street shooting that came too close."

"Crap." She twisted the sheet between her fingers. They didn't feel as nimble as usual. They felt big, clumsy.

"A dinner out that ended in the hospital with lifesaving measures."

"Food poisoning?" she ventured.

"Simply put, a poisoning. My cousin Jack Arundel is a police detective—"

And didn't that say every damned thing about his family?

"—and he said unless we could figure out who, they were going to get better at planning, while we would inevitably fail in our protective measures, and the killers would finish the job." For a guy who was as attached to his mother as Dante had appeared to be, he'd been amazingly stoic.

She put her hand on his arm. "You *can* cry, you know. She was your mother."

He shook his head. "I can't cry. I need to discover who wanted her dead."

"Who do you suspect?"

"Traditionally, I'd suspect you."

She had to unclench her teeth to speak. "Can we dismiss that suspicion?"

"Yes. You've exonerated yourself."

She touched the still-warm skin on her face. "Gee, thanks."

"And put yourself into the path of the killer."

"What?" He looked serious. "Why? Because I saved her?"

"That, certainly. An assassin wanted no body to remain, no trace of Raine Arundel left on this earth."

"Obliteration."

"And a move back to the old ways."

"Will they kill you next?"

"Not easily." He smiled chillingly. "I do hope they try. That would simplify the task of finding the traitors, but it seems unlikely."

"Why wouldn't they try to kill you?" She answered the question herself. "Because they believe your mother's death will serve as a warning, make you reconsider the move to the legal and moral. Which is not as profitable?"

"Not as easily profitable. Not for people who want to break the rules."

"Maybe they think the move to respectability was made on your mother's insistence. Now you'll be out from under her influence and—"

"They can influence me instead."

"Have they *met* you?"

"I assume. There's a good chance they're related to me, although that's not one hundred percent. If that's the case, it means they hate you because you're a Daire. Romani. We're back to the blood vendetta and yet another reason to end your life." He was such a straight talker.

Why? She'd lived with this her whole life. She knew the ugly facts. "Did your mother recognize me the first time I worked for her?"

"She suspected."

"Why?"

"You have the look of the Daire Romani. And to…" He hesitated.

Now he was being delicate? "To who?"

"You have a striking resemblance to that old portrait of Vlad Tepes."

Vlad Tepes. Vlad Drăculea. Romanian prince of such cruelty and fame he inspired the fictional character Dracula. "I have never impaled anyone."

"Nor have I, although I cannot promise that in the past some Arundel has not."

For safety measures, she had changed her appearance, but the complexion, the eyes, the mouth—nothing could be done to disguise them. Not that she should want to. Not that she should need to. But something about knowing that how she looked could result in explosions and gunshots, execution and blood-shed, made her think cutting her distinctive dark red hair was no great sacrifice. Wearing reading glasses she didn't need was a subtle subterfuge. Attracting no attention had been her goal… and now she had flung herself into the forefront of the blood vendetta by attempting to rescue Mrs. Arundel…and sleeping with Dante Arundel.

She put her hand to her forehead. What she'd done over the past twenty-four hours had been nothing but events in her life… and they would possibly end it. How had a few hours managed to gain such importance?

She looked up to see Dante watching her, his somber expression telling her all too clearly he knew what thoughts possessed her. "What convinced her that I was...the little girl?"

"She had me watch the security video. I remembered you."

"I remembered you, too."

"You knew me at once."

She sighed. It wasn't something she wanted to admit, but... "Yes. I recognized you. It's all in my mind in flashes of memory. Except at night, in my dreams, it's a video. My mother had told me what to do. She had instructed me over and over, but I was...stupid, young. We came into that magnificent room. That man with the mean face laughed at me and I cried. Then I was playing and I glanced up and you were watching. You were frowning. The nice man gave me lemon candies."

"Our butler, Andere. He was injured in the blast."

"I'm sorry to hear that." She was. She'd eaten one candy, slipped the rest into her pocket, and that night they were all she and Aunt Yesenia had to eat.

"We did look for you," Dante assured her.

"I never doubted that."

"Not to kill you."

She had nothing remotely civil to say to that.

"The family is legitimate now. The deaths and chaos caused by...your mother convinced my mother it was time. According to Arundel tradition, she should have retired to a convent and worn a widow's veil to mourn Benoit until the end of her days."

"Medieval," Maarja muttered.

He stroked her fingers as if to give her strength. "If she was going to remake the organization in her vision, if she was going seize control from among the contenders, her sight needed to be omniscient, her reach had to be far, and her justice had to be swift and brutal."

Again her perception of Raine Arundel shimmered and shifted. "Yes. I understand. I think."

"I have a number I want you to memorize."

"Number?" Where had that come from?

"A phone number. In case you need me for any reason."

"Like if someone is trying to kill me?" She really hoped that wasn't what he meant.

He kissed her fingers. "Or you're pregnant."

She also really hoped he didn't think that. "Listen. If I am, you don't have to worry about it. If there's one thing I know from my upbringing, it's how to raise a child alone. You don't have to be involved." She was trying to be reassuring, but found herself pressed into the pillows, a big angry, broad-shouldered man leaning over her.

"Do not even—" he separated the words into individual threats "—think that's going to happen. My child will have two involved parents who love and guide him or her or *them*."

"Okay." She hadn't been afraid of him before, but this made her wonder what trigger had been tripped. "But we don't have to—"

"Live together? Yes, we do." He shook her a little. "You understand?"

She got a panicky, trapped feeling. "Calm down. We're not talking about a child, we're talking about a supposition."

"You'll call me if you're pregnant."

"Yes. Yes, of course." She looked around. "My phone—"

"Is being replaced."

"Oh." She hadn't thought, but somewhere along the line, when the emergency room personnel had removed and discarded her clothes, her phone had vanished. "Was it...?"

"Broken. I'm surprised you're not more broken." He leaned back, but he watched her as if he was ready to pounce—again—and recited the phone number.

She recited it back to him. Several times. Until he pronounced himself satisfied, tucked her in, and rose to start his day. "Sleep as long as you can. My mother says it's the best way to heal."

His mother didn't say anything anymore. She was dead.

But Maarja felt no urge to remind him. She didn't even want to remember that herself.

CHAPTER 12

When Maarja opened her eyes again, it was eight thirty in the morning and the Bay Area fog was lightening outside the window. She rolled over, the aches and pains inflicted by the previous day made themselves known, and she groaned as she stood and hobbled toward the bathroom. She must have banged her knee, because it felt swollen and stiff. Her neck ached as if she had whiplash. She was pretty sure the bruise on her hip went all the way to the bone, and she must have landed with her arm skewed because her shoulder ached as if it had been twisted.

She was also hungry.

How could the grief and disbelief about Mrs. Arundel linger in the background, yet be supplanted by the real physical parts of life? Body functions, bruises, hunger, thirst? It seemed impossible, but all very real.

Boy shorts and a lace cami bra rested in a basket on the counter, and a long loose, light dress of deep amethyst hung on the robe hook with her name safety-pinned to the hanger. She had to sit down to pull the underwear up her legs, and her shoulder ached as she raised her arms to struggle into the bra. The dress draped well, and she supposed the wraparound styling was easier than a pull-over-her-head type, but she had to work to get her arms in the sleeves and shrug into it.

Movement sucked.

On the other hand, this dress looked *fabulous darling*, so fabulous she wanted to take it off and check the label. But she couldn't face going through the twisting motion again, so she would assume she probably wouldn't recognize the maker, anyway. She didn't shop at Saks Fifth Avenue, or even Off 5th. Good peasant stock, that was her.

The hospital had suggested an over-the-counter pain reliever, and she intended to find some.

Because…the morning after losing her virginity was no stroll through the park, either. She was sore, and between that, glancing at the shower where the plastic jar of massage oil hung on the wall, and remembering Dante's earlier alarming conversation, she couldn't move without being very aware that her advanced age hadn't helped her easily slip through the ritual deflowering. First-time sex was everything the novels had promised: painful, shocking, invasive, mind-blowing, pleasure-driven, and if there was a baby, life-changing.

She clamped down on that last thought.

She'd barely be concerned if Dante hadn't been so insistently throwing around terms like *unbreakable union* and suggesting they had somehow been manipulated by fate to be the ones who would end a centuries-long and bloody feud through, you know, primitive fucking and massive reproducing.

Although it would be nice to never again be afraid for her life…

As she exited the bathroom, a tall broad-hipped woman bustled in holding a tray. "We were listening for you to wake. Mr. Arundel wanted you to have a hearty breakfast before you took your pills, then he's got his personal stylist waiting in his office for you to fix up your poor hair." The woman surveyed Maarja's head and tsked sadly. "Such a pretty color to have singed so badly. But there's always some sacrifice when you're a hero, and I know dear Raine would—" The woman's voice trembled and caught, then she forged on. "I'm Fedelma Arundel Lambert, Mr. Benoit Arundel's cousin. When my husband was killed, I took over the household management for the Arundels. You're Maarja Daire and you're with—"

Maarja tensed.

"—Saint Rees Fine Arts Movers."

"Right! Right." Maarja had thought Fedelma was going to say, *You're with Dante.* She wasn't. When she could, she'd be out of here and she would never look back, and never mind the internal voice that said, *Like he's going to put up with any disappearing act I could perform unless he damned well wanted to.*

"Sit here, Miss Daire." Fedelma put the tray on the desk and pulled the metal dome off the plate. "Since Chef didn't know what you liked, he prepared a variety of foods. Irish oatmeal, bacon, a soft-boiled egg, a bowl of fresh fruit, a bread basket with toast, rolls, and croissants."

"Wow." Maarja could get used to this.

Someone knocked on the door. Fedelma opened it and accepted a second tray laden with two insulated jugs, and small pitchers of orange juice, grapefruit juice, and tomato juice. She returned to the desk and at Maarja's indication poured a cup of hot tea and a glass of grapefruit juice. "There's butter, jam, and honey, and Chef is standing by if you have any special requests."

Maarja picked up her fork and speared a raspberry. "This is perfect, thank him for me, and thank you."

"Don't hesitate to ask. We feel privileged to serve the young lady who put her own life on the line to—" Fedelma choked again, and this time she whipped a white handkerchief out of her skirt pocket and wiped her eyes.

Which made Maarja tear up, which made Fedelma pat her shoulder and say bracingly, "None of that. Ever since her husband died, Raine has been busy and happy. This isn't how I thought it would end, not now, but we all know for the Arundels, an early death is always a possibility."

Savagely unwilling to admit the possibility, Maarja asked, "Why? Why is it a possibility? If Dante has really moved the family into legal enterprises, what could anyone achieve with murder?"

"Memories are long."

"Ridiculous!" Maarja sprinkled flake salt on her oatmeal, added a sprinkling of dried cranberries, and mashed them into the warm cereal. "Mrs. Arundel wasn't even really an Arundel. She simply married one and I'm not surprised to hear it was an unhappy union. Did she even have a choice?"

"No. We never... None of us..."

"But you said you were Benoit's cousin. Your last name is Lambert. You weren't forced to marry an Arundel."

"My husband was part of the organization. As a reward, Benoit gifted me to him."

"That's medieval." A word Maarja had heard too often this morning. "Did you fight it?"

"The marriage? That's not how it works. They look for pretty girls who love their families and whose fathers or mothers or brothers or sisters—or all of the above—are in trouble. Deals are struck. Sacrifices are made. No one escapes, and if they do, they escape alone." Fedelma stood with her hands clasped at her waist, a solid woman of good sense whose exterior never hinted at her difficult hidden past. In a portentous voice, she said, "Maarja, you know of what I speak."

Maarja's father was dead. Her mother was dead. But she had found a family and a job, she wasn't alone, and she resented Fedelma's belief that she was. Yet how could Maarja tell this woman who had suffered through a marriage with a thug that she could have escaped that particular prison? Fedelma's circumstances differed. *Her* mother hadn't blown up Benoit Arundel to give her daughter a chance at life.

It was all a matter of perspective.

A thought occurred to Maarja. "Wait! You don't think

I'm somehow stuck in the same—" *trap* was the wrong word "—situation as you were?"

"Of course not."

Maarja waited for more.

"Not long after the wedding, my husband was killed on a mission." Fedelma lifted the teapot. "Can I freshen your cup?"

The conversation made Maarja view the massive mounds and variety of foods with a different perspective. Maybe this breakfast wasn't merely a thanks for trying to save Mrs. Arundel. Maybe this dress, expensive and flattering, was more in the line of enticement for the woman who Dante saw as his predestined mate.

A surge of horrified rebellion made her push back the chair and bound to her feet. And stagger a little when her hip twinged.

Fedelma caught her arm. "Are you all right?"

"I just…remembered I have an appointment today…at the dentist's office."

"What's your dentist's name? I'll call and explain that you have to cancel. Do you want me to schedule a different day?"

Maarja stared at Fedelma. Was she acting like an assistant? *Her* assistant? "No. I'll go…to the dentist."

"Miss Daire, you can't go to the dentist. Your skin looks sunburned from the heat of the blast and if you had to open your mouth wide, your lips and your cheeks would crack. You need a gentle facial and Dante has arranged one for you." Fedelma pushed her back into the chair. "I know you're hungry. You haven't eaten since, at best, lunch yesterday. Finish your breakfast. I'll take care of everything. Now, what's the name of your dentist?"

Maarja sat and tried to think, but her stomach growled and her fingers trembled. She needed the over-the-counter pain reliever Fedelma had placed on her tray, and she remembered the doctor's lecture to have something in her stomach when she took them. Picking up a cinnamon roll, she peeled off the outer layer, and before she popped it in her mouth, she said, "I was lying about the dentist. I wanted out of here."

"Ah."

One thing about Fedelma: she didn't require a lot of explaining to. Her experiences meant she understood, or at least so Maarja supposed. While Fedelma moved about the suite, straightening and picking up, and for sure not leaving Maarja alone, Maarja ate until she felt she could take the pain relievers. Then she ate a little more—the chef, whoever he was, knew how to prepare a toothsome breakfast—and with a sigh put down her fork. Taking a breath, she announced, "I'm ready."

"I'll let Dante know." Fedelma seemed so stuck in some kind of old-world serving mode Maarja was startled to see her pull a phone from her skirt pocket and message. She immediately got a beep back, and she chuckled. "He's impatient." She helped Maarja to her feet—the painkillers hadn't kicked in yet—and led her through the door.

A man in a gray suit, white shirt, and red tie walked toward them, frowning intently.

Dante.

No! Maarja did a double take.

Not Dante. Handsome, younger, unscarred: he was Dante as Dante would have been if the explosion had never happened. His full upper lip was shaped like a heart, with an indent that went well with the sexy half smile he developed when he saw her. He changed directions to intercept them, and not for the first time in her life, she saw the full seductive force of a man who thought he was God's gift to women.

Before he reached his goal, Fedelma stepped between them, spitting such a rapid stream of non-English invective that Maarja, who had taken four years of French, caught merely a word here and there. But the tone was clear; *This woman is out-of-bounds.*

He stopped in his tracks, and for a moment, his expression turned ugly. He wiped that away so quickly it was almost a mirage. That half smile returned, and he chucked Maarja under the chin. "When he's done with you, I'll call."

As he strode away, Maarja stared after him. "Unbelievable! Back to the 1950s."

"That's Connor Arundel," Fedelma told her. "He's a second cousin to Dante."

"Connor? That's quite a name. I can tell he's related, because of the looks, of course, but he's got the attitude." The asshole attitude, and mean with it.

"He's been much spoiled. He's childish when he's crossed, and a wild card Dante holds close." Fedelma lowered her voice. "Between you and me, he can be dangerous. Avoid him when possible."

Maarja nodded. "I'll do my best to avoid them all."

Too late, Maarja. You messed that up yesterday when you let the old memories lead you to risk your life for an Arundel. God, when she considered what she had started, she wanted to clasp her hands around her head and squeeze some sense into herself.

When she looked up, Fedelma was waiting patiently for her to return to the present. "Ready?" She acted as if Maarja's momentary breakdown was entirely to be expected.

Maarja supposed that was true. The last twenty-four hours had been like some black comedy, the kind sophisticated people laughed at and she winced about. "Ready as I'll ever be."

Fedelma led her down the hall to what must have been designed as a massive dining room now turned into an equally massive office.

Maarja had barely enough time to take in the high ceilings, filled bookshelves, broad fireplace surrounded by an odd seating arrangement, the oddly stark standing desk before the windows, and the looming man's shadow behind it before Dante said, "Maarja, welcome to the heart of my business domain."

Said Hades to Persephone.

CHAPTER 13

As Dante walked out from behind the desk and away from the bright windows, he came into focus, a handsome man who smiled as if he knew exactly what was in her mind. Uncomfortable concept, especially when her mind had become a flaming dumpster of suspicion, grief, wariness, and the consuming need to hightail it out of here.

He stopped two feet short of her and looked her over as if she were an art object of which he'd recently taken possession. "As I hoped, the gown looks lovely on you." Stretching out his hand, he touched her cheek and winced. "But your face bears testimony to yesterday's act of bravery. I hope you'll let my facialists care for your skin."

Facialists? Was that some kind of cult?

He didn't wait for her consent, but turned her, and with a hand on her spine, propelled her toward the fireplace. The odd furniture arrangement turned out to be a portable massage table. The two white-coat-wearing men fixed their gazes on her face without actually seeing her; they saw nothing but her skin. Both made shocked clucking noises. The taller one took her hand and started to pat it, then brought it close to the lamp and shook his head at his partner. In absolute silence they wrapped a plastic cape loosely around her neck, gently adjusted a plastic cap around her flame-receded hairline, switched on some gentle flute music, and with a gesture invited her to lie down on the table.

She glanced toward Dante, but he'd already returned to his desk and frowned at a paper in his hand.

She glanced at Fedelma, who smiled encouragingly at her, seated herself on a rocking chair, and pulled yarn and a crochet needle out of the bag beside it.

The short facialist moved a screen between her and the rest of the office.

Maarja had fallen down the rabbit hole into some place that was definitely not Wonderland, more like a Grimms' fairy tale. She slid onto the table and reclined with a grimace while Shorty slipped a pillow under her head and one under her knees, then patted her arm. "Don't fret. I'm Vincent, Frederick's assistant, and he is a genius. Your skin will thank you."

These guys could not be for real.

Vincent placed a weighted bag over her eyes, the scent of lavender wafted over her, the heated table warmed her back, and while Frederick delicately applied cool lotions to her face and hands, Vincent explained about the organic ingredients and the purity and the...

Maarja woke with a start. She opened her eyes and looked around without turning her head. The weighted eye bag was gone. She was still on the massage table in Dante's office. The facialists and their capes and caps had vanished, her face and hands felt refreshed—and she felt stupid, lolling around behind a screen in broad daylight in a working environment, probably snoring, certainly drooling.

She could hear the murmur of male voices, then Fedelma's soft voice, then Dante saying, "Excuse me."

Maarja turned her head and watched as he moved the screen aside. Leaning over her, he smiled as if she were a pet that amused him. "You fell asleep before Frederick and Vincent were halfway through the skin treatment. They were so flattered, I didn't tell them the pain reliever had probably kicked in. Do you feel better?"

She rolled to one side and he helped her sit up. "Yes. Thank you. I do." She wanted to tell him she didn't need his assistance, and to stop smirking at her, but her real goal was to get out of here without causing a fuss, so she stood and said, "My skin feels much better. Please thank Frederick and Vincent for me."

"They have been thanked."

"If you'll let me borrow a phone, I'll call Saint Rees and he'll send someone to pick me up—"

"Kristoff has been waiting for you to wake so he can cut your hair. Right now I'm afraid you look spooky."

"And not in a good way?"

Dante laughed and indicated the beautician's chair that had been set up nearby. By...someone? While she'd been snoring and drooling, had everyone in the building come in to view her?

She glanced at the man who stood beside Dante's desk. He wore a dark suit, crisp white shirt, a loosened red tie, and scuffed shoes with thick soles. In San Francisco, it was a given he walked a lot, because the traffic constantly sucked. He didn't merely watch her; he examined her, and his gaze was not friendly.

"After your haircut," Dante said, "Jack wants to ask some questions about what happened yesterday."

Jack. The cousin/police detective. "How many cousins do you have?"

"The Arundels breed successfully." He paused to let her take that in; it seemed that everything he said had a subtext. "Can you talk to Jack without undue distress?"

Do I have a choice? "Yes, of course."

"I'll get him some lunch while he waits. Cops can always eat." Dante glanced at Jack. "Food will soften his mood. He's very fond of my mother, and not at all happy about the explosion."

"Who is?" she asked softly.

"Someone." Jack sounded like a dog at the end of his chain, growling and unfriendly.

"Right." She gave a quick sigh. "Right."

"Here's Kristoff. He's a genius with a razor."

Maarja watched a white-coated female appear, pushing a wheeled stainless steel tray loaded with a stylist's tools, and another thin tall man dressed all in black walking behind her. "Another cousin?"

"Snippy," Dante observed. "And no, no relation."

The assistant pushed the tray to the side of the chair.

Kristoff waved as if to bless the whole proceeding, then his vision fixed on Maarja and he froze in horrified disbelief. To Dante, he said, "This? You want me to fix this? I'm a hairdresser, not a miracle worker! It cannot be done. No stylist could work with this, this, this, inglorious cruelty that was delivered upon this head."

"In all of San Francisco," Dante said, "only one man can liberate my darling Maarja from the pitiable outcome of her headlong rush to rescue my mother."

Kristoff patted Dante's hand. "Dear Mrs. Arundel. Dear, dear Mrs. Arundel. In her memory, I will make a transformation…" His eyes narrowed and he paced toward Maarja. "A new look. Yes! A whole new fashion. A high forehead Renaissance look. What do you think?"

"I guess. Anything you can do…" Maarja trailed off when she realized he wasn't speaking to her, or even looking at her. Not really. She was more of an object he would deify with his talent.

The white-coated assistant clasped her hands. "Yes! The young Queen Elizabeth the First. This one is blessed with that dark, dark red."

This one?

"Perhaps, dare I say it, a tint on the ends?" the assistant suggested.

Kristoff gasped in horror. "Ingaborg, how dare you suggest

such a thing? Look at the texture on this growth. Prepare the Kristoff masque and—" he plucked at the ends of Maarja's hair "—add my secret ingredient. One tablespoon only! The line between hair health and hair death is a fine one."

His assistant leaped into action, mixed and applied, set the timer, and in less than a minute the entire room filled with a stench that reminded Maarja of an angry skunk.

While Jack staggered out the door and Fedelma pressed a throw pillow to her face, Dante cackled. "The expression on your face, Maarja!"

"It hurts to be beautiful," Kristoff said crisply.

"My mother says that." Dante paused, then corrected himself. "*Said* that."

For the first time, as Dante turned toward the window, Maarja saw a crack in his mask of detachment. Grief? Fury? She didn't know, but she wanted to go to him and hug him, tell him the sorrow would never go away, but it would fade... And he would tell her it would fade only when he won bloody justice for his mother.

At least hugging him would distract him, because her own eyes were watering, and not from sorrow. The stench was growing.

The timer dinged, and Kristoff and the assistant took Maarja under her arms, pulled her to her feet, and rushed her to the bar sink. They rinsed, shampooed, rinsed, shampooed with an urgency that made her hope she had hair left for them to style. They blotted her head, pulled her up, marched her back to the chair, and Kristoff went to work with scissors and razor.

She didn't understand how it could take so long to trim as little hair as she had left, but forty-five long minutes later, Kristoff stepped back, his assistant blotted his forehead, and he swiveled the chair around to face Dante. "Well?"

Dante strolled over. He circled her, nodding slowly. "Maestro, you're a genius."

Fedelma and the assistant oohed and applauded.

This whole being-an-object thing irritated the hell out of Maarja. "Can *I* see?"

The assistant actually had to search to find a handheld mirror, and while she held it for Maarja, Kristoff launched into a two-minute demonstration of what product to use, how she could change the style, what to do as the area around her face grew out, and told her when her next hair appointment would be.

Then Maarja was out of the chair, Kristoff and Ingaborg whisked themselves out of the room, and Fedelma took a cord-less vacuum out of the closet, cleaned up the clipped hair, and left Maarja alone with Dante.

CHAPTER 14

"What do you think of the look?" he asked.

"It's...like I...did this on purpose." She knew she sounded stunned, but those glimpses of herself in the mirror inspired awe and amazement. Somehow she had gone from an invisible female in frumpy coveralls to a woman battered by an explosion and grief to a lead in next season's fashions.

For a woman who preferred to blend into the scenery, that could not be good.

She didn't look at Dante. She was too aware of the awkwardness of meeting the guy she'd slept with and acting like it was no big deal. So she wandered over to the overflowing bookshelves. The hardcovers included architectural history, business and relationship advice. The paperbacks, SF and cozy mysteries, were well-read. Enshrined in its own lighted case, a richly decorated edition of *A Thousand Nights* held the place of honor. She drew near, put her nose almost to the glass.

"Would you like to hold it?" Dante stood at her side.

She briefly considered he knew a lot about seduction and seducing her in particular, and wished she had the good sense to say no. "May I?"

He opened his phone, typed in a code, and the case went dark. He lifted the glass lid and stepped back.

Her hands were clean and dry, and when she hovered her fingers over the leather, she sensed its age. Gently she carried it over to the window into the light. But not the direct sunlight; that would fade the colors, the ink. She leafed through the pages.

"Sixteenth century, leather-bound, beautifully illustrated, in Persian," she told him. The gold work on the page edges glittered dully. The end papers were a feast of gold leaf, rich green abstract plants, and ultramarine animal eyes that peered from the page. A single carmine smear marred the page.

"It's stained," Dante said. "The only flaw."

She stroked her fingers over that stain. In that touch, she smelled a curl of flavored tobacco, tasted the printer's sweet pleasure in his completed masterpiece, felt the prick of the knife's point on his finger and the smooth slide of the paper as he used his blood to mark the book... "It's not a flaw. It was deliberate. His blood on his creation, forever."

Dante viewed her with something like awe. "I was afraid you'd tell me the book was a fake."

"No. It's very, very real." She returned it to its case, smoothed her fingertips across the binding one last time, and observed while Dante covered it with the glass and set the alarm.

He said, "When we marry, it will be yours."

"No."

He took her hand. "Come and sit on my stool."

"Is that a euphemism?"

"So suspicious." He led her behind his desk and to the ergonomic drafting chair he had pushed against the wall. "Up," he said.

"Why?"

"You look so fragile a zephyr could blow you away, and we have to talk."

She didn't want to talk. She wanted to leave. But with Dante's police-cousin waiting in the wings, she supposed she had no choice. She climbed onto the seat, which, not surprisingly, was as comfortable as an elevated office chair could be. She adjusted the back and the arms to fit her, then looked up with a grin, half expecting him to be irritated with her for changing his settings. Irritating him was, after all, her intention.

Instead he tilted her chin back, leaned in, and put his lips to hers. If he'd been forceful, she would have resisted, but the sneaky bastard softly, gently reminded her of what had passed between them. When he lifted his head, he smiled into her wide eyes.

She cleared her throat. "That's not talking."

"Nonverbal communication is the foundation of any relationship."

"We don't have a relationship."

"Do you always speak in the negative?"

"No."

He laughed, picked her tightly gripping hands off the padded arms, and kissed each of the palms, then gazed into them. "You have a long, deeply etched life line, and look, one love of your life."

"The heck you say." She tried to take her hands away to look at them.

He tightened his grip. "How's your cunt?"

She was getting the rhythm of him. Touch, kiss, joke, use his gaze to caress and praise, ask inappropriate questions... He'd be a good cop. Probably where he'd learned the method, from his many arrests. "My *coochie* is fine, thank you, and thank you for in the future not calling it...what you're calling it."

"The French word is *chatte*."

She could translate that. "Cat? Like pussy?"

"Um. Yes." He smiled at her as if he knew something she didn't.

"I'll look it up!" she assured him.

"Do." His lids lowered, but he had matters on his mind other than arguing with her. "Sore?"

"Not bad."

He lifted his eyebrows and slid his palm up her thigh.

"Not good, either," she admitted.

He slid it down again and sighed. "I wish I felt like a heel."

"You're strutting."

"Like a peacock with a living-color rack of tail feathers." He leaned in to kiss her again.

She backed up against the wall—and someone knocked on the door.

"Saved," he teased, and called, "Who is it?"

"Jack." His voice came out of a speaker somewhere. "Look, can we do this? I have to go back to work!"

Softly Dante said to Maarja, "Jack has already interviewed me. Now he needs to do the same with you. He needs to know everything you saw and heard yesterday. Tell him everything. Don't be intimidated." Stepping back from her, he raised his voice and called, "Come in."

Jack stuck his head in and sniffed. "Is it less smelly now?" He focused on Maarja and started. "Wow. You look better."

"Gee, thanks. You Arundels are *such* charmers."

Jack cracked a half smile and started in on his interrogation.

He asked the questions, she answered them, and she realized Dante had placed her in a position of advantage. She was seated in the lone desk chair; Jack and Dante remained standing. Jack kept trying to pace around her; he was frustrated by her back against the wall, and she thought he would have liked to tower over her, but the elevated seat put her almost at his height.

He interrogated her about her activity before the explosion ("I was moving Mrs. Arundel's art"); why she was doing that ("I'm a fine arts mover"); what event led her to return to the library in the first place ("I left my reading glasses").

At which point Dante said, "Son of a bitch."

"Yes," she agreed, knowing he would realize she meant him.

"You're positive about that?" he asked.

"Yes."

"Would you two quit flirting and concentrate?" Jack asked in irritation.

Startled, because she had never as far as she knew in her life been caught flirting, and embarrassed, because she thought he might be right, she blurted, "I left my reading glasses, Mrs. Arundel wanted to be alone so I left her again, before the elevator opened, I heard the blast... No wait." She had to think. "I heard a crash, like she fell out of her chair. I turned—and the explosion knocked me down. Or...the explosion roared over top of me, and I threw myself down on the floor."

"You don't seem very sure of what happened." Jack hadn't been friendly before. Now he was positively accusatory.

"I do remember. I just think... I think I must have been unconscious for a few seconds. Then. Then I wanted to—"

"Rush right in and save Mrs. Arundel." No one had ever sounded as nasty as Jack Arundel.

She shook her head. She was sweating, and she felt lightheaded.

Dante offered her a handkerchief.

She couldn't take it. She trembled, clutched the arms of the chair, and she didn't dare let go or she would topple off. "I was afraid. I was too afraid. If I hadn't used precious seconds being scared, I might have saved her."

Dante put his arms around her and pulled her face into his chest. He aimed all the old Anglo-Saxon curse words at Jack, then went on to French.

Vaguely, through the mist of nausea and well-remembered fear, she heard Jack answer, "It's my job to be an asshole. You know that, Dante. Hell, she could be the best actress in the world—"

In a fit of anger, she shoved Dante away. "I could be, but I damned well picked myself up and ran into the flames, and she was alive when I dragged her out of there. She was *alive* and she *was* talking to me. I wish… I'd give anything to have not hesitated, but I did, and I can't undo what I did. I'm the one who has to live with it." She closed her eyes against the focus of their gazes.

A moment of silence, then from Jack, "Right. Good actress or telling the truth. Miss Daire, please remain in the area—"

"My home is in Gothic." Just off the Pacific Coast Highway.

"Close enough," Jack conceded.

"I work moving fine art to different parts of the country."

"I will ask that you stay within the California borders." Jack wasn't really asking. He was telling.

She thought about that, and nodded. "I can do that. For a few weeks. I'm sure that going forward, that won't be necessary."

Jack gave her one last considering stare, and left.

Dante handed her a hankie. "I'm sorry he was a jerk, but—"

"I'm a suspect." She blotted her face. "You're right. He's upset that his aunt has died, and he's frustrated because he doesn't know how the explosive was set. I appreciate that. Who is supposed to do this kind of investigation? The local police? The FBI?"

Dante shook his head and sighed. "It seems as if every department and agency is involved, and no one trusts the other. With the multiple attempted assassinations, the confusion and frustration seems to get worse and worse."

"When will there be results?"

"There's lab work to be done." He stopped.

"And?"

"It's all technical, and of course I can barely pry information out of law enforcement—"

"*You* can hardly pry information? What about your contacts?" She gestured toward the firmly shut door. "Like Jack?"

"The days of the Arundels being able to bully and bribe have come to an end. I ended them." He put emphasis on the last sentence.

"You're wealthy and influential. I have trouble believing you can't tap into some source for information on your own mother's violent death!" She examined him, the way he stood, his still expression, and understanding dawned. "Ohhh. You don't want to, or dare to, share that information. Why didn't you say so?"

"It's never good to say too much." He sounded so noncommittal.

"The less I know, the better."

"There is that, too." He put his hands on the wall behind her head, leaned closer, and in a low vibrant whisper said, "I promise, I'll tell you everything as soon as it's safe. There's so much at stake here. The Arundels are going to be completely legitimate and there will be cooperation—or bodies. Nothing in-between."

She stared into his eyes, chilled by the bleak intent she saw there. "But what if—?"

"Nothing in-between," he repeated.

Someone yanked the door open.

Nate said, "You need permission to go in there!"

Saint Rees paid no attention. A man in his late forties, her boss was broad-shouldered, round-bellied, and tall, a former professional African American football player, and he tossed off Nate's body block and marched into the room.

Dante slid his hand into his jacket.

Maarja gripped his arm. "No!"

Saint Rees ignored Dante. Chin lowered, fists clenched, he looked at Maarja. Just looked at her in sorrow and in warning.

She slipped off the seat. "What happened? What's wrong?"

His deep voice came out of the depths of his belly. "The van didn't arrive at the rendezvous point."

CHAPTER 15

"The van? With Mrs. Arundel's art?" Maarja's mind clicked away from Dante, the office, the hovering lure of security, and snapped into her guard mode. Ignoring Nate's menacing advance, she jumped off the chair and hurried to Saint Rees. "You've heard nothing from Alex? From Serene?"

With her peripheral vision, she saw Dante wave Nate to a halt.

"No communication, but the van has been found along 303 Bartlett Springs Road." Saint Rees took her hands. "Blood everywhere, no Alex, no Serene, no art—"

"Whose blood?" Maarja's voice rose. "Is it Alex's?"

Saint Rees nodded. "Alex's."

"What about Serene?"

"None of her blood."

"Unlikely," Maarja said crisply.

Serene. Maarja had worked with her for over a year and still didn't know her at all. Beneath that meditative facade, there could be depths of ruthlessness and cruelty. Yes. She could take a commission to steal the finest art and hurt the finest person, plan and execute it flawlessly, and never flinch.

"It looks as if she was waiting for just such a circumstance as this tragedy." For the first time, Saint Rees acknowledged Dante with a nod. "Mr. Arundel, my teams are scouring the area. We've got copters in the air, men on the ground. Experts and trackers. The art will be found." His eyes, big and richly lashed, shifted to Maarja. "Alex is our first priority."

Maarja's gaze clung to his. "Alex…" Her sister of the heart. They'd spent so many hours of their lives together, being dysfunctional teens (were there any other kind?) and brave adults as they ventured into the world and left their torn pasts behind. Then logic took over from emotion. "Serene could be that kind of opportunist, I agree, but it's more likely she's been hired by the bastards who killed Mrs. Arundel. The coincidence is too unlikely." She turned to Dante, expecting agreement and concern.

Instead he stood, arms loose, fingers flexed, his face blank, cool, unreadable.

Yet she could read it; the lover who talked of a fateful union had vanished, leaving Dante Arundel of the vengeful and aristocratic Arundels. His lips barely moved as he spoke. "The unbelievable coincidence is that *you*, Maarja, packed *la Bouteille de Flamme* and now it has been stolen."

She felt like she'd been slapped by a lover. By her first lover, her only lover. Her knee-jerk reaction was to punch back. "And I gave up my virginity to distract you. Right. Logical. How could I ever have been such a dolt as to imagine that I could fool you, the magnificent Dante Arundel?" By the time she finished, she was on tiptoe, in his face and shouting.

"Maarja. My God!" Saint Rees grabbed her elbow and pulled her back, and put her behind him. "Mr. Arundel, I know you're upset, and rightfully so, and I apologize for the loss of your belongings. They will be retrieved. But Maarja is of sterling character, has been in my employ longer than any of my movers, and if she were going to be involved in a theft, there have been other better opportunities. I beg you, believe me. Please don't hurt her."

She realized he was afraid Dante would put out a hit on her.

If she were intelligent, she'd be afraid, too. She would be, if she wasn't so angry. "Asshole," she muttered.

"Miss Daire does not need to worry about any life-threatening accidents that originate from me." Each word had been chipped from Arundel ice. "However, we have discussed she might be in danger from other quarters. She should take care what she says, and to whom."

"She will be," Maarja snapped. "I need a phone. I've got to call our mother."

Dante walked to his desk, picked up an iPhone, stepped around Saint Rees, and handed it to her. "It's new. It's yours. It's set to your number, opens with your fingerprint, and includes your apps."

She looked him right in those brown eyes, and noted the heated gold still moved beneath the surface. She had somehow equated that to passion...for her. Now she knew it meant nothing, it was simply who he was. In a voice kept carefully neutral, she said, "Thank you. Is it set so you can track me when I carry it?"

"What kind of a fool do you think I am? Of course it is."

"I can always change phones."

He nodded. "You can."

She heard what he didn't say; changing phones would make no difference. He would always know where she was.

Saint Rees pulled a large white handkerchief from his pocket, wiped the sweat off his long forehead, and spoke to Dante. "As I said, we're searching by every means possible to find the thieves and your art. This has only happened one other time; within twenty-four hours we recovered everything intact."

Maarja swiped the phone open. The home screen looked exactly like her old phone, and she didn't waste time wondering how he'd managed that. Instead she took a breath and texted Octavia. Mom, phone ASAP.

It wouldn't do Maarja any good to call now; every week at

this time Octavia held meetings for the Oakland Golden Neighborhood Community Festival in person and on camera. She expected everyone to attend and give it their whole attention, and she by God followed her own rules.

Saint Rees rumbled a distraction toward Dante. "Because of the uniqueness of your possessions, the thieves will be hard-pressed to sell them without attracting notice. I cultivate my channels of communication most assiduously—"

That was an understatement. The man knew everybody, had contacts everywhere, and today and every day, that counted for a lot.

"—and I will receive notice when the objects surface. If you hear anything, please let me know right away."

Maarja's phone rang, and as soon as she answered, Octavia's frantic voice sounded in her ear. "What's wrong with Alex? Ever since last night, I've been thinking about her, so I called her, and called her, and called her… She's not answering!"

Maarja realized she didn't even know what to say. She had to swallow around a sudden lump of tears before blurting, "The van was stolen. Alex's missing. The art's missing. There's blood…" She found herself squatting on her heels, resting her elbows on her knees and holding the phone in both hands. "Mama, do you think she's dead?"

"No, honey. No, I don't think that. I can't. Somewhere she's hanging on by a thread. Saint Rees is searching for her?"

Maarja rocked back and forth. She nodded, then cleared her throat. "Yes, on ground and in air." No sobs, but she was dripping tears off her chin.

Dante's hands lifted her by her elbows while someone slid a chair under her behind. He pressed her down into the seat, then gestured her attention toward Saint Rees, who was on his phone talking and barking instructions. Mid-sentence, he looked at Maarja. "We've found Alex. She's alive, critical condition, received treatment at the Colusa Medical Center. They're medevacing her to UC Davis Sacramento."

"Did you hear that, Mom?"

"All I heard was *alive*." Octavia's voice grew strong and hopeful.

Maarja gave a wobbly laugh. "Yes. But critical condition. We'll come and get you, take you to her."

"I'll get myself ready." Octavia hung up before she finished the last word.

Maarja shook away Dante's grip and rose to join Saint Rees as he strode toward the door. "Where was she?"

"Colusa Wildlife Refuge on CA-20. Those bastards beat her and flung her out into the marsh, figured she'd drown or worse. She crawled back to the road. A farmer spotted her, thank God, because the guy had experience with injured animals and after he called 9-1-1, he worked on her. Medical personnel said he saved her life, but, Maarja—" Saint Rees stopped walking "—it's not good. She might not make it, and if she does, she might never recover from her injuries."

She nodded, dripping tears again, but without the sobs because she couldn't spare the energy. "I'll see if Mom can wrangle one of our neighbors to meet me just across the bridge, and we'll drive in from there."

"We'll pick her up in the helicopter." Dante's words stopped them in their tracks.

Maarja didn't even turn back. "No. I—"

"You don't like me. I know." Dante's voice dripped ice. "You don't want any favors. But if there's a chance Alex won't survive, I can get your mother to Alex's side in time."

CHAPTER 16

Discovering the Oakland neighborhood where Maarja had spent her adolescence explained a lot about her personality.

Meeting her mother explained even more.

Dante's pilot set the helicopter down on the high school lawn, if it could be called a lawn. It looked like a war zone, brown except for the weeds and pockmarked with holes. He removed his headphones and spoke directly to her. "This was your school?"

Maarja followed suit, hanging the headgear on the hook beside her. "My alma mater. The school building's been condemned for years. Sheetrock down, insulation all over the floor, leaking toilets. Crime rate commensurate with the neighborhood. Official name is Casas Bonitas. All of the kids call it Cacas Boners."

Dante winced.

A skinny Vietnamese man waited under the portcullis beside a fit, broad-shouldered, gray-haired woman in dark glasses. He held her arm and spoke while she nodded, and Dante knew from the way Maarja's face lit up that was Octavia Maldovitch.

He admitted to some trepidation at meeting her. He and Maarja had a relationship, one based on suspicion, distrust (his), heroism and hurt (hers), and one mind-blowing fuck. What would her mother have to say to him? Nothing, he supposed;

during the ride, none of Maarja's attention had been focused on him. For her, now, he was nothing but a convenience, a way to get her and her mother to her sister's bedside.

"That blade is rotating above. Keep your head down." He slid the door back so Maarja could jump out and run to her mother. The two women embraced, held each other as if exchanging strength, and spoke, then Maarja and Octavia waved at the man who'd escorted her here. "Thank you, Mr. Nyugen!" Octavia called.

He waved back and walked purposefully toward the gang of hostile youths headed toward the helicopter.

The gang parted like the Red Sea.

Hm. Something about Mr. Nyugen made them wary.

Putting her hand on Maarja's arm, Octavia walked with her toward the helicopter.

The shock shivered through Dante.

Octavia Maldovitch was visually impaired. He hadn't understood why she couldn't make her own way to Alex's side, but he'd been willing to play whatever game they wanted to play. No game; the dark glasses protected those eyes, and yes, he was an asshole. He got out and spoke. "Mrs. Maldovitch, I'm Dante Arundel."

She extended her hand and took his in a strong grip. "Good to meet you, Dante. I'm Octavia. Thank you for offering the use of your helicopter. If not for you, we'd be hours getting out of the Bay Area and to Sacramento and in that time—" She caught her breath. "Let's go."

Maarja provided a visual of the helicopter for her mother: the pilot in front, an empty seat beside him, two seats side-by-side and one small cramped one in the back. Dante helped Octavia into the seat that Maarja had occupied before, and as he made sure she had clicked her seat belt, Maarja climbed into the back, leaving him to sit beside Octavia. He helped her explore her headgear before she placed it on her ears and adjusted the microphone.

Donning his, he spoke into the microphone. "Can you hear me, Octavia?"

"Yes! Clearly, thank you." She turned her head back toward Maarja. "Are you belted in, sweetheart?"

"I'm here, Mom." Maarja had started dripping tears again, that soundless crying that didn't seem to affect her voice or efficiency.

"Don't cry, Maarja."

How did Octavia know that?

"Alex's going to recover. We'll make sure of it."

"I know, Mom." Maarja wiped at her cheeks.

"I've arranged to have the helicopter land at the hospital. We'll be there in about thirty minutes, depending on the air traffic there." Dante handed Maarja tissues and signaled to the pilot to lift off.

Octavia tapped on her watch, setting the timer.

As the helicopter rose, Dante saw the gangs who'd been advancing on it scatter...and they hadn't been a welcome committee. What did they think, that they were going to strip down the helicopter? Or take possession and go for a ride? Scary place, this part of Oakland. Again, another insight into Maarja's mind. He already knew her well enough to realize she wouldn't like him being in her head.

The helicopter headed east across the Bay Area, over clogged freeways, industrial areas, and subdivisions that stretched toward the horizon.

Octavia turned to Dante. "Dear, I'm so sorry to hear about your mother. It was all over the news. The videos are wrenching to listen to."

"Thank you. Her death has led to a lot of discord and speculation and...lifestyle changes." He meant Maarja and him.

Octavia picked right up on that. "Are you two together?"

"Yes," he said.

At the same time, Maarja said, "No!"

Octavia turned to Maarja. "Dear, I'm so proud of you for attempting to rescue Mrs. Arundel, especially knowing what I know about your past. If you were able to find comfort with Dante—"

"Temporary comfort, and an illusion." Her steadfast scorn would do well in the Arundel family.

"Dear, if I recall, you were untouched. The feeling of closeness must have been powerful to overcome such long-held reluctance. To have at last thrown away the shackles of the past and embraced a freedom to try a new world of sensual experiences must be delightful."

Octavia gave off old hippie vibes, and he moved to immediately correct her free-love assumptions. "Octavia, Maarja will try this new world in my arms."

Maarja promptly said, "Mama, he imagines I engineered the theft of his art."

He interceded swiftly. "Merely a moment of genuine doubt. You must admit the suspicion is logical. Also, be aware, Maarja, I think before I speak, and speak only when I think the words will be reported. Why do you think I would make such a cruel accusation in my office for all to hear?" She refused to look at him. He leaned back and, cupping her chin, turned her to face him.

She met his gaze for one moment, then slapped his hand away.

Octavia listened, head tilted, hearing everything they said and probably more.

He'd given Maarja something to think about, and satisfied, he asked, "Octavia, how did you come to care for Maarja and Alex?"

"Ah!" Octavia launched into a story she'd obviously told many times. "I was fifty-three years old before I accepted the directive to have children. Not children from my womb. At that age and in my unconnected state, that would have been impossible. But when Mr. Caruthers brought that skinny, skittish child to my front porch, I recognized Maarja as the first of my children."

"Mom, don't…" Maarja objected.

Octavia paid no heed to her daughter. "Alex was next, another wounded child, needing someone to take her from abandoned to transformed. I knew I didn't have the skills, but Mr. Caruthers had a way about him. He knew things, and I believed when he said these girls were mine."

Dante was fascinated, both by the story and Maarja's vast discomfort with the telling. She didn't want him to know her family; he wanted to know everything. About this, like everything, he would get his way.

"My big old house has three bedrooms and one bathroom. With the two girls and me, the bedrooms were full, and the bathroom was constantly occupied." Octavia chuckled. "That's when I discovered the truth of the adage, how long a minute is depends on which side of the bathroom door you're on."

He chuckled with her.

"I thought that was all the daughters I could handle. Then Chrispin arrived on a summer day, a child without a voice. I told Mr. Caruthers no. No, I said!" Octavia slapped her fist into her open palm. "I'm a person who prides myself on being shallow. I didn't want to deal with a mute child and all the trauma inherent therein. But while I was arguing, Alex and Maarja took her by the hand and led her in, like I was some goddess of kindness and generosity."

Maarja had a quirk in her cheek. "No one thinks that, Mom."

"I would damned well hope not." Octavia huffed. "Chrispin slept in Alex's room."

Maarja chimed in, as if drawn to the narrative. "On our second Christmas Eve, she sang *Silent Night* in her pure, sweet voice and our little family had our reward."

Octavia added, "And the mystery of her past deepened."

"Does she speak as well as sing?" Dante asked.

"Yes, to us, and eloquently, but not about her life before she came to us," Maarja replied. "She's still reticent in public."

Octavia picked up the story. "I had three girls, the house was crowded, then Emma arrived, her backpack slung on one shoulder, her face screwed into a defiance that spoke more than words."

"Did Mr. Caruthers bring her, too?"

"Mr. Caruthers died," Maarja said. "Sooner or later he was going to anger the wrong person, and he did. Chrispin found his body in the dumpster and notified the police. For a while, I was afraid she'd end up in the dumpster, too, but she had a reputation as the spooky deaf-dumb girl, and Alex and I convinced the street guys she was on the spectrum. She couldn't—"

"Wouldn't," Octavia corrected.

Maarja continued, "—talk to the cops. Anyway, all of them thought she was crazy."

Dante was fascinated to see that while they spoke, Maarja had relaxed. She still dripped the occasional tear, and she glanced down at the passing scenery as if urging them speed, but she joined the conversation without her previous distance. He had no doubt if he reached out to her now, she'd slap him away again, but he also knew she'd think about what he'd said and perhaps let loose a little of her disdain for him. "Four daughters," he said. "All teens?"

"All within two years of each other. One week, three of them had their first periods." Octavia used her voice of doom.

Maarja made a protesting sound.

"Dear, the man knows about periods!" Octavia said to her.

"I have some experience, although not with girls of that age." If their mission hadn't been so dire, Dante would be enjoying himself. "I'll bet that was a difficult week."

"Emma was so thin it took her another two years to catch up. Then I had four girls cycling together. Every *fourth* week was a difficult week."

Maarja closed her eyes as if she couldn't bear to look at him. Nope, even with the dire situation, he was enjoying himself. "Tell me about it. How did you handle sudden parenthood? My mother always said the reason God presents your child to you when they're a baby is because if you got them as a teenager, with all their smirking and smart mouths, you'd lose faith in the goodness of the Lord."

"Not my girls. It was the opposite. I used to wonder—why were they all so silent? Why did they defy the tropes? Why would four adolescent girls be silent?" Obviously rhetorical questions.

"Will Chrispin and Emma hold vigil at Alex's side, too?" He needed to know, to arrange lodgings, to prepare protection for them all.

"I'm afraid that's not possible. Emma is in the military, on assignment somewhere doing something she doesn't tell us about. Chrispin left to find her roots and we…haven't heard from her lately." Octavia's voice broke.

Maarja shot him an angry glance as if he'd deliberately caused Octavia upset. Nothing could be further from the truth. This lady deserved to be coddled and cared for; he didn't yet know her whole story, but he suspected she had taken care of herself for her whole life. She needed him just as Maarja needed him. Neither woman yet realized how much their lives had changed.

He looked sideways at Maarja. Although she had begun to comprehend. All she needed was time and space. He hoped he could give it to her.

Octavia's watch gave a buzz and she straightened. "We're close."

"We're over Sacramento," Dante confirmed.

The true atmosphere revealed itself. Octavia reached out her hand to Maarja, who grasped it tightly. "She'll survive, Mommy."

"She's a fighter." Octavia's voice quavered.

That's when Dante realized Octavia worried Alex would not survive. Yet she'd been so willing to chat, to tell him about her girls, he hadn't realized... And Maarja had suffered a brief breakdown in his office, but other women he knew—Béatrice, Fedelma—wept loudly as if to offer proof of their grief. Maarja dripped brave and silent tears, and that reminded him of...his mother. Of Raine Arundel of honored memory, whose funeral had been prearranged right down to the hymns and the flowers. Not too much longer to wait, and that last duty would be done, and his beloved mother would be free at last.

The helicopter had to wait to land; Life Flight had right-of-way and the hospital's helipad was busy. But at last they walked the corridors toward intensive care where they washed up, gowned up, consulted with the doctors, and finally stood beside Alex's bed.

Maarja leaned forward to speak into Alex's ear. "Mommy and I are here." She put Octavia's hand in Alex's. "That's Mom's hand you're holding, and she's giving you all her strength. You know what that means. It means you're plugged into a light socket and the power of the universe is yours to draw on." Maarja questioned Octavia with her gaze.

Octavia shook her head. No press of the fingers, no response at all.

Maarja continued, "We talked to the doctors. We know your condition. Do you know? You've undergone emergency surgery for internal bleeding. That was simply for your survival. You need more surgeries, but your condition has to stabilize. Mom and I want you to work on that first."

Octavia shook her head again.

"Now I'm going to tell Mom about you. What I see—" Maarja got a little choked, then steadied her voice "—and what I think right now. So..."

Maarja told Octavia about Alex's face, so broken it was unrecognizable. She told her about the tube down Alex's throat that allowed her to breathe past the swelling, the fluids and the drugs that gave her sustenance and pain relief, the bruises and the cuts from boots that kicked and knives that slashed. The broken bones the doctors had already explained, and how only a strong will, skillful surgeries, and the correct physical therapy would get Alex on her feet again. If the villains had shot her, they would have killed her, but Serene and her crew had enjoyed their savagery too much to make Alex's death easy or painless.

Dante had many times seen swift and violent death, but this... this was hate and vengeance incorporated, and Alex's survival was a testament to gritty determination. Seeing Maarja's grief made him realize Alex was not a sister of the blood, she was a sister of the heart.

Stepping out into the corridor, he pulled out his phone and made the first and most important call to his first and most important advisor. "Who is Serene?" For she was the key. She was the unexpected player, and why? What was her stake?

The answer shouldn't have surprised him, and when it did, it left him cold with contempt. "All right," he said. "The game has changed. You know what to do." When he hung up, he straightened his jacket and returned to Alex's bedside.

With this theft, an unforeseen move had been made on the playing field. And if he could be said to be riding a horse named Fate, his enemies would soon realize—he held the reins, and this game of fortune favored the ruthless.

CHAPTER 17

For three of the longest days of Maarja's life, Alex hovered on the brink of death while Octavia and Maarja spoke to her, held her hand, cried silent tears, and prayed for a miracle.

Peripherally, she knew Dante had hired a firm of trusted private nurses to monitor Alex's care, and she suspected he'd hired guards to mingle with the staff. She didn't ask why. She knew why. If the hospital administration was not happy, and she suspected they weren't, he would have no one "interfere" with Alex's continued survival.

Maarja wholeheartedly endorsed that.

When, on the fourth day, the private nurse announced, "She's made an improvement," and Alex's eyes fluttered open, Maarja burst into tears, which brought Octavia off the cot where she slept. As she had learned to do, Maarja swiftly controlled her outburst to explain to Octavia they'd turned a corner, and Octavia held Alex's hand and cried on Maarja's shoulder, and Alex seemed to recognize them and respond to their joy.

Within moments, the room was full of doctors and nurses and Dante. He stood with them, against the wall and out of the way, but he watched with that cold judgmental air that grated on Maarja's nerves like a metal rasp.

Within moments, Alex was scheduled for an MRI, and within

hours, for her first surgery. From now on, all procedures would be aimed to secure and hasten her recovery.

That was the news Maarja and Octavia had wanted.

Dante waited until Alex was asleep once more, then he came to Octavia's side and asked, "I have a two-bedroom suite in a nearby hotel. Can I coax you to go there and sleep in a comfortable bed?"

"No. I'll stay with Alex, but you must take Maarja."

"Mom!" What was Octavia thinking? Maarja didn't want to go with him.

Octavia paid her no attention. "Maarja is still recovering from that explosion and every time I ask her, she says she's fine. I can tell by her voice she's exhausted." Before Maarja could object again, Octavia turned to her. "Please remember I spent months in a hospital and rehab environment. I'm used to this bustle. I can sleep through the comings and goings. Strange people make you twitch, and you need your rest." She put her arm around Maarja's shoulders and walked her toward the door. "Go with Dante, dear. You trust him."

Dante took over from Octavia so smoothly Maarja knew they'd discussed this. He guided her through the labyrinth of corridors to an elevator, his hand resting on the small of her back in that proprietary gesture that made her want to smack him. He murmured in her ear, "Your mother's always right, *ma petite amie*, or so my mother always told me. Octavia has been caring for Alex. You've been caring for them both. If you don't rest, you'll collapse and frighten Octavia and perhaps set Alex's recovery back."

As they descended to the first floor, he maintained that contact, as if he thought if he didn't stay close, she'd faint or run away or...or she didn't know what he thought, but she knew he irritated her.

He walked her through the lobby and out to the hospital's portico. "The car's right here."

She blinked at the sunshine. She hadn't been outside, she realized, for days.

Nate waited beside a black sedan. Dante helped Maarja into the rear seat and slid in after her, and as the car drove off, he pulled her close to rest on his shoulder.

She wanted to ask what he thought he was doing, handling her like this, but the harrowing days and nights caught up with her and she was asleep before they got to the hotel.

When she woke, she was alone and ensconced in a lovely king-sized bed with fluffy white linens that smelled faintly of lavender, and she felt better than when she'd arrived. That was to say, better than dirt. She wore her panties. Huh. She didn't remember removing clothes, but she might have. Or Dante might have. Or he might have hired someone to... Naw. No matter what he thought of her, and she was confused about that, he'd do that himself.

Outside, the sun was shining, so it was either later the same day or the next morning, and she was pretty sure it was later the same day because she didn't think she could have blacked out for so long, not with all that was on the line.

Sitting up, she reached for the phone, but found a note propped up that said in black ink, *Alex is through surgery. The doctors are congratulating themselves. Octavia is rested and well-fed. Sleep more or find me in the sitting room.*

Dante's handwriting. She knew without even having seen it before. She was no expert, but she could read his character in the sharp scrawled edges. The words themselves seemed to offer her a choice: *Sleep more or find me in the sitting room.* But she noted this was not a choice of freedom, not an offer to return her to the hospital or provide a meal. She could sleep. Or she could speak with him.

She didn't want to do either one of those things.

Defiantly she showered. Not one of the choices—but a rebel,

that was her. She dressed in the, again, new clothes she found hanging on the hook on the back of the bathroom door. Whoever Dante was consulting had great taste, for the dress clung comfortably to her, the dark red matched her hair roots and emphasized the color, and three rhinestone daisies climbed the lapel to give it pop. She brushed her teeth, fluffed her dubious coiffure, applied moisturizer and sunscreen, and went out to the sitting room—which in her world was big enough to be called a living room—where Dante sat at a desk surrounded by computers and screens.

An attractive unknown woman bent to speak to him, and she slanted a look at Maarja that clearly told her she was an intruder.

Dante flicked his fingers to dismiss his assistant. "Go, Tabitha." When she didn't immediately remove herself, he looked at her. She froze, her eyes widened, then she backed through the open door and into the kitchen—really this was a massive suite—and started rattling pans.

He didn't raise his voice to say, "Tabitha, you're no more than a temp. You can be replaced. Shut the door."

She heard him, for the pocket door slid closed...most of the way.

Maarja knew what Tabitha had seen in his eyes; that flat black, utterly without molten gold gaze would suggest the chill of the grave. If Maarja had any sense, she would pay attention. Instead she said, "Charming as always." She knew the basics of negotiation; she should force him to speak first. But she wanted this finished. She wanted out of here. She wanted to go back to the hospital, then return to normal life. "I'm better. Alex's better. We'll be fine without you. Go home. Grieve for your mother. Find her killer. Take your revenge."

His smile mocked her dismissal. "And you—what will you do?"

"Wait with my mom. Help Alex recover. Work. Wrap and

protect art objects. Watch for Serene and when she appears, kill her."

In a voice as flat and black as his eyes, he asked, "Have you ever killed anyone?"

She looked out the window.

He took that as a no. "It's not as easy as you think. Most people, even if they're threatened, even if they're attacked, hesitate before they injure the other person. If done correctly, vengeance is cold, well-planned. You use any means at your disposal: a knife, a fist, a firearm, a garrote, to end the life that seeks to destroy you and yours."

She turned back to him and told him the truth, although she knew he wouldn't listen. "An explosion."

"Yes. An explosion. It's personal, and once you've started, you can't stop or the other will recover, and you'll never be safe again."

He'd killed people. She got it. "I understand. But brutalizing my sister and leaving her to die so horribly means I'll never be safe, anyway. Serene knows Alex. She knows me. She knows what she's begun."

He leaned back in his chair, studied her as he slipped a black-and-gold fountain pen between his fingers. "You can stay here. I'll take care of you."

A crash sounded from the kitchen.

Maarja almost laughed. Another hope dashed, for his gaze never even flicked in that direction.

Nor did Maarja's. All her focus remained on him. "Four nights ago—or five? I don't know—you were all about cruel fate and unifying marriage and inevitable consequences. Now, without a hint of passion or even humanity, you're offering me a position as your mistress."

"Four nights ago, you rejected all that I offered. Why would you want more now?"

"I don't want it. I'm pointing out your inconsistency."

"Aren't we a couple of inconsistent dupes?"

She got it. He was right. "Fair enough. But I'm not staring at you as if you had just crawled out from under a rock." Out of the corner of her eye, she saw Tabitha inch the door open and lean forward enough to listen. "I assume by your current judgmental behavior you still think I had a hand in the robbery? That I gladly gave my sister over to brutalization and death? Or that both of us were complicit without realizing the consequences of throwing our lots in with such inhuman beasts?"

"It's time for you to tell me the truth. All the truth."

Her heart stopped. Just for a moment. Just to give her a pretaste of the death he would provide for her. When her heart started again, she saw the knowledge in his eyes. He knew. Somehow, he knew. Somehow in the last few days he'd managed to pry into her deepest, most thoroughly forgotten secrets and weave them into a cloth that he would put over her face and use to smother her.

She stepped back, clasped her hands behind her, and in a formal tone said, "There are many truths in this world, Dante Arundel, and I know a few of them. To which one do you refer?"

"Cast your mind back. Back to that moment when your mother blew herself apart to kill my father."

"Yes. She died so that I would survive."

"Such a careful answer. You reply without denial or affirmation."

Her supposition had been right. This was a setup. Why, she didn't know, but she was sure these were the last moments of her life. Her heart thumped like a bass drum, but without any rhythm, unless fear had its own rhythm. She wanted to beg, cry, remind him of the night they'd spent together, offer herself without pride or hope to be used as he wished.

She bit down on her tongue. If she was going to die, she didn't need to waste precious breath on humiliating herself. "You're angry in a way you weren't when we arrived here at the hotel. What has happened?"

"Today while you slept in that massively comfortable bed, I received a video taken on that fateful day in my father's throne room."

"A video survived?" Another frightened breath, another heartbeat that announced her day of reckoning had arrived.

"The Arundel security videos were kept in the hopes that someday, as technology advanced, they could be recreated from their twisted remains."

She nodded as if approving of the foresight.

"One of the things no one could ever figure out was how your mother triggered the explosion. It was suggested by our people who were there and survived that she had shoved explosives up her *chatte*."

Maarja took a deep shocked breath.

"In my judgment, that was possible, but seemed risky for a woman so desperate to end my father's life."

"To save mine," she reminded him quickly.

"To save yours," he agreed as if that truth had no meaning to him. "It was suggested and most agreed that she ingested the explosive, knowing or gambling on the fact that the Arundel security didn't include an X-ray of that kind."

"I don't remember what Mama did for preparation, but—"

He slashed his hand like a karate chop.

She flinched as if he'd slapped her.

He continued, "It was suggested that once she had the explosives in place, at the moment of my father's threat, she used her abdominal muscles to detonate the bomb."

She didn't make the mistake of trying to interrupt his monologue again.

"On that fateful day when I saw you in my mother's library, and identified you as the Daire child, my memories blasted me, unfaded by the passage of time. I knew they were there, waiting for me, but the events which unfolded left me with no time to explore them."

The explosion, he meant. His mother's death. The hospital. Her collapse in his bed. Then—

He said, "Then we fucked."

In the past, she'd thought he used the word because he inhabited a realm where men ruled by intimidation. Now she thought—*for you, it's just a verb...and you've never made love in your entire life.*

So yes, they had fucked.

"Afterward, I was exhausted, exalted, and while I watched you sleep, I recalled each second of that day in my father's throne room in real time. The scene, the people, the moments are etched in my mind." In a sudden motion that shocked and frightened her, he flung the pen toward the kitchen—and it stuck in the Sheetrock wall exactly beside Tabitha's protruding head.

Tabitha froze, her blue eyes so fixed and wide her mascara scraped her hairline.

Maarja swallowed. It had to be a pen with a blade. No way he could do that normally. But still...impressive aim and scary as all hell.

Tabitha retreated into the kitchen.

Maarja heard a hard thump, and a retching sound. She understood both reactions.

Dante continued his monologue without taking note of Tabitha's reaction, or Maarja's, or even that his pen had penetrated exactly where he intended. "Your mother didn't detonate the bomb."

She'd spent her life anticipating this moment. Fearing this moment. "No."

"Someone else in that room did."

"Yes." Oh, God, yes.

"Your mother had a conspirator."

"Yes, she did."

"And that conspirator survived."

Her mouth was so dry she could barely croak out the answer. "Yes."

"It can be only one person."

Every muscle in her body clenched.

"Andere."

She almost collapsed where she stood. *"What?"*

"Andere was hurt badly enough that no one suspected him, thus he assured himself a place in our organization."

Feebly she said, "Wait..."

"He hasn't been seen since the explosion that killed my mother." Dante's attention shifted to his phone. He picked it up and began to dial.

Maarja had only a split second to make the decision; let Andere of the French lemon candies suffer and die, or admit the truth. With all the strength of her convictions and in the belief these would be her last words, she confessed, "You're wrong. It was me."

He looked at her as if she were speaking a foreign language.

She clarified, "I detonated the bomb. I killed your father."

CHAPTER 18

With Dante, Maarja never knew whether or not she was being played.

This time, she knew. He was not playing her.

He sat, holding his phone, carbonite frozen in shock. His eyes flared gold, a giant blast that exuded no heat, no emotion except shock and realization.

It couldn't last. She waited for his hand to dip into his jacket, to pull out his pistol and blast her into oblivion.

Instead his lips parted to release one word. "How?"

She stared at him, his features, his eyes burned into her retinas. It was like looking at the sun without protection, waiting for the predicted eclipse.

Behind those eyes, his brain clicked through the possibilities and, of course, came up with the right answer. "The video game."

She nodded.

Now the pistol. Now the bullet. Now the long sleep and the end of the feud.

"Get out."

She didn't move. She didn't understand. Did he want to shoot her in the back? Why... "Why?"

"Why let you go? Why not kill you?"

"Yes."

"Because you carry my child."

"I do not!" Possibly not her brightest moment.

"You'd better hope you do."

"A baby would save my life for nine months. After that I'm easily replaced." Why was she even discussing this?

"Forever. You are bound to me forever. I hold your life in my hands. You hold my son in your body."

His gentle smile chilled her. She wanted to shiver...but she was afraid to stir, afraid that the merest movement or whisper of denial would trigger violence. Maybe not a bullet, maybe... something that would leave her scarred, body and soul.

His lips barely moved as he said, "Maarja, everything that has happened started with you. You could have run from that explosion. Instead you chose to save my mother. That gave Serene her chance to rob me. That's why Alex was beaten. That's why we fucked, and that is why you're carrying my child."

She shook her head. "That's stupid!"

"The real world runs on repercussions."

"I don't live in that world. I refuse to live in the old ways!"

"You're in over your head in the old ways. You're drowning in the old ways." His voice and his face were cold, impatient, certain. "When you rescued my mother, that act alone enlisted my protection for you. That bravery can't be canceled by this newest revelation. I am not my father. I am not Benoit Arundel. Be grateful for that." He flicked his hand at her as he'd flicked his hand at Tabitha. The message was clear. She was no higher than an employee, and she had taken as much time as he cared to give her.

Nodding stiffly, she turned with military precision and headed toward the door.

Before she stepped across the threshold, his voice brought her to a halt. "Maarja."

She wavered. She really didn't want to surrender to the command in his tone. Not to mention he was ruining her absolutely perfect exit from the room and from his life.

On the other hand, she knew, absolutely knew, he wouldn't let her leave until he was damned good and ready, and she wasn't of the mind to test her strength against his. Not today. Not after this revelation, not after telling him her great secret, and of his easy turn to possible brutality. Turning with the same military precision, she faced him. "What?"

"Repeat the phone number."

Not what she expected, in so far as she expected anything. "The phone number?"

"The one I made you memorize."

She wanted to say *No* and *Why*, and *I'm never going to call you, not ever, no matter what.* But the barbarous vendetta that had haunted her for her entire life had at last trapped her. She was caught. Her foster sister Alex had been swept into the hostilities.

So Maarja could say none of those things. Instead she looked just past Dante's right ear and recited the numbers, and when he said, "Very good. You may go," she did.

CHAPTER 19

Like most graveside services in California, Mrs. Arundel's took place on an incongruously sunny day under dappled leaves of the old and gracious Alta Mesa Memorial Park. Maarja arrived late, hoping to miss any pontifications and testimonials, and in that she succeeded, but she never expected the large crowd of black-clad mourners to still be pacing past, examining the contents of the coffin, dropping flowers onto the body, then lingering in clumps around the site and speaking in low voices. It had been ten days since the explosion; Maarja supposed that length of time made it possible for the Arundels to gather from far and near.

As she approached, she saw Dante sat under the awning that protected the family from the sun, scrutinizing each person in the line from under heavy-lidded eyes…and waiting for something, although Maarja couldn't imagine what. Not her, because although she felt his gaze touch her, he showed no recognition or approval.

Not a problem. She was here to show her respects to Mrs. Arundel, not to bow to him.

A red-nosed Béatrice sat beside Dante, sniffing into her wrinkled handkerchief. Andere sat beside her, looking more like the undertaker than the undertaker, and Fedelma sat beside him, head high, expression blank. Maarja had witnessed Fedelma's tears for Mrs. Arundel; she wondered now at her stoicism. Had she perhaps too often been a participant in an Arundel family funeral?

A suit-clad Jack sat on Dante's other side, at the end of the row, also observing, but in an analytical way. He seemed to be watching for twitches and tells, and to Maarja's casual, uninformed eyes, there were plenty of those: older men and women who smirked inappropriately, older men and women who looked almost too grieved, young men and women who watched Dante watch them, bored young men and women who were there because by Arundel protocol they were required to be.

Behind the immediate family, Nate stood with his arms crossed over his chest, scrutinizing the entire scene.

This funeral line, so filled with French aristocrats, all holding single red and white roses, seemed to Maarja like the lineup for execution by guillotine. Somebody, and maybe a few somebodies, were going to end up dead.

On that thought, she joined the line and, with down-turned head, she inched forward. She wished so fervently she'd thought to bring a rose that at first she didn't notice the hush that rippled up the line, then over the rest of the crowd. All she wanted was to get past the coffin, pay her respects, and return to Sacramento to help care for Alex. Yet when she could hear the rustle of leaves and bees humming as they visited the fragrant funeral wreaths, she realized all the low-toned conversations had died. Except for two hissed words that wafted from deep inside the crowd. "Benoit's assassin…"

She lifted her head and glanced around.

Every eye was fixed on her. Critical eyes. Cruel eyes. They were like a single entity, a cobra waiting to strike.

For the first time she recognized what she was to these people.

Romani. Daire. Enemy. *Prey.*

How had they discovered she was the one who'd been Benoit's executioner? Had Dante told them?

No. He would never hand over information to the unworthy.

Maarja allowed her gaze to probe deeper into the crowd.

There she was. Tabitha. The temp who eavesdropped. Tabitha smiled as if she'd won the prize.

Maarja had told herself the old ways didn't concern her.

Dante had made it clear she was a fool. Why hadn't she believed him? She should have stayed away. Now she stood alone, thinking she could easily accompany Mrs. Arundel into the open grave, and no one would ever know.

She met Dante's gaze.

Nothing stirred in those dark cold eyes, yet he lifted his hand and gestured as if blessing her—and the people in line in front of her moved back, grudgingly, one at a time, allowing her to go ahead of them to the casket to view the body.

The hair on her arms and the back of her neck lifted. Sweat trickled down her spine. If a trapped animal gave off the scent of fear, she was exuding it. She walked slowly, because she wanted to run. She breathed carefully, because she wanted to gasp. She looked ahead rather than around to meet the dozens of hostile eyes.

She reached the coffin, and at the sight of Mrs. Arundel, she stopped and stared. They'd dressed her in a lovely dark blue silk gown, and the roses covered her in scattered profusion from her shoulders to her feet. Her crossed hands held a rosary, and she looked good. Pleasant, as if her passing had been painless.

Maarja's own sob caught her by surprise, loud in the hostile silence, and she whipped out a tissue and pressed it to her lips. She glanced up at Dante, who tilted his head back toward the way she had come. She leaned over the coffin, placed her palm over Mrs. Arundel's cold hands in a last, fond farewell. She lingered an instant, then began her trek back across the lawn, walking around the line as it moved back into place, meeting no gazes, ignoring the prickling, back-of-the-neck knowledge that danger stalked her, and this crowd with their knives and kicks and jeers would assure she died slowly and in agony.

She passed the last of the crowd, she thought she'd escaped without hurt, when she heard running feet thumping behind her. She half turned—and Dante's cousin Connor Arundel caught her arm and whipped her to face him. "What did you do with the bottle?"

Out of the corner of her peripheral vision, she saw Dante rise and stride toward them. She kept her attention on Connor: blond, blue-eyed, smooth skinned, and as scary as a fight-trained pit bull. She knew better than to lose eye contact. "*La Bouteille de Flamme*, the holy bottle, was stolen in transport."

"Arranged by you."

"By me? My sister was on that truck. She was almost killed!"

"She isn't your *real* sister, she's not your kin, and close almost only counts in horseshoes and hand grenades." Connor was so angry she stepped back, not out of fear but to escape the flecks of saliva flying at her. "The bottle is gone. It's ours, our family's. Your mother gave it up for the chance to kill our leader. To murder Benoit Arundel. The bitch murdered him!"

She stepped forward again, into spittle range, and went toe to toe with Connor. "*My mother* died in that blast. My whole family, real or not, has suffered to protect the bottle containing the blood of Jånos, the revered founder of my tribe, he who fought evil and won. I don't know who has stolen it, but the curse will strike them down as it struck—"

Dante grabbed Connor by the arm and yanked him back hard enough to make him stumble. "You will not dishonor my mother's remains or the woman who saved her from the blast. Back off, *boy*, or take the consequences."

Now Connor stepped forward to go toe to toe with Dante, but he hadn't a chance against the man who had, as Benoit's heir, forcibly moved his criminal family into legitimacy.

"Maarja, go with Andere," Dante instructed.

She glanced around, surprised to see Andere beside her.

"Come, Miss Daire, I'll walk you to your car." Andere took her hand with calm assurance, put it on his arm, and covered it with his own. "Which way?"

"I'm parked there." She pointed and Andere began to walk, and she had no choice but to walk with him. "But—" She glanced back at Dante and Connor.

Dante spoke to Connor, then with one hard fist, he smashed his cousin in the face.

Connor's head cracked back, he went down hard, and he didn't stir.

Dante looked at her, his eyes glowing with a dark unholy cruelty tinged with bitter brown.

She turned around and kept walking.

He didn't want her here.

She had caused problems at his mother's funeral, and she hoped never to see him again.

CHAPTER 20

Maarja's mind and body had been invaded, shoved from the top of the trapeze and flung into a series of flips and maneuvers that left her dream world in shambles. Every night she hated to go to sleep. She dreamed all the usual dreams: returning to high school and not knowing her locker combination, living in a house that stood on the sand and watching the ocean waves sweep the foundations away, seeing her mother but not being able to hear what she said after "On your life, remember this, Maarja."

Ah, that was the worst. For years, that had been the worst.

Now, she also dreamed about Dante. Wonderful dreams, where he came to her as a supplicant, kissed her toes, her fingers, her mouth, her breasts, between her legs until she spasmed in ecstasy…

And there were dreams where he looked like Dante, but he wasn't, and he raped her and slit her throat.

Every night was another procession of teen embarrassment or vivid horror or orgasm…then she rose in the morning and went to work.

The theft had been a blow to Saint Rees and his business; when moving fine art, trust was all.

Alex's beating had both broken Maarja's heart and ignited

her anger. Despite Dante's warning that dealing death required a callous touch, when she found Serene and her bevy of thugs, they would suffer for their crimes and brutality. She was determined of that.

For three weeks, Maarja worked too much, trained so hard in self-defense her master commanded her to step back, spent time at home reading Christmas books and girl-bonding stories, watched for clues to another heist, waited for the moment she could take vengeance and find justice for her sister, and talked to Octavia and Alex daily.

She also looked up *chatte* on Google Translate and discovered it did mean *cat*…and also *cunt*. She was not in any way surprised.

Yet on all the fine art moves across California, she saw nothing, heard nothing. She felt no hint of disturbance in any of the objects she handled. It was as if the crime had never happened… except that Alex lived in pain as she recovered from one treatment after another, one physical therapy appointment after another, prepared to face one surgery after another, and struggled to learn to walk again.

How long could a person remain on high alert? As the days ticked past with no word of the art being sold, Maarja began to believe the thieves had gone, vanished to Mexico or Canada or anywhere but California where they would be recognized and eliminated. Because no one could maintain that level of tension forever, she relaxed her constant vigilance.

Three weeks…

Then…she came home.

The house in Gothic had been built in the late 1930s: one bedroom, one bath, a kitchen, living area, front porch, back porch. It was spare, it suited Maarja, it was *hers*—her first home since the explosion that had killed her mother and Benoit, rocked her world, and changed her life. Sometimes she was gone for days, driving across Nevada or Pennsylvania or Texas with a load of rich people's stuff, but when she stepped through her own door, security and comfort enfolded her.

Usually.

When she parked her car in the tiny garage off the alley, the sun had just set, twilight slid across the land, and the car clock said 7:09 p.m. She gathered her duffel bag with its three days of accumulated dirty laundry, trudged across the walk and up the steps onto the back porch. She dumped the bag and stripped off her white overalls; after three days, they were more grubby gray than white, and the shorts and pink T-shirt underneath were nothing to brag about, either.

She looked at the washer and dryer. Laundry. Tomorrow. Morning. It had to be done. But not now.

She untied her running shoes and replaced them with the wool slippers she kept by the back door, and inserted her key in the lock.

As soon as she stepped through the door into the kitchen, her senses clanged like a cracked bell.

Someone had been in the house.

An enemy. Someone who left a trail of gleeful malice from the back door into the kitchen and...where?

Someone had left her a message. And it wasn't *Happy holidays, enjoy your bookmarked Hallmark movie.*

She flicked on the overhead light.

Nothing had moved. Nothing had changed. She checked her security system. No one had set off the alarm for the doors or windows. Her video showed no intruder.

She took a deep breath. Home and calm and happiness permeated the air.

Yet a current wicked intent shoved her toward the bureau in her bedroom. She turned on that overhead, too, and her bedside lamp.

Nothing lurked in the shadows. Whoever it was didn't fear

the light. Exposure meant nothing to them. Of course, because somehow they'd removed themselves from her security camera.

She looked around, up at the corners, at the fixtures and furniture, anywhere a camera could be hidden. Were they watching her now? Did they see her open the second drawer—she knew without a doubt it was the second drawer—gingerly lift her fuzzy blue wear-around-the-house socks—and find it?

The bottle. *La Bouteille de Flamme.* Ancient red glass, made in Murano, stoppered with wax and containing the blood of her ancestor.

She didn't lift it; she didn't have to. She knew it, its very existence had formed her life, and she knew what she had to do.

Call Dante Arundel.

She knew the number. Whether she wanted to or not, whether she thought she would ever have reason to call or not, she had repeated it every night before she went to sleep.

She dialed.

In less than one ring, Dante picked up. "Are we going to be parents?"

The assumption startled her. She hadn't thought about that silly belief of his, and if she did, which she didn't, no way, she thought he'd realize how ridiculous he was being. "No, I... No, it's not that."

"Then what?" Clearly he couldn't imagine what else she would call him for.

"Not something so..." She had to steady her breathing before she could speak. "The bottle is here."

He didn't answer.

She said, "The red bottle."

"I know what you mean." His voice was emotionless, unreadable. "In your house?"

"In my house. In my home. In my sock drawer." Like it made a difference whether it was her socks or her silverware.

"Is it real?"

"Yes."

"I'll be there at once. Don't touch it."

She spoke into the phone. "Like I would be that stupid."

He had hung up.

No, she wouldn't put a fingerprint on that bottle.

CHAPTER 21

Forty minutes later Maarja had turned on all the lights in the house. Yet when someone rang her front doorbell, she froze in place, then deliberately relaxed and checked her phone app. The porch camera showed Dante Arundel on her front porch, dressed in a dark business suit, starched white shirt, and a charcoal tie, loosened at the neck.

She opened to him at once. "How did you get here so fast? Transporter beam?"

"Helicopter." In a shrewd sweep of dark-eyed intelligence, he assessed her physical health and her mental distress. "You have to invite me in."

Like he was a vampire. "Come in," she said, not because he compelled her, but because she actually knew why he wanted the words spoken aloud. Her front porch camera recorded conversation, and for a wealthy man like Dante, permission must save on lawsuits.

He walked in and back toward her bedroom.

A black sedan was parked at the curb, and the unmistakable form of Nate lurked beside it.

She shut the door. "If you came by helicopter, how did you get here by car?"

Dante looked back at Maarja. "We set down at Angelica Lindholm's helipad."

Angelica Lindholm essentially owned Gothic.

"She graciously allowed me to keep a car for my use in her garage." He walked into Maarja's bedroom.

Angelica Lindholm also didn't graciously allow anyone to exploit her, her influence, or her facilities without good reason, which meant Dante had...paid her? Threatened her? Commanded her? Maarja took a breath to ask, then exhaled and hurried after him. She had other more important questions, like "Why would you do that? Keep a car in Gothic?"

"I thought this day might come." He stood by her chest. "Which drawer?"

"Second one. What day?"

"The day you called me." He opened the drawer.

"Left side." He was talking about her, and him, and pregnancy. "I had a period. A little late, I think, but there's been a lot of trauma so it's not surprising."

He lifted her socks and looked, nodded, then put them back. "You could have told me."

"I did tell you. I told you when we had... When you brought it up..." Shit. She was fumbling this big-time. "Afterward, after we...were in the shower, I told you I wasn't pregnant."

"Hm." He gave his opinion clearly in one syllable, like he had no faith in her previous assurances and still didn't quite believe her.

But she *had* had a period. It was as simple as that. Bleeding, cramping, moodiness...more moodiness...more moodiness. Her hormones had been hell-bent on reminding her of Dante and his prediction of fate and babies to unite the families and, oh, my God, the dreams for those nights. Talk about a horror show, complete with the entire cast of hostile characters from the funeral, her sword-wielding mother, and some assassin who kept showing himself, but without a face.

Oh, and a baby she had to feed and change, and she had no experience and no way to support it…

Fine. Her conscious mind refused to consider the chance of a child. Her subconscious mind was not so easily coerced.

"You have a security system," he said. "Nothing and no one shows on the video, so whoever placed this commandeered your system. I've got my people looking into it."

"How do you know what's on my security system?"

"It's basic home security, nothing fancy, good enough for most situations, but also easy to hack as needed. I needed."

She wasn't speechless, exactly. She just didn't know what to say. "I'll…upgrade."

"Not tonight." He stood with his head down, clearly thinking. "You got home. You came in and walked right here to find the bottle."

She didn't know what to do first. Combat outrage that he'd hacked into her camera and watched her recent movements? Or be glad he cared enough to come so quickly and investigate so conclusively? And keep a car here to come to her when she needed him… She remembered his expression when he heard the shipment had been stolen, the ruthless cast of his face, the chilling manner in which he'd weighed her involvement and found her guilty. Worse was that moment when she'd admitted she killed his father…

She had blood on her hands. His father's, and she did not care about that.

But her mother's.

Dear God, Mama.

All his preparation had been in case she were pregnant, yet she was not and he was here, now, anyway. What did it mean… other than the fact she didn't understand Dante Arundel? She didn't understand him at all.

"You knew *la Bouteille de Flamme* was here. Maarja, how did you know that the bottle was here?" The way he spoke, she thought he'd asked more than once.

"I told you. In your mother's library. Remember that day? I told you I have a sense about these things." Yet his first thought might not have been that he knew that, but that she'd somehow set it up herself.

He said, "The Chinese scroll you said was a fake? You were right."

Ah. She'd proved herself. "I know. Usually I have to touch something to sense its past." She half smiled. "The Chinese scroll didn't have much of a past."

"But tonight, you don't have to touch the bottle."

Yeah. Proving herself wasn't so easy to this doubtful asshole. "Inside the glass is the blood of my blood. I know when it's near." *Believe me or not.*

As swiftly as a snake striking, his hand reached out and gripped her wrist. "Do you know where the stopper is?"

"Nobody ever told me."

"Do you *know*?"

He'd spotted her prevarication, damn it. "I know. I didn't until I held the bottle the first time, in your mother's library, then I understood what I'd only sensed." She shook herself free, went to the jewelry box that sat on her dresser, and in an act of great courage, lifted out a necklace. Courage, because she was alone with an Arundel, the son of the man who'd been willing to kill a woman and a four-year-old child for this, and Dante could casually take her life, dispose of her body, and no one would ever know what had happened to her.

Dante's gaze narrowed on the shiny stone that hung on the sturdy gold chain. "Of course. You were wearing that the day your mother—"

"Yes. That morning, she put the chain around my neck. She told me it was my heritage, the only thing she had to leave me. She told me to remember her when I wore it. None of it made any sense to me at the time, but I have treasured it." Maarja cupped the stone in her hand and stepped close to show him. She lowered her voice when she spoke of it, using the reverent tone one used in church. "Viewed close, it really didn't look like much, a black stone with a hole in it. But it's not black, it's a blue so dense it seemed to be impenetrable. A hole was carved, not by human hands, but by water." Her eyes fluttered closed as she sensed the tumult of a cascading waterfall, relentlessly grinding the stones at its base until this one broke free. "Years and years it traveled down, down toward the sea. The waves found it, played with it, smoothed the stone—feel it—" Blindly she reached for his hand and guided his finger to the rock's silky surface. "A girl discovered it. Many years ago she found it, glinting in the bright white sand. She took it to the glassmakers on the island, and they created the blood-red vessel to give it purpose, and the girl carried it to her tribe, to her father."

"What happened?" Dante's voice coaxed Maarja, lulling the portent of anguish.

"She was the daughter of Jånos, our founder, our visionary. He foretold that we would come to a place where we could live at peace with man and nature, high on a cliff overlooking the ocean. When he spoke, we could almost hear the waves crashing, imagine a life of fishing and farming. The tribe traveled north and west, walking, pulling their wagons, caring for their horses, seeking the home that Jånos foretold. When they came to the land of the Normans, the man who called himself Lord of the lands, Èrthu Arundel, saw the girl and wanted her...for a moment only, for he had a wife great with child. Instead Jånos offered the glass bottle and stone stopper. Èrthu took the gift, raped the girl, slit Jånos's throat." Dante's fingers flexed in hers, offering his strength. "As her father died, the girl captured his blood in the bottle, and thus it became a holy object to us."

"What happened to Èrthu Arundel?" Dante's voice barely pinged into Maarja's consciousness.

"Jånos's sons castrated him as they would have an unruly horse or a wayward ox. He lived, but it was too late. His wife gave birth to a boy child, Èrthu raised him in cruelty and vengeance,

the years of battle and blood had begun, and for a thousand years
the bottle and the stopper changed hands, were separated, sought
each other, until…today…"

Taking a deep breath, Maarja opened her eyes. She looked
right into Dante's face…into the face of a fiend.

His complexion had bleached to a waxy tint, with furious red
on his cheeks and lips. His nostrils flared, his cruel white teeth
were bared. His eyes…heavy-lidded, dark-lashed, with a gold
flame lit deep within.

She was a fool. This man was dangerous to her, more dangerous than even she had known.

Still holding the stone, she tried to step back.

He caught her arms. "Do you always see so much?"

"Never. Only now, when you're touching…me." Maybe it
wasn't him who was dangerous to her, but the *now* of knowing.

He looked toward her bureau, then he scanned the tops of
her windows. Or maybe the edges of her coved ceiling where
her camera lens watched and recorded. "We'll do this thing."
He seemed to be talking to himself.

What thing? She didn't speak out loud. She still felt as if she
had one foot in the past, and somehow he had taken a step away
from her and into the future.

He took her by the shoulders and positioned her so she stood
at right angles to the light from her bed lamps. Going to her
bureau, he opened the drawer, and while she whispered, "You
said not to touch it," he took it out from under her socks and
brought it to her. Holding it cupped in his palms, he gazed at
her from those fierce, dark, fiendish eyes. "Free your stone from
the chain. Unite the stopper with the bottle. It is, after all, what
both have been seeking all these centuries."

CHAPTER 22

Dante was right. The one had been created for the other, out of the bones of the earth, stone and sand, heat and fire, the artistry of God and man, working together.

Dramatic. Absurd. And true.

Maarja opened her chain, slid the stone free, slipped a finger through the hole, and considered the bottle.

"The wax," she said. She meant the wax that sealed the bottle, the temporary replacement for the stone that had lasted for generations.

Using a magician's trick, a bone handle appeared in his right hand, and with a flick and a click, a sharp thin steel blade appeared.

She flinched.

Stiletto. She guessed it had come out of his sleeve or his belt or... She didn't know. Didn't want to know.

With a frightening efficiency, he slipped the point under the wax and popped it out.

They both waited, wondering what kind of odor would come from the long-unopened bottle reputed to hold the blood of a martyr.

Dante took a long inhale. "Cedar. Lavender. Thyme. He's not in here." He sounded almost disappointed.

"Blood of my blood," she reminded him. "The other scent is honey. Whatever they preserved of Jånos is mixed with scents that would pleasure him in the afterlife, and the honey preserves him and the plant material."

"How do you know that?" Dante wasn't doubtful, just curious.

"The Egyptians used honey to preserve small bodies, because honey is antimicrobial and antibacterial. It doesn't spoil."

He flicked the wax from the tip of the blade, and the stiletto vanished with a sleight of hand as efficient as its appearance. "You know the oddest facts."

"I could say the same about you."

He observed too much of her reluctance to mate the stopper to the bottle, yet he waited on her without reproach.

The scents rose in her brain, blurring the edges of reality. "I don't know how to make the stone fit."

"You don't have to *make* it. With a little care, when you maneuver it, the stopper will slip into place." Once again, he cupped the bottle in both his palms. "I know this. Don't you?"

"Yes… The stone feels warm in my hand, as if it understands the momentousness of this event."

He used that deep, gentle, soothing tone he'd used during her seduction. "Do it. It's time. Past time."

"Yes." Her fingers shook a little as she fitted the stone into the bottle's collar. It was like a jigsaw puzzle; it had to fit exactly right, but he was right. She maneuvered it, and with a small clink it was seated as if the stone and the glass had never parted.

Dante smiled with so much satisfaction he might have been created for this moment. "Take it."

When she reached with one hand, he pressed it into her palm, then took her other hand and wrapped it around the bottle, too, so she cupped it in both her palms as he had before. He enclosed her hands in his, so a layer of him supported her, and a layer of her supported the now joined bottle and stopper, and inside the bottle the blood of Jånos rejoiced. Even more than the sex between her and Dante, even more than the click that signified the bottle and stopper had mated, the mere act of *holding* while so entwined seemed like it meant…something…

Dante leaned toward her, his breath softly caressing her skin. "After so many years, they are one. Maarja, can you feel their celebration?"

Mesmerized by him, by the sense that together, they'd created something greater than themselves, she nodded.

"Maarja, shall we celebrate, too?"

She thought he would close in on her, kiss her, be that kind of masterful upper-hand I-took-your-virginity guy that he actually was.

He waited. He wanted her to lean into him.

In a distant corner of her mind, she was aware this was probably not wise.

He was the enemy.

He handled a knife like a professional executor.

Yet nothing about this, from the moment the explosion blasted her to the moment she gave herself to this dangerous stranger to the moment she'd reunited the bottle and stopper, had been wise. She gave herself over to the dizziness of knowing that together they had made history, and stood on tiptoe to lightly touch his lips with hers.

His fingers clenched around hers, holding her holding the bottle. The glass ignited with such heat she felt as if the whorls on her skin had been dissolved and rearranged. His mouth applied a firm pressure, his lips opened, and what she had thought would be a soft accord sizzled with lightning so bright it blinded and thunder so loud it deafened…yet her mind unwillingly comprehended the brand that burned them. Without words, an ancient wrong had been righted, a new vow had been made.

CHAPTER 23

Maarja whiplashed herself back, away from this…this…this omen. "What was *that*?"

Dante's lips were red and swollen, his eyes smoldering in a primitive display of ownership. "You know what that was."

Did she know? In that ancient part of her brain that sucked in the knowledge of an object's past, did she comprehend what he'd done? "Did you perform some kind of voodoo marriage?"

"*We. We* performed an ancient ritual that wiped the ancient stain clean and restarted our worlds. This is it. This is all. You and me—we began in fire and explosion. We continue with sex and union. Now…now we are fused, together, one."

We? No! "*We* did not!"

He lifted her hands and the bottle to her eye level. "You're not the only one who knows a few of the bits and pieces of history. The Arundel family has always known the past could be resurrected and changed."

"The *fuck!*" She wasn't usually a hardline swear-girl, but by God, this situation required it.

"Yes. The fuck will happen." Dante smiled, all half-crooked-up corner of the mouth, sexual anticipation, and amused, smiling eyes. "It'll be good, too. If I could, if we had time, I'd shove our pants down and push you against the wall, and together we'd celebrate our new world."

She clenched. Thighs pressed together. Breasts nipply and hard. Coochie, damp and flexing.

Damn him. He had her thinking like him, reacting to him, wanting him.

He knew it, too, but he knew what she didn't, and he got serious in a hurry. He glanced around at the walls and again at her cove molding. "We don't have time. We've got to get out of here."

She looked, too. Her cam…yes. He had definitely positioned them for optimum viewing, and all of this had been recorded. For whom? *They?* Why did *they* care? "Why do we have to get out of here?"

He turned her toward the back door. "I told you—I'm not the only one who can hack your cameras. They saw us do this."

"As you meant them to!" *Who were they?*

He didn't argue. "They're our witnesses, and they'll want to kill us and destroy the proof of what we did." He plucked the bottle out of her fingers and did that stiletto magic disappearing act with it. "Not everyone believes in fate, and if they do, they also believe they can change it. They think they can be Èrthu, and seize the future for themselves. If we let them. We will not let them."

They turned away from the monitor that showed the interior of Maarja's bedroom, and faced each other. "Dante's move to bring this Romani into the family signifies a change in plans. We cannot permit that. We have to eliminate him, too, before she carries his child."

"Too? We didn't eliminate Raine. Somebody else did."

"There are more participants playing this game than we realized. Think like Benoit. We'll eliminate them all."

"Benoit died."

"We will survive. We will conquer. They will all die, and we will own our world."

CHAPTER 24

Dante grabbed a pillow off the bed and handed it to Maarja, who looked at it and him in alarm. Shrugging out of his jacket, he tossed it around her shoulders and pushed her ahead of him toward the front door.

They were escaping.

She fought, distracted from her thought of some kind of absurd, primitive, life-changing marriage ceremony to the here and now. "You can't let them take my house!"

"What? Why?" He glanced around.

She did, too.

It was small and old, dated in its plaster walls and high ceilings and all the accoutrements that marked it as a late 1930s construction. But—"This is my house. My home. The first place that is mine. You can't let them burn it, or bomb it, or whatever you think they're going to do."

He urged her onto the front porch.

She set her heels and turned to him.

He had his phone out, talking to somebody. "Protect the Gothic house. If anything happens to it, I'll hold you responsible. Yes. Untouched. Make it so."

She thought about objecting to the idea that one person in Dante's organization would now extend their dark wings over her home, but…she loved this place where her heart beat in warmth and safety, this home where she relaxed in wooly socks and listened to the storms off the Pacific, where her past was just that, the past, and cast no shadows.

He held his phone. "Walk to the sidewalk. Take a right. Step into the shadows of the trees. Stay there." He directed her every movement.

She did. Hit the concrete and headed right. What kind of dumbass wouldn't? He had the whole thing figured out, and *she* figured he wasn't going to marry her and kill her in the same night. If he wanted to off her, he'd have done it a long time ago.

Behind her, Nate jumped the limo's hood—that man was scary athletic—and slid into the driver's seat. The motor purred and the vehicle smoothed forward.

Where the shadows deepened, she stopped. Dante caught her from behind. She didn't startle; she knew it was him. "Give me your phone," he instructed.

She fumbled it out of her pocket and placed it in his palm.

He took the pillow out of her arms and handed it and the phone off to…someone who lurked there. A woman, dressed like her in a pink T-shirt and shorts.

So creepy.

And a man, dressed like Dante in his suit, white shirt, and loosened tie.

The female handed over a blue hoodie.

Dante whipped his jacket off Maarja's shoulders and tossed it over her shoulders. The male shrugged out of his jean bomber jacket, gave it to Dante, and took his phone.

To the casual eye, the impersonators resembled Dante and Maarja. They stepped forward into the light cast by the streetlamp.

Nate stopped the limo, hurried around, and opened the back passenger door.

From the porch across the street, Mr. Cummings called, "Nice ride, Maarja!"

The female gave a wave of acknowledgment. Flinging the pillow into the car, she leaned in and was swallowed by luxury. The male followed, Nate closed the door, returned to the driver's seat, and the car sped away.

"Perfect," Dante breathed, and shoved Maarja farther off the walk into the darkness. He helped her into the hoodie, pulled on the jacket, removed his tie, and stuck it into his pocket. He rumpled his hair into a frenzied mess, pulled something from the jacket pocket—lipstick?—and with his finger smeared some around his mouth, then around hers. This was, she realized, an elaborate charade to fool...them. Him. Her. Whoever had started this.

From farther up the road, another car, a black sedan, started its motor and cruised after the limo.

For the longest three minutes of her life, Dante held her in place, watching, waiting... "That should be enough," he said in her ear. He twitched the hood to cover her distinctive hair and flung an arm around her shoulders. "Let's start walking. Up the hill. To the Live Oak."

The Live Oak Restaurant and Inn, the five-star restaurant in this one-horse town, with luxurious suites taken by celebrities who wanted privacy and mostly got it.

"Of course. The best dinner on Big Sur." She walked, wandered, really, scrunched up against him. He stopped her every few minutes to hug her, kiss her, and always his focus was on their surroundings. These embraces held no emotion, no passion; they were merely camouflage that gave the impression of nonchalance while Dante took the time to survey the street around them.

"A lot of people are looking out windows at us," he commented.

"It's a village. Not much to do on a Tuesday but watch the tourists suck lips."

"They don't recognize you?"

"I'd say not, or there would be some catcalls."

"Good. That's good." He increased their pace. "Here's the house I rented. We can get in a little bit more of a hurry now."

"The house? I thought you said the Live Oak…"

"We'll go in the front door, turn on the light, cast some interesting shadows on the blinds, turn off the lights, leave. I chose this house for the side door. If *they're* watching—" whoever *they* were "—they'll probably miss that one. Rich people don't know much about small old houses and how they're constructed."

"And they don't yet realize you had this planned down to the nth degree." She didn't know what she thought about that. His security measures put an end to her turmoil about his primitive wedding ceremony—no, not primitive, *phony*—and flung her into another set of confused emotions. Worry. Anger. That niggling discomfort that she'd been constantly observed while unaware. More anger.

"Precautions are necessary for our continued good health, and in this case, elaborate precautions are in order." He spoke in an instructive tone, like he was teaching her what she needed to know in the future.

Which led her back to the anxiety about the wedding ceremony and what he expected was going to happen with them in between what he'd already mentioned happening against the wall and, she supposed, on the bed and in the shower again and back on the bed and, if her friends were to be believed, on a trapeze while using Crisco shortening.

Meanwhile, Dante ushered her inside the tiny house, turned on the lights, lowered the blinds, made sure they were positioned correctly to cast silhouettes, and pulled her close, body to body.

He was not as focused on their safety as she thought.

Or he was really good at multitasking. Because that was a big boner he tucked against her.

In a hushed tone that sounded wickedly tempting, he said, "If the neighbors are watching anyway, we might as well give them a passion to aim for." Bending her over his arm until she threw her arms around him to keep her balance, he kissed her in light dry brushes that both confused and enticed her. His warm breath smelled dark, like black licorice and bitter chocolate fudge. His tongue, when he slid it across the seam of her lips, made her jump. He shushed her, clutched her waist more firmly, cradled her head, and kissed her with such depraved skill she floundered under the breaking wave of *too much*: too much heat, too much craving, too much Dante.

When he began a slow retreat, she followed, trying to entice him back to her, back to the magnificent hunger between them, but he was inexorable, and when she stood erect and opened her eyes, she found she held his head between her palms. Snatching her hands away, she stepped back…and he let her. She retreated. He moved to the lamp and the click as he darkened the room sounded loud and rude.

"There," he said softly.

There what? There, he'd fooled *them*, whoever *they* were? There, he made her wet and frustrated? There, the neighbors were grabbing for their vibrators and their roommates?

He caught her hand and tugged her toward the short hallway between the living room and the bedroom. He stopped in the dark. "Here's the bathroom if you need to use it."

"Thanks." She went in, did *not* slam the door, flicked on the light, and peed. The man really knew how to knock the lust right out of her. She'd driven home, found the bottle first thing, and never again thought of her bladder. Until now, when he pointed it out, like a big ol' fat nasty uncouth rude boy who should mind his own genitalia.

She came out, he went in—apparently he *was* minding his

own genitalia—and she realized this pause, and the normalcy of having the bathroom light go on and off, would portray the couple in this house as doing the natural thing proceeding bedroom activity. *They*, if they were still out there, would move on rather than continuing to watch.

Damn it. She *was* beginning to think like Dante, like an Arundel.

Going into the bedroom, she turned the lamp on low, tossed the covers down, and straightened the sheets, knowing her silhouette was doing its part to create the right scenario. When he appeared in the doorway, he said, "Very good." Walking over, he turned the lamp back off and grasped her wrist. "Five minutes, and we'll move."

She nodded. He couldn't see her, but she was still feeling hot and bothered and not all that cooperative.

He spoke, maybe to fill the silence, maybe so that anyone listening at the door would hear him murmuring in a slow deep, seductive voice. "I would kiss you more, for the pleasure of you in my arms, answering me, seducing me—"

She gave an incoherent grumble. Seducing him, indeed.

"But if I kissed you, I wouldn't be able to stop. Not again."

Her irritation eased. Maybe she wasn't the only one helpless in this cycle of needing and wanting and mindless…lovemaking.

No. She wouldn't call it that. That would indicate intimacy, engaged emotions, a relationship. Better to call it fucking, and she told herself one time did not mean mindless fucking.

Her other self pointed out, logically and with great precision, that thinking about the fucking every night while she was alone in her bed constituted mindless…something. Mindless horniness. Mindless need. Wanting to touch herself now, in the dark, while he stood beside her…that constituted lust.

She was not married to him. She was tagging along so she didn't get killed because of that damned… "What happened to the bottle?"

"Not to worry, I have it," he assured her. "Let's go out the side door. It's right here."

She grabbed his lapel. "Wait. A month ago you hated me. I was the villain. I had stolen *la Bouteille de Flamme*. I'd killed your father. My sister's blood meant nothing. You judged me. Why now? You make some kind of phony marriage to me? You believed me when I said someone came into my house and put the bottle in my drawer? Why? Why now?" She was so angry. The bastard. The Arundel. Dante. Always the same. Injustice and death and…and fucking.

And she was the one being fucked. *A pretend marriage.* Damn him all to hell.

"You could have been the one who they sent to kill me," he said. "You could have been the one who planned the theft of *la Flamme*. You're smart enough. You're the apex of the Daire family. You could own the world. I knew it. But I didn't believe it."

"Because I was a virgin."

"Because you risked your life to save my mother!" He took a long breath. "I made you memorize the number. The last thing I did was make you repeat it. What does that mean to you?"

"It means you're hedging your bets."

"I only bet on sure things." He put his face close to hers. "You. Need to. Remember. That."

CHAPTER 25

She would remember that. Maarja remembered everything Dante had ever said to her, because it was safe. It was important. If she was going to live through this, she needed him. He was either going to save her...or kill her.

A man who was going to kill her wouldn't perform a wedding ceremony with her.

Would he?

The side door wasn't normal-sized. It was narrow and short, made to fit a hobbit or maybe to give the 1940s milkman somewhere to put his deliveries. Dante held her elbow as she stepped onto the slick concrete stairs and down the steps. He followed her at close quarters. He opened the gate that led into the next house's backyard and shoved her through. They walked through somebody's backyard, avoided their handkerchief-sized garden, went through another gate into the next backyard, then down a narrow side yard, through another gate, and...they stood at the back of the Live Oak Restaurant and Inn.

The brick building was old, and long, and thin, a former brothel converted into a world-class restaurant and a few suites expanded to rent for fifteen hundred dollars a night. And up. Most people who lived in Gothic couldn't afford to stay here. Certainly she never had. But she'd eaten in the dining room, rubbing elbows with movie stars and jet-setters who traveled to Gothic to enjoy Señor Emilio Alfonso's Spanish creations.

With his hand on her spine, Dante directed her into the side door here, as narrow and low as the last one, and she found herself in the small restaurant kitchen, aflame with cooking burners and full of ovens toasting iron pans of bread, cheese, vegetables, and thin slices of exotic meats that, oh, God, smelled like heaven to someone who planned a cheese and veggie plate before falling into bed.

Señor Alfonso, justly famous for his four-star restaurant in Barcelona, Spain, directed his small staff with energy and enthusiasm. Catching sight of Dante and Maarja, he shot them a welcoming smile and gestured them toward the small table in the far corner of the kitchen. Not in the dining room, the kitchen! They were as private as it was possible to be. No one could see them or know they were here. How had Dante arranged this in the convenient here and now? Maybe *he* had put the bottle in her sock drawer?

She chewed on that thought as he seated her on the bench against the wall, slid the table closer, then snuggled against her, effectively trapping her and touching her. Leaning in, he asked, "What's wrong?"

In a low voice, she said, "Someone tried to frame me for theft. You involved me in some bizarre ceremony—"

"Wedding ceremony," he corrected.

"You seem to think my house needs protecting, that I need protecting."

"I will always protect my wife."

She took a breath and let it out. *One battle at a time, Maarja.* "You have people impersonating us, dressed like us, leading *them*, whoever they are, astray. You rent a house we can walk into so it looks like we're people we're not—"

"Bought it."

"And we sneaked through dark backyards to have dinner in

the Live Oak Restaurant kitchen!" She leaned forward, got in his face. "What's wrong? Really, Dante? What isn't wrong?"

Oblivious to the moment, Señor Alfonso appeared at the table carrying his *gambas al ajillo* served in a miniature cast-iron skillet sizzling with olive oil. He placed the shrimp in front of Maarja where the scent distracted her with its garlicky goodness. "The señorita loves these, I know." Pulling a corkscrew and a bottle from his expansive apron pocket, he expertly opened the wine, producing two glasses, and poured a taste for Dante. "From Rioja, as you requested."

Dante tasted it. "Excellent. One of my favorites."

One of the sous chefs arrived with a cutting board with small wedges of *tortilla Española* surrounded by toothpicks of Manchego cheese topped with pimento-stuffed Gordal olives, and a basket of crusty bread.

Already the tiny table was getting crowded.

Already her stomach growled.

Señor Alfonso gestured. "Eat! While we prepare more!"

What could Maarja do? Her hostility toward Dante was completely understandable, but Señor Alfonso didn't deserve the anger overflow. She smiled and thanked him, and while she did, Dante tore off a small chunk of bread, dipped it in the bubbling oil, and when she turned her head to glare at him, he put it to her lips.

Him, she could be rude to, but Señor Alfonso and his sous chef stood beaming and waiting, so she let Dante feed her and… she collapsed against the back of the bench. Man, it was good. For one moment, while she chewed, she closed her eyes to allow the full fruity taste of the salty oil and the tough bread fill her senses…and when she opened them, the chefs had retreated and Dante was looking at her as if he craved sex rather than food…

"Shrimp?" He didn't wait for her agreement, but used the tiny fork to spear one. He blew on it to cool it, then took it in his fingers and put it to her lips. She tried to take it from him, but he coaxed, "You'll love it. Señor Alfonso said so. Just a bite."

It was a shrimp.

It was also surrender.

But she was tucked into the corner behind a table with a big broad-shouldered guy leaning toward her, who smiled like he knew stuff he shouldn't know, which probably he did, considering he'd been watching her on her own damned video camera… She bit into the shrimp and chewed and moaned.

"Fuck." He shifted as if he was uncomfortable.

"No," she snapped.

He wasn't listening, he was too busy choosing the best bits for her, murmuring about the briny olives and the six-month-old cheese and the way the bread crust crumbled and fell into the oil…and each word was foreplay. Señor Alfonso and his staff kept bringing tapas, hot and cold. Ludwig, the restaurant's stuffed shirt continental waiter/maître d', poured wine, keeping their glasses topped off, while she mellowed and admitted secrets like, "These *patatas bravas* are fabulous, but I really love a big baked potato with bowls of crisp bacon, sour cream, grated cheddar, and Irish butter lined up in front of me." And, "Now that I've tried *Jamón ibérico*, I can die happy."

Dante nodded and looked as if he filed it all away for future reference, which niggled at her in a worrisome way.

Finally, she had to lean back and shake her head. "No more."

Dante chuckled, loud and deep in his chest. "We've just begun."

CHAPTER 26

Maarja slapped her hand on the table hard enough to make the glasses jump. "No!"

Señor Alfonso, headed for their table with a plate of cream-filled *miguelitos*, made an abrupt turnabout.

She might have had too much wine. Or her frustration had boiled over. Or both, because the easiness caused by the good food turned to confrontation, and she made the accusation that haunted her. "Maybe *you* put the bottle in my drawer."

Dante had the guts to look surprised. Then he followed her train of thought and nodded slowly. "Because I had all *this*—" he waved a hand around "—planned."

"Yes!"

"I can see the logic, but I didn't have the bottle, and I don't know who did. You'll have to take my word for it, because I can't prove that." He leaned closer again, blocked her in with his shoulders and his intensity. "I'm good at preplanning. I knew it might be necessary to get you out of your home in a hurry, so almost before you left the hospital with Alex, I handled it. I'm fast on my feet; the appearance of the bottle gave me the opportunity to mark you as mine. Not casual-lover mine, but this-is-serious-and-if-you-hurt-her-you'll-be-sorry mine."

"I'm not *yours*. I'm not a thing to be marked. Or possessed."

"*They* don't think that way. A woman is definitely a thing to be possessed and a pawn to be used."

She spotted it right away; he hadn't addressed an important issue. "*They* think of me as a possession. What do *you* think?"

One side of his mouth quirked up. "That you're mine."

He didn't lie. She had to give him that. He stared her right in the eyes and told her what he thought…and felt.

She needed out from behind this table, away from this sense that fate, in the guise of Dante Arundel, had her trapped. "Time to go." She pushed at his shoulder.

He slid backward off the bench, moved the table out to make it easy for her to stand, shook Señor Alfonso's hand, and thanked him for the lovely meal. She did the same, then turned toward the back door.

Dante took her arm. "We have a room here."

Somehow, she hadn't seen that coming. She thought there'd be a car waiting to whisk them away somewhere…somewhere where she could explain to him where she stood. Where they stood.

As it was, she listened while Señor Alfonso assured her they would occupy the most secure suite in the house, on the third floor, that he had hosted celebrities who needed a time away from the limelight and she and Mr. Arundel would be completely private during their time at the Live Oak.

She thanked him again, for the fact of the matter was—she needed that security. She'd seen the faces at Mrs. Arundel's funeral. She'd suffered under Connor's fury and acrimony. She'd felt the malice that had invaded her home to place the bottle in her drawer. If she wanted to live tonight, she would stay where Dante had arranged.

Ludwig led them toward a coat closet, or what she thought was a coat closet. But no; he used a small key to open the lock, and handed it to Dante. "The other doors have been programmed as you requested." He stepped back.

Dante gestured her into the dim space lit by a single bulb hanging from the ceiling.

Ludwig shut the door behind them.

The right hand wall was lined with shelves of canned goods; a camouflage, she supposed, as well as storage. The other two walls were flat and blank, and Maarja took a quick, frightened breath. Was this like the Haunted Mansion at Disney? Was the floor going to sink or rise or go sideways? Not that she was particularly claustrophobic, but this close, airless space with Dante Arundel made her feel trapped and wary.

Dante reached into the shelf at eye level and tapped in a code. "The same as the number you memorized," he told her.

A door opened to the left.

Breathing a deep breath of relief, she stepped through into a small foyer lit by a glass and molded iron sconces on the walls.

With a soft click, the door closed behind her.

She looked back.

Dante ran his hands over the door, securing it against intrusion. She supposed she should appreciate the feeling of safety, but...he was on the side of the door with her. He laid claim to her. He believed she was his. To own? To do with as he wished?

Oh, hell no.

Two closed doors stood between them and the kitchen and here, in the space between real life and its consequences, existed the chance to make her position clear to Dante. She could not allow that moment in the restaurant control what happened between them.

She took one step up—the high ground—and turned to face him. In icy tones, she said, "I am not yours. I would not be even if this *marriage*—" because Maarja was really angry, and because she knew it would irritate him, she used air quotes "—were legitimate or legal. Such an idea, that you can own me, is insulting to me as a human being."

He didn't nod or acknowledge her words in any way. He watched her, narrow-eyed, unsmiling.

Which made her want to rush at him, make him afraid of her punches and kicks. Only the strong caution her martial arts master had instilled in her held her back. That, and the knowledge Dante probably had more experience, undoubtedly was more ruthless, and obviously had a longer reach.

She used her words, because before they shared a suite, he should by God acknowledge her dominion over herself. "Your mother could never have approved of such an outdated belief of human ownership. Would be ashamed of you for holding such a view."

"Did she tell you that?"

"No, but *especially* your mother, who in her own marriage was nothing but an object and a possession. I'm convinced she taught you to be more enlightened."

"She did try." He barely seemed to move his lips.

"You can get over the idea I'm going to fall into your plans and sleep with you out of some misplaced sense of obligation."

"Obligation."

"Because you saved my life." That sounded churlish. "Not that I'm unappreciative—"

"You appreciate that I didn't leave you to be murdered."

She hesitated. When he repeated her words, especially in that cold emotionless tone, they sounded insulting. "Are we sure someone was going to murder me? The bottle in my drawer... They were trying to frame me."

As if seeking patience, he looked down, a slow motion, deliberate in its purpose, then up again. His eyes, dark fringed, faintly glowed as if the gold in their depths had grown molten with heat.

The heat of impatience? Or anger? Or...

He wasn't listening to her. He was refusing to hear what she said, or believe that she meant it. Prickly with frustration, she turned her back on him and climbed the stairs.

She'd reached the first landing when he said, "Frame you? Yes, but who would they send to discover the bottle? Which of my relatives would strangle you with his bare hands, seize the reliquary, and use that to claim mastery over the Arundel organization?"

She turned. "You don't have to be so—" She'd intended to say *brutally frank.*

The sconces lit him, the dark hair, the sculpted face, the body he'd created with the constant vigilance of training, and she couldn't speak. He still stood, legs braced as if he stood on a deck in stormy weather, hands relaxed at his side. A long forgotten memory flashed through her, of Benoit Arundel on his throne, his cold green gaze resting on her, assessing her, weighing her worth and finding her nothing more than a burrowing tick to be eliminated. To Benoit, she had been the last of her family; he hoped to count her death as the ultimate Arundel victory.

Only her mother's sacrifice had saved her.

She hadn't realized it before, but while Dante's hair and eyes were dark rather than light, he had the look of his father: ruthless, intent, a great dark beast, twitching with the need to...not hurt, but to dominate...her. She could object and deny, but together they had joined the bottle to the stopper, they had kissed and experienced the flash of heat and triumph, and Dante would now have his way...unless she got into the suite before him.

He remained on the ground floor.

She was up one flight. She had a head start.

He took a step toward her.

She turned and fled, around the corner, up another flight, around a corner, up another flight, to the waiting door with its electronic numbered lock. She heard the light thump of his footsteps as he loped the stairs after her. He didn't race; no, of course not. The beast hunted, and never doubted his success.

All she had to do was key in the right number, and get inside the room. And shut it behind her.

Use the security bars.

Pile furniture in front of it.

The number. The one he'd insisted she memorize. She pushed each button firmly; she didn't have time to flub it. The lock clicked.

She'd won! She pushed the door open, hurried inside, used her whole body to shove it closed...

Almost closed. He hit it at a run, knocking her backward.

She recovered, braced her feet, straining, leaned against it, heart thumping, teeth gritted with determination. Like any of that mattered. The door inched open until she gave up and leaped backward, and he crashed into the room. She darted around him. He caught her by the waist, swung her in a circle. Like they were dancing, and he would lead where he liked.

She caught a whirling impression of the suite; wide windows open to welcome the storm, golden hardwood floors, large rugs of neutral weaves, a tall gas fireplace, flames flicking, warm lighting, and a giant bed that dominated the room with its airy light pink curtains. Chocolates and two black silk sleep masks on the pillow. Romance and seduction and—he kicked the door closed.

She lifted both her feet and slithered out of his embrace, braced her hand on the ground, and kicked the legs out from underneath him.

She didn't have time to exalt.

He flipped as he fell, a smooth acrobatic roll that brought him around to knock her flat on her back and bring her beneath him, beneath his weight. "Stop," he said.

The shock of heat and muscle and man—and knowing he'd handled her all too easily—made her listen. Not to his command, but to her own good sense. He'd taken her down with a minimum amount of fuss. She wasn't going to win that way.

"You said you had never raped a woman. You said you wouldn't rape me!"

"Never rape. Not between us." Standing, he offered his hand.

She looked at it, longed to grab and twist, but she knew him; he was prepared.

She put her hand in his and let him pull her to her feet, close but not too close.

He performed that magic trick, the one where the stiletto appeared in his hand. Gripping the neckline of her T-shirt, he clicked the blade out and used it to slice the thin material from top to bottom.

Not that the T-shirt was anything to brag about, but...damn.

"Don't move," he advised. "That bra will take finesse, and the knife is very sharp."

Resist? Oh, hell no. She barely breathed as he cut through her sports bra, then almost without pause he slipped the point under the elastic waistband of her shorts and removed her last chance to stay un-naked. Except for her panties...which were plain cotton, the kind she always worked in...

Fine. She hadn't survived this long without craft and cunning. She took her time looking him over from his toes to his forehead. Intimidation was her goal, although she wasn't entirely successful. In her strongest dealing-with-a-difficult-client voice, she said, "Give me the stiletto."

His eyebrows lifted. He looked down at his white starched shirt, at the buttons that closed it, and presented the knife to her, bone handle first.

The ass. He had all the faith in the world she wouldn't slit his throat. She could. She would. She'd do what she needed to do to make her point...as it were.

She gripped the stiletto with a Maleficent smile. Slipping the blade into his neckline, while he flinched, she pulled and jerked and cut the buttons.

When she put the point of the blade to the skin over his

heart...he laughed in a kind of exaltation. "What a woman I've chosen!"

Which made her fingers clench on the bone. Did he not comprehend how much she longed to carve him into little pieces? "I cannot be *chosen*."

"Yet here you are." With another one of those sleight of hand gestures, he pulled *la Bouteille de Flamme* from somewhere up his sleeve. Stepping away from her and the blade, he set it on the dresser and turned on the lamp.

The glass caught the light, warming to a crimson glow.

When he returned to her, she tensed, preparing for him to grab her wrist, and thinking what countermove she would make.

Instead, hands relaxed at his side, he stepped right into the tip of the blade. "You have two choices now. Consummate our marriage. Or cut out my heart."

CHAPTER 27

Maarja couldn't look away from Dante's face: his faint confident smile, the gold that flowed beneath his bitter-brown eyes, the determined jut of chin, the carved stone of his bones.

"That's not a choice!"

"In our world, it is."

"It's not our world, it's yours!"

"You are a Daire. *The* Daire. You are one of Jånos's tribe. Think what you like; you were born to this world, same as me."

"You don't think I'll use this knife on you."

He toed off his shoes. "I have no doubt you will do it in the right circumstances. But I'm not afraid to die, and you won't kill to preserve your own skin. For you to kill, it's got to be a higher cause."

Was that true? How could he know that about her when she didn't know it herself?

He moved forward, slow enough to not impale himself on his own knife, but fast enough to challenge her. "Two choices, Maarja. Blood and freedom. Or sex and knowing you're bound to me until the day we die. Because you're mine."

Her eyes narrowed. His insolent assurance pushed her to the edge of a precipitous cliff. She put pressure on the tip of the blade, just enough to bite into his skin over his breastbone. Blood welled up, trickled down.

He no doubt felt the pain, but he didn't seem surprised, and he didn't stop, maneuvering her toward the giant bed. He added, "And I'm yours."

She came to a halt.

He came to a halt.

He shrugged out of his shirt. His hands went to his belt; he unbuckled and unzipped, dropped his pants and stepped out, closer to her.

The knifepoint slid farther beneath his skin. It bumped up against hard bone.

"Mine." She tasted the word. He claimed her and wanted her to claim him. Possession worked both ways...if she agreed.

She looked him over.

He was beautiful. A Viking's body: tall, long-limbed, with warm brown skin marred from previous battles...and the explosion that killed his father. His face, stony cold and without expression, could frighten a woman if she failed to look deep beneath the surface, but Maarja saw what drove him: the metal-sharp resolve to extricate himself and his family from the endless cycle of vengeance and murder. He had the intelligence to do it; all he needed to do was outmaneuver his enemies, to make them reveal themselves so he could neutralize them.

He trusted her to be at his side.

For a good reason—she'd risked her life to save his mother.

And for a stupid reason—because he'd taken her virginity.

He stood with one foot in the Old World; he believed in fate. She might think that was ridiculous, but...six hundred plus years was long enough for the cycle of possession and murder to exist. She trusted him to finish this vendetta.

She needed to clarify only one thing. "You and me, forever. No one else, ever."

"Forever isn't long enough for me to learn you: your mind, your body, your heart."

"So yes?"

"You and me forever. No one else," he promised. "Do you believe me?"

"You may be a ruthless bastard, but you're not a liar."

He barked a laugh.

She took the blade away from his chest and presented it to him.

He accepted it and without looking, threw it so hard she heard the thump as it buried itself in whatever target he'd chosen. That half smile on his face would frighten a lesser woman, but Maarja... Well, yes, she was afraid. A little.

"Why are you afraid?" Putting his hands to her shoulders, he pushed the remnants of her T-shirt and bra to the floor. "I don't want to kill you."

Either he was reading her mind or she was talking to herself. Probably talking to herself, the drawback of living alone for so long. "No, for what you want, I must be alive and pliant."

"Eager would be nice."

"But—"

"But you're new, barely touched." He slid his hands down her spine to her bottom, rubbed her panties as if the smooth cotton and the shape underneath pleasured him. "I hurt you once. You'll have to trust me not to hurt you again."

She cleared her throat. "It might be...not easy."

"To trust me? Or to take me?"

"Yes?"

"Those are my jobs. To prove myself to you. And to make it easy, this second time. To make it good. I know how to pleasure you."

She stood naked, bare...well, except for her panties and house slippers. Yet he didn't look at her body. He focused on her face,

molten gold flowing beneath the dark stone of his eyes. He compelled her, and she couldn't look away.

"Maarja, it's not all about the pain, is it?"

Hypnotized by his voice, she shook her head.

"You're letting me touch you, and this time you're not driven
by grief and need for comfort." His hands slid up her spine, his
fingers spanned her waist, and he pressed as if he wanted to support her as her knees weakened. "You're thinking coolly, wondering about the long years ahead. Even more than that, you're
revealing yourself, and you're trusting me not to injure your
body or mock your passions."

She nodded. For a man, he was insightful. She did fear embracing him, letting go of her reserve.

"It comes down to trust, Maarja." He pulled her tight against
him. Blood from his wound smeared her chest, and his boxers
didn't provide much of a barrier against his erection. He was hard
and hot, and she knew she'd had him inside her, but he seemed
impossibly big. "Do you trust me to make this good for you?"

Funny. Trusting him to be good in bed wasn't an issue. This
guy had that look about him. Maybe it was the way he walked,
or his swift reactions, or his slow hands. Probably it was the
way he concentrated on her, as if no one else existed for him,
as if the world could end and as long as he was in her arms, he
wouldn't notice.

"I trust you. This is about me. Last time, I was out of control.
You used your tongue on me—"

His hands flexed. His dick grew. He breathed through his
open mouth as if he needed all the air in the room. "God, yes."

"I made a lot of noise, and I let you do things I'd read about
and heard about, but… Well, most of my friends say most men
are in such a rush to get to the main event that they don't do
the good stuff."

His lips barely moved as he asked, "Are you worried I won't
do enough good stuff, or that I'll do more?"

"I don't know if you're going to do more or less, but I think that you're going to make me lose my sense of self and scream. In a good way. When I come back to myself, I won't be the same." She started to feel foolish, unable to explain what she felt. "I'll have left part of myself in you, and I know I said I'd belong to you as long as you belong to me, but I don't want to be the only one who has emotions invested here."

"You want me to leave a part of myself with you, and when we're finished, I'll be so deep inside you I'll never leave. You'll know my mind and soul. Since the first time I saw the little girl you were, I wanted you to grow up. I imagined you were mine. I've been waiting so long. Now, here you are. Here I am." He nudged her chin around. "Look at the bottle. Look at the way that little lamp brings the red glass and the blue stone alive. When the two of us mate, we'll create a different color in the world, one that has never been seen before."

CHAPTER 28

Dante was right. The glow melded and flowed, turning a rich purple where the stone and glass met. It was a message, and not a subtle one.

"Maarja..." He nuzzled the side of her neck, her ear, the hollow of her shoulder, her breast.

Goose bumps shimmered across her skin, and she ran her fingers through his scalp, the black hair so dense she could feel it in the texture and the weight. And when he clamped his mouth around her nipple and sucked, she clutched at his neck and bit off a moan.

He whispered against her skin. "All the things we didn't do the first time, we'll do tonight. From your scalp to your toes, Maarja, I'm going to taste you."

"I got home from work. I haven't had a shower!"

Not worried at all, he chuckled, and moving to her other breast, he sucked again. "The scent of a woman, my woman... is an aphrodisiac."

"You're crazy."

He smiled like an evil genius. "You don't know what your own *chatte* tastes like, do you? Because you've never had a man suck you, lick you until you scream. I like your flavor; it's as if you were created to my preference. Primitive and salty."

"I, um, may have…" *TMI! TMI!! Shut up, Maarja!*

"Put your fingers into yourself and licked them?" The gold in his eyes heated and flowed, merged into golden delight and hot desire.

"I was a virgin, not a nun. I own a vibrator, you know!" If she thought that would put him in his place, she was sadly mistaken.

Instead his voice descended another octave. "How many speeds? How many different vibrations? How often do you use it? When can I use it on you?"

Really, she talked too much.

"Let's try this." He left her standing there, went to the bed, removed the chocolates and one black silk sleep mask, and tossed the covers onto the floor. He dropped the chocolates onto the nightstand and came back to her. "I won't hurt you. I won't betray you."

"I know."

"Do you trust me?"

She began to have an inkling of his intentions, but she answered steadily. "I do."

Slowly, so she could stop him if she wished, he slid the mask over her eyes. She froze in place. The darkness was absolute, every vestige of light blocked. She stood in her panties and slippers, deprived of her sight and dependent on Dante.

In a soothing tone sure to tame the wildest creature, he said, "I love your footwear, but I'd like to remove them." When she merely nodded, he asked, "Maarja, is that all right?"

"Yes."

Again he knelt at her feet. Taking her hand, he placed it on his shoulder and lifted first one foot, then the other. With two soft thumps, he tossed the slippers, and she found herself standing barefooted on the rough-textured rug. Sliding his palms up the backs of her legs, he cupped her bottom and held it in one hand, then used the other to strip off her panties. "Doing okay?" he asked.

She nodded, then remembered he wanted her to speak. "Yes. But I feel very...nude." As if she stood on a stage with the spotlight on her, and she couldn't see the audience.

"Gloriously nude," he crooned. "Magnificently nude. For me. For me alone. Spread your legs for me. Maarja, a little more. So I can... Yes, like that."

She waited, jumped when his fingers touched her, opened her, and jumped again when he put his mouth on her. He tongued her and in less than ten seconds, he took her from wariness to ninety-miles-an-hour arousal. She braced her feet. She gripped his shoulders. She fought for breath. She fought to keep silent. She didn't know why that was important, only that it was. She was on the verge; another moment and she'd be lost in an orgasm so brilliant it would light up the dark.

He pulled away. "Not yet. Darling, not yet. Can you wait a little longer?"

She shook her head. "No. Now."

She was getting anxious, or was it awkward? All the emotions were piling in here, urged forth by the dark and her nudity and his slightly clothed state and her barely halted orgasm. "Are you going to take off your underwear?" she asked.

"I did. Given incentive, this man can move swiftly."

She reached out.

He stepped back. She didn't know where he was, damn him. Damn him! She lifted her hands to throw off the mask.

He caught her wrists. "Trust. Remember?" He danced her backward. "The bed is behind you. Sit down."

She hesitated.

"The sheets are clean and white and taut, and they smell as if they were dried on an outside line. Half a dozen pillows are stacked against the headboard, their cases crisp and waiting for the indents of our heads...or our knees...or we could use those pillows in any way we like." He whispered, every word rife with

insinuation. "Would you like to know how inventive I can be…
with merely a single pillow?"

She sat.

"Is the sheet cool?" He knelt and picked up one of her feet.
He kissed her toes, then smoothed something across the sole,
around the ankle, over the bones that had suffered such abuse
from her workouts.

As he massaged, at first gently, then more deeply, she wanted
to moan for the pleasure of this unique seduction.

He prompted, "The sheet? Maarja? Is it cool against your
bottom?"

She struggled to divide her thoughts. "Um, yes. And against—"

"Yes," he crooned. "Concentrate on that. You're flushing.
From your chest to your cheeks, you're getting rosy with desire."

"Am I?" It startled her to comprehend how her body responded to this care he lavished on her, and even more to realize he observed her so closely.

He slid one oiled hand up her leg, her hip, her belly to her
breasts, and massaged her nipple with his thumb. "Your breasts
are swelling, and—" he smoothed up her chest, her throat, to
her lips "—your lips. Are you swelling below? Where you touch
the sheet? Can you feel that?"

"Yes…" She heard the moan in her voice.

"Yes." With his fingers, he outlined the shape of her mouth.
"Can you smell the lavender in the oil?"

"Yes."

"Lavender promotes serenity. Are you serene?"

She was sightless. She was aroused. She was amazed. Anticipation gripped her… Serene she was not. "No."

He chuckled. "No. Nor am I."

Was that supposed to give her a sense of affinity?

His fingers disappeared, then reappeared on her foot. Moving
her with extravagant care, he lifted it and placed it flat on the
bed against her bottom. Which meant, with her knee crooked,

one sole flat on the sheet and one foot on the floor, she was open to his view.

For a long torturous moment, he said nothing, moved not at all.

Abruptly uncomfortable, she tried to close herself.

He caught her. "No." His voice was husky. He cleared his throat and more clearly said, "No. You're so beautiful. Your clit, your labia beckon me to touch, to taste, to come inside and fuck you until I'm mindless."

"Why don't you?" Her husky tones matched his.

"Oblivion. We're seeking oblivion for *you*." His hands grasped her other foot and began rubbing again. "We're not there yet."

CHAPTER 29

A fresh wave of lavender rose toward Maarja's head. She fought the urge to lie back, to relax against the pillows and allow Dante to pleasure her with his skillful massage, his restrained passion, and the knowledge he was, slowly but surely, chipping away at the shackles that held her bound to reality.

"Go ahead." As before, he read her mind. "Beds are to be used. For sleep, for resting…for sex. Let me rub this foot while you recline."

"That's too—"

"Revealing? What are you afraid of?" One hand slid up the inside of her leg. His fingers dusted the ends of the hair that protected her so inadequately. "That I'll be driven to touch all the parts of you, enter you with my fingers, my tongue, my dick…my mind? Because I've already done that…or have I? Each time between us is new, never tested, never tried in the history of the world."

As she listened to him, she realized he was unhurriedly lifting himself to loom over her, all the while still holding her foot and massaging it. So as her leg was rising, unfolding, she was unbalanced…she was revealed.

"All my dreams are about you. What I'll do to you, what

you'll do to me, how we make each other feel. You're unprac-
ticed—"

"Hey!" *True, but...*

"And yet you move me as the moon moves the tides."

Poetic. She relaxed back onto the bed. He eased her toward
the middle of the mattress. She got a peek of light, then he adjusted her mask and again she was in night. The mattress dipped
as he joined her, one knee between her thighs. "You're incan-
descent with desire, the most beautiful thing I've ever seen."

He smelled...so good. His hair, his skin, his breath...he exuded pheromones that made her whimper and grope her hands
along his shoulders.

He spoke in her ear, his smooth voice a seduction in itself.
"This first time—"

"It's not the first time."

"It feels like the first time. This time, you know who I really am."

"Do I?"

He chuckled. "You trust me, so you know all you need to
know."

"I suppose."

"You *suppose?*"

"All right, I do. I trust you not to tell me everything."

His voice grew serious. "I'm not patronizing, but it's safer
for you if you don't know everything." With gentle hands, he
pushed her hair off her forehead.

"In case I get captured by one of your...vengeful family."

"Yes."

A little of her lovely glow faded; she had to stop encourag-
ing Dante to talk.

Yet Dante had promised oblivion; he proved himself a master
of distraction. He bent his head and kissed her mouth. He taught
her to get lost in the pressure, the taste, the movements of tongue
and teeth. It was wet and rich, delicious in its decadence, and

when he pulled back, she tried to follow. But he nuzzled at that spot where her jaw met her earlobe, then followed her throat down to her breast to suckle so urgently she dug her heels into the mattress and lifted her hips in supplication.

"What do you want?"

"You."

"My mouth."

"No." She touched his chest. It was bare. Slid her hands down to his hips. They were bare. Reached for his—

"My mouth," he said firmly.

She no longer held him in her hands, for he was between her legs, suckling again, but this time on her clit. She twisted, cried out, moaned, and when she hurtled toward climax, orgasm, he stopped her, calmed her, petted and massaged her, described to her how much better it would be if she held on to the thin edge of control until he was inside her. He asked if she agreed.

She shook her head, took a breath to shout, and whispered, "No."

"Think about it," he coaxed. "You've held yourself in control for so long—"

She snorted. He'd held her in his control. He'd taken away her sight, leaving her dependent on him, opening her other senses. Every gentle touch of his fingers stroked the fire in her nerves. The aroma of the sheets, the lavender oil, his skin, filled her mind and brought her the faint scent of her own arousal. Each nuance of his voice both comforted and provoked her. And his taste—she wanted to kiss him, lick him, suck him until his control vanished and he—

The beast was still talking. "Your *chatte* is swollen, damp, waiting, throbbing. Isn't it?"

She nodded sullenly.

"When I push inside, what do you think will happen?"

"I'll come. But I would come, anyway!" Why couldn't he see that?

"The sensation is building, Maarja. Every moment you wait, it's building." He took her hand, put a packet in her palm, tore it open so she could follow his movements as he rolled it on. "Because your *chatte* is so tight, so hot, so ready, the lubricated condom will help my dick pulse into you."

Her hand crept down to touch herself, to see if he was right.

He laughed, caught her fingers, kissed them.

"No. Wait." She got her elbows under her and tried to sit up. "When will we—?"

"When the pleasure heats you, when you melt in my arms, it'll be just you and me, the wetness, the pressure... So much pressure. Like *Bouteille de Flamme* and the dark blue stone, we'll merge and be reborn in strength and glory. Wait for it..."

She bit her lower lip until it hurt.

He licked it, scolded her softly, then continued in that crooning voice, building pictures in her mind. "When I press all the way inside to touch the deepest part of you, that moment will trigger...what, I wonder?"

The idea lingered in the air, a promise and a story to which she knew the inevitable ending...but she wanted to hear the words.

This time, he didn't describe. He didn't enhance. Instead, as if she'd spoken, he said, "Good. I agree. This first time, at least—"

Her brain pinged. He was back to calling it the first time.

"—I want to see your face when you come. I want to hear your moans in my ear." As he told her what he intended, he elevated her hips, used his fingers to open her and to guide himself into position. "I'll control the pace, keep you waiting, then drive you from peak to peak." He pressed into her, not far.

She took a breath and held it. He was right; anticipation and frantic need had created an ache so strong she was almost afraid. She hovered on the verge of pain. She whimpered.

He shushed her. "I'm not going to hurt you. I would never hurt you. We'll take this the way we've taken everything. To-

gether, and at a leisurely pace…" He dragged out the words as
he pulled out and pushed in. A little farther. A little farther.

She whimpered, groped for him, grasped his butt, urged him
to hurry—my God, would he never finish this?—but he closed
the gap between them by lowering her to the mattress. He rested
his weight on top of her, and he seemed heavier than before,
muscular as if he'd spent hours in the gym working off his sexual frustration. His skin burned, giving a lie to his cool composure. She strained to move him, but with his hands under
her knees he lifted her, and pressed into her, and lifted her, and
pressed into her…

"Are you ready to…lose yourself in ecstasy?" His voice lingered like a sexual promise, triggering anticipation, trepidation,
and—

He sank into her body, all the way in. His dick expanded her,
the tip touched deep inside… She braced her heels against the
mattress, pushed her hips tight against his, and she came. And
she came. And she came. Now beneath the mask she could see:
pleasure so intense it painted fireworks in the dark.

Placing his palms flat on her hips, he slid them up, up over her
waist to her breasts. The calluses of his fighter's hands scraped
across her nipples. Another orgasm had her fighting to regain
control, of him or at least herself.

Without success, for he rode her, pressing up and in, keeping
their bodies tight, his heavy, heavy weight dominating her as
his palms continued their climb up her body. He slid them up
her arms, raising them over her head. In one hand, he held both
wrists against the sheet. The other moved from her bicep to the
side of her face and slowly pushed the mask away.

The wispy, swaying bed curtains cocooned them in a pink
glow. She blinked into his face. His crooning voice had conveyed passion, yes, but also encouragement and an almost de-
tached patience.

A false impression.

No wonder he'd covered her eyes. His cheeks were a hard red, his swollen lips parted to show his white clenched teeth, and through golden molten eyes he viewed her the way a lion viewed its downed prey, waiting to quash any attempt to escape.

In a startled panic she did try to escape, struggling to free her wrists, pushing against him as if that would accomplish anything but a return of pleasure.

Both hands returned to her arms. His fingers intertwined with hers. He was so close. So close. "Put your legs around me. Open to me. Maarja. Please." He trembled with the effort to hold still, but he'd lost control of his voice. No longer hypnotic, it was deeper, more guttural, and held a desperation that she comprehended above all else.

Yet he'd chosen to remove her mask, to reveal himself to her, knowing what she'd see. It was a gamble on his part.

In a rush she accepted him, all the way, thighs wide, legs embracing him.

She thought he tried to smile at her, to thank her without words, but it looked more like a painful grimace as he eased out of her again, and eased back in.

She adjusted her hips, trying to smooth the way and—

His eyes flared and she saw it happen. At last he slipped the leash he'd set on himself. He set a pace that demanded and gave. At once he brought her back to the precipice, to that point of almost climax. As her body reached and yearned, tears slipped out of her eyes and into her hair.

He bared his teeth as if he suffered in agony, making him more of a beast, and the sight of this man driven out of control for *her* was all she needed. Her climax engulfed her in flames and ice, in color and heat, in the fear she'd been unalterably changed and the conviction that he was right; fate had led them here, to this moment, and nothing could ever be as glorious again.

Except, with Dante, the glory would be theirs for as long as they lived, and beyond.

★ ★ ★

Afterward, in the shower, Dante said, "I love the color of your hair. The real color." He ran his fingers through the short strands. "Dark red, like the bottle and in the right light, it glows. When you feel safe, will you grow it out for me?"

She liked the way he phrased it, comprehending that she kept it short so if she had to fight, her opponent had little chance to grab her hair and use it to control her.

And he said, *When you feel safe.* It was an unspoken promise that better days would come for them both; they would see to it. "Yes. When I feel safe, I'll grow it out for you."

CHAPTER 30

In the wee hours of the morning, Maarja half woke as Dante spooned her, his cock stirring against her bottom, his hand cupping her breast.

She moaned, not in ecstasy but because she'd really like to sleep some more. Between a hard day's work moving art, being scared and threatened, screwing the lid on Dante's bottle, running over half of Gothic in the dark, and being claimed on the bed and on the bathroom counter après shower—that marble had been cold—she was still tired.

He massaged her shoulders and back, pressed his arms under her belly and lifted her to her knees, stroked oil between her legs and buttocks, rubbed himself against her like a great cat marking his territory, and she moaned in a different tone.

What did she know? Maybe all men were like this, wanting and needing and coaxing and pleasuring. Her friends' reports didn't agree with that theory, and she enjoyed a moment of feeling special, a desire magnet, the woman that tugged at the powerful Dante Arundel and subdued the beast.

Yeah. Femme fatale, that was her.

She was enjoying that thought, and the pleasure of his touch, when—

The bedside hotel phone rang.

She jumped.

He swore viciously, thrust the covers aside like a man driven by a force outside himself, fumbled with the receiver, and finally answered. "It's four thirty in the morning, and I'm about to get laid. *What?*" His voice crackled with irritation.

Maarja slid onto her belly, closed her eyes, wishing last night had never happened, wishing it could all happen again, wishing he wasn't so sure of himself he had to tell some contact in his book he was about to get laid. She might have told him no. She might have!

"Fuck!" Dante threw the phone across the room. He leaned over her, stroked her hip, and in a totally calm tone, said, "Come on, Maarja. Life is a bitch, and the bitch just had puppies."

She didn't sit up. "What happened?"

"My cousin Connor has been executed."

CHAPTER 31

Maarja didn't know what to say. *I'm sorry that bully relative of yours is dead* seemed inappropriate. "Connor? Your cousin Connor? Why him?" seemed safer.

"I've disappeared off their radar. They know this will flush me out of hiding."

"They'll kill a man to bring you to the surface?"

"He's a minor player, but he's my minor player." Subtext: once Dante claimed you as his, you were his forever.

She slid from beneath the sheets. "Let's do it."

He gave a laugh. "I should have known you'd be prepared."

She pulled a hotel robe off the hook. "I'm not the one who did whatever happened, if that's what you mean."

"I know that. But I didn't order the hit, so who did?"

He seemed to be dismissing her abilities, and that irritated her. "Why do you know that's not me? Anyone can arrange a hit, and after that scene at your mother's funeral, I could be perceived as having motive."

"If you were going to kill somebody, you'd do it face-to-face. For instance, me." He put his hand to his chest where, after their shower, the blood welled up again and formed a smear of crusty reddish-black over his skin. "Suitcases are over there. Yours is packed. Car's out back. I need my cell phone and that knife I tossed last night when you—"

She pointed at the suitcases.

"Son of a goddamn bitch!" He stared at the knife hilt buried in the cloth side of the wheeled briefcase.

She grinned at him. After that display in the hotel room in Sacramento, sticking his writing pen into the wall to scare Tabitha the snitch into a faint, Maarja knew he must be able throw a *knife* and hit his target 100 percent of the time. Right now, he was down to 99 percent because he'd wanted to get in her—

"All I wanted was to get into your *chatte*."

"Pants." She took a calming breath. "You wanted to get in my pants."

"I don't give a damn about your *pants*." He lifted the matte gold hardside suitcase onto the bed.

"I'm simply saying—"

"I know." He opened the zipper, pulled out a compressed packing bag, and handed it to her. "You want me to use some manners when I talk to you."

"Do you know how?" she snapped.

"I know how. I like to see you flinch when I say the bad words." He grinned at her the way she grinned at him. "Get dressed, take a piss, and we'll get going."

She sighed in mighty exasperation. "Do we have to call it that?"

"What girlie thing do you call it?"

She cackled a little.

"What? What do you call peeing? Pissing?"

"I'll tell you if you promise to use that term from now on?"

"You call it *taking a winkle* or something, don't you?"

Still smiling, she shook her head.

"Okay, I promise, what?"

He really wanted to know, and she really wanted to hear

him use this euphemism. "After Chrispin graduated from high school, the family took a trip to France. We were exploring a park in Alsace–Lorraine, we watched the sunset, we wandered toward the parking lot—and the gates were closed. Locked. No one around. We hiked to another gate. Locked. We wandered until Alex snarled, 'I don't care, I've got to take a leak.'"

He was getting the drift, and grinned.

"She headed into the bushes, dropped her pants, and for the first time, a policeman showed up. He yelled, *'No make à le pipi!'* and we've called it that ever since."

"That sounds like pee-pee to me."

"Yep, but it's spelled differently in French."

"You want to me to call taking a piss *make à le pipi* in front of my tough-guy relatives?"

She crossed her arms and waited.

He stared forbiddingly. Sighed. Said, "Go *make à le pipi.*"

She went into the bathroom and shared a smirk with her reflection. She and Dante had started a relationship—she refused to call it a marriage—and they were testing each other. She supposed that was what couples did and at this point, she refused to worry about that. Staying alive had a way of rearranging priorities.

As she slipped out of the robe, she saw the smear of his heart's blood between her breasts, and she was right back to the conflict of being a modern woman who half believed all his talk about fate.

She came out wearing black leather leggings, a body-hugging sleeveless camo T-shirt, and a black leather jacket. Black boots completed the ensemble.

He smiled when he saw her. "I told Andere I wanted an outfit you could fight in. I'd say he's been watching too many biker movies."

"Or dominatrix movies!"

He winced. "Please. I don't want to think that about Andere and...no. Please no."

He, she was displeased to note, wore brown cargo pants, a midnight blue golf shirt, a brown jacket (probably to cover the bulge of his pistol), and brown running shoes. "You look comfortable." The bottle was gone from the dresser, so she knew the jacket concealed that, too.

He grabbed a NOLA baseball cap, pulled it on his head, opened the door, and gestured her into the corridor. "Are you not comfortable?"

"Physically, yes." Every bit of the leather was buttery soft, easy to move in. "Mentally I feel as if I'm missing a whip and some chains." She ran down the flight of stairs, glanced up to see Dante standing, staring at her as if it wasn't only Andere who enjoyed the random dominatrix fantasy.

Ha! Danger permeated the air, each breath could be her last, and something about the prospect of death balanced by the prospect of sex enhanced every aspect of this moment. She took the corner and started down the next flight of stairs, then popped back to catch him in mid-stride. "The pants are tear-away," she said.

He missed a step, jumped, landed, stumbled again, and when he righted himself, he moved so swiftly that if she hadn't been prepared, he would have caught her and—she didn't know what he would do. Tear away the pants?

She sprinted down to the ground floor and into the dark quiet kitchen. Catching her as she bolted for the closed back door, he pulled her close. "Stop," he said. "Quiet."

His body was tense; she didn't know how to read that. Wariness as they prepared to leave? Or sexual need that must be reined in? She guessed the answer to both was *yes*.

He opened the door, stepped out ahead of her, did a visual check, then gestured her out. "That car." His voice sounded perfectly normal, the tone conversational.

That car was an SUV, a couple of years old and a generic sil-ver color.

Rain splattered her as she hurried to the passenger door. "I thought it would be the limo."

He walked close behind her, and with his hand on her elbow, he helped her in. "They won't be looking for this car."

"That's for sure. It looks like a soccer-mom car."

"I have my soccer-mom fantasies." Now that he had her in the car, he lingered as if he didn't have a care in the world. "Will you wear rolled-down cotton socks and white tennis shoes for me?"

"I'm wearing tear-away leather leggings and you're lusting after cotton socks and white tennis shoes?"

He pointed his thumb at his chest. "Midfield defender."

He had surprised her. "You played soccer?"

"In high school. Why do you sound surprised?"

"Team sports seem so…normal."

"High school was normal. Team sports were normal. How do you think guys get soccer-mom fantasies?" Leaning in, he kissed her surprised mouth. He shut the door and came around. "Make sure you're belted in."

"Of course." She clicked the seat belt. "Out of curiosity, what are you expecting on this trip?"

"Nothing. But I haven't lived this long by not anticipating everything."

My God. The world he inhabited.

She heard his voice in her head. *You are one of Jånos's tribe. Think what you like; you were born to this world, same as me.*

Damn him. She didn't want his voice in her head.

He put the vehicle in gear, pulled out, and drove without headlights up the road to Angelica's estate. The gates opened.

He drove in.

He parked.

He drove out.

The gates closed.

She didn't know why, but she figured he knew what he was doing. He'd better; this SUV had a manual transmission. He shifted gears from first to second to third to fourth to fifth… She knew how to drive a stick, of course; that was one of the requirements for her job, to be able to drive vans and trucks of all sizes. But most people couldn't, and darned if she could figure out why he didn't have an easier-to-drive vehicle. Except… if a person knew what they were doing, driving a stick gave a control that couldn't be duplicated with an automatic. He liked control. He demanded control. She almost asked if he would ever allow her on top…but he drove without headlights until they turned onto California Route 1, the Pacific Coast Highway, and she didn't want to distract him. Intermittent rain splattered the windshield, and without stars or moon, the night was so dark it *loomed*.

When he did turn on the headlights, she breathed a sigh of relief. People who had a lick of sense didn't drive the Pacific Coast Highway at night; it curled and twisted in switchbacks, took dips and rises like the roller coaster in Santa Cruz, and experienced regular slough-offs that would expectedly take the (mostly) two lanes of asphalt into the Pacific Ocean.

Maarja and Dante headed north in the deepest dark of night with fog curling through the valleys and rain squalls dusting the heights. The southbound lane clung to the edge over the Pacific, but they were tucked up against the cliffs, which provided a greater sense of security about not toppling into the waves *and* at the same time a niggling worry about boulders tumbling off the cliff sides and smashing them flat.

She didn't even know how to be properly afraid.

She started giggling.

"What's so funny?" Dante asked.

She mimicked him. "It's four thirty in the morning, and I'm about to get laid." In the faint light of the dash, she could see him smirk.

"It was. And I was."

"*I* was sleeping."

"Afterward, I was going to let you sleep late."

"And wake me up how many more times?"

He shook his head. "Three's my limit."

The inexhaustible lover: another romance myth shot to hell.

He continued, "After that, you'd be too sore."

So…inexhaustible and considerate. And bossy and conniving.

"Sleep now," he suggested. "I'm driving."

"On this road? At this speed?" Because he wasn't wasting time. The headlights flashed, illuminating pavement and cliffs and dips at an alarming velocity. "I can sleep when we get where we're going. Where is that, by the way?" *Subtle, Maarja.*

"My office in San Francisco. I'll drop you off there. You'll be safe while I check out the situation." He didn't even pause for her to come up with an answer. "Is precognition a common gift among the Rom?"

CHAPTER 32

That would teach her not to go to sleep on his suggestion. Now she had to speak about the difficult stuff. "I don't know. Aunt Yesenia used to say things sometimes, but mostly when she'd been drinking, and I was too busy trying not to get caught with a backswing to pay much attention."

"What happened to her?"

"She died in Florida. Liquor and weed. Bad boyfriend." Her voice broke a little. "Barely made the news."

"You don't mourn her, surely?" He was clearly incredulous.

"She was my only living relative. My mother's sister." Having his attention focused on the road rather than her made it easier to address issues, and darkness hid most of her feelings. "She wasn't always drunk and mean. When I was little and crying for my parents, she cuddled me and made me hot chocolate. Eventually the constant moving and fear broke her down. She used to say before she got saddled with me, she had prospects. She had a rich boyfriend, she could have gotten married, she could have had her own children to care for. All true, I think, and another tragedy in this long line of tragedies."

"I guess I understand." He spoke slowly, as if he was really making an effort. "I can't imagine being alone in the world, I'm so overwhelmed with relatives who eat and give me advice and scheme and want me to pay them for support." She felt him glance toward her. "I share them with you. You're welcome."

Because of the bottle and stopper. Because they were now married. He really, really wanted to impress that on her while she really, really intended to pretend it had never happened. Which she did by answering his question about precognition. "I always had a sense for old books, and I used to go to the library to read and feel the connection with the other people who had read that particular story. When I was a teen, I remembered some stuff and I wanted to know who I was and why... it all had happened."

"Do you remember it all?"

"Enough. The high points. I don't remember my father. I remember my mother in snapshots. I remember that day when we...killed your father...vividly." She waited to see how Dante reacted to her choice of words.

As far as she could tell, by the dim light of the dashboard, he didn't.

She said, "You were scarred by the blast." Across his forehead and cheek, the divot of the wound looked like a shadowy canyon.

"Broken collarbone. Broken wrist. Unconscious under the rubble for hours. Nate found me first, and when he lifted me, that brought me to consciousness." He grimaced. "While I was screaming, Andere found my mother. He thought she was dead. I looked over and saw him holding her body, and I thought she was dead, too. That was the only thing that could have shut me up."

Maybe that's why he had shown no signs of grief over his mother's death; he'd already suffered through it.

"When she moved ever so slightly—"

She could hear the relief, the joy, in his voice.

"By the time I got stitched together, even if I wasn't tough, I looked it."

"You could have had plastic surgery."

"No."

"Tough is good, huh? In your business?"

He grunted, which was no answer. But when he turned the dash lights off, plunging the interior of the car into darkness, she looked out the windshield to see—"Those headlights are coming right at us!"

CHAPTER 33

"Yes." Dante flipped his headlights to high beam.

"Don't! That driver—" Maarja's remonstration disintegrated as with a twist of the steering wheel, Dante threw the SUV into a skid.

Tires shrieked.

At full speed, the other car slammed into their right rear fender.

Metal crumpled. Glass broke.

Maarja's seat belt yanked her so tightly against the seat she couldn't breathe, but that didn't seem to matter because she still managed to shout, "No! What the—?"

Dante twisted the wheel again, headed them north on the wrong side of the road, then one-hundred-and-eighty degrees and they were behind the other car. His headlights flashed into the rear window of the low fast black car right before he smashed into the tiny trunk and blasted the window to pieces.

Maarja could smell scorched tires and flop sweat.

The sweat was hers.

The black car hit the accelerator and leaped ahead.

Dante hit the accelerator and the SUV leaped after it.

This was no ordinary soccer-mom vehicle. Whatever he had

under the hood kept them gaining on the sports car—on the straight stretch.

She was an idiot. When she'd seen those headlights flash on and come at them, she thought the other driver was drunk, on drugs, had a heart attack and lost control.

But no. It had been a murder attempt.

Now it was a duel.

In a conversational tone, Dante said, "There are sunglasses in the console. Get them for me, please, Maarja."

Why sunglasses? There wasn't a hint of light except from their headlights and… Oh. The other guy. She nodded, not that Dante could see her, found the glasses, hesitated, then wiggled around to place them over his nose and around his ears.

"Thank you, darling. In case of emergency, you do a marvelous job of keeping your head." He sounded so composed, so pleased she responded to help him. "In the right circumstances, light can be a weapon. Something for you to remember in the future."

Maybe some of his other relatives would scream their heads off. Maybe they all weren't dangerous and scary. Maybe a fair number of them were like Béatrice the Shrieker. In its way, knowing she managed to stay poised was a comforting thought. Although…if this continued for too long, calm might dissolve and hysteria take its place.

"You're doing well." Again it seemed Dante read her mind.

The highway started up and into a series of hairpin turns. He hit those curves hard, but here the low-slung sports car showed off its advantages. It full-throttle hugged the corners, getting farther and farther ahead of the high-profile SUV. At some point, the lights disappeared…

Had the sports car topped the cliff? Had it pulled off and lain in wait? Or did Maarja remember correctly and—"Dante, on the way north, did we pass a turnout at the summit? Because if that driver—"

"Yes. And I know."

He sounded as if he were ticking a box in his mind.

Turnout? Check.

Chance for sabotage? Check.

Dante reshaping destiny? Most certainly.

At the turnout, even before the sports car's headlights flashed on, blinding Maarja, Dante turned the wheel toward the guardrail that hung over the ocean.

Dante had not been blinded. Dante was wearing sunglasses.

The sports car ripped onto the road, missing them by inches, and recovered immediately, skidding around to get on their tailpipes. The SUV's tires spit gravel. The sports car followed. Dante drove the perimeter of the turnout so fast and so close to the guardrail she should hear metal shrieking against metal. But he never made a wrong move. Not until that spot on the far edge where the guardrail hung right on the edge of the cliff. Then he turned the SUV to the right, toward the drop-off, toward the ocean, toward the long fall and inevitable death.

At the moment the SUV crumpled the guardrail, he smoothly moved the shift into Reverse. Maarja's head jerked back and forward on her neck as the tires spun, then caught, reversing them and giving the attack car clear access to the place where they'd been.

In the sports car's headlights, she saw the newly broken guardrail dangling in midair, the ground still attached to the post. The driver of the black car slammed on their brakes, but too late—Dante's maneuver had put weight and strain on an already stressed and faulted cliff. With a deep groan from the earth, the massive boulder that supported the turnout broke away. The attack car almost seemed to show a human personality as it fought to hang on, but more and more ground gave way until gravity won, taking the car—and its driver—bouncing down the cliff. The car exploded. The blast shook the ground. Light flared across the Pacific Ocean.

Maarja gasped in relief. Dante had saved them from the assassin.

Dante said, "Fuck!" in such a tone of conviction she looked again.

The already-dangerously broken cliff had been hit, shaken, broken, and it was crumpling, falling, eating away at the turn-out and the road.

"Dante. Dante..." she chanted as he maneuvered the car in a fast three-point turn while the edge came closer and closer to their front wheels. "Faster. Faster!"

They weren't going to make it. What the assassin had not been able to accomplish, Mother Earth would complete.

Maarja took her last breath on this earth—and Dante whipped the car around facing toward San Francisco and drove like a bat out of hell.

Her eyes hurt she held them so wide. Sweat rolled down her spine, wet the back of her hair, coated her palms where they gripped the seat. Her heart pounded in her ears, yet she heard Dante call Caltrans, the California Department of Transportation, to report a rockslide that had taken part of the Pacific Coast Highway, give the milepost, and hang up. "Road crews are on the way." He made conversation as if nothing extraordinary had happened.

In a broken whisper, she asked, "What happened back there...? What was that?"

"Sabotage." Dante sounded calm, as if those four dangerous, horrifying minutes were nothing out of the ordinary, as if behind them the car blaze didn't light up the waves, as if he hadn't just won a vicious battle against an assassin sent to kill them. "Are you hurt?"

Her knee had made contact with something: the dash, the console, the door, who knew? Her head ached, but in the bigger scheme of things... "I'm fine."

"Good girl." He patted her as if she were a faithful dog. "This put us behind schedule. Try to get some sleep."

She disregarded that with the scorn it deserved. "Where did you learn to drive like that?"

"Defensive driving school. When this is over, you'll enroll."

"Why?"

"Because if I hadn't trained, we'd be the ones over the edge of the cliff burning to death. You're obviously a target because you're a Daire, and double because you're mine now."

Sound reasoning...

A brief spurt of fury caught her by surprise. "Damn it! Why did you drag me into this?"

He only snorted, yet said so much.

Hostile and perturbed, she snapped, "I suppose you'd say I dragged myself into it?"

"No one dragged you. You took every step without hesitation."

"Blindly! Without knowing the consequences!"

"Unless you know more than you're telling me, unless you can see the future, too, we all walk blindly. The best we can do is watch where we step." Humor lightened his tone. "As my mother used to tell me, you have a choice between a pile of dog poo and a land mine... Take the dog poo."

"What a helluva philosophy."

CHAPTER 34

As they neared Dante's condo, the door to his private garage sensed something about the vehicle and opened smoothly, and as it did, the lights inside came on. He drove in, down the ramp into the underground space, and the gate shut behind them. Like all underground garages, it was utilitarian: gray concrete and dim light. He housed six of his cars down here; no one else had access.

He turned off the engine and took his first full breath since he'd seen those headlights coming at them. "We're safe."

"Really?" Maarja glanced around. "In here?"

"Very safe. The garage door is reinforced and so is the access door. A private elevator is keyed to my hand print and goes directly from the garage to my floor." He viewed her expression. He didn't understand what he was seeing. Fear after what they'd gone through? No. Disbelief as she comprehended the changes in her life? That didn't look right, either. He patted her shoulder, hoping to provide her a little comfort and reinforce his reassurance of protection. "We'll go up now. I'll check things out, make sure it's okay for you. Then I'll head to—"

She grabbed his fingers and squeezed. "No."

"No?" Did she want to talk here?

"Get out of your pants."

What the hell? "What do you think—?"

"Unzip. Remove your pants." She turned her head to look at him, her expression fierce, angry, determined. "We were almost killed. Your car is crunched. I'm seat-belt bruised and God knows what else. I deserve a bonus." She ripped off her leather pants like a stripper about to perform the Gypsy Rose Lee maneuver for an appreciative audience.

He *was* an appreciative audience. Oh, God, he could not be more appreciative.

Somehow she got rid of her panties and projected herself over the console between them. She used the levers to push his chair back from the steering wheel, and lowered his seat back a few inches.

"Wait," he said. She wanted to do it *now*? No kissing, no fore-play, no prep? "This is not a good idea."

"Yes, it is. We almost got killed. We almost *died*. You're going to give me what I want. Take. Down. Your. Pants." She balanced above him with her boots on either side of his hips and unzipped him. She took his erection between her palms and lightly stroked. "Down. Jeans."

He wanted to laugh, to protest more forcefully, to point out that yes, they had almost been killed and while the garage was secure, his home was more secure and surely they could wait the five minutes it would take to get in the elevator and—

She placed the head of his cock between her legs.

She'd never manage this. Every time they'd fucked he'd used a lubricant. A woman as new as she was... God, she was wet. She pressed down.

He slid inside those first few inches and, caught by surprise, he groaned.

He never groaned. It revealed too much.

Using both hands, he caught her bare butt and held her still. "You're out of control."

"You mean, *you're* not in control."

She was mocking him. This *girl* was making fun of him.

She batted at his hands. "I'm doing this. All you have to do is sit here and think of England. Can you handle that?"

He didn't know how she was doing it or even if she was doing it on purpose, but her cunt rhythmically flexed on him, pulling him deeper...centimeters at a time, like some kind of medieval torture designed to drive a man to the edge and beyond.

It was working. He teetered. He let go of her and gripped the door and the console hard enough to leave fingerprints. He thrust up, trying to seat himself.

"Don't move," she snapped. Gripping his shoulders, she eased herself down.

He wanted to instruct her, explain how a little back-and-forth made the process flow more naturally, but he recognized her expression: it was resolve mixed with lust mixed with the satisfaction of being in charge.

When she'd taken him to the hilt and her bottom rested on his legs, she leaned back, her hands on his thighs, and smiled into his eyes. "I like this."

"I see you do."

The timer on the automatic lights clicked. Darkness enveloped them.

As if that was a signal, she fucked him. Hard and deep, lifting and falling, breaking him with sex. Physically, her body was strong and taut, developed by her job and her unceasing workouts. Inside she was tight with a texture like velvet. Right now, this moment, she fulfilled his every teen fantasy. His brain rediscovered an adolescent joy in drenching pleasure, the insanity of the now where the past had never happened and the future didn't matter. To hell with not revealing himself with a groan; he could only manage caveman grunts that aptly conveyed his wholehearted consent to whatever she chose to do.

What she chose to do was pause at the top as if they'd reached the highest point on the roller coaster...for one suspenseful moment he waited in agony... Then, like the roller coaster, she sped into the drop that stole his breath and stopped his heart. She pounded down on him, her cunt squeezing, clutching, sucking on him. As if it was all too much, she sobbed as she came, demanding he come, too. As if last night had never been, he pumped semen into her, to fill her, to satisfy her, to claim her as his.

Damn it. She *was* his. She might resist, but she was learning.

He only hoped she didn't kill him during the lessons.

For a woman with so little experience, she showed a remarkable aptitude for debauchery.

Was this what he had to look forward to for all the years of his life?

Dante fervently hoped so.

CHAPTER 35

Maarja collapsed on top of him. Her legs shook from the strain. She gasped, unable to fill her lungs with enough air to give strength to her body. He seemed similarly affected; she'd mastered him, or so she told herself with satisfaction.

One of them had to speak. Him, probably. The darkness was absolute, but she could still imagine the self-satisfied quirk of his mouth as he spoke for the sole purpose of pointing out how violently she had possessed him.

What would she say? That kind of male dominance required a snappy repertoire and right now she didn't have it. Apparently her body had a rule. Try to kill her, and she'd fuck Dante. Every...damned...time.

She took a breath to speak and head off him and his inevitable wit—when a vibration shook the garage accompanied by a rumbling that made her all too aware of being below ground. The parking garage's emergency lights flickered on, dim and yet almost blinding for their night-accustomed eyes.

"Earthquake!" It was San Francisco. She'd been raised in the Bay Area; she'd spent her life waiting for The Big One. *Now was not the time!*

As the garage settled back into stillness, he said, "No. No." His face in the dim light didn't display the intoxication of sexual satisfaction, rather an intent shift to lifesaving awareness. "Someone exploded...something." He looked into her eyes. "Probably the elevator we were supposed to be on."

She gaped at him in horror...and inevitably, in acceptance. "Yes. Of course."

He pointed into the darkest corner where a crappy, beat-up, faded green 1960s Opel Kadett was parked. "We're getting out of here—in that."

"That?"

"Who would chase it?"

"I don't even want to ride in it."

"Exactly." He lifted her up, separating them.

They both groaned.

The synchronized spontaneity made her want to smile, but her mouth couldn't move like that. What they'd done was too much, too intense. Not to mention that, now that it was over, she remembered what she should never have forgotten.

Last night, he'd been careful to use a condom, conveying the clear message he would not get her pregnant so she'd be forced to accept him.

Today, on the other hand, she'd totally given in to stupid, careless, mindless screwing. Inside her, his little swimmers were no doubt heading up, all excited about meeting the ovum of their dreams. She'd dodged the bullet—or the baby—once, but she couldn't ever be so careless again. Today they'd totally missed any chance at being careful about the potential of being parents. Maybe since she'd been on top...

"Leave everything." He glanced at her legs. "Except your pants. Go to the car. Get in. We're gone." While she haphazardly attached the pants around her waist, he came around, opened the door, helped her out, and held her steady until she had her feet.

He didn't need time to steady himself, damn him. Grabbing her hand, he ran to the feeble excuse for a car. She pulled herself away and got into the passenger seat; she didn't need a man helping her in. They needed to get out of here undetected, al-though she didn't know, if someone had exploded something above, how they'd leave without being seen.

Dante tucked her leather pants, still torn apart at the seams, in around her legs, and shut her door.

So much for not needing help.

He got in the driver's side, dug around under the floor mat, pulled out an old car key, put it in the ignition, and started the engine. It purred like a well-groomed cat. He grinned at her startled expression. "Had it souped-up years ago," he told her. "Just for such an occasion."

From the glove compartment, he produced a garage door opener. He pressed the button and directly in front of them the concrete wall slid aside. A dark hole gaped in front of them.

That did it. She was impressed. "How James Bond of you."

She wasn't so impressed with the gearshift in the middle, the clutch on the floor, or the low dark tunnel. The ceiling almost touched the roof of the tiny Opel. Pieces of dirt and clay fell out from between what looked like old beams and bricks.

He must have sensed her dismay and questions, for he said, "During the Prohibition when my great-grandfather ran liquor, he built his share of tunnels below the city. Not many of them survive; as you said, earthquake. But this one should get us to the next building's parking garage, and from there we can get on the street and out of the area."

Should was not the word she wanted him to use, but it was honest. "Then where?"

"I have a safe house."

"If your enemies—"

"Our enemies."

"If our enemies tracked us into the garage and measured the approximate time it would take us to get out of the car and go up to your office, then they're deep in the belly of your orga-nization." She started the arduous process of reconnecting the leather into some semblance of pants. "So no, you don't have a safe house."

"Fuck. You're right."

"It happens," she said acidly. "At least that narrows the number of suspects."

He looked at her. "Fuck. Yes!"

"Eyes on the tunnel," she shrieked.

He faced forward.

Abruptly the tunnel came to an end. He slammed on the brakes and they faced a blank concrete wall. He pressed the button on the garage door opener. Once. Twice. He slapped the opener on his palm.

She started to hyperventilate at the thought of being buried alive.

At last the garage door opened in jerks and fits.

"I'm going to have to come down with some WD-40." While she cackled hysterically (but really—dangerous, debonair Dante Arundel using a can of WD-40?), he drove into the parking garage under some other building on some other San Francisco street. He pressed the button to shut the door behind them, watched until it closed completely. He waved at the lady who was standing outside her car, purse over her shoulder, gaping at them, and drove up the ramp and onto a morning rush hour street.

The appearance of the Opel Kadett caused a blare of derisive horns, and he waved at the drivers, using one finger and looking so much like a defiant aging hippie she covered her eyes. They were so blatantly conspicuous no one in his organization would ever look to them as the escaped Dante Arundel and his newly-wed-by-glass-and-stone wife. "Does anyone in your organization know about this car?" she asked.

"No one alive today," he answered coolly.

What an uncomfortable answer. Yet…if he was right, she'd live through this drive. "Let's go to my mom's."

"In Oakland? What the hell would we do there besides convince someone to set her house on fire?"

"It's Oakland. You saw it. Crummy old neighborhood. Former mansions subdivided into dingy apartments. Bathroom down the hall. High crime. Only a few private homes left intact. Mom's is one. She's always been the force in the neighborhood. She takes care of people. They take care of her." It was nice to be able to tell him this. "They'll take care of us. We can hide there while we prepare. And then—we'll leave as fast as we can. We'll face whoever it is with all our weapons in hand."

He didn't answer, his face hard and unreadable.

"Do you have a better idea?" she asked.

"No. But if something happens to Octavia, how many people are going to want to kill me?"

"All of them."

"Then let's do this, first."

"Where are we going, if not to Oakland?"

"Connor's house."

"I thought he was dead." The newly created Maarja found herself asking, "Is he?"

"Perhaps. We'll find out, won't we?"

"When you got the call, I assumed while I was in the bathroom you'd check up on it."

"I didn't have my cell. Remember?"

"Oh. Right." He'd answered the hotel phone to get the news about Connor from…someone…because he'd given their phones to the fake Dante and Maarja. She'd thought he had a replacement, but in light of this…

"Why didn't you call Connor from the hotel phone?"

"I did. No answer."

"He didn't recognize the caller ID."

"Or he's dead." Dante anticipated her next question, for he told her, "I got the information from someone I trust implicitly."

"That someone has betrayed you."

"Never. That person has received bad information. From who? How was it conveyed? When I get to a phone, I'll find out."

He was so sure that the person who'd told him the news was blameless and she couldn't imagine who that would be. "Who do you trust with your life?" she asked.

CHAPTER 36

"Two people." Dante smiled at her. "You're one."

She didn't want to experience the warmth of knowing this man trusted her. Yet she smiled back and said, "Yes. You can trust me."

"Do you trust me?" he coaxed.

She wanted to think about it, the ramifications of trusting him, the consequences of admitting it, but there it was, flowing through her veins, a rock-solid certainty that he'd put his life on the line for her. Again she fussed with putting her tearaway pants back in order. "Yes. I trust you."

He touched her cheek. "Shy? Now?"

"No." *Yes.*

"Why won't you look at me?"

She glanced at him.

He met her gaze for one swift moment, his eyes all golden warmth, then turned back to the traffic.

She blushed and faced forward.

It didn't change a thing. They were up shit creek without a paddle. Still...through all the difficulties and anguish, trust had grown between them. That was nice to know.

Just like she knew he hadn't forgotten to tell her who the other person was, and that meant he wasn't going to. If he truly trusted her, and she knew he wouldn't have said it unless he meant it, then only the sensitive identity of that other person stopped him. And that made her think…

He said, "I know Octavia is going to worry when she can't contact you, but I promise as soon as it's viable, I'll contact her and assure her of your safety."

"Thank you. That's good of you to think of her."

"She's my mother-in-law. Alex is my sister-in-law. Because of what happened to Alex, I already had placed them under protection. That order won't be rescinded until I feel sure of their safety."

Maarja's breath caught. All that had happened: *la Bouteille de Flamme* in her drawer, the fake wedding that Dante took so seriously, the flare of heat from the bottle and stopper (she looked at her palm, which still did *not*, she told herself, tingle with sensation), this fear that drove them—all made her aware that someone, somewhere could capture Mom and Alex and use them to control her.

As she absorbed that truth, this trip took on new urgency. She had to get somewhere, do something, to protect the ones she loved.

All the ones she loved.

She didn't love Dante.

She didn't love Dante.

She didn't love Dante. He was a strong man, a Boss with the capital B, but he could be taken, tortured, killed. She'd seen death. She knew its face. She didn't love Dante, but she didn't want him wearing that face.

Beat. Beat. Beat.

Theoretically Dante and Maarja were driving *out* of San Francisco, *away* from the morning rush hour, so the traffic shouldn't have been terrible. But not terrible for the Bay Area equaled solid suckage, and no cell phones meant they couldn't use GPS to find a better route. They weren't going anywhere, merely staring at miles of brake lights while Maarja fiddled with her leather pants.

"The legs won't go back together?" Dante asked.

Maarja sighed in exasperation. "Not in this car. It's so small I can't maneuver."

"Leave them. I like it."

"Because it looks like a leather skirt slit up to my vajayjay."

"Of course." He was such an unabashed male animal.

She scooched and adjusted until the leg slits were on the side. "There. Now it's slit up to my *hips*. That's a little less…southern exposure."

"You have great hips. Great legs. However you want to show them to me is a boy's wet dream." He sounded so ravenous and *happy*.

"I'm not showing them to you, I'm—"

He smirked.

She smoothed the leather over her knees. "Anyway, you're supposed to keep your eyes on the road."

"I am."

Someone honked behind them.

"No, you're not."

"It's your fault." He gave the finger to the car behind them. "Your legs make me think of your *chatte*. Are you still wet? I came like a boy and now I want to do it again."

"Traffic is moving!"

In a happy tone, he said, "You already nag like a wife." He drove forward at twenty miles per hour.

She wasn't going to win, so she subsided into silence.

After half a mile, he braked again. "Wow, I even got to put it into second gear! Are you sulking?"

"Similar. I'm thinking. The reappearance of that bottle—does that mean things are coming to a head?"

"Yes. I have been waiting for them to make the next move. Which they did."

"Why did they?"

"Pending deals that require me to change my policies. Potential allies who are questioning their competence." He nodded in satisfaction. "Impatience."

"Serene is part of the conspiracy to depose you. The bitch."

Dante ceased tapping his fingers on the steering wheel. "Why do you say that?"

"I thought she was an opportunist who used the explosion to steal the art to sell, but since the bottle arrived in my bedroom, she's got to be working for…whoever it is."

"Or she sold it to them."

Maarja so badly wanted Serene to be more than a thief, but… "I didn't think of that. I'm so angry at her."

"About Alex."

"Yes. Stealing and betraying a trust is one thing. Beating someone and leaving them to die is another. Serene was always, oh, so…pressing palms and *namaste*." She said the last word as if it were an insult.

He inched the Opel ahead a few inches.

She glanced at his granite face. "You don't think that's it, either."

"Previously, her reputation was spotless, right? Saint Rees thoroughly investigates his employees, no?"

"Right, and he's uncovered some pretty heinous applicants who buried their backgrounds in a deep grave. He's good at what he does." She put her hand on his. "Really, Dante, I know you believed you'd been bamboozled, but Serene bamboozled us all. Her and her fucking Zen." Oh, no. She snatched her hand away. She was starting to talk like him.

He didn't say anything about her cussing, but his mouth quirked. "In that case, one other thought. If it was her first time at robbery, she may have tried to make a deal to sell the objects and—"

"And they were stolen from her!"

"You can't steal from a dead woman."

Maarja turned and stared at his indifferent face, feeling innocent and foolish. "You think she's dead? You know she's dead?"

"I do not know, but if I was betting, I'd come down on the side of a soon-to-be-discovered corpse, a recovery of all art except for one small bottle, and a successful closing of the case by the police."

She faced forward, at the barely-inching-along line of cars, and swallowed. He was right, of course. If Serene was really a novice at theft and violence, she could very well have run afoul of the more experienced villains who objected to the attention her activities had brought to them.

A parallel could be drawn between her and Serene. In over her head. And sure, she didn't like Serene, but she wanted her to go to jail, not be dead. Too much pain and ruin hovered close. Alex, Raine Arundel... "That works if someone killed Serene for the bottle. A relative of yours. Why wouldn't they sell off the rest of the art?"

"Because it's my art, and it's always good to hedge your bets."

"Oh." She needed to remember Dante was the ultimate bad guy. "Whoever is doing this knows that if you survive all the assassination attempts, the return of your art might pacify you, you won't be moved to widespread speculative vengeance, and they'll be able to take another run at overthrowing you."

He inclined his head.

"You won't mention the bottle because it's already in your possession."

"It's actually in *our* possession. I'm merely the one who is protecting it until such time when it's no longer an object sought by anyone but museum curators."

She thought about that. "When this is over, you want to give it to a museum?"

"That would be safest for *la Bouteille de Flamme*, don't you agree? We can give it to someone with the stipulation that it must be displayed and protected, and on our anniversary, we'll visit it and hold hands." He cast her a flirty glance as if trying to lift her sadness.

She was not sad about Serene. She hadn't liked her in the first place, and when Serene and her henchman hurt Alex, she discovered how to hate as a Daire should hate.

She was a little sad about her own loss of naivety. It seemed the further she got into this, the more she was bruised, not just in her body, although all the aches and pains from the early morning's crashes had begun to make themselves known. But the woman she had thought herself to be: savvy, cynical, street-savvy, no longer existed. Compared to this place she now inhabited, before she'd been cocooned in safety. The world was both worse than she had believed and—she looked sideways at Dante—better.

"Hey, look!" He shifted gears. "We're speeding along at thirty-eight miles per hour!"

"That's great. How much longer to Connor's?"

"At this speed? We might get there by eleven."

"We really need a cell phone."

"Not yet. Let's stay off the grid for a while longer. Until we're prepared."

"For what?"

"For what's going to happen."

CHAPTER 37

Connor lived—if he lived—in a nice average-looking place: suburban neighborhood, large lots, full-grown trees, ranch-style mid-century modern with a few tweaks like a pop-up mother-in-law suite over the garage.

As Dante and Maarja pulled into the driveway, Maarja said, "Not at all what I expected."

"Most days, Connor works from home, so they added the space over the garage to keep him out of Owen's hair."

She looked at Dante. "What does Connor do for you?"

"He's my accountant."

"Well, of course he is."

"What did you think?" Dante's mouth quirked. "He was my enforcer?"

"I figured he had to be good at fighting because he's such a big-mouthed, rude, unbearable—" She did a double take. "Wait. Who's Owen?"

"Owen is Connor's spouse."

Obviously Maarja hadn't heard him correctly. "Owen is…?"

"Connor's partner." Dante got out of the car.

She did, too, although more slowly and with the knowledge she hadn't come out of that duel on the highway without bruises, and spoke across the car roof. "Owen is a…man?"

"Most definitely."

"They're gay."

Dante's mouth quirk grew to a smirk. "No need to sound so astounded."

"Connor came on to me!"

The smirk disappeared. "Do not tell Owen! He'll beat the snot out of Connor."

"I would hope to hell! What would Connor have done if I'd taken him up on his offer?"

"Connor played on both sides of the street most of his life, then he met Owen, fell in love, and... Well, he still flirts."

"In between being a jackass!"

"Some would say that runs in the family."

"You're not a flirt." She started up the front walk.

At her deliberate omission, he gave a bark of laughter and followed close on her heels.

The way he kept close to her gave the appearance of protection, but it didn't feel like security. It felt as if he wished to keep her within arm's length at all times. It felt like stalking. "What kind of accountant? Like, as in money laundering?"

"As in, someone who has handled all the changes in the corporation, including moving us out of money laundering and into laundromats."

"You own laundromats?"

"No. It was a figure of speech. We buy successful companies and leave them alone to make profits, for as long as that works. Connor's very good at recognizing graft and turning that over to me, and I handle it." She wanted to ask if Dante whacked people, until he tacked on, "Legally. It starts with firing and ends with prosecution for their crimes." Apparently he knew he should reassure her.

"Connor has a reputation as being mean."

"Who told you that?"

She had to sort through all the tumultuous events of the last few weeks, and finally traced it. "Fedelma."

"Oh."

"What?"

"Fedelma is dedicated to the family. She feels she must safeguard our reputations as the most vicious sons of bitches in the Western world. As an accountant, Connor falls below that standard."

"That is such a weird behavior. Is she a suspect?"

"Of course," he said matter-of-factly.

She recalled Fedelma's obvious grief. "She seemed to honestly love your mother, to be grieved by her death."

In a flat tone he said, "You cannot know what motivated the explosion that took my mother out of the picture."

"I guess, but—"

They arrived on the broad front porch. Dante pointed to a spot to the side. "Stand there and don't get in the way."

This could not be good.

He rang the bell.

The door opened and a very alive Connor said, "Dante, hey, what's—"

Dante did that magic trick where all of a sudden he pulled his stiletto, clicked it, and aimed the point in Connor's face.

Connor leaped out onto the porch, somehow passing the blade while landing a stunning blow to the side of Dante's head. Dante twirled like a ballet dancer to face Connor. In a similar magic trick, Connor had a knife in his hand, pointed at Dante's heart.

It all happened so fast Maarja was left standing, gaping in shock.

When Dante backed into the house, Connor followed. After a moment of glancing at the car and thinking that this would be a good time to make her exit, that trust between her and Dante reared its ugly head and she followed the men through the foyer into the living room.

She should get a medal of bravery, or at least a ribbon for being not the brightest.

The house inside was welcoming, with comfortable furniture, rugs that splashed colors and natural fibers across the oak floors.

Connor was all growling guard dog. "What the fuck do you think you're doing, coming to my home, blade pointed at my throat?"

"Fucking traitor set me up to die like a horse driven off a cliff. Me and my woman."

"What?" Connor shouted.

Maarja glanced at the thin, fit man of forty who stood in the door of the kitchen, staring in astonishment at the violence happening in his living room. "His woman?" she mouthed to him.

Owen—she assumed it was Owen—rolled his eyes in sympathy.

To Maarja, Connor looked genuinely shocked. "I would never betray my true lord and leader, but you—"

Dante interrupted. "In the face of such treachery, you can't claim your home as sanctuary."

They sounded as if they were reciting dialogue so formal it was written in the Middle Ages. The guys went into half crouches, circling each other like a dance from *West Side Story*. They snarled, actually bared their teeth, and breathed in strong hisses.

"Okay, that's it." Maarja had had enough. She walked toward the kitchen. "Owen? I'm Maarja." She offered her hand, and they shook firmly. "Do you have a pistol? I'm not going to shoot anybody."

"Of course I do. Married to him, it's required." He went into the kitchen and came back with a small-caliber gun. As he handed it to her, he said, "I'd ask why, but I suspect I don't want to know."

"Probably not." She took it, aimed it at the ceiling over Dante and Connor, cleared the safety, and pulled the trigger.

The blast and the shower of plaster brought the shouting to a halt.

"Maarja, what the hell was that?" Dante shouted.

"Is she crazy?" Connor demanded of his cousin.

"Bad impulse control," Dante said. "I guess."

She pointed the pistol at the ceiling again. "Shut up."

They did, although probably more for fear of what she would do next with the firearm and less out of respect for her fierce pronouncement.

She asked, "You both have a gun on you, don't you?"

They snorted like angry ranchers who'd been insulted by the resident lamb. "Yeah."

"Stop posturing, pull your firearms, and kill each other. You're boring Owen and me." Maarja clicked the safety on again and carefully transferred the pistol to Owen. To him she said, "Be careful. The barrel's hot."

Owen put his arm around her shoulders and steered her toward the kitchen. "I made some iced tea. Would you like some?"

They got through the swinging door and out of sight, then stopped to listen. They heard the thump of fist against flesh, then another, then—

"You've got the hardest fucking face." Maarja could almost see Dante shaking his fingers. "I hurt my fist every time."

"Next time you decide to attack me for no fucking reason I'll put on my *squishy* face." Connor sounded like the meanest, most bewildered son of a bitch on the planet. Also, as if he'd been hit in the nose and was congested. "What the hell's the matter with you, man? Why the attack?"

"I got a call you'd been exterminated."

"The hell you say? From who?"

"An impeccable source. Turns out it was a way to lure me onto the PCH and run me off the cliff."

"You look alive to me."

"I'm not that easy to sabotage."

"I'm not that easy to kill, either. Why did you believe the call?"

"Where were you at 4:43 a.m. when I called to verify?"

Silence.

Owen dashed back into the living room. "He was busy!"

"I was busy, too, but I answered the phone," Dante said icily.

Maarja stalked out. "If you'd been fully busy the way they were and answered the phone anyway, you'd be here alone. For the rest of your life."

Both Dante and Connor were white with ceiling plaster and red with blood smeared on their faces, and they stared at Owen and Maarja like two guilty boys.

She and Owen swiveled and marched back into the kitchen.

"Connor just vacuumed." Owen mourned his formerly pristine living room while he placed the pistol in a kitchen drawer.

"Sorry about the gunshot. I was afraid they were really going to hurt each other."

"I know. Thanks for the quick thinking." He poured tea from a stout pitcher and gestured around at the plates and utensils stacked on the countertops. "Pardon the mess. I'm in the middle of renovating the kitchen, I'm a contractor—Rainbow Contractors, you'd be surprised to know the people who actually think that means I'll color their house—and of course our work comes last."

"I like the cabinets." She rubbed her hand on the dark gray highlighted with dark yellow gold. "Unique. And the breakfast table matches!"

"My designer is top-notch." He headed for the cooking center.

"I have range envy!" She admired the hefty six-burner gas cooktop.

"I like to cook. Hungry?"

Her stomach growled loudly. "Toast if you have some. I haven't eaten anything today."

"I can do better than toast." Owen laid bacon in the frying

pan. "The smell of this will heal the breach and bring in the boys. Bread's in the box. Knife's in the drawer."

Maarja sliced bread and placed it in the toaster, set the table, and chatted with the kind of comradery people experience when they have shared experiences. In the case of Owen and her, the sharing consisted of being partners with two murderous dirtbags.

Within a few minutes of sizzling and scents, Owen's prediction proved true, and Dante and Connor shoved each other through the door.

"You're not eating at my table looking like that! Plaster and blood. No, sirs!" Owen pointed toward the back door. "Go use the hose!"

Maarja grinned as Dante and Connor trudged out into the yard.

"You have to be firm," Owen told her.

"I'm getting that," Maarja replied.

CHAPTER 38

Outside on the grass, Connor grabbed the hose and adjusted the sprayer. "What are you doing with her, man? She killed your father!"

"Good. Am I allowed to say good?" Dante turned on the water at the faucet. "Or how about…I don't care. He was a fiend who brutalized my mother and me and your mother and every person around him. A psychopath of the first order, from a family of psychopaths stretching back generations. Someone needed to kill him. Good for Maarja's mother for planning so meticulously, and let's show some sensitivity for the poor little girl who was used as a pawn."

"If you command, my liege." Connor gave a mocking half bow. "But good luck on getting the rest of the Arundels to cooperate."

"She triggered the explosion, but she didn't know, and innocence has to be a shield."

"That's not in the code."

"Show me where it's written down."

"It's not, but we all know it." Connor waved his arm to indicate the greater family. "Anyway, given a choice, she'd do it again now."

"So would I. So would you. Give me that." Dante wrestled the hose away from him. "Do you remember Benoit?"

Connor shook his head. "Not really. Except...he made my mother cry."

"Did you never wonder if we're half brothers?"

"My mother was his cousin!"

Dante sprayed him with the hose. "Get real."

Connor wiped his face, smearing plaster and blood. "Thanks for putting that disgusting thought into my head."

Dante used the hose like a shower on himself. "He loved hurting people, especially people who couldn't fight back. Especially family. Especially women."

Connor took the hose back and did the same. "If you insist on having Maarja, she's going to cause trouble forever."

"The family will damned well learn to deal. I'm done swearing off her. She ran into an explosion to save my mother. She cried when Mère died. She was a virgin." Dante shouldn't have confided that last, but Connor had been his friend forever and—

Connor seemed unfazed. "You only liked her for like fifteen minutes, then you went into that deadly silent cold-eyed glare you've perfected."

"I thought she was involved with the theft of the bottle. Then she told me she'd been the one who detonated the bomb. I'm a dickhead. It's required, especially now."

Connor did a belated double take. "She—"

Exasperated, Dante said, "Don't say she killed my father again."

"She was a virgin?" Connor's voice rose.

Crap. Dante should have remembered Connor's slow reactions. "Could you be any fucking louder?" He glanced toward the house, twisted the sprayer to jet, and hit Connor in the face again. "Don't tell her I told you!"

Undeterred, Connor questioned, "A virgin? You found a... You slept with the last remaining member of the Daire family and she was a virgin?" He raised his hand to protect his face. "No. No way. She fooled you."

"How? Tell me, oh, enlightened one. Explain—"

"Plastic surgery. Something… I don't know! That's too much—"

"Don't say it!"

"Like fate."

"I *told* you not to say it."

"Tell me you used a condom."

Dante stared at Connor. Let him take the hose. Spray him in the face.

"What the fuck were you thinking?" Connor shouted. "What the fuck were you—"

"I wasn't thinking. I was… It had been a tough day and she… I… She cried. And I'd been waiting for her all my life and…" Dante wiped at his eyes. "Oh, just spray me again."

Connor let the hose dangle, too horrified to even take advantage. "Is she pregnant?"

"I'm an enlightened being. A product of the twenty-first century. I'm not superstitious. It was one time."

"*One* time?"

"Yes!" Dante remembered that morning in the parking garage. "Except this morning."

"What the hell?" Connor shouted again.

"Probably the wrong time of the month." Dante was aware he was babbling. "She *shouldn't* be pregnant."

Connor sprayed him in the crotch. "That's no answer!"

Dante flinched and protected. "She says no."

"Did you see her take a pregnancy test?" Connor read the answer on Dante's face. "Do you believe her?"

"I believe I've got to get this situation under control damned fast before…"

"Before the baby bump is so big she's waddling?"

Dante inclined his head.

"Are you going to marry her?"

"I already did." Dante reached into his sleeve.

Instinctively Connor flung the hose aside and pulled his stiletto.

Dante produced *la Bouteille de Flamme*.

The stiletto disappeared back into Connor's sleeve, and he reached out with tentative fingers. "Is that…?"

"Yes. Yesterday someone put it in her house."

"To frame her."

"Yes. To get her killed by someone, I assume someone in the family who could be trusted to overreact either with purpose or as a tool." Dante gently transferred the bottle to Connor's cradled hands.

Connor viewed it with a mixture of awe and terror. "How did you find out?"

"She called me."

"Did she? How terrifically interesting." Connor frowned at the bottle.

"I went at once, of course. I recognized the machinations, if not the hand behind it."

"Are you sure she's not playing you?"

"Positive. Because I also recognized…her. Who she was to me. Fate is not the bitch I'd imagined, because for the first time in three weeks, I felt whole. In my heart." He was saying words he hadn't even thought before, but they came out easily, as if he'd always known and finally admitted.

"Ah." Connor nodded judiciously.

Dante felt a little chagrined. "That's all? Ah?"

"You're in love."

"I wouldn't go that far." Knee-jerk reaction. And he didn't do knee-jerk reactions.

"When I met Owen, I didn't want to commit. I didn't want to fling myself into a marriage. Especially a gay marriage. My God! I knew the havoc he would cause in my life, my associations. My mother! I tried to walk away, I really did. I walked so far I almost didn't get back before... When I came to my senses, he didn't want to listen to me. He didn't trust me when I said I loved and needed him. I had to prove myself before he would enter the relationship again." Connor took a discomfited breath. "I had to beg."

"Ah." No wonder Connor used that single syllable; it said more than Dante ever imagined.

"I understand what you feel." Connor wore that *misery loves company* face. "Did you beg?"

"No time for that. She was in danger in her own home—and she had the stopper."

"I see that." Connor touched it with one fingertip. "You got her to...?"

"She joined them while I held it."

"Witnesses?"

"Whoever had taken control of her security camera."

"Now you've done it." Connor laughed. "Did she realize what she'd done?"

"As soon as it was joined."

Connor surreptitiously glanced toward the house. "I'll bet that went well."

"Not immediately." The understatement of the century. "Connor...when she kissed me, the bottle and stopper gave off this flash of heat."

"Like...like they'd been waiting all these years and... You are shitting me." Connor glanced around as if in this sunny suburban backyard he saw the Daire and Arundel ghosts watching him.

Dante comprehended the feeling. "Not sure...but I suspect the stopper fused to the bottle."

Connor gently twisted the stopper.

It didn't budge.

Connor stared at him in consternation. "The fifteenth century for the win!"

"I've got to stop challenging fate." Dante glanced toward the house. Was Maarja carrying his child? Why would she say no?

Because—lowering thought—she didn't want to marry him. Couldn't she see the advantages?

He was rich. He had a few scars, but last night she'd enjoyed his body. He'd made sure of that. The way she responded… Oh, yeah. He would definitely make sure she craved him time and again. That was only fair, since he craved her. He could keep her safe…although she wouldn't be in such danger if she hadn't been there for the explosion… "If she isn't pregnant from the first time, she's probably pregnant from what she did to me after the attempt to run us off the road."

"What she did to you?"

"You know. Death too close and all that."

"Yes, I know." Carefully Connor handed the bottle back to Dante. "Congratulations, man. You picked a good one. Or fate picked a good one for you."

Dante placed it on the glass patio table in the sun. Together they stared at it, at the blending of colors, blue to purple to red, all rich and glorious, casting shimmering rainbows in circles around its base. "It's a promise of peace," Dante whispered.

Connor hummed softly, then seemed to make a decision. "Okay. Okay. Okay. Okay." He paced each repetition of the word as if he needed the seconds between to clear all the circuits in his brain. He stripped off his T-shirt, his pants, and underwear, and jumped naked into the pool. "Come in. It's easiest. No one close. No one wearing a device." It was a subtle accusation at Dante. Connor didn't necessarily trust him.

Good point. No matter how you arranged the letters in Arundel, they always spelled *corrupt*. Dante stripped off and jumped in. "Son of a bitch! Your pool heater is broken?"

Connor grinned evilly. "Don't have one. Did your dick shrink to the size of a peanut?"

"When you hit me with the water, yeah!"

"Come on. Into the middle."

They swam to the center of the pool.

"Who are your suspects?" Connor demanded.

CHAPTER 39

Owen watched out the window fondly. "Look at them. They're getting along so well!"

"Goodie. I'd hate to see them break up." Maarja refused to look. Instead she shredded cheese and beat eggs.

With his first sign of snappishness, Owen said, "You would. In this family, you need every ally you can get."

"I'm not of this family." She could do snappish, too.

"Maybe you should have explained that before I let you blast my living room ceiling!"

"Fair enough." She took a breath. She was a fool if she let weariness alienate the guy who was cooking her breakfast. "Did I see you at Mrs. Arundel's funeral?"

Owen grimaced. "I'm objectionable to some of the less enlightened family members, and I wanted that dear lady's sendoff to be lovely and as peaceful as she deserved." He hugged her shoulders. "Thank you for trying to save her."

"I wish I..."

"I wish, too. I loved her dearly, as did Connor, and now that she's deceased, the crooks and killers in the family are restless and jockeying for position." He took a breath. "If I'd been at the funeral, Connor would have had to behave like a civilized person instead of the Arundels' biggest mouth."

"Biggest ass," Maarja muttered.

"Ha! Yes, exactly. My thanks; you've certainly taken the pressure off me as the unwanted in-law!"

"Glad to help." She had always done sarcasm well, but she was becoming one of the world's leading experts.

"What exactly is going on?" Owen wanted a rundown.

"I don't know where to start. What have you heard?" When he told her, it was almost everything, so Maarja filled him in on the details of the previous night: the bottle, the ceremony, the escape without cell phones—she let him fill in the blanks about what happened after the dinner in the Live Oak kitchen—their wakening to the news of Connor's death, the calamitous drive up the coast, and the explosion of the elevator.

As she spoke, Owen was on his phone looking stuff up. "Caltrans reports a slough-off on the Pacific Coast Highway. A car went over the edge and burst into flames."

"May they burn in hell," Maarja said fervently.

"You must have been tossed around by that stunt driving." Owen looked at the length of her bare leg. "Honey, you've got bruises!"

She pulled the leather aside and winced at the ladder of black and blue climbing up her thigh. "In the adrenaline rush, I didn't realize."

"Connor had laser surgery, so I've got ice bags in the freezer, a bottle of extra-strength Tylenol, and a year's supply of arnica." Owen shot her a wry grimace. "He is such a baby. Go into the bathroom and strip down. I'll get you a robe, and we'll check you out."

She looked at him like, *Huh?*

"I said I was a contractor. If I had a nickel for every framer who's ever needed his boo-boo fixed on the spot, I'd have a shitload of nickels. Now go." He waved his hand at the bathroom beside the kitchen. "We'll make you more comfortable."

When she and Owen came out of the bathroom, Connor and

Dante stood in their damp boxers and stared at them, at Owen's dark blue bathrobe wrapped around her.

"Connor, get the ice bags out of the chest freezer. We've got to stop the swelling in her elbow and her hip." As Connor headed into the utility room, Owen glared at Dante. "Someone didn't take good care of his new wife!"

Dante didn't protest his innocence, but instead drew Maarja gently into his embrace. "You should have said something."

"I'm okay," she mumbled. "I've been bruised before."

"Saving your mother!" Owen snapped at Dante.

Dante helped her to the table and sat her down. Kneeling beside her, he said, "Maarja, you have to tell me. I'm here to care for you, always."

He actually looked guilty. Anxious.

"You must be hurt, too!" she said.

"Swimming in that frigid pool took care of my bruises," Dante assured her.

"Sissy." Connor dropped eight ice bags on the table. "Let me know if you need more."

Dante looked at her knee and clucked like a mother hen, then examined her elbow and helped Owen attach the ice bag with a long elastic strip.

When she'd taken the Tylenol, and Dante was satisfied Maarja had been made as comfortable as possible, they settled down at the round table while Owen poured coffee for the guys. He told Maarja, "You're tired and we don't want caffeine to dilate your capillaries, so you drink water and milk."

She wanted to object that she needed caffeine, but...he was right, and she liked the mothering. "Thank you," she said meekly.

"I looked up everything Maarja told me." Owen placed wheat toast, scrambled eggs, crisp bacon and sausage, and a huge bowl of fruit before them. "San Francisco cops are investigating a suspicious explosion in the Arundel building. The elevator blew up. People were trapped on all floors. Dante Arundel has been reported missing."

Heads nodded. As the platters changed hands, they were quickly emptied and everyone dug in.

Maarja found herself feeling better with every bite—amazing how medicinal food could be to a too-long empty stomach—and when she smeared blackberry jam on her toast, she broke the silence. "This stuff is great!"

Owen beamed. "Connor is a lousy cook, but he makes the pickles and the jam! Oh, and he cans the garden tomatoes!"

Maarja looked at Connor. "I had no idea you had a talent that didn't include—"

Connor clamped his hand over hers and looked at her appealingly.

She finished, "—yelling at me in public."

He lifted her fingers and kissed them. "It will never happen again. I've been taught better manners."

Maarja thought he meant today, with Dante's fists, but Connor turned to Owen and they exchanged a smile.

"I can make jam, too." Dante used his deep sexy voice. "What kind do you like?"

"I like them all, but…peach. And apricot." She could see his brain store the information away. Connor and Owen exchanged another smile, and she thought rather uneasily that Dante was… Well, he was courting her. With homemade jam, since he couldn't yet give her a peaceful life.

Maarja smiled as she ate, and when she had put enough in her belly to allow her brain to kick in, she said, "Someone managed to infiltrate the Arundel home and set the explosives to kill Mrs. Arundel. At the same time, all Mrs. Arundel's art was highjacked by Serene and her gang, and my sister was badly hurt. That all speaks to a coordinated effort by a person or persons deep in Mrs. Arundel's confidence."

"I never believed they could kill her." Connor sounded prosaic, but his voice broke.

"They tried before," Dante pointed out.

"Food poisoning. A runaway car. Nothing that could be pinpointed as an assassination. But an explosion in her own house! So public, so powerful, so unquestionably a murder!" Owen stood and started stacking the plates so vigorously one chipped. He swore and kept stacking.

Connor stood and poured more coffee for the men. "Some of the family and the hangers-on aren't happy about Aunt's efforts to move the Arundels into legal and less easily profitable methods of earning a living."

"I told you, Connor, it's not about money, it's about power." Owen spoke with certainty.

"Money is power," Connor replied.

"Not everybody with money chooses to crush their opponents into the dust. Every person given power becomes like Sauron, determined to rule them all and bind them in darkness." Owen saw Maarja look longingly at the coffee.

Dante observed the interaction through lowered lids that might have meant he was weary, but Maarja knew also meant he was sifting through the facts. "Someone has been trying to kill Mère for a while, thinking that when that occurred, I'd be malleable and eager to return to the old ways."

"Because you're a weakling easily led by others." Connor couldn't have sounded more sarcastic.

Dante gazed at him. "I have been careful to give that impression."

Connor looked dumbfounded. "You...you actually think anyone will believe that?"

"Not completely, because since the explosion no one has come forth to offer their advice and support." Dante managed to remain still, not a flicker of the eyelash, yet radiated danger.

Or perhaps Maarja knew him too well.

"Maybe because they know you're totally pissed off about your mother's death and would look suspiciously on the first person who offered advice." Connor stood and started cleaning up the dishes. "They might think you can be manipulated, but you're still deadly."

"The person who offers the deal is the traitor," Maarja recited.

CHAPTER 40

The men looked at her like, *Huh?*

"*The Godfather.* The movie," Maarja explained. "That's what Don Corleone says to his son. The person who offers the deal is the traitor. It could apply here."

Dante beamed as if his golden retriever had achieved his graduate degree. "You're right. I'll remember."

She did not bark and wag her tail, but only because she needed to glare while she shifted an ice bag to her hip.

Owen deposited a cup of hot chocolate in front of her. "A little caffeine, enough to help your headache but not enough to do more damage."

She took a sip and sighed. She could get used to being spoiled.

After digging around in a kitchen drawer, Owen came back with a battered tablet and a pen. "Who are the suspects?"

"Dante and I discussed that," Connor said, "in the pool."

Owen tapped the pen. "Any conclusions?"

"Nothing definitive," Dante said, "and I could use insight from you both. You'll see people differently because you weren't raised in the culture."

"The culture?" Maarja widened her eyes. "Is that what we're calling it now?"

Dante ignored her sarcasm. "In no particular order—Jack. I

like Jack for the next self-appointed crime lord. He went into the police to get a grip on the department, and during training, we lost him. His primary loyalty switched to the department. He'll only give us what he considers *appropriate* information, and he's been as pure as the driven snow."

In a dun–dun–DUN tone, Connor said, "Or at least…so he says."

Owen scribbled on the paper.

"Can we put Béatrice on the list?" Maarja asked. "She is so whiny, she's not even real."

Owen scribbled again, putting down names and notes.

"Sure. Not real is suspicious." Connor nodded. "Not to mention she's annoying. Jack is your *primary* suspect, Dante?"

"I said in no particular order." Dante's expression became still and dangerous. "Andere."

Maarja fought dismay. "I told you it wasn't—"

"You told me *you* killed my father, not Andere."

"And that bitch Tabitha heard me confess and told everyone." Owen scribbled.

"I didn't mean she was a suspect," Maarja told him.

"Who did she tell?" Owen asked sensibly. "Who passed it on from there? Who put her in place to listen? Tabitha's a link."

"And a stink." Maarja touched her forehead with one finger. She hadn't had enough sleep and she had a headache, and she was tired of being suspicious of everybody. Someone had to find a way to flush out the bad guys. Someone had to find a solution to this hard-fought and surreptitious battle. Soon.

Owen patted her hand. "You'll get the hang of this sooner or later."

"Sooner would be better, huh?" Like immediately. She turned back to Dante. "Why do you say Andere?"

"Because of your confession, I can acquit him of killing my father. Yet Andere came from a long line of sycophants to the Arundel family. He never wavered in his devotion to my father, regardless of what evil deeds Benoit performed. Andere suffered in the explosion and recovered, and I never questioned that his loyalty transferred to me. He has done whatever Mère and I required to enforce the changes we demanded." Dante spoke to her as if she were the only one at the table.

She got the message. "Andere's well-acquainted with evil deeds. He can torture. He has killed."

Dante leaned back. "He has."

"Who in your organization hasn't?" She thought that was a sensible question.

No answer.

"The women don't. For the most part, right?"

Shrugs all around.

"Sure, your mother, Raine Arundel." Maarja wanted to put a cap on the evil. "But she didn't have a choice. She had to take control!"

Nods.

Still not a genuine response. "At least not Béatrice!"

"*You* offered her as a suspect." Owen pointed his pencil at his notes.

"Because she's annoying and I don't like her. All that melodramatic shrieking." Maarja admitted, "I wanted to contribute something to the conversation."

"You don't have to do that, sweetheart," Connor said. "You sit there and look pretty."

She punched him hard enough that he rubbed his shoulder and told Dante, "She's mean!"

"Remember who she is. She can fight." Dante handed her a fresh ice bag for her knee. "Although maybe not right now. Fedelma has worked for my mother and me for as long as I can remember, so she's on the list of prime suspects."

Connor looked down at the table.

"That's Connor's mother," Owen told her.

Maarja leaned back in astonishment. "Fedelma is Connor's mother? But she said—"

"What did she say?" Connor asked.

Maarja looked at Dante. She'd already told him this.

Dante nodded, giving her the push to release the information.

Maarja swallowed. "She said, *Between you and me, he can be dangerous. Avoid him when possible.*"

"We have a conflicted relationship. I can't remember a time when she didn't push me to be Dante's best friend, then whisper in my ear that I could replace him." Connor seemed to be dealing with the mother issue very calmly. "She lusts for power, and I'm a sad disappointment to her."

"Especially since I came along," Owen added.

Connor patted his hand. "Yes, dear, that goes without saying. She wanted a manly man, and she got me. Good ol' loyal accountant and company man me." He glared at Dante and slapped one of the ice bags on his swollen nose.

The conversation went a long way to enlighten Maarja about Connor's pass at her, then his attack at Mrs. Arundel's funeral. He had a lot to live up to and a lot to prove, and he never could.

"What about Nate?" Maarja wavered on where to place a new ice bag. "Dante, your bodyguard has been in the thick of the action. Last night he delivered you to my house and took away our doppelgängers."

Dante was still unconvinced. "What's the motivation?"

"Money and power." Connor touched his nose and winced.

"Possible. He is my father's son." Dante took the ice bag Maarja handed him and put it on his fat lip.

"My God, how many of us are there?" Connor couldn't have been more dismayed.

Surprised, Maarja looked at Owen.

Owen looked at her.

Silently they consented to leave that subject for another day.

"Who's *his* mother?" Connor asked.

"I don't know."

"Why not ask Nate?" To Maarja, that seemed like the obvious answer.

"Until he acknowledges the relationship, I can't," Dante replied.

She placed the ice bag on her forehead.

"It's a guy thing," Dante explained. "I only know because Fedelma told me my father deliberately bred a male to be the bodyguard to care for the legitimate heir—me—he would have with the wife he had already picked out—Mère."

"That is so awful." Maarja's heart softened toward the impassive Nate.

"*Where's* his mother? She's a woman who escaped Benoit?" Connor obviously didn't believe that.

Dante confirmed what Connor's tone suggested. "No concubine ever escaped him. She cooperated, she's in hiding, or she's dead. Somehow. Probably not an accident."

"None of that removes Nate from the suspect list," Owen pointed out.

Maarja lifted her head. "Dante, is that why your mother didn't like Nate? Because he, um, was the unofficial older heir?"

"Mère didn't like him because he never warmed to her. Warmth is not in his job description. In general, Nate's not a cashmere sweater."

Maarja grinned at the description of the big, grim man.

"Was Aunt Raine a good judge of character?" Owen asked.

"She married my father." Dante obviously considered that a reason for doubt.

"Blackmail, though, right?" Maarja asked. "That's what Fedelma told me."

Dante looked at Maarja as if he'd never heard such a thing. "She said that? No. Mère was dedicated to keeping him happy."

"Yes, because he hurt her if he was unhappy. You said it, Dante! You said—"

"I know what I said." Dante drank his coffee with a concentration that said he needed it. "But even after he was dead, she refused to speak ill of him."

"To you. To his son," Maarja said sensibly. "She didn't want to besmirch his memory."

"Hard to do. He smirched it enough all on his own." Yet Dante seemed willing to consider that explanation.

"Anybody else?" Maarja looked around the table.

"Only everyone else in the family. Everyone who profits from our activities." Connor told the truth, but clearly he didn't like it.

"Someone in the inner circle planned the elevator explosion. That narrows it down considerably. Is there anyone in the family who's a ballistics expert?"

Heads shook.

"We hire that done," Dante said.

"The first explosion killed Mrs. Arundel. The second explosion was supposed to kill us." Maarja took that with ill grace.

"Someone doesn't have the imagination to come up with a variety of murder weapons." Connor had the guts to sound amused.

"Or we're dealing with a copycat," Dante said seriously.

Maarja used her fingers, cold from the ice bag, to massage her forehead. "Do we have a front-runner in the way of suspects?" She wanted answers.

"Andere," Dante said.

"Nate," Owen said.

"Jack," Connor said.

"We're getting nowhere." She tapped her fingers on the table and said fiercely, "We've got to force their hand."

Connor gingerly patted her arm. "Okay, boss. Got a plan?"

"Yes." Maarja waited until everyone focused on her. "We—" she pointed at her own chest, then at Dante "—are going to get legally and very publicly married."

CHAPTER 41

The objection came from an unexpected source.

"You are not going to make it that easy for—" Owen pointed at Dante "—him! Make the bastard court you. Lead him around by the balls. Seize your chance to be bridezilla!"

Dante said nothing. He was too busy watching Maarja with an expression that indicated...something. Desire, probably. Affection, maybe. Possession, for sure.

"I will," she assured Owen. "Later. Now we need to end this before someone gets dead."

"In a weird sort of way, it's a good idea." Connor stood, got a bottle of champagne out of the refrigerator, and went to work on the foil. "A wedding between the Arundel boss and the one remaining Daire will bring out the bastards."

"Ha!" Maarja got an adrenaline rush that almost felt like affection for Connor.

Dante remained silent and enigmatic.

Connor continued, "We have to have it some place where we control the venue."

Maarja sat up straighter. "My mother's house in Oakland."

"Would that work?" Connor asked Dante, and popped the cork.

Dante nodded slowly. "Octavia and Alex are in Sacramento while Alex works on her physical therapy and prepares for her next surgery. That will keep them out of the line of fire. Those people I saw in Oakland are dangerous in their own way. Octavia is loved—"

Maarja interrupted. "Mostly. She's made a few enemies of some of the less savory characters who populate the neighborhood."

Dante nodded his acknowledgment. "Our people will be invaders, isolated by that community. It's a good idea."

"The event will bring everyone out to see, and complain, and fake smile, and give some kind of inappropriate gift, and in the middle of the solemnity, before the vows can be finalized, somebody's going to try and take control of the business via a coup." Connor poured champagne into flutes.

"And kill Maarja," Dante said.

"They can try." Connor might be an accountant, but he obviously relished the chance to outwit their enemy.

Maarja felt Connor was a little too blithe. "I'd as soon skip that part."

"What do you think's going to happen if we go through with this plan? Some of the family support me no matter what I choose to do with the business. They follow me out of long-held loyalty. Tradition!" Dante thumped his own chest as if providing a drumbeat for the word. "But those same family who treasure tradition consider it an abomination that I would do anything more than use Maarja before I slit her throat. Maarja, killing you will be their goal, their endgame. The Arundel family is so close to eradicating your family. Only one Daire left…"

"Don't sugarcoat it!" she warned.

"Who are you going to use for security? Everyone we would normally employ we no longer trust." Owen made a good point.

The answer came easily to Maarja. "We'll use Saint Rees Fine Arts Movers. Those of us who pack and drive are scary folks, mostly women, who excel at blending into a crowd. It's natural." Maarja took the flute Connor handed her. "Besides, Saint Rees needs the creds to get the business rolling again. This robbery was devastating, and we could use an endorsement from somebody wealthy and important. Like Dante, here."

Connor distributed the flutes, put his hand on Owen's shoulder and lifted his flute. "To a long and happy marriage for Dante and Maarja."

Maarja lifted her glass, took a sip of champagne, and put it down. "Thank you, that's lovely, but if the bride doesn't get some sleep soon, she's going to fall on her face out of sheer exhaustion."

Owen leaped to his feet. "Come with me, dear. We'll put you in Connor's office over the garage, and we won't disturb you while we plan your future." As they left the kitchen, he said more quietly, "When I get done with those boys, they're going to make sure you have the wedding of your dreams."

"I don't want the wedding of my dreams. I never had those dreams." She climbed a flight of stairs. "I want to be safe, and I want Dante to be safe, and I want to make decisions about my life not influenced by fear. Can we just do that?" Her voice rose with each word.

Owen held her arm and patted her hand. "Then you'll have the wedding of *my* dreams, and when it's over, all the choices of the world will be yours."

CHAPTER 42

Maarja woke up to roll over, because she couldn't roll over without pain and careful planning. As she moved, one inch at a time, she observed that the sun was setting, the room over Connor's garage was both a spacious office and a spare bedroom, and someone behind her was snoring loudly. A slow glance over her shoulder showed Dante, naked and sprawled on his back, eyes closed, head tilted and mouth open.

He was bruised. He had a fat lip. He was cute.

That betraying thought made her wrench herself around, and groan as every joint protested.

He woke immediately and smoothly sat up, like being knocked around by his own stunt driving posed no problem for *his* movements. "You okay?" he asked. "Whiplash? Need help to get up and take a piss?"

She narrowed her eyes at him.

He sighed as if much put upon. "Need help to get up and *make à le pipi*?"

She wanted to make fun of him, but she was still too tired to fight.

Her restraint made him look carefully into her eyes. "You aren't concussed, are you?"

"No, I'm not concussed." She wore a soft denim shirt but-

toned up enough to cover the essentials. The shirt was probably
Owen's. He'd probably helped her into it. She sort of remembered that. "Yes, please help me to my feet and I'll use the facilities." Which sounded so straitlaced after his blunt language.

He grasped her around the ribs, which interestingly enough
weren't bruised, and gently lifted her off the bed. Quite a change,
since he was usually pressing down on a bed. As she hobbled
toward the bathroom, he asked, "Are you going to be okay by
yourself?"

"Yes!" She drew the line at that intimacy.

"When you come out, we'll talk." He shut the door behind
her.

That sounded ominous.

She couldn't read the man. Was he upset with her?

As she used the facilities, brushed her teeth, splashed water on
her face, and did a little light stretching, she tried to figure out
how to reassure him about whatever he was perturbed about.

When she came out, he was barefoot, wearing a torn T-shirt
and faded jeans that hugged his thighs so well she could see every
muscle and sinew. Her mouth dried. He looked ready to play his
role in *The Innocent Gardener and the Seductive Exchange Student.*

And she needed to get a grip on her fantasies. They were spinning out of control and she was in no shape, physically, to tackle
him. Instead she tackled the first uncomfortable subject. "You
didn't say anything when I said we should get legally married.
I'm not trying to trap you." She fiddled with the buttons on her
shirt. "It doesn't have to be forever, you know."

"Maarja, I know. The number of times you've assured me
that I don't have to marry you and you don't want to marry me
and our union isn't ordained by fate or blessed by love…could
cause dents in the ego of a lesser man." He sounded snappish
and turned toward the door. "Owen asked if you want a bath in
some herbal concoction he prepared to ease your aches. I'd say
yes if I were you. You'll hurt his feelings otherwise."

He was definitely snappish, and her feet dragged as she made her way toward him. "If someone will be there to haul me out."

"I'll be there. I can see you without clothes without fucking you."

"Without *wanting* to fuck me?" She laughed at him. She hadn't had enough sleep, so it followed that he hadn't had enough sleep. Probably that was the reason for his grim mood.

"Look. I can see you naked without fucking you because you're hurting and it's my fault."

Dismayed, she protested, "Not your fault! Your driving saved us."

He paid so little attention she might not have spoken. "But I can't see you naked without *wanting* to fuck you, without thinking what it's like when I'm inside you and all I want to do is come inside you and yet never finish, because it feels so damned good and so damned right. My skin against your skin, the way you clutch me, your voice when you get that little sob that means you're on the edge... There's never been a woman like that for me. Put on your robe—"

"Owen's robe."

"And I'll help you to the guest bath with the soaker tub."

He helped her slide into the robe, and he sounded impatient, but the words he said! Not poetry; that wasn't Dante. Blunt, earthy, sexual. Life was precarious and all she could think of was...fucking. He made her want to pull him on top of her. He made her want to sit on him and ride him. She wanted to press her legs together to ease the ache. Instead, as he took her arm and walked her down the stairs, she was lasciviously ready and wondered if he had plans to join her in the tub. Hoped he had plans...

As hopes went, hers were unfulfilled.

He ran the hot water, dumped in Epsom salts and a linen bag of what looked like dried weeds, tested the temperature with his elbow. The scent of lavender and chamomile wafted up, carried on the steam. As impersonal as a lady's maid, he helped her undress, get in, and tucked a bath pillow under her neck. "Owen says to relax for twenty minutes. That should give me time to catch you up."

She did not ask how she was supposed to relax when he used his corporate president voice, or why he couldn't get in the tub and talk at the same time. She knew the answer.

Time was the thing they didn't have. Utilizing her bath to discuss their plans made sense, so she arranged her washcloth over her nipples, because her nipples broke the surface of the water, and used her hands to swish the water in the futile— okay, silly—hope of concealing other body parts. That made her pubic hair wave like seaweed on the tide.

Great. Just great.

Dante pulled the dressing table stool over to the tub and placed it to the side and behind her head where she couldn't see his face. "I called Octavia," he said.

That drove the weirdness of this situation totally out of her head. "Thank you. My poor mom! Was she frantic after our disappearance?"

"Yes. I reassured her, told her you were safe, if a little battered. Explained in depth what had happened, gave her the whole background of you and me—"

"Oog." She sank deeper into the tub, trying futilely to conceal herself from his words.

"And asked for your hand in marriage."

Maarja stopped rippling the water.

"Octavia lectured me on a woman's right to control her own body and destiny, advised me that in her experience, fate is nothing compared to love and support and vows spoken in earnest." A significant pause. "And she gave you to me."

"My God," Maarja whispered.

In a more humorous tone, he said, "She also said if I ever hurt you, she would personally remove my junk and since she's vision impaired, that could get messy."

"My God," she repeated. Any relaxation created by water, salts, and herbs vanished in Maarja's need to leap to her feet and run.

"Let's warm up that bath a little more, shall we? You're looking tense." His hand appeared to flip on the hot water. "You do realize *you* proposed to *me*, right?"

"Yes, but I didn't think you'd—"

"Go through all the forms?" He sprinkled more Epsom salts and a handful of loose herbs and dried flowers under the faucet. "Swish that around," he instructed.

She did, and when the water was warm again, she turned off the faucet. "Better," she said. "Did Mom tell you she's performed quite a few weddings in her backyard?"

"She mentioned that. I assured her we'd stream the ceremony to her and Alex and she could officiate from the safety of—"

Maarja laughed and shook her head at his foolishness.

He paused to gather his thoughts. "She's not going to stay in Sacramento, is she?"

"Did you not get to know her at all? That woman believes in facing down the bad people of the earth. She's fearless. She wasn't born blind, you know. She had a talent, she taught people joy in their creativity, and was struck down for it." Maarja relaxed back into the tub and grinned for the fierce joy of knowing she'd have at least part of her family with her on her wedding day. "Mom will be there in person. Alex, too, if she can manage it. My other sisters, no. I wish, though! Did you call Saint Rees? He's fond of my mom. She'll add a layer of distraction for him, but he'll make sure she's safe."

"Right." Dante contemplated the complications he had set in motion. "I did call Saint Rees. Smart guy."

"He's more than that. He's a good guy."

Dante accepted her chiding gracefully. "A rare combination.

At once he saw the advantages of providing security. He went into sales mode, promised to concentrate all the California crew in Octavia's neighborhood."

"You'll pay him well."

"Maarja, I'm not thrifty."

She realized she had insulted him. "I know."

"I understand the advantages of binding people to me with loyalty, with kinship, with money. However, in the case of Saint Rees, there was no need for any of that. He considers you, Octavia, and Alex family." Dante scooted the stool closer to the tub. His voice grew quiet and intense. "He also gave me information I had never considered, information he had uncovered while searching for and investigating Serene."

CHAPTER 43

Maarja slowly sat up. The washcloth slipped into the water. She swiveled to face Dante. Remembering his earlier conversation with Connor, she guessed, "She's your...sister?"

"If only it were that simple."

Maarja leaned her arms on the bath pillow and fixed her gaze on him. "Tell me."

"What do you remember about your aunt after the explosion that killed my father?"

She clutched the pillow to her chest. For the first time, she tried to grasp the fragments of memory that eluded her...or she had ignored. "We lived in an apartment. It was okay. It was nice. We didn't go out. Ever. It wasn't safe. Aunt Yesenia hugged me. She cried with me. She..." From her four-year-old mind, she dredged recollections that had meant nothing to the child she'd been. "She couldn't hold me in her lap. I told her to sit back in her chair, but she laughed and her voice broke." Maarja closed her eyes to bring the memory forward. "She was pregnant."

"Yes. She was pregnant."

Maarja's eyes sprang open. "With Serene?"

He nodded.

"Your father was her father?"

"There's no doubt. Saint Rees had her DNA done."

"Serene is found? She is dead?"

"Yes. And yes. She didn't survive her contact with the world of art theft."

Maarja didn't feel grief for the cruel young woman. As far as she was concerned, Serene deserved her fate for her betrayal of Saint Rees and her treatment of Alex. After assembling the truths Dante had presented her, Maarja said, "Your father sought out Aunt Yesenia, my mother's sister. She spoke of him so bitterly I thought she was angry because of the devastation he'd rained down upon my family. But he wanted information, so he romanced her."

"A sound assumption. Actually the old blond bastard couldn't keep his cock in his pants and if he could actively ruin a woman's life while screwing her, he counted that as a win-win." She'd thought Aunt Yesenia was bitter. When Dante spoke of his father, he was dark chocolate bitter, the cooking kind with no sweetness to lighten the horror.

Maarja was still thinking through the scenario. "He romanced her with the intention of convincing her to give up information about my father, the last surviving male Daire and the object of Benoit's obsession. He succeeded, because my father was ambushed and killed. My mother realized what had happened and she created her plan to destroy Benoit with the clear knowledge she would die with him, and she forced Aunt Yesenia to promise to rescue and raise me."

In an emotionless voice, he said, "The results of the DNA test are all the proof we have of anything. Everything else is speculation."

She shot him a stern glance.

He conceded, "I believe you're correct."

"My aunt was pregnant, and some months after the explosion, she gave birth to Serene and gave her up for adoption." Maarja sank deeper into the tub. "No wonder she turned vicious. Her baby was gone, and all she had was me, the child who she'd had to give up her life and hopes for."

"No! She had you, the child whose parents she had betrayed, and she didn't want to pay the price of reparation." He leaned forward, spoke in her ear, a fierce no-nonsense man who understood human motivation all too well. "No, Maarja, feel no guilt or pain for your aunt. She promised your mother to raise and protect you. She resented that promise. When she abused you, when she abandoned you, she betrayed that promise."

"I know, but—"

He was uncompromising. "She was weak, and she produced a daughter who traced her roots—probably another DNA test. Serene was determined to exploit her connection to you and Benoit Arundel, and she was so morally bankrupt she relished the opportunity to leave a trail of pain behind her."

"Still, I wonder what Serene's upbringing was like? Were her foster parents indifferent? Abusive?"

"I don't care. We all make our choices. Her choices were cruel and manipulative, and she's dead because of them." He stood. "Time's up. Let's get you out of the tub." Reaching in, with his hands under her shoulders, he pulled her to her feet, helped her out of the tub…and smiled a pained and crooked smile.

"What?"

"You have flowers in your hair." With a light hand, he ran his fingers through the short ends around her face and behind her head. Still smiling, he brushed herbs and blossoms off her shoulders, her breasts, her thighs. And finally he used his thumbs to stroke blossoms out of her pubic hair. "There," he said unsteadily. "All clean and relaxed."

He had a funny definition of *relaxed*.

Stepping forward, she pressed her wet body against his, ran her fingers through his hair, down his shoulders, over his chest. "Sadly, you seem tense all over. Let me see if I can help." She kissed his mouth until he clutched her and rolled his hips against hers, demonstrating how unrelaxed he was. He was a man driven by desires, and she embodied those desires.

Pleased with herself, feeling like the femme fatale he seemed to think of her as, she took a bath towel off the heated towel rack. She dried herself, one careful part at a time, well-aware he watched as if he couldn't look away.

"There's a word for women like you," he said.

She grinned. "What?" She thought he would call her a tease. Instead he said, "Lovely."

His eyes heated with golden molten lava, melting away her amusement and leaving her bare and needy. She took a step toward him.

He took a step toward her. Then—something seemed to catch his gaze, distract him. He glanced around. "Damn. I forgot to light the aromatherapy candles. Owen gave me strict instructions. Don't tell him!"

CHAPTER 44

Dante and Maarja stayed the night at Connor and Owen's, the four working far into the wee hours, doing a deep dive into all things related to relatives and associates of the family business. Connor found a long, slow money leak originating from Dante's office, confirming suspicions that the problem originated among his inner circle. Yay for Connor.

When Maarja yawned, Dante announced it was time to quit, but before they did, he sent out a manifesto to the Arundels announcing his continued survival and his intention to wed Maarja Daire. With the marriage, he decreed the long feud would be ended, and he commanded them to Octavia's home in three days to witness his nuptials.

Then he showed his teeth in a hostile parody of a smile and predicted that he'd ended a great night's sleep for many. Amid the general agreement, he took Maarja back to their bed, gave her a luxurious massage that eased her pain, and eventually eased her into arousal. He pleasured her with his mouth until she heard herself moaning those long luxurious moans that meant she'd found the ultimate pleasure.

Lifting himself from between her legs, he smiled into her face. "Go to sleep now, darling."

"After that?" She slid her fingers into his dark curling hair. "I can't sleep."

He chuckled and wrapped her in his arms.

To her chagrin, she fell asleep in seconds.

Maarja woke alone, wandered down to the kitchen, and found Connor snoring with his head on the kitchen table while Dante worked on Connor's laptop. She poured herself a cup of coffee and one for him, and sat. "Any closer to finding the embezzler?"

Dante stretched. "With so many software blind alleys and hack U-turns, I'm spinning my wheels. Connor is a wizard at this stuff. He'll figure it out eventually, but he was up all night and no good to us now."

"Should we put him to bed?"

"I'm going to help Owen drag him in there. Owen was up half the night, too, ordering clothes for us and luggage to carry it in."

"And having a marvelous time!" Owen trilled as he came in from the backyard.

Maarja wondered briefly when she'd lost control of her own wardrobe.

Oh, yeah. When she'd rescued Mrs. Arundel from the explosion.

Owen came over and started massaging Connor's shoulders. "I ordered electronics, too. One computer, two phones, one tablet. That should set you up for the moment."

"As soon as the packages arrive, we'll drive to Oakland to your mom's house and you can start doing wedding things." Dante waved a vague hand as if he wasn't sure what those would be. "I'll answer the six million calls, texts, and emails from the family and put the fear of Dante in each and every one of them who dares question my decision to marry you."

Maarja sipped the coffee. "I can only imagine."

"I'll also let them know we've discovered an embezzlement and I'm not going to be too picky about punishing the right person." His malevolent smile caused a small frightened flutter in Maarja's own heart.

"Just a thought, but isn't that going to cause possible panic and maybe someone getting hurt who's innocent?" she asked.

"I doubt it, and if it does, Dante's justice is swift and painful." Connor raised his head. His eyes were bloodshot. His words dragged. But he sounded certain. "It will flush out any other attempts at embezzlement and cause panicked finger-pointing, which is always revealing."

"In case of finger-pointing, who are you suspicious of?" This whole labyrinth of moves and countermoves confused her and confirmed she was right in her decision to avoid playing chess.

"The pointer, of course." Connor yawned, a magnificent jaw-cracking yawn. "I've got to go to bed. Owen and I will be at the wedding venue as soon as I can regain consciousness."

"I hate to miss any of the wedding preparations, but Connor's right." Owen hoisted Connor to his feet. "He's vile if he doesn't get his sleep, so we'll stay here until he's his usual loving, cheerful self."

She stared at Owen, then at Connor. Somehow Connor had made Owen believe that. Love was really a miracle worker. She looked sideways at Dante. If this powerful, dark, intense man loved her, her knees would buckle, he could sweep her away, and she'd be happy, holding him in her arms and heart. She would know she'd discovered what most people never did: a mate who clearly saw into her soul and loved the person she was.

But Dante was more than a businessman and more than her lover. He was the head of a family—Family with a capital F. Family like gangsters and godfathers, people who made decisions with fists and bullets. Based on his canny sense of human nature, he made judgments and passed verdicts. He enforced his will on the reluctant. He knew how to terrify, and he knew how to soothe. He suffered no challenges from any upstart and he never ever took his gaze off his endgame.

"In less than an hour, the clothes and bags will be delivered by messenger. Help yourself to breakfast." Owen waved his hand around the kitchen. "We'll see you later today!"

As the two guys disappeared toward their room, Dante contemplated her. "Why are you looking at me like that?"

She simply didn't quite understand his endgame in reference to her. Or she did understand it—he'd told her often enough—but she could not comprehend quite why.

"Thinking," she said.

He cupped her cheeks and looked into her eyes. "Stop. You're doing it wrong."

Maybe, but she couldn't stop.

She wasn't beautiful, she wasn't charming, she wasn't tactful, she didn't flatter him. She was the last remaining Daire; the last remaining enemy of the Arundels. Sure, he wanted to sleep with her. That was clear. After that night in Gothic, more than clear. But why the rest of it? Why want marriage? Why claim her and cause such trouble among the already contentious Arundels?

He was going to kiss her, so she asked, "Fast-food breakfast okay?"

"Hm." He caressed her lower lip with his thumb. "We've got time. You put ice on your boo-boos." He opened the freezer and tossed her two ice bags. "And I'll pop the toast in and make us PB and Js."

"That sounds good."

He stuck his head in the refrigerator and came out with all-natural peanut butter. "Damned hippies," he muttered.

She smiled, because he wanted her to, and pressed the ice on her bruises.

In the end, all the events past, present, and future came down to one question: Did this man toy with her like a crafty cat with an unwary mouse? When she embraced him, did she embrace her own destruction?

After all, Benoit Arundel was Dante's father. Nothing could change that.

As Dante and Maarja drove away, clothes in the trunk, she asked, "Do we trust Connor and Owen completely now?"

Dante laughed shortly. "I attached an app to Connor's computer that reports all his activities to me."

"So, short answer, no. What about his other computer? I assume there's more than one. Or Owen's computer?"

"All the electronics in the house and probably a few beyond respond to the app." Dante rubbed her thigh. "I'm proud of the way you're thinking like an Arundel."

She answered tartly, "I'm thinking like a survivor who's recently suffered too many close calls."

"As I said, an Arundel. We have a lot in common, Maarja. Not just an ancient blood feud. Not just a bottle reunited with its top. We have the same instincts, we think alike, and in the far distant future, long after the wedding, when we've been together for all our lives, we'll even look alike. Wait and see."

"I don't see that there's a lot of choice," she muttered.

"No. We no longer have any choice." On that cheerful note, Dante hit the freeway toward Oakland.

CHAPTER 45

Dante parked the Opel Kadett on the curb in front of Octavia's Oakland home. "No one will steal this turd," he said with satisfaction as he pulled their new neatly packed luggage out of the trunk.

"They would if they knew what was under the hood." Maarja got out and looked around.

The yard looked pretty good; Mr. Nyugen rented the attic for himself and the dilapidated backyard gazebo for his karate school, and on the side he handled the gardening.

On the other hand, the house looked... Well, if a word could be found to describe it, that word would be *sagging*. Built in the early twentieth century during a brief period of prosperity, the former mansion had two stories, two bathrooms (one up and one down), a large front porch, and tall double-hung windows. The furbelows that decorated the eaves had once been multicolored, and fragments of paints still clung in the crevices. Overall, the white paint was peeling and bare boards rotted, but it was home.

She opened the front gate, also sagging, and stepped carefully along the broken chunks of concrete walk, up the steps, and across the porch to the door.

Upon going inside, she stepped into a riot of conversation and movement: in the foyer, the dining room, the living room, on the stairs were neighbors, members of Oakland Golden Neighborhood Community Festival, Octavia's sisters-in-law who she kept as friends after her divorce, their kids (also friends), Mr. Nyugen, and some kids in white karate gi, balancing on ladders and decorating with garlands of flowers. People from Saint Rees Fine Arts Movers mingled and helped, blending in as they did so well and at the same time monitoring the activities for unusual behavior.

Beside her, Dante dropped the bags. "Your mom and sister must be home and preparing for our wedding."

"So it would appear."

"You were right."

"Keep that in mind."

"Darlings!" From the center of the crowd, Octavia waved in their direction. "We didn't think it wise to wait for you before we got started on the arrangements. With the wedding so soon, there is so much to do. One question only Maarja can answer—what kind of flowers do you want in your bouquet?"

Before Maarja could even begin to gather her thoughts, Dante answered, "She wants orange blossoms."

"She does?" Alex sat in the foyer, in a wheelchair at a card table covered with planning paraphernalia.

"I do?" Maarja stared at him.

"Orange blossoms are traditional. Our wedding is to be traditional in every way." He made his pronouncement like he was the king marrying the beggar girl.

Not like Maarja cared. She hadn't even thought about the wedding as an event. But wasn't the bride supposed to have some say in—

Octavia bustled toward them. "Yes, of course traditional, in the way that a wizard's wedding is traditional. Maarja always loved wizards and I have the robes left over from a wedding I performed a few years ago—"

Dante spoke loudly and clearly. "I'm not wearing a wizard's

robe and neither is Maarja. She's wearing a pure white wedding gown."

Maarja tried to intervene. "Pure white isn't my best color and—"

Octavia cut her off. "Dear boy, white is so passé. She would be lovely in a sapphire blue and if you're trying to subtly impress on everyone her recently lost virginity, since medieval times, blue has been associated with the Virgin Mary."

Dante didn't even deign to answer that. "She'll wear white."

Maarja met Alex's rueful gaze and wandered over by her sister. A brief gentle hug, and Maarja seated herself at the chair nearby. She knew better than to reproach Alex for leaving the hospital. Instead she asked, "Is this too much for you?"

"It helps," Alex answered frankly. "I'm not constantly thinking about what hurts or my next physical therapy or my next surgery and what's going to hurt. I'm the official organizer... Although from the sounds of things, all the stuff Mom had decided is about to change. It's the battle of the Titans over there." She tilted her head toward the ongoing vigorous discussion between Octavia and Dante. "Who do you think will win?"

"They'll both convince themselves that they won," Maarja answered.

The sisters cackled.

Maarja jumped when a familiar high voice caroled at her shoulder. "Hellooo!"

Maarja swung around and stared in astonishment at the wispy woman who had been Mrs. Arundel's annoying, inefficient assistant. Her basset-hound face looked the same: thin blond hair, pale pink lipstick, bright pink blush. She was continually sniffing in that annoying manner that made Maarja want to hand her a tissue and tell her to *blow*. But somehow she looked different, less morose, less self-pitying, more interested and involved. Maarja asked, "Béatrice? What are you doing here?"

"When the commandment came from Dante that the family was to attend his wedding to you here at Octavia's house, I told Fedelma we should come and help."

It took Maarja a moment to identify the expression on Béatrice's face.

The formerly glum Béatrice was beaming.

Would miracles never cease? Maarja glanced around. "Fedelma is here, too?"

"She couldn't come. The poor dear was in Dante's condo when the elevator blew and she thought he'd been killed. When she heard he'd survived, she got down on her knees with her rosary to thank God, and she's barely been up since. She has always been very devout. Meanwhile, I was in British Columbia on a whale-watching tour. I didn't even hear about it until I flew home and by then Dante had sent out his commandment. So I came here and I'm helping!" A mere smile changed Béatrice's face from long, thin, and vacant to something resembling beauty.

In light of her previous laziness, Maarja found her support highly suspicious. "What are you doing to help?" she asked the woman who valued her manicure above all things.

"Actually I'm here to get an assignment from Alex. I need a new task!" Béatrice beamed some more.

"You finished the tortilla roll-ups already?" Alex was clearly impressed. "You can either clean the silver or prepare another appetizer."

"Not the silver!" Béatrice's moue made her look more like her old vapid self. Then she ruined Maarja's condemnation by saying, "The cleaner is bad for me and bad for the environment. Instead, shall I make my famous snickerdoodles?"

"Sure! Snickerdoodles are my favorite." Alex smiled as Béatrice headed for the kitchen, then stared hard at Maarja. "Why do you have that expression on your face?"

"What is she really doing here?" Maarja ground out.

"She told you. She got here, introduced herself, rolled up her sleeves, and went to work."

"Work. Really." All Maarja could remember was Béatrice taking advantage of Mrs. Arundel's generosity. "Isn't she afraid she's going to break a nail?"

"Maarja!" Alex sounded shocked. "What's wrong with you? She's done a lot, *and* she takes special care of me and Mom."

"She's a screamer."

"Hasn't screamed once," Alex snapped.

"Fine. But—" Seeing Alex's indignation at what she considered Maarja's unreasonable prejudice, Maarja said, "Fine." Which meant, *Fine, but I'm going to keep my eye on her.* Because Béatrice was on the list of possible villains, and Maarja didn't believe she could have a personality transplant so soon after Mrs. Arundel's death.

Dante arrived leading Octavia with her hand on his arm. Both were radiating satisfaction.

"Dante, the dear boy, listened to reason," Octavia said triumphantly, "and the wedding party will be dressed in medieval garb and the bride and groom will be in a traditional suit and gown."

Dante began, "Octavia, the dear girl—"

Octavia laughed.

"—has graciously agreed to allow Maarja to wear the antique white lace veil that came down from my mother's family, with a wreath of fresh orange blossoms from the tree in the backyard." He slid his arm around Octavia's shoulder. "She'll make the wreath herself."

Maarja took her mother's hand and kissed it. "Thank you, Mom."

Octavia hugged her. "I'm so glad one of my girls is settling down with her true and loving mate! Of course, you two are so different, you're going to need to delve deep within yourselves to work through the next seventy-five years together!"

"Yes, but we're both so stubborn we won't give up." Dante met Maarja's eyes. "Isn't that correct, beloved?"

"I'm not stubborn," she told him, "I'm just always right."

"She means yes," he told Octavia.

"I know what she means," Octavia replied, eyes twinkling. She lifted her head and sniffed. "Someone's making something with cinnamon. I'll have to go check that out!"

"On the way, tell Mr. Nyugen to stop that kid from hanging on the chandelier in the dining room. That old ceiling could come down." As if Alex's words were magic, plaster began to rain down and the little girl jumped to the floor, crying, rolled, and came to her feet like the green belt she was, and pandemonium reigned.

Octavia clucked and hurried toward the commotion.

Dante, Maarja was surprised to see, smiled faintly as he watched what looked like mass confusion. When she lifted her eyebrows at him, he said, "When Mère and I visited her family in France, it was absolute chaos all the time. Just like this. It was so different from home. I loved it. I always said when I grew up and had a family, it would be loud, loose, and happy."

Of course, his words touched her tender heart. "How long since you visited?"

"Not since the explosion that killed Benoit. After we're married, I'll take you and Mère—" He snapped his mouth closed.

Even more touched, Maarja realized he'd relaxed enough to forget he could no longer talk about his mother as if she still existed on this earth.

Even Alex felt for him, for she patted his arm. "Maarja, I put you in your old room. I'm sleeping downstairs with Mom because I still need help, so Dante, I put you in my bedroom. It's a twin bed. You're going to hang over the end, but I'm sure that's good for your character."

Maarja waited for Dante to object, to demand they share a bedroom, but he nodded. "I'm going to need somewhere fairly quiet to park myself with my computer and phone so I can get this wedding ball rolling."

Alex gestured at the piles of paper, the pens, the cell phone, the computer, the tablet. "What do you think I'm doing here? Coloring with my crayons?"

Maarja waited, smirking.

In surprising diplomacy, Dante said, "You're taking care of the thousand and one things that precede a wedding. I'll take care of the big wedding prep stuff and I've got some business issues that need to be dealt with." He nodded at Saint Rees when he appeared out of the crowd wearing white overalls.

Alex observed the byplay. "Ah. That explains why the Saint is here. I had wondered." Leaning forward, she asked, "Are you going to keep Maarja safe?"

He leaned into Alex's face. "If I have to fling myself in front of a bullet or swallow the poison meant for her, she will be safe."

"Okay, then," Alex said. "You have my blessing."

Dante accepted with a respectful bow.

The whole thing was getting ridiculous. Blessings and bows, knife fights, and rituals. Ancient feuds cherished in the modern world, and a single chance to heal the breach that had taken so many lives. All unthinking, Maarja put her hand on her belly and for the first time consciously considered the possibility of a baby. When she met Dante, her whole life changed. If she got pregnant, it would change again. Nothing would ever be the same, and in a moment of self-doubt, she wondered how she would face so many challenges.

She didn't see her sister and the man who had helped her create her possible offspring observe her and draw their own conclusions.

When she came back to herself, Alex and Dante were fighting about whether or not Alex, as maid of honor, would be seated during the ceremony or lean on a staff as part of the wizarding/ medieval ceremony.

Maarja interceded. She would have her way in one thing, at least. "Alex will stand and use the staff, as will your best man. Who is…?"

"Best men. Nate and Connor," Dante confirmed.

Maarja continued, "We'll make our vows brief, succinct, and to the point. Won't we?"

"I can do that." Dante gripped her hands and pulled her to her feet. "Although possibly not without the use of Old English four-letter words."

"Like what?" Alex was puzzled. "Why would you swear at your own wedding?"

"Because when Maarja's beside me, I can think of only one thing, and that's—"

Maarja put her hand on his mouth.

"Oh." Alex ran her gaze over him and laughed. "Lucky Maarja."

CHAPTER 46

As they climbed the stairs, Maarja asked Dante, "How come you're okay with separate bedrooms?"

He carried their luggage and grimaced at the question. "Your mom came at me from the angle of if I want a traditional wedding, I should behave like a traditional bridegroom and spend my nights in miserable horniness."

"My mom said *that*?"

"Not exactly that, but based on that logic, I did promise I wouldn't fuck you before the wedding day."

"You said *that*?"

"Not in so many words," he allowed. "Not fuck. I may have used a euphemism."

"I didn't know you knew any euphemisms."

One step from the top, he stopped climbing, placed their bags on the landing, and when she turned to face him, he wrapped his arm around her waist, pulled her close, and kissed her, a deep marvelous, sexy kiss that made her press against him hard enough to meld into his bones. When he slowly pulled away, a healthy amount of applause from below made her glare at him. He murmured, "I know so much more than I've shown you; you don't need to worry about my vocabulary. It's your vocabulary that's going to expand." His gaze slid to her belly. "Among other things."

The question popped out of her mouth as if she'd been thinking it all along. "What if I'm not pregnant? What if I'm infertile?"

The man looked astonished, as if the idea itself couldn't be conceived. "It's a little early to worry about that."

"No. It's not too early." She gestured down at the people still smiling up at them, and the people who had returned to their tasks. "It's actually very late. We're getting legally married in two days. If I'm not pregnant, if I can't conceive, if I don't want to have children, what is your reaction? For all that you believe we're destined by fate to end this stupid-ass vendetta—"

His mouth quirked. "What do you really think of the feud, Maarja?"

"We live a modern life in modern times. All of this—" she gestured around "—is tangible. We don't *have* to get married if I'm pregnant. We don't *have* to have babies if we get married." Reality bubbled out of her, a reality beyond family and ancient grudges and an imagined homage to their star-crossed destiny. "What do you want, Dante? Do you want me, or simply our progeny for the peace they provide?"

He truly seemed dumbstruck by her outburst. Dante without words—and how rare was that?

His lack of response gave her the impetus to pick up her suitcase and walk around him toward her room. "Let me know when you figure it out. We can trap a threat without going through with the ceremony. We. Don't have. To get married." She slammed the door behind her, not because she was angry, but because she wanted to provide an exclamation point for her statement.

Somebody had to say it.

They both needed to know.

By late afternoon Nate had arrived and taken up his station in front of the dining room where Dante worked behind closed pocket doors.

A barrage of gifts arrived at regular intervals, gifts that were promptly removed from the premises, inventoried, x-rayed, and examined by bomb-sniffing dogs.

Not that anyone was suspicious.

Workmen swarmed the house, scraping, painting, replacing old siding and old plaster, trimming trees, and planting flowers.

Octavia sought Maarja, caught her at Alex's desk, and demanded, "Why are there so many hammers? And saws. I can smell new paint. And solvent! I heard someone in the backyard discussing the fountain. I don't have a fountain! Caterers in the kitchen talking about new appliances! What is Dante doing?"

Alex intervened. "Mom, I'd say that he's being a good guy, but that doesn't seem his flavor. I suspect it's prep for the wedding."

Octavia swung on her. "It's a backyard ceremony, not a royal gala!"

"Actually," Maarja said, "in Dante's circle, he is a kind of royalty."

"The killer kind," Alex mumbled.

"When he's done, I'm not going to know my house!" Octavia wailed.

Maarja didn't really want to go and see if Dante would grant her an audience. Not after this morning's stairway confrontation. But—"I'll talk to him, remind him who you are, make sure he understands there are restrictions." Although when Dante intended to do something he believed needed to be done and would improve a life, Maarja didn't expect him to pay attention.

Nate stood before Dante's makeshift office, arms crossed.

From inside she heard a man shouting.

Nate looked over the top of her head and spoke a single word, "No." As if she'd asked to enter.

The voice was muffled, but not enough to stop her from hearing, "...You crazy?...Can't go through with this...Already upset the enemies!...Lost your mother, lost your mind...Shit show! A woman! A piece of...Suspect!...Do you know what you're inviting?..."

Dante spoke in a soothing tone, but she couldn't make out the words.

Nearby, she heard someone whimper. Béatrice stood against the wall, watching the door and wringing her hands. She looked a little like the Béatrice Maarja had first met: pale, hunched, with a pinched mouth that had never seen a smile. Yet she'd seemed so different here, at Octavia's house, in this safe, busy environment.

Well, of course. Béatrice shut down in the face of adversity. Maarja had made unkind judgments about her and about Mrs. Arundel for tolerating Béatrice. Mrs. Arundel had seen what Maarja hadn't bothered to see; away from…away from constant fear of fire, explosion, pain, and death, a different Béatrice lived a different life, a whole life.

From inside the office, they heard another shout, clearly a condemnation.

Béatrice cringed and whimpered again.

Behind Nate, the door was flung open and Cousin Jack, San Francisco police detective, stepped out. His red face and wild eyes displayed his mood only too well. He caught sight of Maarja, stalked over, and, with his hand open, straining and cupped like a claw, reached for her.

Nate caught his wrist. "No sir, Jack. Not on my watch."

The whole house full of neighbors, family, and hired workers stood very still and watched the scene from a distance. No one wanted to interfere. No one wanted to attract attention. Everyone knew the Arundel reputation and in this part of town everyone had too much experience dodging bullets.

Jack drew a long breath. "I'm fine." He tossed his wrist and when Nate let him go, he pointed his finger in Maarja's face. "*You*. Should have never. Been born. *You*. Should have never. Lived. *You're* the ruin of him. Give him what he wants and let him go!"

Maarja thought this guy was demented…and remembering

the lesson she'd just learned from Béatrice, she told herself he was driven by concern for his cousin. Gently she said, "I'm not holding him."

"Then why is he staying?"

She didn't know how to explain when she didn't know herself.

"You've got your teeth into him," Jack accused.

From the office door Dante said, "Jack, it's simple. I'm in love with her."

A gasp came from the front of the foyer.

There Connor held a briefcase to his chest and gaped like a dying fish.

Owen stood beside him, holding two grocery bags full of what looked like flower garlands. "I told you so."

Nate shut the sliding doors, protecting Dante's office privacy.

Jack violently shook his head. "No. Don't tell me you've fallen into that old trap. She's merely a woman. Who can tell one from another?"

Dante viewed his cousin in pity.

"You're too strong for that!" Jack was shouting again. He looked around and, seeing Béatrice, he stalked toward her. "Mother, what are you doing here? I thought all you wanted was to be free of the Arundels. Remember? You said that in the note you left before you waltzed out to your whale-watching in Canada."

Maarja viewed Jack, then Béatrice, then Jack again. His *mother*? Downtrodden, fearful, and depressed Béatrice was his *mother*? By who? By the boyfriend who left her after the explosion that killed Benoit Arundel?

No. By Benoit himself.

In Jack's face she saw the madness and malice of old Benoit, and in Béatrice's cringing fear, she saw a woman who had been cruelly taken and used by Benoit, and who feared her own son for the pain he inflicted.

As Nate had said, *Not on my watch*. She moved swiftly to intercept him, and found herself abruptly halted by Nate's grip on her arm.

Dante moved between Jack and his mother. He didn't say anything. He simply stood there, feet braced, hands at his hips, challenging Jack in his presence and stance.

The moment smelled ripe with the scent of potential bloodshed.

From somewhere in his scarred soul, Jack dug up some semblance of good sense, and with visible effort, he stepped back from the encounter. "I'm leaving, and I'm not coming back. You can use your feeble organization to shit flowers out your ass for the whole world to smell. San Francisco is my home now, and the police force is my family." As if he suddenly realized what he was missing, he groped under his jacket. "Dante, you bastard, give me my service pistol!"

"I'll keep it for now," Dante replied. "Until you've calmed down."

"I won't calm down. *In love.*" Jack snorted. "You'll make us a laughing stock of the business world." As he left, he was weaving, making a wide path, looking for someone to shove aside.

He left without accomplishing his goal.

CHAPTER 47

Only Béatrice's shivering sob broke the stillness in the house.

With a soft word, Maarja freed herself from Nate's grip and hurried to Béatrice's side, but when she tried to put her arm around the white-faced woman, Béatrice shrank back as if Maarja had somehow acquired the patina of heartlessness from her association with the Arundels.

Maarja sort of understood. "Mom," she called.

Even without sight, Octavia had read the situation, for she was already on her way. She slid her arm around Béatrice's shoulders and whispered encouragement as she led her toward the kitchen.

Alex was on her feet, leaning against her desk, white around the lips. She, too, had been too recently involved in violence, and this scene had brought back the horror. "Was that man drunk?"

"No." Dante stared after his cousin. "Something else."

"Meth?" Connor suggested. "It's got to be something aggressive for him to speak to you like that."

Dante grunted, then nodded to Connor and Owen. "Glad you two made it. Any more light on our little financial issue?"

"No," Owen said. "When Connor woke up, we got in the car and I drove. Took us an hour and twenty minutes to go thirty-eight miles. He slept like a baby."

"Those Taylor Swift songs you were singing weren't lullabies!" Connor groused.

"You could have driven!" Owen said.

"I could have!"

Maarja met Dante's gaze. The little tiff had brought a relaxation to the crowd, and slowly movement returned as everyone returned to their tasks.

"And fallen asleep at the wheel! No, thank you!" Owen was clearly cranky.

Dante intervened in the quarrel. "So no?"

The couple stared at him blankly.

He expanded his question. "No more light on our little financial issues?"

"Not the main one." Connor lifted his briefcase. "I'll get on it right away. The good news is, two others have been revealed. One straight-out confession. One finger-pointer who when I advised him I'd be able to trace the money trail, admitted guilt. Before the week is out, I expect a few others to be called to my attention." He smiled with every appearance of real enjoyment. "Good times."

Octavia had returned. She waited for the end of the discussion, introduced herself to Connor and Owen, took them into the kitchen for refreshments, and came back alone. "Owen, the dear boy, observed the state Béatrice is in and assumed control of the kitchen. Tonight he's calling out for pizza and he'll create something for snacks for our worker bees. Connor commandeered a corner of the table and went right to work. What a lovely couple! Dante, I do like your family."

"Wait until you meet the rest of them before you pass judgment," Dante advised.

She laughed. "You can pick your nose but you can't pick your relatives. Words to live by!"

"I do know." His voice was compassionate as he asked, "How is Béatrice?"

Octavia sobered. "She's in such a state. I never imagined a woman could collapse so completely. What in the past has happened to her? Is it what I think?"

"I'm afraid so." He led her to chairs set against the wall, showed her the seat, and sat beside her. Maarja followed. "My father was not a man to admire. Not in any way."

A confirmation of what Maarja had suspected.

"Your father? My poor dear Béatrice!" Octavia turned her face toward the kitchen. "You and Jack seem nothing alike."

"Béatrice collapsed after he impregnated her. She had to be institutionalized, and he bitterly despised her for weakness, for making a fuss over something he considered his right."

Octavia and Maarja shuddered in unison.

Dante continued, "He took the baby away from her, donated a huge sum to an orphanage, and placed Jack in their care."

Maarja ventured a guess. "He dumped Jack because he was afraid his son would inherit her hysteria, and he didn't want it to infect his life?"

Dante nodded, and for Octavia's sake, he said aloud, "You sum it up well. He despised nothing as much as frailty, and frailty in a son could not be borne. It wasn't until after my father was killed and my mother had regained her health that she brought Jack back into the family, and we saw how very much he resembled Benoit."

Maarja's memory flashed with a glimpse of Brat Benoit, he with the golden mane of hair and cold green eyes. "Your father would never have made a scene the way Jack did."

"You remember my father?" Dante asked in surprise.

"Not…really. Only that he sat so still, like a figure frozen in ice. Except for his eyes, and they burned like…" Maarja stared at nothing.

"Like golden coals, alive with the hate that fed his soul," Dante said.

She glanced at him, startled at how well he knew her thoughts.

"Yes. I only looked at him once. I wanted to run, but Mama said…" she closed her eyes "…to stay…" Her eyes snapped open again, and she repeated, "Dante, your father would never have made a scene the way Jack did."

"No." Dante's expression mirrored the one he'd worn as Jack marched out. "Perhaps there's more of Béatrice in him than we realized." But Maarja could tell he doubted that.

Octavia patted his arm to get his attention. "Béatrice is afraid to ask, because it goes against your order as the Arundel leader, but she wants to leave before the wedding. To escape what's coming. She fears…what's coming." She didn't approve of Dante's patriarchal position and she couldn't comprehend, this fierce woman who'd faced so much, why Béatrice feared this plan to out their villain. But Octavia didn't judge Béatrice; she understood not all people were warriors.

Dante granted permission. "Of course, she can go. Perhaps back to British Columbia?"

"She'd like that, I think. She has spoken with such rapture about the whales and the wildlife!" Octavia's face took on a wistful cast. "She describes them so well I can almost see them."

"An Alaskan cruise," Dante decided. "One of the National Geographic cruises. Béatrice will be out of danger, in among people who appreciate what she loves."

Maarja relaxed a tension she didn't realize she felt. Yes. Béatrice would be safe on a ship.

Dante took Octavia's hand. "You look worried. Is everything okay?"

As if he lent her a feeling of safety, Octavia scooched her chair closer to him. "So many people in my house and outside my house! They're all doing things. I didn't hire them, and some of them are taking over the jobs like cleaning up the flower beds, the things my friends and neighbors volunteered to do to prepare for the wedding. Why are they here?"

Maarja liked that, given the chance, Octavia felt comfortable enough to task Dante with her concerns herself.

"If we're going to be ready for the ceremony, we've got to bring in professionals." He was like a boulder that stood against the everlasting crash of the waves, strong and sensible. "Are they assuming too much? Pushing your friends out of the way? I can speak to them."

"No, it's simply that...new appliances, Dante?" Octavia gestured toward the kitchen. "For a wedding?"

"The caterers require the best to create a reception we can all enjoy. Surely you didn't think that when we brought our event to your doorstep, we would expect you and Alex to handle everything by yourselves?" Dante put his arm around her. "What kind of son-in-law would do such a lousy thing?"

Most of them, Maarja thought.

Octavia beamed. "Son-in-law. How lovely! Your family will be absorbed into ours. Now I don't want you to wear yourself out."

"I'm good at delegating, I'm used to being busy, and I know you probably don't like this, but we must have security for the wedding." He used his practical voice. "When dealing with the Arundels, there's no use using temporary measures."

Octavia screwed up her face and began to speak.

He talked over top of her. "When we're married and head off on our honeymoon—"

"Our honeymoon?" Maarja asked.

He met her gaze while he talked to Octavia. "You'll have permanent security in place. Octavia, I'm sad to say, becoming a relative of mine involves some risk. I can't have Maarja worried about you or Alex." Dante had gone into full charming mode. "If you have any other concerns, you're to come to me immediately. Nate will usher you in."

Nate rumbled an agreement.

Octavia said, "Thank you, Dante, that's all very reassuring, and you are certainly full of the blarney."

Maarja grinned. Mom could spot sweet talk when she heard it.

Octavia walked briskly away, then returned to say, "I meant to say, thank you for bringing in such a comprehensive physical therapist for Alex. I hadn't realized how angry she is about Serene and her treachery. She seems to be handling the pain and problems in her body better than her rage. Although…" Octavia paused to think. "I should have remembered." She wandered off, leaving Dante and Maarja watching her.

"You have a great mom," Dante said.

"She is. You had a great mom, too. It's something we have in common." She put a comforting hand on his arm.

He put his hand over hers and walked toward his office.

Nate opened the doors, and as they walked in, he shut them behind them.

She felt like a queen. A queen of…what? A consort of the king of the underworld? "Did you think on what I said?" she asked.

"About whether or not we will have children? Can have children?" He led her to the massively comfortable chair behind his desk and pushed the seat under her butt. "I've thought of little else."

She sat and put her hands on the padded chair arms. She examined the stacks of papers, the computer screens, the pens and keyboards and trackballs. "You get busy when you're thinking."

"Fall down eight times, get up nine."

She liked his philosophy. And his determination. And his thoughtfulness.

"Did you think of what *I* said?" he asked.

"When?"

He tilted his head toward the door. "There. When Jack challenged you."

It's simple. I'm in love with her.

"Yes. I…" She discovered in herself a huge streak of cowardice. She couldn't work up the nerve to say it back to him. She, who had taken a huge hurdle with him, balked at completing the race.

On the other hand, he watched her with a half smile, as if he saw something in her hesitant discomfort and the blush that lit her nose and made her ears hot.

She plunged into a conversation that had nothing to do with fertility or future or...love. "Why are you throwing so many workers into what is a potential crime scene? When every one of them could be an assassin?"

"I consulted with your Saint Rees. He agreed with my plan. He and his crew are watching. Observing." He glanced out the window at the crew trimming the bushes. "We're hoping to lure the killer with the appearance of carelessness. Let him onto the premises among the other laborers. Tempt him by the chance to do the deed early."

"I thought the wedding—"

"Do you imagine I want our wedding to be ruined by a killer?" Dante pushed his face close to hers. "Do you really think I would use you as a front to flush out the son of a bitch who wants to take me down?"

Obviously she wasn't the only one who could ask difficult questions. "I think we do what we have to do."

"Using the wedding is your idea, Maarja."

"If it works, I'm glad for that."

"Remember—we can see the finish line. We won't stop now until it's over."

She slowly nodded, comprehending and yet wanting it all laid out. "If some construction guy points a knife at my throat?"

"Take him down, Maarja." He sat with his hip on his desk, to all appearances relaxed and confident.

The way Dante viewed her... As if he expected her to save herself. To save them both.

She could do that. She had practiced her self-defense moves until she knew them as well as she knew how to breathe.

He continued, "Then we'll be married by your mom the way she wants it to be—all peace and love and forever. That will do for us. That is who we are. We are not enemies. We are lovers until the end of time."

She kept trying to inject modern life and reality into their lives.

Dante kept taking them back to the fogs of myth, the memories of a time before where love created life and justice was won by courage.

She was starting to like his way of looking at life. And him.

From the practical standpoint of getting shot or stabbed or framed, from the moment she ran into the flames to rescue Mrs. Arundel, she had known she'd steered herself into perilous waters.

Yet the physical danger she'd faced was nothing compared to the emotional complications. Her feelings for Dante veered from one extreme to another. He annoyed and attracted her. He exuded menace; people were rightfully afraid of him, yet because of her actions, he'd extended the umbrella of his protection over her. He also believed, apparently in all sincerity, he had a right to her. As if she were a possession he owned.

No. Wait, that wasn't right. As if she was part of him…and he was a part of her.

She had never in her life imagined she would have the courage to be paired with any partner, much less a powerful man who believed in destiny.

Of course, how could she have foreseen that the old fears for her own safety would fail in comparison to the turmoil of emotions that now dominated her mind and heart?

CHAPTER 48

Maarja's clock said 2:11 a.m. when she heard the floorboards squeak and Dante slid into her narrow bed behind her. "It's our wedding day," she whispered. "You promised Mom."

"I promised not until the wedding day." He kept his voice low, too. "Technically that's today. It's after midnight."

"Hm." Splitting hairs, but sure. *"Traditionally—"* she injected a little sarcasm into the word "—you're not supposed to see the bride before the ceremony."

"I can't see you. I can't see my hand in front of my face."

"Fog," she told him in an instructive tone, as if he didn't know. "It happens in the Bay Area."

"That, and most of the streetlights are shot out." He snuggled behind her, wrapped his arms around her waist, made her aware of his nudity and his desire.

She asked, "Did Mr. Diddly-Hump wake you up?"

He made a strangled noise. "Mr. Diddly-Hump? My cock? Where did you hear that?"

"I made it up."

"To pay me back for calling your Miss Tittle-Twat a cunt?"

She grinned into the darkness. "Could be. What do *you* call your banana splitter?"

He came up on one elbow. "My cock. My dick. In my teens,

I called it a woman's best friend, then a girlfriend told me in no uncertain terms that was a vibrator with fresh batteries."

She covered her head with the blankets and giggled as she imagined the young Dante's indignation.

"And…" He hesitated.

She sensed a great secret. "You can tell me," she coaxed.

"I call my cock *Loki*."

"Loki? Like the Norse god?" She groped for an explanation. "Because he's a mischief maker?"

"Because Loki says, 'Love is a dagger, a weapon to be wielded far away or up close. It's beautiful until it makes you bleed.'" The way Dante spoke, all deep dark velvet tones whispered right in her ear…he sent chills down her back.

"That's so…poetic."

"Yes, well, also… Loki's dagger is long, powerful, godlike." His tone changed, became humorous. "When I saw the show, I named it. You're the only person I've ever shared that with."

She slid around to face him and put her arms around his neck. "I won't tell anybody."

"I trust you." Three words that were now, before, forever his true wedding vow.

Using all the skills she learned from him and all the techniques she ever imagined, she kissed him, reveling in his taste, his scent, the knowledge that she held a powerful man and could make him tremble. When she drew back, she whispered, "Did you shut the door?"

"God, yes." He began the long gradual descent of her body, learning her in the dark through touch and taste while she muffled her moans in the pillow she held to her face. When he suckled on her breasts, when he sucked on her clit, when he thrust his strong tongue into her, tears leaked from the corners of her eyes…and when he came up and into her body, and began the leisurely in and out that told her without words that he wanted this pleasure to last…all her senses shut down. There was only the two of them in this bed, skin to skin, breath to breath, dancing to a rhythm only they knew. When at last outside the faintest hint of dawn pierced the fog and climax united them, the glow of *la Bouteille de Flamme* enveloped them, and they inhabited a new world they had created together. Only them. Only forever.

At 5:45, with a great deal of unnecessary smoothing of material, Dante helped Maarja back into her nightgown and reluctantly returned to his own bedroom. He left Maarja staring at the sunrise-embracing fog with a smile. This marriage between them was being performed to keep the peace and to heal an ancient grudge. More important, he told her, they did this to ensure her safety, it was a trap for Dante's enemies, and—hey, it was her idea! Yay, Maarja, for sheer brilliance while facing danger and death!

Yet, although those practical reasons existed, she smiled because she was getting married today. She looked forward to donning the gown Dante had ordered, which she had not yet seen—a light cream, because he'd assured her she could have whatever she wanted as long as it was some variation of a white wedding gown—and his mother's veil with its newly made crown of fragrant orange blossoms. She looked forward to having Alex stand beside her as her maid of honor, holding her wizard's rod, while Octavia performed the ceremony. Maarja felt like a bride, and this marriage felt real. She and Dante could make a go of it. They had emotions, moments, attributes in common no one else could ever have, they had passion, and they had love.

That thought made her breath catch.

Did they have love? In front of everyone, he had said that he loved her. He had proudly declared himself to his cousin/half brother Crazyass Jack. Was it rhetoric to flush out the part of his family who would kill him for such a sentiment? Was it a way to change the target from her to him? So many doubts, yet...

She trusted him, and he said he trusted her. For him to say

such a thing meant something momentous. The poets wouldn't agree, but she thought trust from a man like Dante was worth all the pledges of love from every other man alive today or ever.

The question she had to answer was—did she love him?

Her heart began to thump like a bass drum, as it had when she told Dante she'd killed his father, as it had when she believed she looked on the face of death, and that death wore Dante's features.

Did she love him? If she did, what stopped her from telling him?

Life is brief. From the moment of the explosion that killed her own mother, she'd known that. To hesitate now was a crime. What would he do if she came to him to tell him? Was there any doubt that he would welcome her?

As if to answer her, she heard a creak of the floorboards. She took a calming breath, smiled, and whispered, "Is Loki making mischief?"

When Dante didn't answer, she glanced toward the door where she knew he waited. In that instant she caught the scent of that malice that had invaded her home on the day she found *la Bouteille de Flamme* in her drawer. As the knife slashed down onto the mattress, she rolled in the blankets off the far side of the bed.

The thump onto the floor knocked the breath out of her. She struggled to drag herself out of the blankets, to escape before the knife-wielding assassin could vault over the bed after her. She untangled herself, leaped to her feet—and into a cruel grip that lifted her to her toes.

Somehow a man had made his way to the far side of her bed.

His arm wrapped around her throat.

The point of a knife tucked under her chin.

Jack's icily intent voice spoke in her ear. "Scream, Maarja."

CHAPTER 49

This was not the writhing malice she'd felt reach for her as the knife slashed down. This was Jack, a man so cool in his concentration she felt his grip on her like ice in her veins. Yet something linked him to the masked and camouflaged figure who had stepped back against the wall opposite, a collaboration so ugly Benoit Arundel himself seemed to have risen from his grave.

Jack pressed with enough force for the sharp tip to pierce her skin.

She jerked, trying to get away. "Don't," she whispered. Warm blood slithered down her throat.

In that scarily instructive tone, Jack said, "Maarja, scream. Scream for all you're worth. For years, I've been groomed to kill Dante."

His phrasing caught her attention. "Been groomed? By who?"

"By my mother, of course." He laughed as if he told a great joke.

"I don't believe you." She wanted to shout, but she kept her voice low. In case she survived these next few minutes, she wanted the information only he could give her. "Béatrice doesn't have it in her."

"My mother hides in plain sight. Haven't you realized that's possible? You'd better wise up in a hurry, Maarja, or you'll die young." He mocked her without a trace of mercy. "Oh, wait... too late. You'll die before the sun rises."

She couldn't help it. She looked out the window, wanting to see a lightening in the gloom, but the tendrils of fog clung to the house and shriveled all hope. If she screamed, as he wished, she would bring Dante to be stabbed from behind by...Béatrice? "Béatrice is cruising to Alaska."

"Thank you for that information."

He'd been lying. Fishing for information. She'd been a fool to give it up.

Yet if the figure against the wall was not Béatrice...who was it? Not his mother. Then who? Maarja strained to see that other being in her room—what person had been willing to stab her while she slept?—but in the dim light she could see nothing but a tall figure wearing a mask and cap and dressed in desert camouflage up against the wall beside the door. "What do you hope to accomplish? You and...that person?"

"I'll take control of the Arundels. The moment is now. We know that. Soon everyone will know that." He pronounced each word like a directive. "We'll be feared again. We will be great again."

The knife tip sank a little deeper. "Scream and live another few minutes," Jack said again.

This was not the same man who had publicly thrown a temper tantrum. This was the real man; it hadn't been meth that caused his outburst to Dante, but the need to publicly misdirect his intentions. She remembered how Dante had watched Jack as he left; he had doubted Jack's performance.

Smart man. Had he maintained his vigilance over the last few days? Where was Saint Rees? *Where were Dante's precautions?*

Jack's preternatural calm sent the right message. So did her own swift intelligence.

She was not alone in her home. She drew breath to shriek—

Dante leaped through the door and flooded the room with

white light that blinded her and, by the way he staggered, Jack, too.

Dante's wedding present to Maarja was opportunity. Sightless, and in perfect sequence, she performed the moves her self-defense master had taught her.

Pull your head back. Tuck your chin. Slide it under his elbow.

Left hand: slam his junk with your fist.

Right hand: grab his wrist and twist until his elbow breaks behind him and his grip opens. Catch the knife and—

Jack's elbow cracked, a horrible sound that made her want to vomit.

She took possession of the knife and—

Dante cut the light.

Jack swiveled in a move that too clearly told her he'd had the training to match Dante's—and unsurpassed pain resistance.

She lost her grip, but gained the first vestiges of her sight.

So did Jack, for he grabbed at her again.

She held the knife in both hands, a maneuver designed to make her look like an amateur.

He watched her through cool eyes, so different from his previous behavior. He had been camouflaging his true self, using a feigned reckless rage to hide his true intentions. He intended to hold her hostage—or kill her.

She intended to survive.

Like an amateur, she went easily into his arms and, when he grabbed for the hand with the knife, she punched him in the sternum with her right fist. She used the knife she gripped in her left to shove it up under the soft part between his jaw bones, into the flesh, placing the sharp point into his mouth and sinuses and brain.

Jack's eyes bulged in surprise.

His grip on her loosened.

He gave up his death rattle.

Dante snatched her back against him, leaving his cousin to

crash to the floor. He pulled her toward the door, away from the corpse.

Maarja's knees collapsed, but she shouted, "The other one. Get the other one."

Footsteps tapped as the accomplice fled along the corridor and toward the stairs.

She pushed at Dante. "The other one!"

Dante let her go. He dashed out, following the sound of foot-steps.

She slipped to her knees.

Then—

Alex's shout. Octavia's cry of terror. A slam. A thump. An-other burst of adrenaline brought Maarja to her feet. Grabbing her robe, she raced down the stairs after Dante.

Dante's commanding voice yelled, "Halt!"

A gunshot.

Maarja stopped in her tracks.

Breaking glass.

Dante shouted again, his voice strong, calling for Saint Rees's security force to join the chase. He gave commands and Maarja could breathe again. That gunshot had not injured him.

Yet from the thunder of feet and the yelling outside and in, it was obvious the knife wielder had not been apprehended.

Maarja found Alex and Octavia in the hallway helping each other to stand, and both wore the shocked, dazed expressions of people who had been wakened into a world of unexpected violence. As Maarja assisted them back into Octavia's big bed, she babbled stuff like, "Are you badly hurt? I shouldn't have come home. Let me get ice and a pain reliever. I shouldn't have involved you…"

Octavia interrupted to say, "Shut up, Maarja. This is your home. All we need to make us feel better is a few of the apple fritters from La Patisserie and some hot coffee."

"Really, Maarja, since when won't apple fritters fix all our problems?" Alex teased.

Which made Maarja burst into tears. She crawled on the bed with them, cried and cuddled and gave them the rundown on what had happened upstairs in her bedroom. Amid their exclamations of horror at Jack's intentions and their admiration for Maarja's actions, Alex used her own rolls of gauze that rested on the end table to blot the cut on Maarja's chin and reassured her that she needed only a few stitches.

"A few stitches are of little importance," Octavia decreed.

"She can't see the blood," Alex said to Maarja. "And the pain isn't hers. That's why she's so sanguine. You can cry if you want."

Predictably, Maarja laughed. With tears on her cheeks, she laughed.

Determinedly upbeat Octavia declared, "We were knocked down. You were cut. But the only bad omen we needed to worry about on Maarja's wedding day was the fear that the bride and groom would be married and buried within a few hours. Now due to our own darling Maarja's fighting skills, she's defeated the enemy."

"Someone got away." Maarja wiped her nose on the tissue Alex handed her.

Outside, sirens approached, their wails muffled by the fog.

"We don't know that yet," Octavia said. "They might be captured."

From the doorway, Dante said, "So far, we haven't apprehended him." He strode in, took Maarja's hand, pulled her close, and with gentle fingers tilted her chin. He peeled off the bloody gauze to see what had been done to her, then replaced it. "When I do, they'll pay."

CHAPTER 50

Dante concealed his fury with a kiss pressed to Maarja's fore-head and handed her back into Octavia's and Alex's loving arms. He ran up to Maarja's bedroom. There the coroner and EMTs clustered around Jack's body, doing the stuff they had to do for form's sake.

If it were up to him, Jack would go in a dumpster.

Taking the arm of the EMT in charge, Dante said, "You're needed downstairs."

"Did you find another body?" The name badge said Zion, and he looked as weary as any guy who'd been on duty through the night shift should look.

"Not a body. My woman needs stitches." With one finger, Dante sliced under his chin.

"Not life-threatening?" At Dante's nod, he said, "I can't leave this scene for that!"

"Jack's dead. He doesn't need you." Dante was cold with con-tempt: for Jack, for daring to threaten what was his, and for him-self, for not foreseeing what Jack intended. "He took a knife to my bride, she's bleeding, she needs her wound closed *now*. You do know how to suture, right?"

"I'm an EMT. I'm not officially trained for that. Two hundred miles offshore I won't get in legal trouble, but here—"

"If you know how, I'll make sure you don't get into trouble, legal or otherwise." Dante used his mob-boss voice.

Zion glanced at his people working the murder, spoke to the coroner, and walked with Dante to Octavia's bedroom.

The women wore robes and serious expressions.

Officer Guerrero of the Oakland Police Department, who was (not surprisingly) a friend of Octavia's, had found them and was doing her preliminary questioning. She moved aside to let Zion photograph Maarja's wound, numb the area, and suture it. He grumbled as he worked, complaining that he was a critical care paramedic, not a plastic surgeon, and his sutures were for emergencies, not for a bride on her wedding day.

Officer Guerrero seemed startled to find a homicide at Octavia's home, but not as startled as she might have been that it had been that particular San Francisco cop. Apparently Jack had been making a name for himself around the Bay Area as the guy to avoid.

When Zion finished and Officer Guerrero requested Maarja accompany her to the station for interviews, Dante was prepared to step in. As it turned out, he didn't have to. Octavia coaxed the officer with an account of the wedding that would take place this afternoon and the promise that they'd all be available tomorrow for questioning.

When she got a call there was a shooting on the docks, Officer Guerrero surrendered. "I'm needed elsewhere, so I'll use my judgment and postpone correct procedures." She eyed Dante. "Although if anyone at the station ever discovers I did that for an Arundel, I'll be busted back to patrolman."

"No, you won't." He would make sure of that. He escorted her down to the front door, providing information he knew she would need, and when he returned, Zion had finished and left, and Octavia and Alex were comforting Maarja, pressing an ice bag against her cut, assuring her the bruising could be covered with makeup, at least until after the wedding ceremony.

He felt like he was intruding on a primitive feminine pre-wedding ritual, yet when he caught a glimpse of the bond that united his wife with her chosen family, he relaxed a little more. She was his. She was theirs. That made him theirs, too. He liked that feeling of belonging, and he hated to interrupt their bonding, but when Maarja opened her arms to him, he rushed to hold her against his chest, to rock and comfort her.

Comfort himself, too. That was too close. He'd almost lost her.

He noted that Octavia and Alex stepped out to give them privacy, and he appreciated that, for they had to speak of what had happened.

She'd had to kill. That was an ordeal he'd never intended her to face.

He leaned back, stroked her hair, looked into her face. "You killed Jack."

"I'm not sorry." Her voice trembled.

"It's not easy to take a life." He knew that better than most.

"No. The sound and feel…the blood on my hand…to see life leave his eyes…" She breathed deeply as if she wanted to vomit. "That will live in my nightmares. But, Dante, he held me close, and I *saw* him. Inside him. He was willing to threaten me for the opportunity to kill you. He wanted to murder you first so I would suffer. After that, he meant to use and kill me. All his life, he dreamed of blood and death and pleasure and vengeance." She caressed his cheek. "Dear Dante, I'm so glad I ended him. He was Èrthu Arundel returned to life. Mad with rage against the world that didn't provide him with everything he wanted. Furious with his mother for depriving him of his father. Cruel to his bones."

Holding her, hearing her, he saw with her eyes into the past and to the French lord who had started this vendetta with his warped and vicious malice.

"Besides, better me to kill Jack than you, Dante. I had no

fraternal feelings toward him. You do. I feel the devastation of ending a life, but no guilt. The man deserved to die."

This was not the time to grin—but he did. Her voice had changed, had become brisk with practicality. She would be changed by the morning's events, but her mind wouldn't linger over them. No wonder fate had chosen her for him.

Still in that no-nonsense voice, she said, "I can go forward with this wedding today, if you can."

He put his forehead against hers. "Yes," he breathed. "Please, yes."

CHAPTER 51

Behind him, Dante heard a limping step and the sound of a walker, and Alex cleared her throat.

He turned, and Maarja peeked around him.

Octavia and Alex had returned, and Alex pinned him with a pointed stare. "With all your security measures, how did two killers get in our home undetected?"

As his sister-in-law and the woman who'd been knocked down by an intruder, he acceded her the right to question him. He didn't like it—but he accepted it.

Maarja slipped from his arms and sat on the edge of the mattress. "And did the other one get away?"

Dante looked sharply at her. She sounded a little slurred. But she looked better, less tearful, with more color in her face and a sparkle of interest in her eyes. "He escaped out a window in the…studio?" He didn't know what room he'd been in, but there had been half-painted canvases and tools, pigments and brushes that had been put down and never again picked up.

"Mom's studio," Maarja told him.

"I should clean it out," Octavia said. "I've never been so hopelessly blind that I could convince myself to do it."

"Those wood prints. On the cloth. You have great talent and

vision," Dante told her sincerely. "You must have made quite a name for yourself."

"I was on my way as an artist and a teacher. My husband got jealous and…" She shrugged. "My mistake for accepting less than the best."

"He hurt you?" Dante was outraged.

"Rather badly." Briefly Octavia covered her eyes with her hand. "But Maarja isn't making the same mistake." She was willing to let the intruder question go.

Not so for Alex. "How did they get in? Your cousin whose body the Oakland police are currently removing from Maarja's bedroom? And his accomplice who jumped into our backyard and…vanished?"

"That scene in my office and the foyer was unusual behavior for Jack." Dante had been over the scene so many times in his mind, and now he understood what had niggled at him. "He's controlled, might lose his patience but doesn't lose his temper."

"He was a cop. He had access to drugs." Alex wavered. She'd been pushing herself ever since she'd left the hospital. Today she'd been knocked down, she was worried, and she had a role to play in the wedding.

Dante strode to her side and helped her lower the seat on the walker and seat herself.

"I hate this," she muttered.

"I know." He touched the scar on his face to assure her he had reason.

She nodded in appreciation. "Misery loves company. But… Jack?"

"Jack showed none of the physical signs of drug use. Call me a suspicious bastard, but I watched. Those are difficult to fake. Assuming he was putting on a scene, what was his motive? What was he trying to accomplish by behaving counter to his usual behavior? Since he joined the San Francisco police, he made it clear he'd transferred his loyalty from his family to the force."

Dante perched his hip on Octavia's dresser, and he spoke to the three women with respect, explaining himself without excuse. "I don't ignore my doubts. I didn't like his behavior. I thought it artless, and I didn't believe that. I suggested to Saint Rees that his people keep a light watch, and if Jack appeared, to let him in to make his way to my room. I miscalculated his goal. I thought he would *first* come after me. Instead he used Maarja to get access and take control in the most ruthless move possible."

"You *thought*? You put your confidence in what you thought?" Alex reacted like a snarling dog.

"His accomplice knocked out my bodyguard. Nate was out cold, hit and kicked with such force I'm worried about a concussion. Or worse." Worry pulled at him in all directions, but the fear that his bodyguard had suffered a brain injury was the worst. Nate was one of his people, always there, stolid, silent, supportive—and yes, a suspect. But not. "A second unit of EMTs are with him."

"Not Nate!" Octavia looked so grieved. "He's a good man. Too closed in, of course. But that's his job, and his mother is a horror."

Dante and Maarja exchanged looks.

"How did you get him to talk to you?" Dante asked.

"She was interested," Maarja and Alex said at the same time.

"That's her secret," Alex added.

Maarja nodded. "Everyone talks to Mom."

Dante realized his mistake. He had believed that Nate, who had stoically sacrificed his personal life to preserve Dante's, deserved his privacy. Dante hadn't asked the right questions; why would any man allow himself to be condemned from his earliest days to such a career? Who had set him on such an unwavering path, and why had he never once rebelled? Now Dante realized he was missing a crucial component in solving this mystery, and perhaps Nate would now share his story—but Nate had been knocked unconscious by an unknown assailant. Urgently he asked, "Octavia, do you know who his mother is?"

"Not by name, but the pressure she put on Nate his whole life!"

"Pressure to do what?"

"He didn't say, but she doesn't deserve a son like him." Octavia picked up her phone and texted. "There. I've alerted my prayer group to assist in his recovery; he'll be cradled in love."

"All my life, he's been there. For me. I'm suspicious of him— I'm suspicious of everyone—but when I saw him laid out, his muscles slack, that bruising as if someone had stomped on his face in a fury... He and Connor are supposed to stand up with me, but he is... I don't know if he can be at the wedding today."

Maarja took his hand. "Dante, you're the guy who makes the tough calls—and sometimes...you're wrong."

Alex snorted. "Say it's not so."

Maarja ignored her. "With this new information—what do you see when the pieces next move on the chessboard?"

"I see a reveal at the ceremony today." Dante stood and headed out the door. "Let me call off the hunting dogs. We need to reveal our enemies, and as you suggested, a peaceful, hopeful wedding ceremony should draw them out."

"Should we worry about an explosion?" Octavia asked.

Dante decisively shook his head, then said, "Whoever this is, he wants to make a statement. He wants to be in charge. He must make an appearance."

"Or she," Alex said.

"Or she," he agreed at once. "I have thought... Well, there's no use in wasting time with speculation. We'll find out soon enough."

When he was gone, Maarja turned to her mother and sister. "Every little girl dreams of a white wedding with flowers and friends and family. I get all that and the chance to be the bait in a trap to catch a killer."

"I always knew when you found the right man, he would be unique and wonderful," Mom said.

"He's unique, anyway." Alex was acerbic. "We should cancel this event right now."

"No," Octavia said.

Alex stubbornly continued, "We've all been through a lot and it's a marriage Maarja doesn't have to make."

"You heard Dante about the reveal." Octavia had that stubborn jaw set that her kids knew meant business. "Maarja's idea to bring everyone together was the right plan, we've already proved that, and I refuse to allow a little trauma postpone what will be a marvelous and eternal union."

"Marry in haste, repent at leisure!" Alex retorted. But with Maarja not stepping into the disagreement and Octavia being so adamant, she clearly knew she'd lost this battle.

Maarja touched the bandage on her chin. "I hope the Novocain wears off soon. I've got vows to recite and the back of my tongue is numb."

CHAPTER 52

The fog lingered through the morning, muffling sound and limiting vision, a situation Dante apparently found unsatisfactory for he occasionally paced into the bedroom, muttering, "Great. Just great," at intervals designed to irritate.

Maarja was beyond irritation. The time had arrived. They had the license. Mom would perform the marriage. Alex would lean on her staff and be Maarja's maid of honor. Connor would stand with Dante. And they'd lived through the night.

Now all they had to do was live through the ceremony.

At last Dante managed to irritate Alex enough that she banned him from the house altogether, and Mom and Alex began the barbaric ritual called *dressing the bride.*

Mom told Maarja to lift her arms and close her eyes, and when she did, they dropped the wedding gown over her. The material rustled with a warm, deep sound of wealth. The sleeves slid down and the seam rested on her shoulders. She lowered her arms, and they fastened the rows of buttons at her spine and pushed her over to the mirror where they commanded she look at herself.

Despite her best efforts, she'd been unable to effectively grow out her hair since the explosion. Yet the ruffle of dark red curled slightly as it framed her face, her eyes shone more violet than blue, and she felt exuberant.

"What do you think of the dress?" Alex sounded so excited. "Isn't it gorgeous? Dante picked the velvet so Mom could enjoy the texture, and this tone of white perfectly accents your skin tone!"

Maarja looked down at herself. The flat jeweled bodice pressed against her ribs and lifted her breasts above the sweetheart neckline; the velvet hung in rich folds from her waist and draped into a train that dragged behind her and demanded an entourage of fairies to carry it.

"It's even got pockets!" Alex could barely contain her glee.

"It's perfect," Maarja said and then, "I thought you didn't trust him."

"He's got great taste in clothes." Alex did love good clothes. "I hope he does as well with jewelry."

"Jewelry?" Maarja didn't get it.

Alex pointed at her ring finger. "Have you seen what he got for your wedding ring?"

"No?" She hadn't even considered it. "My God, I didn't get him a ring!"

"Don't worry," Octavia soothed. "He's handled everything else, I'm sure he's handled that, too."

That did not comfort Maarja at all. She was bad at this being-a-bride thing.

"Wait until you see this veil!" Alex placed the orange blossom wreath on Maarja's head like a crown, then draped the long fall of old French lace down over her shoulders and back, and lifted it gracefully so it floated down over the train like winter snow in the Sierras.

"How does she look?" Octavia sounded as excited as Maarja felt.

"So pretty, Mom," Alex said. "She's shining with a glow from within."

"I really am." Maarja supposed she ought to be embarrassed to describe herself with such enthusiasm, but many times she used her vision to provide Octavia with a view of the world and now, looking in the mirror, she could scarcely believe the woman who stared back at her. A smile trembled on her lips. "I'm the most beautiful bride ever."

Octavia sighed in delight, then perked up, always ready to offer advice or...a small paper bag, which she handed to Maarja. "Alex and I—"

Alex interrupted. "It was Mom's idea!"

"*Alex* and I—" Octavia put an emphasis on Alex's name "—decided you should take a moment to discover if a baby is on the way."

Impulsively Maarja crunched the bag in her fist. "If I am, what? Knowing won't change anything." She peeked into the bag at the light green box and felt slightly nauseated. Not morning sickness, she assured herself, just nerves.

Alex wiggled her fingers at Maarja, urging her toward the bathroom. "It is a good idea. If you're not, no big deal, and if you are—"

Maarja dug in her heels. "I don't wanna!"

"It's so unlike you to be a coward." Alex never pulled her punches. "You have to *make à le pipi* before the ceremony, anyway. Just do it."

"Maybe," Maarja grumbled.

"Perhaps you're glowing for more than one reason." Clearly Octavia was in no doubt.

"Maybe," Maarja said again. She did have to go, and unwillingly she took the bag into the bathroom, opened the box, and read the instructions.

It only took a few moments, and she sighed in relief.

Octavia and Alex were right. She was glad to know the truth. Now to figure out how to tell Dante.

CHAPTER 53

From an everybody's-looking-at-me standpoint, taking her first steps down the aisle was nerve-wracking.

Taking her first steps down the aisle aware of the virtual target on her chest and her back was worse. Maarja's bouquet of orange blossoms did not tremble. She kept her chin up, her spine straight, and she smiled. Smiled as if she had not a worry in the world.

Dante used the same posture, but wore a stern expression meant to scare someone.

It was working. Maarja was scared. Just not of him, the most dangerous man in Octavia's backyard. A backyard that had had its grass mowed, its trees trimmed, and bountiful vases and planters of flowers placed in fragrant abundance. New shrubs, tall and short, had been planted in the wide strip of dirt in front of the newly repaired and surrounding wall. The sun had banished the fog, and light glinted through the willow branches and tickled the climbing roses until they emitted their old-fashioned fragrance.

As she walked, a suspicious murmur swept over the Arundels. The vast assortment of family members watched with possible amazement. Maybe horror? Definitely disbelief. After all, she was a Daire, and the only other reason they could imagine for the ceremony was not true; no way she had captured Dante with her beauty.

Dante's forbidding gaze swept the assemblage, and it was as if he had commanded them aloud. With various poses, sneers, and some clear reluctance, the Arundels rose to their feet.

Her unbeauteous lips twitched in amusement.

For all that they were incredulous, on Dante's command, they were by God here for the event.

On the bride's side of the aisle, she saw Mr. Nyugen, the neighbors who weren't hostile to Octavia and the ones who were (but showed up for the free food), the Saint Rees movers who doubled as security, and friends scattered here and there. Maarja's friends gaped in disbelief to see her marrying a guy who had a reputation as a crime boss.

Yep. Lots of disbelief going on here. She understood that.

As the groom, Dante should have been watching Maarja, admiring her beauty, but his gaze skipped across the crowd, watching for any hint of an attack.

Saint Rees, who was to give her away, kept them marching steadily forward, but he, too, observed the gathering.

Maarja had to admit, so did she. She should have her gaze fixed to the dais where Octavia stood under the arch, waiting to marry them. There, Connor stood beside Dante and on the other side Alex waited in her amber velvet gown supporting herself with her wizard's staff.

Owen sat in the front row, next to Nate. Nate's skin looked like parchment, his head was bandaged, and his face was a mass of cuts and bruises. He shouldn't have been out of the hospital. Maarja was almost certain he'd walked out to be here. To protect...who? To face...what?

An elderly couple, married by the way they stood shoulder to shoulder, stood against the wall where they could advantageously view the ceremony. The woman leaned on a walker and wore an old-fashioned hat with a cheek-sweeping pink veil, and the man wore a fedora low over his face.

Because the last weeks and days and night had taught Maarja to view everything and everybody with suspicion, that couple made Maarja suffer a pang of concern. Why weren't they sitting with the rest of the families and friends? Were they deliberately hiding their faces? Were they a danger to her, to Dante, to the others? They might be elderly, but she would never make the mistake of confusing age with weakness and she knew not to underestimate the Arundels.

Another glance made her want to stare at them more closely. Something about them seemed familiar…

She saw Tabitha, her petulant mouth drooping as she watched Maarja walk down the aisle. Petty, yes, but Maarja knew she would always recall and enjoy that incredulous disbelief that Maarja rather than Tabitha had won the prize.

Who from the inner cadre of Arundel administration was missing?

Béatrice was on an Alaskan cruise. At least…Maarja believed she was. She certainly wasn't here.

Maarja didn't see Fedelma. Three days should have given her time to cease thanking God for Dante's survival, get up off her knees, and hie her butt down here to witness the wedding.

Both women were tall. If they were here, she'd spot them.

She didn't see Andere, and he matched Dante in height. He, too, should be clearly visible.

Too many prime suspects were nowhere in sight, and this morning someone had escaped from Octavia's home and somewhere they were lying in wait for their chance. Had they somehow managed to conceal themselves and a weapon among the decorations? Had they forced their way into a neighbor's house and even now watched from an upstairs window?

She glanced up and around.

Saint Rees observed and leaned close. "The neighbors were glad to let us place guards in their homes."

She nodded, then glanced at the people who attended and the guards who lurked around the perimeter.

Truth be told, she still suspected Connor, although why would he have waited so long to kill her and Dante and take control?

The answer was easy enough. Because on the dais, he could make an unforgettable exhibition of Dante's assassination and her own bloody death, proclaim himself victor, vanquisher of the final Daire, and head of the Arundel crime family.

In all the history of all the brides that had ever walked down an aisle, had one ever been as watchful and wary as she?

Maarja and Saint Rees reached the base of the dais. As she handed off her bouquet to Alex, she met her sister's gaze. Somehow she'd thought Alex would be mirthful, amused to see Maarja marrying after so many years of celibacy. Instead she smiled with tears in her eyes and nodded.

Wow. Approval from Alex. Maarja never expected that.

Dante stretched out his hand and Saint Rees placed her hand in his.

Right. Traditional.

Octavia gestured them up onto the first low step. They'd agreed that would be best so everyone could see Octavia over Dante's broad shoulders.

Dante had been unable to convince her she didn't want to wear her wizard's costume, so he'd had it copied in rich black and gold velvet with a ruff that lent her an imposing and queenly presence. From somewhere he'd procured a heavy scepter that appeared to be solid gold with a jewel at the end, which looked like a cabochon ruby.

Maarja hoped it wasn't actual gold and ruby, and hoped more her visually impaired mother wouldn't have to try to bash some-one over the head with it. Although by the way Octavia caressed the scepter in her arms, she appeared to be having pleasant thoughts about the idea.

In her most stern leader-of-the-neighborhood-association voice, Octavia told everyone to silence their phones. Then, when the scrabble to obey had calmed, in her most warm old-hippie tone, she welcomed the bride and groom, their families and friends, the city of Oakland, the whole Bay Area, the state of California, the United States of America, the oceans and countries around it... By the time she got to the whole universe, and invited every tree and stone and creature to witness this happy occasion, Maarja could only imagine what was happening behind her. Among her side of the aisle, most people had known exactly how the ceremony would start. They would be sanguine and no doubt amused at the reactions from the Arundel side of the aisle. Now that she thought about it, for all their criminal activity, the Arundels were a bunch of boring stiff-necked conformists.

She glanced at Dante, expecting to see him still glancing around, seeking the one that would harm them, or maybe looking patient with Octavia, but he watched Mom intently and respectfully. As conformists went, he knew what was important.

Maarja liked that. She liked him. He could be one scary asshole, but this powerful man was more than that. He appreciated her humor, honored her makeshift family, protected all the ones loyal to him, worshipped her body, and freely admitted he loved her.

So when Octavia invited Maarja to share the vows she had prepared, she faced Dante and wondered how he would behave when she made her vows. Would he smile in triumph because he believed she was his? Would he frown because she'd fought him for so long? Would he be tender or gleeful or masterful?

She couldn't tell what he felt, only that he watched her with such intensity she felt as if she were speaking to his soul.

She spoke clearly. "This morning, very early...you remember—"

His mouth twitched the tiniest bit.

"—I wanted to tell you what was in my heart. I was frightened of so much emotion spilling out of me and...I've been a coward. When I was four years old, terror arrived, and I discovered life is brief and uncertain and to *not* speak is to miss an opportunity that might never be given again and leave the words—"

Dante's focus shifted away from her, behind and over her right-hand shoulder.

"—unspoken." She immediately comprehended what his sudden attention adjustment ordained, and she both cut her vows short and rushed her words. "I say them now and please listen for one more second."

He glanced back at her, and nodded curtly.

"I love you." There. She'd said it! Out loud. In front of everyone.

"I love you, too." He'd said it out loud in front of everyone, too, as clearly as he'd said it the first time. Now he reached out and pulled her to his side, and as he held her hand, she felt him slip something cool on her ring finger.

She glanced down.

A plain gold band. Of course. Tradition.

Alex would be so disappointed.

She looked up to face—Fedelma.

No longer on her knees praying, if she had ever been. No longer wearing a matronly dress that expressed without words her desire to serve.

This woman stood where she'd hidden herself, in the sniper pit she, or Jack, or someone who labored in the gardening crew, had dug in the soft dirt between two of the new shrubs. Fedelma wore camouflage fatigues that shed dirt and leaves. Grime and blood smeared her face. And she held a rifle steadily against her shoulder—pointed at Maarja.

CHAPTER 54

With the speed of a fullback, Nate got to his feet. "No, Mother! I told you no! Don't do this!"

Dante's fingers spontaneously compressed Maarja's.

"Fuck me a-running." Behind them, Connor sounded shocked.

How amazing the human brain could be. Maarja faced the round black hole of a rifle pointed at her chest. She absorbed a revelation she'd never imagined. She heard gasps, then the clatter of folding chairs as everyone on the Arundel side flung themselves to the ground, and, a few moments later, everyone on the bride's side (her side) realized the implications and followed suit.

She observed that the members of Saint Rees's team remained on their feet, and they began to move in a prearranged pattern to remove Fedelma.

Yet in a split second, her mind ran through the possibilities and certainties.

Four sons: Dante, Nate, Connor, Jack.

Three mothers: Raine, Béatrice, Fedelma.

One father: Brat Benoit Arundel.

When Benoit decided he would wed a woman to produce an heir, he'd first chosen to take a woman who could carry a boy who could be trained to be his heir's bodyguard. He wanted someone who could be as ruthless and determined to advance the Arundel name as he was, as he would train his heir to be. What followed was logical to him. The son to protect his heir would carry cruel Arundel genes from both parents.

He'd forced himself on his cousin Béatrice. She had been a young innocent woman. She'd collapsed, mentally unable to deal with his uncaring rape. For that, he scorned her and the son he'd conceived with her.

That was Jack. He was warped. He was dead. Scrub him off the face of the earth.

Benoit hadn't given up. After Béatrice's collapse and even before Jack was born, he turned to his cousin Fedelma. Or she offered herself to him. Because here she was, and Nate was born. Benoit took the boy away to train him, then used Fedelma to make Connor.

After his failure with Jack, Benoit was hedging his bets, making sons rapidly on a woman who was unbalanced, ambitious, and unhealed from the first birth.

Who cared? He didn't.

Within months and weeks, Raine had given birth to Dante, the legitimate Arundel heir.

Then the glitch in Benoit's scheme was exposed.

Fedelma, as ambitious and as merciless as Benoit, had no intention of allowing either of her sons to be nothing more than a bodyguard and companion for Dante. She was an Arundel. She had been given to another man, a member of the organization. She wanted the top man. She wanted Benoit, and she had aspirations.

Like Dante, like Connor, Maarja had assumed Nate's mother to be an unknown, lost in time, disposed of or perhaps a runaway. But no. Nate's mother was here, now, at Maarja's wedding, and like the Arundels of the past ages, she was willing to kill. She *wanted* to kill.

Fedelma took a tall step out of the pit and onto the level ground. She swept the rifle around, and the members of Saint

Rees's team halted where they stood. "Dante, call them off," she commanded. "No lackey is going to sabotage me."

"Leave her alone." Dante spoke to Saint Rees. "This is a family matter."

Saint Rees gestured.

His team backed away.

"I'm glad you see it that way, *boy*." Fedelma gladly pointed her rifle at Nate. She hated him, her son. She hated everyone here. Her eyes, so much like Dante's, glowed gold with a fanatical zeal. She wanted, she intended, to end this day in blood. "Ungrateful son. Always you deny your duty to me! I should shoot you where you stand."

Nate stood with his feet planted on the lawn, "You already knocked me out and kicked me with such joy I suffer and the doctors fear for me. Why stop at shooting?"

"When I kicked you, I disciplined you as I should have done more, and sooner. You. And him." She flicked a hand and a glance of scorn at Connor and Owen as they moved swiftly to take Octavia and Alex off to the side, away from the line of fire. "My sons. The sons of the great Benoit Arundel. Like the Arundels of the past, your father was the god of death, fear, and cruelty. Neither of you are worthy of the blood that flows in your veins. Only Jack. Only he had the ambitions and the wiliness to take the place as the leader of this generation, and he wasn't even the son of my loins."

Dante spoke right to her. "You should consider that *you're* the weak link."

"I am. I know it." She smiled, and the effect was horrible. Her broken teeth, her bloody mouth, the flakes of dirt drying on her skin. The jump through the window glass and the landing on the ground had been obviously painful and devastating, and hiding in the pit gave her the appearance of an oozing monster. "All these years of scheming, for nothing. It ends today. I die today." For one moment her rifle swung wildly.

Screams erupted from the gathering. A scattering of people panicked and ran for the house.

Fedelma ignored them and pointed her rifle at Maarja. "But I won't kill an Arundel. I won't slaughter my own blood. I'll kill *her* and stop this marital abomination."

Maarja spoke right to the atrocity the Arundel heritage had created. "You can't kill me. I carry the Arundel heir."

The gasp from the assemblage almost lifted the orange blossoms from Maarja's head.

Dante gripped her hand and, as if Fedelma wasn't there and pointing a rifle at them, looked Maarja full in the face. "Truly?"

"Yes." She brought the peed-on and washed stick out of her skirt pocket and waved it. She nodded at the same time, as if she needed all the ways to assure him. "I don't know how it works, I'll have to look it up, because I really did have a period. It was weird, bleeding and wild emotions."

He took the stick from her and stared at it as if a baby was some unexpected miracle when in fact, all along he'd been insisting on its existence.

Maybe he wasn't as certain and as powerful as he proclaimed.

She'd knocked him for a loop.

And she was nuts for being thrilled at a moment like this.

"Hey!" Fedelma yelled, wild, impatient, unable to believe the all-important Dante Arundel could ignore her in her big moment. "I'm here and ready to kill...someone!"

From the wall, a full-throated woman's voice said, "Then kill me, Fedelma."

Maarja recognized that voice. She turned to see...Raine Arundel tossing her veiled hat aside and, leaning on her walker, stepping away from the wall to confront the woman who had served her for so many years. And deceived her for so many years.

CHAPTER 55

Maarja wanted to rush to Raine and hug her. To dance and laugh with the joy of a life returned to the earth. To congratulate her for being on her feet and ask how it was possible.

Instead she looked, terrified, between Fedelma and Raine.

The breeze waved the willow branches. An incongruously chirping bird broke the utter silence. No one moved or breathed.

"Maarja and Dante, please step aside." Raine stood upright, barely touching her walker, laser gaze focused on Fedelma. "This isn't your fight anymore."

Dante took Maarja's arm and walked with her up onto the dais. Maarja thought he'd leave her there, return to the battle, but he stood shoulder to shoulder with her and watched the drama. She glanced at him and nodded in satisfaction.

In her ear, he said softly, "So that's where Andere disappeared to."

For the first time, Maarja took note of the man who stood beside and slightly behind Raine. Andere, the butler with the lemon drops, the one who had dug Raine out of the rubble of the first explosion, the man Dante labeled as descended from a long line of Arundel sycophants. "That explains a lot," she murmured.

"Doesn't it?" Dante answered in the same tone.

"Did you think I didn't know about you fornicating with my husband?" Raine asked Fedelma. "Did you think Benoit would deign to hide his sexual activities from his wife? He wanted to make me miserable. I didn't care about him, and he wanted to make me jealous. He bragged about using you to make a bodyguard for my son."

"He didn't use me. I offered myself!" Apparently a point of honor to Fedelma.

"He laughed at you for being offended that you hadn't been chosen as his bride. He wanted a virgin and an aristocrat, and you didn't fit in either case." As Raine deflated Fedelma's confidence, she smiled in bitter triumph. "He also didn't appreciate that you'd killed your husband. Lambert was one of his trusted officers."

"He didn't know that!"

"He did. If there was anything to do with slimy, underhanded tactics, Benoit knew all about them."

Maarja softly said, "It's like the shootout at the O.K. Corral...with geezers."

"Female geezers," Dante agreed, "and all the scarier for that."

"He should have chosen me," Fedelma cried. "He wanted to breed children with the superior Arundel genes. I can scheme. I can influence. I was fertile. I would have stood beside him and served him, and the day would have come—"

"Yes. He believed he could breed the son he wanted with the proper breeding cow." Raine used the term in scorn and derision. "If he'd had a sister, he would have fucked her to get the results he wanted. I was Benoit's first cousin, and the next best thing. With me, he intended to breed an Arundel even greater than himself."

The rifle zoomed in on Dante, standing calmly, shoulders relaxed, hands loose. "Your son is as weak as mine. As Nate. As Connor."

"My son is The Arundel." Raine projected her voice like God

giving his commandments to Moses. "Fedelma, Dante is *your* commander. You defy him with your actions. Put down your weapon, and take your punishment."

Fedelma's face contorted. Her rifle swung with swift surety toward Maarja. The barrel paused, steadied… Her eyes narrowed. Her finger tightened on the trigger.

Nate sprang toward her.

"Mother, no!" Connor shouted.

In that split second, Maarja wanted to drop, wanted to run, wanted to do as Dante did, to bravely stand and defy this madness.

Beside her, there was a blur of motion.

A shot rang out. Or was it two?

Fedelma flung out her arms. Her chest exploded. The rifle fell, unfired. She slammed backward and disappeared into the pit that had hidden her since her escape from the house.

Screams erupted all over the backyard.

Maarja gasped, and gasped again, as if the air was life and rescue and sustenance. She looked around to see Raine, handing her pistol to Andere, who holstered it.

Dante performed one of his magic tricks and whatever he held disappeared somewhere on his body. A pistol? Of course. He wouldn't come to his own wedding unarmed. Turning to Connor, he said, "Check on that, would you?"

Connor nodded, tight-lipped and pale. If he was moved by his mother's death, he showed no sign.

Nate sat down hard, but he wasn't tearful, simply weary and injured.

On Maarja's side of the aisle, someone sobbed in fear and panic. Someone said, "Is that woman dead?" in tones of such horror Maarja wanted to snap out a few pithy words like, *Focus!* and *Do you not recognize that this bitch caused this whole murderous kerfuffle?*

Looking as he had looked when she first saw him, Dante pro-

duced *la Bouteille de Flamme* from somewhere on his person—
damn, he was good with those magic tricks—and held it over
his head and hers. In a controlled voice that somehow reached to
the edge of the gathering, he said, "Arundel blood bought this
bottle. Daire courage retained the stopper. Maarja and I united
them. Do you know what that means?"

The groom's side of the aisle were sullenly picking themselves
up off the ground, pretending to be busy, avoiding his eyes.

Dante exuded power and darkness. *"Do you?"*

People stopped clattering the chairs and stood still. Nods and
a few gave voice to a subdued, "Yes."

He swept them with a dark gaze. "Do you who insist on tradition and the ancient feud dare to dispute the reality of this
omen? Come forth and test the strength of this bond. Come to
me and test the strength of the seal!"

One of the teenagers swaggered forward, smirking, challenging him. "I'll do it."

Dante gestured her forward. "When you do, Lucy, when
you find it is sealed, you'll kiss Maarja's wedding ring and bless
her for what she has brought us in peace and future prosperity."

Lucy stopped in her tracks.

Dante was projecting now, the guy in charge who challenged
anyone to defy him. "Maarja brings us at last into the New
World, the land of milk and honey where peace shall reign and
those who wish for dissonance will fade into a world not associated with the Arundel lords. Those who wish for death, for
crime, for war, that is your privilege—but remember, once you
have stepped from beneath the umbrella that I hold to protect
my kin, you can do whatever you wish, but the Arundel shield
is no longer yours." His eyes glowed with gold molten lava and
dark hard rock.

The Arundel side of the aisle stared as if stricken.

The Maarja side of the aisle stared as if they didn't quite get it, but they were pretty sure they were accessories to some scary cosmic event.

Dante took Maarja's ringed hand in his and held it over his head. "Here I have placed the ring of peace. Eat, drink, dance. Pay homage or not. That is your choice. If you wish to handle your life without the restrictions I impose and demand, as is my right as the leader of the Arundel family...leave now. Follow Fedelma and Jack into oblivion." His voice dropped an octave, a threatening tone that sounded bearlike in its intensity. "Follow them to hell."

Maarja looked over the stricken and indecisive Arundels, and she had to have her say. "He's right, you know. You can go to hell in your own way." She met the gaze of the smart-ass Arundel teen. "Some of you will. Please be prepared for the consequences. We *have* united the bottle and the stopper. We *are* married. We *are* producing the next Arundel baby—and she will be powerful. She will be a kicking, screaming, demanding brat of a child who makes you laugh as her father and I wring our hands in despair." She put her hand on her belly. "If you wish to stay and laugh, and be a part of our conjoined families, do so. But do it with a whole heart." She swept the upturned faces with her gaze. "The next person who wishes to play the role of Fedelma—" she gestured toward Connor, who dragged the body onto the lawn "—will answer to me. I am not so kind in my killings. If you don't believe me, you can ask Jack."

"Jack's dead," Lucy snarked.

"Yes." Maarja smiled in her best imitation of Dante's shark smile, and she pointed at the bruised and stitched wound under her jaw. "By my hand." She offered her ring to the teen. "Do you want to be the first?"

Lucy hesitated. That was not the role she'd envisioned for herself in this scene. But with every eye on her, she had to make a decision, and she made the wise one. She came forward, took

Maarja's hand, bowed over it, and kissed the ring. For good measure, she took Dante's hand and kissed his ring, too.

Behind her, an orderly line of Arundels formed, although predictably, a few hung back.

Lucy started away, but Dante called her back. He handed her the bottle. "Test the seal," he challenged.

She did, gingerly at first, then with more vigor. "Fuck! How'd you get it on there so tight?"

Everyone in the family used that word, and flagrantly. Mentally, Maarja dug in her heels. Darned if she was going to learn!

Dante intoned, "The fires of love and fate fused them into one."

"This would be a great video game!" Lucy changed from a smart-ass to a smart kid. "Okay if I design that, Cousin Dante?"

"Go for it, kid," he said.

The tension in the backyard perceptibly relaxed.

The line, which had rapidly become a reception line, moved forward, with hand-shaking, congratulations, some laughter, and a lot of ring-kissing.

"I'm getting sick of having my hand slobbered on," Maarja muttered to Dante.

"Not a problem. We're out of here." He gave her the dark and golden-eyed Arundel stare. "Law enforcement has arrived on the scene."

CHAPTER 56

Officer Guerrero finished taking statements from Dante and Maarja, Connor and Nate, Raine and Andere, and was now packing her briefcase. She looked around them, seated at the large conference table in the dining room/Dante's office, then focused on Octavia and Alex. "Mrs. Maldovitch, the Oakland police see a lot of violence, but this is the first time I've dealt with two killings in one house on one wedding day."

"And one resurrection!" Octavia said brightly. "I know Mrs. Arundel—"

"Call me Raine, dear," Mrs. Arundel said.

Octavia switched smoothly. "Raine and I will be best friends. I like a woman who's prepared to take care of herself and her family!"

The officer replied carefully, diplomatically, "We in the force frown on people handling potential murder with their own weapons, but—yes, she certainly reacted quickly and with great precision. Fedelma Arundel was shot through the heart. Twice."

Maarja knew Raine had shot only once. Dante had also shot. When the police department performed the autopsy, *if* they performed the autopsy (the department was woefully underfunded), bullets from different pistols would be revealed. She didn't feel

obligated to point that out, or that in this crowd Fedelma had
been lucky to be shot only twice.

Octavia took Officer Guerrero's hand. "Won't you join us as
we celebrate this marvelous, healing marriage? We're dancing
and drinking and eating, and you deserve a happy time after
your duties today."

"Unfortunately, I'm on duty, but..." Officer Guerrero looked
out into the backyard where the folding chairs had been cleared
away, a temporary dance floor laid down, fairy lights lit the
scene, and a battered rock band played a barrage of music from
the World War II years all the way to the current war. "I'm off
at ten."

"We'll see you then." Octavia smiled until she heard the door
shut, then sagged in her chair. In a tone of reproach, she said,
"Maarja, you used to be the easy child!"

"Ha!" Alex gloated. "I'm Mom's favorite now!"

"You were always my favorite, dear. As are Maarja, Chrispin,
and Emma." Octavia turned to Nate as if she could see him.
"I'd love to dance while I'm spry enough."

He rose easily to his feet, and Maarja noted that after the crisis today, he seemed to have shed injuries, years, and cares. He
put Octavia's hand on his arm and led her out to the sounds of
music and laughter.

Alex viewed the table from beneath lowered lashes, and recognized it was time to make an exit. "I don't think I can dance,
but I can eat." She turned to Owen and Connor. "Maybe you
could help me to the buffet before the neighbors and the Arundels come to blows over the cheesecake."

Before she could finish the sentence, the two guys were on
their feet and helping her out of her chair.

That left Dante and Maarja alone at the table with Raine
and Andere.

Maarja glanced at Dante, but he shook his head. The die was
cast, a child was on its way. They had to have faith that despite

the heavy weight of the Arundel genes it possessed, with love and good intentions, somehow they would pull this off.

Raine beamed at them. "A baby. I'm so excited about a grandchild. I know you two are wondering about nature versus nurture, and whether the little girl will be an incarnation of Benoit. Especially—" with a tilt of her head, she indicated the backyard where Fedelma had held them hostage "—after this."

Dante gravely nodded. "It's true, Mère. I want this baby with Maarja, and at the same time I think—am I resurrecting Benoit Arundel? Or, God forbid, Èrthu, first lord of the Arundels?"

Maarja put her hand to her belly. "We'll be good parents. We'll make all the difference."

"Of course you will!" Andere agreed. "But…listen to what Raine has to say."

Raine leaned forward, intent on imparting some great news. "Maarja, you know I have Arundel blood flowing in my veins."

"Yes. I had gathered you were part of Benoit's breeding program." Maarja winced.

"Blunt, but true. I am an Arundel. I have my share of the wiliness and determination and, when needed, the ruthlessness." Raine focused on Dante. "The man who captured and claimed me did not sire my child."

It took Dante a moment for that to sink in.

Dante gaped, as stunned and singed as if struck by lightning. "What? Me? Not… I'm not…"

"Benoit is not your father." Raine formed every word to make an impact.

"Wow," Maarja breathed. She had *not* seen that coming.

"So worry no more about whether the babe will be the embodiment of evil." Raine smiled at the newlyweds, enjoying their astonishment and knowing she had given them the gift of fearlessness in the face of looming parenthood. "The baby will be all we wished; assertive, intelligent, forceful, and inventive. My dear boy, I predict she'll rule our world."

"Of course she will." Upright and proper with his old-world courtesy, Andere said, "Allow me to offer my congratulations on your marriage and the upcoming happy arrival. I currently have no gift to present, so let me offer this; please feel free to call on me at any time to babysit. As you both know, I love children." Reaching into his pocket, he brought forth a handful of French lemon candies and placed them in the center of the table as a reminder of who he'd been to them, and a hint of his place in their lives.

In Maarja's mind, the missing piece of the puzzle had been placed on the table, and at last the pieces clicked into place. She took them apart and put them together again. She looked at Dante, wanting to know if his comprehension matched hers.

His lips were pale, his jaw clenched. Shock still held him wound tightly in a tangle of emotions. So…yes.

Maarja recovered first. "Thank you, Andere. The baby, whatever its gender, will be privileged to have both of you in its life."

"I'm glad you understand," Raine said. She exchanged a smiling glance with Andere.

He picked up her hand and kissed her fingers. "*Ma chérie*, you've come so far in these past weeks, working with the trainer. After this arduous day, are you too tired, or would you like to put the therapy to the test and sway to the music?"

"What a wonderful thought. It's been so long since I've danced with you. Yes, let's do that." Raine allowed Andere to assist her out of her chair and guide her toward the dance floor.

As the older man passed, he paused and pressed his hand on Dante's shoulder.

Dante recovered enough to put his hand over Andere's and press back.

His acceptance was enough to bring emotional tears to Maarja's eyes. So many changes! Good changes, mostly. Healing changes. Challenging changes. But she was up to the tasks, and of course, she trusted that Dante would lead the way through every difficulty.

When they sat alone, Maarja unwrapped a candy and handed it to Dante. "Sugar will help with the trauma."

He put it in his mouth and let it dissolve. He closed his eyes and took a long full breath as if it were the first one in many minutes. "I... He... She... Did you comprehend what they...?" He couldn't seem to articulate his thoughts.

Fine. Maarja could help him. "Yes. Benoit Arundel is not your biological father. Your mother, a wise and determined woman, chose a different man, one you and I know to be honest and upright. That does relieve any pressure I feel about carrying a child born with evil welded into its bones."

He nodded numbly.

"I like Andere. He's strong but not vicious, willing to stay in the background until needed, then he steps up to help. Doesn't need to drive a hot car or a big truck. You said he could always do what needed to be done. He's a quiet hero who has nothing to prove." She studied Dante. "Now that I know, I can see him in you."

Dante opened his eyes and stared at her. Touched his own face as if seeking the similarity.

"Not your looks, so much, but, honey, that car that's parked at the curb...that's the antithesis of a hot car."

Dante grinned. "Yeah. But it moves! When it's not stuck in traffic."

Enough of dealing with a topic that would require thoughtful adjustment over months and perhaps years. Time to go out and join the celebration. She stood. "It's our wedding. Can we dance? Before we have to take up the onerous task of allowing *all* the Arundels to kiss our rings?" She looked at her finger. "So much slobber!"

"I'd like that. The dancing, I mean." He glanced up, looked her over as if seeing her for the first time today, stood, and took her arm. "Have I told you how lovely you are?"

"Not yet. But I'm sure you will."

He ushered her out into the backyard. Cheers erupted—wine had been flowing freely—and as they made their way across the lawn, they shook hands while responding to calls of congratulations.

"Now that we know it was Fedelma, Connor has nailed her for the embezzling." Dante talked into Maarja's ear, keeping her entertained while people did indeed slobber on her hand. "Fedelma was stocking up for her takeover of the family."

As they stepped onto the portable dance floor, the band switched to a love song, and Dante pulled her close. He led well, of course, and in a moment they moved together as if they'd been practicing for this dance all their lives. He murmured, "You weren't as surprised about my mother's appearance as I thought you'd be."

"I had my suspicions."

He leaned back and looked into her face. "What gave it away?"

"You said you trusted two people, and I was one."

"Damn," he said softly.

"That made me wonder…who else could the other person be? The only possibility was your mother." Looking back, she was surprised she hadn't realized the truth as the events occurred. "You never grieved. Never were angry with whoever had caused the explosion. Never put all your heart and mind into discovering who'd killed her. That's not like you, Dante."

He rubbed his forehead. "I'm not going to win an Academy Award, am I?"

"Ha! Not you." She liked that about him. He was direct, didn't bother with pretense, and she would always know where she stood with him. "I started thinking back, about how she was alive after the explosion and alive when you carried her down the stairs. Suddenly, you announced she was dead and you held me back from her body. People were on the property, recording everything that happened. I couldn't figure out how the reporters had arrived so swiftly, but they weren't reporters, and if I hadn't been in shock, I would have realized it. They were your people, documenting her death for proof to your suspicious pain-in-the-butt relatives."

His expression was both chagrin and pride. "When you discovered the deception, I thought you were going to punch me. And I would have to let you."

"I would have. I still might take the opportunity. But I knew if what I suspected was the truth, you and she had created the explosion to fool the unknowns who were trying to kill her, to keep her safe and seize the initiative. You knew with her death, they would have to make a move and reveal themselves. I am right, aren't I?" She saw the answer in his face. "Ha! You're going to have to work to stay ahead of me, Dante Arundel!"

He spun her in a slow smooth move. "Instead of staying ahead of you, I'll walk at your side all the days of our lives."

She put her head on his shoulder. "Okay. If you insist. We'll do it your way."

CHAPTER 57

Maarja drove her van up Gothic's winding main street, the setting sun blaring in her rearview mirrors. After her announcement that she was pregnant, Saint Rees had tried to move her into the office—her worst nightmare—and when she resisted she'd been assigned jobs with little risk. Like the one she had just completed, moving a young woman's complete Hummel collection from Eureka to Boston.

Who even knew Hummels were back in fashion?

The packing and inventory had taken two full days of fussiness and the travel and unpacking had been another five days. Every night she conferenced with Dante, but it wasn't the same and right now she found herself as excited as a newlywed. Which she wasn't really; three months ago they'd returned from their Italian honeymoon—which included a visit to Murano—and underneath her white coveralls, her baby bump was plainly showing. When she asked Mrs. Arundel whether Dante had kicked all the time, Raine replied, "No, dear, he was a placid infant, which worried Benoit, may I tell you. I imagine this little tyke takes after you."

Maarja had no one to ask, but she didn't allow that to bother her. She had so much more than she had ever imagined possible. For that, she was grateful.

Her anticipation heightened as she rounded the last curve toward her house...

Her house, which had been transformed by tearing off the front and framing a second story over the living room. A large flatbed truck was parked on the torn-up lawn while a small crane moved trusses off it and onto the studs. A dozen construction workers swarmed the yard, and Owen, her construction guy/brother-in-law, consulted a large roll of plans with Dante.

She braked and gawked like a tourist.

Behind her, Mr. Cummings honked, and Maarja hurriedly turned to drive up the alley to the back of her house. Her tiny rundown one-car garage was gone, replaced by a two-car garage. The open door revealed a vehicle she had no doubt was her husband's. Who else would drive a Mercedes that cost more than Alex's hospital stay? "Dante, you jerk," she muttered.

No wonder he'd been so willing to move his fancy-ass body into her tiny old house. Under his auspices, it was becoming a... well, not a large house, but much more than the old-fashioned one bedroom, one bath she had so cherished.

Okay, fine, he'd had trouble fitting his office staff into the living room, but—he couldn't have consulted with her?

Construction workers fled before her as she stomped in, glowering, and headed toward the front. The living room was in surprisingly good shape for a room that had a beam and plywood ceiling. Or was that the upstairs floor?

She stepped out on the front porch, which was still pretty much the same except the wood floor, railings, and posts were new and, by the smell, newly painted. She walked to the railing and looked down at Owen and Dante.

"Hi, Maarja, did you have a good trip?" Owen didn't wait for an answer. He put his arm over his head and waved it in a big circle. "That's a wrap for the day, folks. Secure it all and let's leave these newlyweds to enjoy their reunion." The coward headed for the pickup marked with his construction logo on the door.

The guys on the crew viewed Dante, who stood looking up at Maarja, and Maarja, who stood scowling down at Dante, and Maarja heard a few "Uh-ohs."

The women on the crew pretended not to watch, but they wore the half grins women always wore when they witnessed a husband about to get his butt kicked.

"Hi, honey." Dante made no move to climb the stairs. "What do you think of my surprise?"

"Your surprise? Is that what this is, your surprise? You take my house apart and make it *bigger* and *better*—" she used air quotes "—and you call it your surprise?"

"My surprise for you. And for our baby. I couldn't see how I could stay home to take care of her—"

They hadn't yet decided whether to find out the baby's gender, but the whole family assumed it was a girl.

"—without a little more space for my office and her nursery." As his enthusiasm and volume increased, he bounded up the stairs and took her hand. "Come on! Let me show you. The city let me expand another two feet on this one side—"

The living room/kitchen was bigger; she simply hadn't noticed as she steamed through the first time.

"—so I could add a spiral staircase up to the second floor." Which was already framed and in place. "I'm going to enclose it for storage and decorate it with your mother's prints. She was thrilled when I asked!" He must have seen something in Maarja's face that slowed him down, because he asked, "That is…if it's okay with you?"

"I'm good with my mother's prints." She was, really she was, but since he'd already asked, it was a damned good thing.

"Great!" His enthusiasm rebounded. "You climb ahead of me."

"So if my big clumsy body takes a tumble you can catch me?" Sarcasm fit her mood.

"So I can watch your butt."

"That's one right answer," she mumbled, and climbed the stairs.

At the top, when she turned, he was definitely watching her butt. As soon as he set foot on the floorboards, though, he burst into more explanations, showing her the window seat and the skylights, framed but not finished, and where the second-story deck would go out the back wall over their bedroom. There they would sit for dinner and watch the sunset over the ocean while their baby slept in her crib. With great sweeps of his arms, he described where his desk would sit in relationship to the rocking chair and crib, how the microwave would heat his coffee and the baby's bottle, how the wallpaper would be washable so his little girl could use her chalk, paint, and crayons like Grandma Octavia.

He was so animated, describing what had been created, envisioning what wasn't yet there, Maarja's irritation eased. She sat down on the floor and waited until he wound down.

When he realized she was watching and smiling, he sat beside her. "I've installed a lot of security, too. Oh! And I made apricot jam today. What do you think?"

"I think our baby is a very lucky person." She leaned against him. "Like its mama."

He put his arm around her.

She asked, "How did you manage to convince the city council and the neighbors and Angelica Lindholm to let you do this remodel?"

In a prosaic tone, he said, "The usual. Bribes, kissing up, paying for the library renovation, promising Mrs. Hannaford next door I'd take her to the beach once a month and let her sit with her feet in the sand."

"She can't climb the cliff. How are you going to do that?"

"Helicopter," they both said at once.

Maarja laughed. "The most expensive remodel in the history of mankind."

"You said it. Owen ain't cheap, and he didn't give me a friends-and-family discount. I called him a fucking bloodsucker and he called me a fucking pain in the ass because I designed this myself and I don't know anything about structure, and I said I could take my business elsewhere and he said yeah, go, you'll be on the receiving end of the biggest fucking of your life—"

She couldn't stand it. "What is it with you guys and your potty mouths?"

"I haven't seen you in a whole week, and at least I haven't said I want to fuck you." He used his most lascivious expression as he viewed her. "Which I do."

Emphasizing each word as she spoke, she said, "You can't use that language around a baby!"

"Okay, I won't. Tell me, what would you call fucking?"

"Making love!"

Dante smiled a slow triumphant smile—and Maarja realized she'd been manipulated. "Yes." He took her hand. "Let's go make love."

★ ★ ★ ★ ★